Valerie Wood was born in Yorkshire and now lives in a village near the east coast. She is the author of *The Hungry Tide*, winner of the Catherine Cookson Prize for Fiction, *Annie*, *Children of the Tide*, *The Romany Girl*, *Emily*, *Going Home*, *Rosa's Island*, *The Doorstep Girls* and *Far From Home*, all available in Corgi paperback.

Find our more about Valerie Wood's novels by visiting her website on <u>www.valeriewood.co.uk</u>

D1386145

Also by Valerie Wood

ANNIE
CHILDREN OF THE TIDE
THE ROMANY GIRL
EMILY
GOING HOME
ROSA'S ISLAND
THE DOORSTEP GIRLS
FAR FROM HOME

and published by Corgi Books

The Hungry Tide

Valerie Wood

CORGI BOOKS

THE HUNGRY TIDE
A CORGI BOOK : 0 552 14118 6

First publication in Great Britain

PRINTING HISTORY
Corgi edition published 1993

7 9 10 8 6

Set in 10/11pt Plantin by
Kestrel Data, Exeter, Devon.

Corgi Books are published by Transworld Publishers,
61–63 Uxbridge Road, London W5 5SA,
a division of The Random House Group Ltd,
in Australia by Random House Australia (Pty) Ltd,
20 Alfred Street, Milsons Point, Sydney, NSW 2061, Australia,
in New Zealand by Random House New Zealand Ltd,
18 Poland Road, Glenfield, Auckland 10, New Zealand
and in South Africa by Random House (Pty) Ltd,
Endulini, 5a Jubilee Road, Parktown 2193, South Africa.

Printed and bound in Great Britain by
Cox & Wyman Ltd, Reading, Berkshire.

Papers used by Transworld Publishers are natural, recyclable
products made from wood grown in sustainable forests.
The manufacturing processes conform to the environmental
regulations of the country of origin.

For my family with love

Acknowledgements

Poem on page 8 taken from *The Geography of East Yorks*, by T. S. Sheppard, FGS, FSA Scot. Reprinted from the *Journal of the Manchester Geographical Society*, parts III and IV, 1913, Sherratt & Hughes, 34 Cross Street, Manchester, 1914.

Sources of general information on whaling and its relevant industry obtained from the Kingston upon Hull Town Docks Museum. Further reading from the Malet Lambert Local History Originals, *The Hull Whale Fishery* by Jennifer C. Rowley and *A History of Hull* by Edward Gillett and Kenneth A. MacMahon.

Grateful loving thanks to my daughter Catherine Wood for patiently reading and re-reading the manuscript and to my family for welcoming the Foster family into our home.

Where life and beauty
Dwelt long ago,
The oozy rushes
And seaweed grow
And no-one sees
And no-one hears
And none remembers
The far off years.

It is the olden,
The sunken town
Which faintly murmurs
Far fathoms down
Like sea-winds breathing
It murmurs by,
And the sweet waters tremble
And sink and die.

1

The dark water slapped against the supports of the wooden wharves and staiths as the whaler drifted silently up the river. The mist which hovered over the water started to lift and, carried by the easterly wind, floated across the wharves and into the gardens of the merchants' riverside houses. Through the quiet streets and alleyways it spread, carrying with it the stench of processed blubber from the Greenland Yards.

On it drifted, spreading wider through the town and reaching into the narrow, grimy Wyke Entry, where it clung to the blackened timbers of the mean old houses that leaned one into another, touching them with dampness.

The entry was silent, save for the rustling and scratching in the heap of rubbish which the wind had blown into a corner, for most of the occupants were still sleeping in the early dawn. Then came the sound of laboured breathing and the pad of running feet which directed themselves into the entry.

Maria wiped her mouth on a corner of the coarse sacking which was tied around her waist. Her grey eyes blinked involuntarily at the tears which had formed as she retched into a bucket by the door.

She'd been plagued by sickness with her other pregnancies and accepted this nauseous condition as one of the ordeals of motherhood to be endured until the fourth month, when miraculously it would disappear.

She straightened her back and took a deep breath. She didn't feel like going to work this morning, the very thought of the smell of the fish which she and the other women had to load into the barrels at the staith side turned her stomach and made her want to vomit again.

But work she must: whilst Will was at sea the money she earned was very necessary. Food was dear, Tom had worn out his old boots and would need new ones this winter, and Will always insisted that money was put by in case the children were sick and needed medicine. Twice last winter cough syrup and poultices had had to be bought for Alice, who at three was a thin, pale-faced child with a weak chest.

Maria smiled when she thought of Will. He had already set sail when she found that she was pregnant again. She prayed that she would keep this child. She desperately wanted one more bairn, one more that they could love and keep and who would help her over the loss of the two babies who had died before Alice was born and who were buried in the churchyard.

Will had been sailing on whaling ships for eighteen years, since he was twelve years old, working for the same company as his father had before him, and he boasted often that Masterson's were the best company in the port, looking after its men and bringing industry into the town with its whale oil and whalebone.

A generous bounty was given to the shipowners by the government, and the men were well paid for their labours. Will would have plenty of money in his pocket when he came home. There were losses, of course, and the men who worked these ships were well aware of the dangers lurking in the treacherous waters of the polar seas. Men were sometimes lost overboard and frostbite was common, with loss of fingers and toes.

Maria poured water from a jug into a bowl and rinsed her hands and face, and was brushing her long dark hair when she suddenly jumped, startled by a loud hammering on the door.

'Maria, Maria!' The voice outside was insistent.

'Who is it?' she whispered cautiously.

'It's me – Annie. Open 'door quick!' She banged again even louder.

She's early, thought Maria, as she unbolted the door.

They were not due down at the Old Harbour side for at least another hour, it was only just daylight. She lifted the sneck. 'Shush, tha'll waken childre'. Don't mek so much row. Alice has had a bad night with her cough.'

'I'm sorry, love.' Annie, her face pinched and grey, stood shivering on the doorstep. 'But it's urgent, I had to come.'

'Come in quick, what is it, what's up?' Maria saw that her friend was distraught, her hair uncombed and without the shawl which the women always wore to keep out the cold river air and the smell of fish from their hair.

'It's 'Polar Star, she's coming up 'river, I've just got 'message.' Annie was breathless with anxiety. 'We've got to go down to 'dock, summat's wrong.'

Maria's face paled. The whaler had set sail barely four months ago and to come home so soon, long before it was due, could only mean that something was seriously wrong.

'Wait a minute while I see to 'bairns.'

She moved quietly to the corner of the room where the two children were still sleeping soundly, undisturbed by Annie at the door. She placed Tom's outstretched arms back into the bed and covered both children more closely with the blanket. Softly she placed a kiss on their smooth foreheads before turning away, her mind in a turmoil.

If there had been a disaster on board the whaler, her children could already be fatherless and she a widow. That thought was always at the back of her mind although she tried not to dwell on it, but she was always conscious of the dangers that the men in the whaling ships encountered.

She wrapped a shawl around her shoulders and the two women hurried out of the narrow Wyke Entry, through the dark lanes and alleys, under the low archway which led into the wider Blackfryers' Gate, and across to the long High Street which ran along the river towards the New Dock.

Although it was still early, lights were beginning to

11

flicker as people prepared for work, and as they passed the big houses in the High Street they saw sleepy-eyed servants preparing for the day, drawing wide the heavy shutters and curtains at the tall windows and making ready for their masters' and mistresses' comfort.

'Come on, this way, Annie.' Maria ran through the narrow Chapel Staith towards the river. She had lived all of her life in the warren of buildings bounding the river and knew every corner, every alleyway.

The mist had risen above the water and swirled around the tall masts of the ships in the crowded waterway, but there was no sign of the whaler.

'Hey,' she shouted. 'Any news of 'Polar Star?'

A seaman appeared on the deck of a Liverpool coaster and waved his hand towards the New Dock. 'Aye. She passed an hour since!'

They picked their way over coils of rope and crates of merchandise that were piled high on the staith, their long woollen skirts brushing against the wet planking, and cut back down the next entry into the High Street.

Annie started to snivel. 'What'll we do, Maria, if our men 'aven't come back? What about our poor bairns?'

Maria took hold of her arm and gave her a none too gentle shake. 'We'll worry about that when we have to, not before!'

But her brave words belied a fear that threatened to engulf her, for in truth she dared not think of life without Will. The hardship of coping without a husband did not deter her, for the whaler wives spent many lonely months whilst their men were at sea, but she would miss the loving and the tenderness which her gentle, honest Will bestowed on her and his children, and she loved him dearly.

They were joined by other women and some children as news spread of the *Polar Star*'s early return, and the sound of their boots and wooden pattens clattered on the cobbles as their numbers grew. Running now, they turned out of the narrow street into the wider Salthouse Lane to avoid the steadily increasing crush of men who were arriving for work at the shipyards and, as they came in sight of the Quay, Maria drew in her breath sharply. 'She's there. They're unloading already.'

Visible at the eastern end of the dock, the masts of the whaler showed black against the brightening sky. The thud of ropes and canvas echoed through the quiet of the morning and a clatter of wood and iron rang out as the barrels of blubber were brought ashore, but the men on board were strangely silent, no whistling or shouting in their usual manner as they went about their tasks.

Maria joined a group of women standing together at the dock side, their shawls clutched tightly between tensed fingers. 'Does anybody know what's happened? What news of our men?'

Some of the women shook their heads indecisively as they waited. Others grumbled that there was no-one around to ask.

'I want to know about my lad.' An elderly woman clutched at Maria's arm. 'He's all I've got now. His fayther went down two year sin'.'

'Where's 'mate?' Maria called to one of the porters. 'Who's in charge?'

'Don't know,' he replied. 'Tha'd best try 'Dock Office. There's been some trouble on board.' He smiled sympathetically at the women and then turned back to load a barrel of blubber on to a wooden sled waiting at the quayside.

They all turned towards the Dock Office, hurrying now that there was a purpose in view, Maria striding ahead of them as if their elected leader. She could feel the women's fear as silently they followed her, the tension spreading amongst them, and she tried to keep calm, unlike Annie who had given way to her emotions and was shaking nervously and wailing to herself as she scurried along at Maria's side.

As they approached the building they saw a knot of seamen standing outside the door, some with bandaged hands, others leaning wearily against the wall chewing

13

wads of tobacco. Some of the women recognized their own men and, crying out in relief, rushed towards them. Maria searched anxiously amongst the faces, but there was no sign of Will, his tall figure and mass of tangled red hair, so distinguishable from the average, was missing from the crowd.

The heavy wooden door opened and a clerk came out. He looked around at the group of waiting men and called out briskly, 'Those who haven't been paid off, come back in an hour to collect tha wages.'

He looked down at a paper in his hand and asked, 'Is there a Mrs Bewley, Mrs Swinburn and Mrs Foster here?'

Maria and Annie both started forward, followed by the elderly woman who had spoken to Maria earlier.

'Come inside please.' He led the way into the building, the men moving away to let them through. Maria recognized some of them as shipmates of Will's and they nodded silently as she passed in front of them.

The three women, united in their fear, sat quietly on the hard wooden chairs in the high-ceilinged hall as they waited to be called. They stared at the windows, the floor, anywhere but at each other, their hands clenching and unclenching.

Presently a door opened and the clerk came out again. 'Mrs Foster!'

She rose unsteadily and followed him into another room, the eyes of the other women following her apprehensively.

'This is Mrs Foster, sir.' The clerk spoke to a man sitting behind a large desk. Behind him, looking out of the window down at the docks, was a tall fair-haired man Maria recognized as the captain of the *Polar Star*. The man behind the desk rose to greet her. 'Mrs Foster, I am Isaac Masterson, and this is Captain de Raad. Please be seated.'

Maria bobbed her knee in a curtsey to the ship-owner and in some trepidation sat down in front of him, her eyes downcast. Will had often spoken of the master mariner who employed him, and she had seen his fine house in High Street, with its rich curtains draping the windows, and had many times reached up above the window sill to catch a glimpse of the gleaming silverware and sparkling crystal on the dark polished dresser inside.

He was speaking to her now, softly and quite kindly. Somehow she didn't expect rich folk to be kind to people like her. She raised her eyes and saw a middle-aged man of heavy build, dressed in a plain grey coat of good cloth who was looking sympathetically across at her.

It seemed as if she only absorbed part of the conversation as he and Captain de Raad told her briefly of the reason for their early return; of the men they had lost and the injuries that they had sustained as the *Polar Star* battled with the ice and the frenzied whales.

'Your husband was very brave,' said the captain in his broken English. 'He saved another man's life at the risk of his own.'

Maria felt faint as they spoke, a black despair threatened to envelop her and she felt herself slipping away. She fought to control herself and as she did so Isaac Masterson leaned over her with a glass of water.

She thanked him and drank, and as she held the glass in trembling fingers asked weakly, 'Is tha telling me, sir, that my husband is dead and his body left out there in 'Polar Sea?'

Mr Masterson took the glass from her and smiled gently. 'No. You must thank God that he is alive and has been brought home to you. He is very ill, but the surgeon says that he is a strong man and will recover.'

Maria stared at the two men, scalding tears beginning to well in her eyes. 'Then what – ?'

'I'm telling you, Mrs Foster, that your husband's whaling days are over. That due to an unfortunate accident, and in order to save his life, the surgeon had no option other than to amputate his right leg.'

Will Foster woke to an onslaught of pain. Not the burning, tearing agony of mutilated flesh which he remembered as the line wound around his leg, but a dull thudding persistent torment below his right knee. He groaned and retched as he tried to sit up to view his surroundings.

A woman came towards him, impassively put her hand on his chest to push him back on to the bed and then walked away.

'Hey – wait, wait on,' he called feebly. 'Where am I?'

The woman didn't answer and kept on walking right out of the room, her long grey skirt swishing and her boots tapping on the wooden floor.

Will closed his eyes as the effort of movement and speech made his head spin. He concentrated on co-ordinating his thoughts and trying to remember the events that had led up to finding himself in this un-familiar bed.

He remembered that he'd been on board the whaler, the *Polar Star*, on her maiden voyage and that they'd set sail during the second week in March from the New Dock in Hull, along with one of Isaac Masterson's other ships, the *Greenland Star*. He'd waved a long farewell to his wife Maria and their son Tom as they'd stood tearfully watching on the wharf side in the grey dawn of that cold wet morning as the ship slowly moved out into the Old Harbour and on into the wide Humber.

He'd stood for a long time on the deck, gazing back at the still sleeping town as the shoreline receded, looking as if for the last time at the windmills and church spires piercing the skyline, the whole dominated by the tall tower of the magnificent Holy Trinity Church.

He recalled that a brisk wind and fine weather had stayed with them as they had entered the German Ocean, but on reaching the Shetlands they had experienced violent gales and lashing seas and had to shelter for nearly a week, the men growing restless and anxious. Then as the gales subsided they took on extra men and supplies from the islands and set sail across the Atlantic for the Davis Straits. For a month they'd sailed north-west until the wind changed against them and the

16

captain, a Dutchman, fearing that they would not reach the Arctic Straits in time for the fishing, altered course and headed for Greenland.

I can remember we reached 'ice at 'beginning of May, he thought, but then his mind became confused, and his head was full of images of threshing whales and blood-stained seas and splintering ice. He heard a voice shouting, 'Is anybody there?' and was bewildered to find that it was his own.

The woman came hurrying back through a door, and as his vision cleared he saw that he wasn't alone in the long room, but that there were other beds besides his, some occupied and some empty.

'Where am I?' he repeated. 'Am I in England or Greenland?'

The woman laughed. ' 'Course tha's in England. Tha's in 'ospital, in 'Infirmary. Back 'ome in Hull.'

'How did I get here? I was on board 'ship – who brought me?'

The words started to tumble out incoherently and his leg twitched in a painful spasm.

'Tha'll have to wait and see 'doctor,' she said, her voice and manner rough. 'I don't know owt about it, they don't tell 'likes o' me. I'm only 'ere to clean up after everybody!'

She walked away to the next bed, but then turning back said in a softer tone, 'If 'tha likes, after 'doctor's been, I'll fetch thee a jug o' beer.'

He closed his eyes and lay back again. The pain was getting worse and he was desperate for water to slake his thirst. 'Nurse,' he called. 'Nurse!' But she either didn't or wouldn't hear him and he drifted off again into an uneasy, tormented sleep where the screams of whales and men intermingled, and the icy Greenland waters washed over him, pulling him down into black-ness.

When he awoke again it was almost dark, the only light coming in from the bay window at the end of the room. There was a man sitting by the bed and as Will turned his head towards him he looked up and gave a gappy smile.

'Hey, Will, I'd given thee up. I thought tha was a goner.' The man cleared his throat and wiped his nose on his bandaged hand.

'Is that thee, Rob? I'm right glad to see thee. What happened? Where are we?' Will again tried to sit up, but he was curiously unbalanced and fell back once again in the bed.

'We're 'ome, thank God,' said Rob Hardwick. 'Though there's some not so fortunate. We lost Richard Bewley: 'e were a good lad, his ma'll miss him. Alan Swinburn. Does tha remember me telling thee he'd gone? Day after thy accident it was. What a way to dee. Killed by a barrel o' blubber! I don't like to speak ill of 'dead, but 'e'll not be missed. 'E were a miserly old pinchgut, stinting on 'is poor bairns and spending 'is bonus in 'dram shop.'

He leaned forward towards the bed, his eyes keen and searching anxiously into Will's face. 'Does tha remember us reaching 'ice and catching a big un?'

Will nodded. He recalled three six-man boats putting out from the whaler. They'd made one clean kill and towed the whale back to the ship for the flensers to do their work of dismembering the carcase and storing the blubber. The following day they heard the cry of other whales and moved off after them.

'Aye, well, it was that day that we made a dock in 'ice and gale started to blow, and we were all fearful of being stove in; but we put off four long boats and set out chasin' again. We knew there was plenty about by 'row they was makin'.'

Will put his hand to his eyes, trying to shut out the vision as recollection returned. The sea was his livelihood, the only one he had known, and he would wish for no other, yet he seemed to be haunted by the memory of the gush of blood staining the water, and could smell the oily reek of blubber. But most of all he thought he could hear the anguished cries as the harpoons struck their victim and see the stricken whale as it dived again and again, turning over and over as it vainly tried to shake off the barbed iron and line, until finally the great threshing body was stilled and it floated, its white belly exposed to the alien skies. The cheers of the men echoed in his ears.

'Well, we'd got two that day,' went on Rob, 'and was just towing them back, when a third one just came out of nowhere, right up 'side of 'boat. It threshed about that much we had all on to keep 'boat upright. Then Richard Bewley threw his iron with such force that he went right over 'side. He never stood a chance. I reckon he went right under 'ice.'

'Aye, aye, I know all that,' said Will wearily. 'But what happened later? Why am I in 'Infirmary with a broken leg? For judging by 'agony I'm in, that's what it is. And why is tha bandaged? Did tha get 'frost?'

Rob fiddled with a loose end of his grimy bandage, his eyes averted from Will. Then he got up from the chair and walked to the end of the bed, looking anxiously down the ward towards the door.

'Tha'll 'ave seen 'surgeon, 'asn't tha?' he asked nervously.

Will's blue eyes, already swollen with pain, narrowed suspiciously as he observed his shipmate, so obviously in confusion. 'I don't think so,' he answered, 'I don't remember.'

A sudden paroxysm of pain convulsed him, causing him to draw in his breath and clench his teeth, sweat running down his face as he tried to control the agony. He put his hand beneath the sheet to take hold of the offending source of pain, and found beneath his swollen, bandaged right knee a void, an emptiness. An emptiness of piercing, burning anguish which sent his senses reeling, and as he drifted into unconsciousness he hoarsely cried out, 'Wilt tha fetch Maria and my bairns!'

Maria sat once more in the hall of the Dock Office, her eyes closed and her head cupped in her hands. Her thoughts were a confusion of relief and despair as she gradually absorbed the knowledge that Will was alive, but she trembled at the realization that her proud, vigorous husband was now crippled.

Annie and Mrs Bewley had been called in together. Annie turned towards Maria as she went through the door. 'Wait on us, Maria, for I'm that afeard.'

A shaft of sunlight slid from the high window and dust particles danced at her feet as Maria sat locked in her loneliness, whilst life outside continued its normal pattern. Sounds of activity filtered through into the quiet hall as the dock workers unloaded cargoes of timber, hemp, linseed, tobacco, brandy and rum on to the quay. Ships from Gothenburg, Hamburg, Amsterdam, Oporto and America were among the many foreign vessels which crowded the busy port.

Then from within the inner room came wailing and a low pitched moaning, and Maria knew that her own suffering was as nothing compared with that of Annie and Mrs Bewley.

By the time they reappeared Mrs Bewley behaved with quiet fortitude, as became an elderly widow. She sobbed quietly into the corner of her shawl, murmuring her son's name over and over, shaking her head to and fro in disbelief. But Annie was distraught, clinging frantically with one hand to the clerk who had brought them back into the hall, and with the other clutching a bag with her husband's belongings, and crying out in hysteria that she and her bairns would starve in the gutter, now that there was no man to support them.

'He's dead Maria! Crushed by a barrel of stinking blubber!' she screamed.

Maria rose pale and trembling from her chair and took hold of her arm.

'Nay, Annie, don't tek on so. Be brave and think on 'childre'. We'll all help thee.' Though God knows how, she thought. The little money saved through her thriftiness would soon be whittled away when there was no wage coming in.

But Annie, she knew, had no money and was probably in debt to the moneylender for she was a poor housekeeper. Alan Swinburn spent his wages as soon as he came home, drinking rum heavily or gambling on cock fights, whilst Annie resorted to stealing coins from his pockets as he lay in a drunken stupor on the bed they shared with their children. There were times when he caught her out and then she was given a beating as a punishment.

Maria sighed. Poor Annie, at least she would be spared that, for many times she had bathed Annie's bruises and fed her ragged, pathetic children.

The clerk tugged at Maria's sleeve. 'When Mrs Swinburn is over 'shock,' he said quietly, 'tell her to go to Trinity House, they'll help her, it's her right. And thee, Mrs Bewley,' he added. 'They'll find a place for thee at Seamen's Hospital.'

At this Annie started to wail again. 'We'll have to go on 'relief. To collect our Sixpences!'

Maria grew impatient. She felt drained of energy, she had an ache in her back, and was sick with anxiety over Will. Didn't Annie think that others had worries too? Life was going to be hard, there was no doubt about it, but they would manage if they were careful.

Trinity House collected money from the seamen's wages – known locally as the Seamen's Sixpences – to give out in relief to the widows and children of drowned seamen, or those who were maimed at sea, and spendthrifts like Alan Swinburn were forced to subscribe. Old people like Mrs Bewley were taken for shelter into the almshouses to end their days. They were given food and clothing and a bed to sleep on and had no need to resort to begging in the streets like some less fortunate souls.

'I'm going home,' said Maria. 'I must see to my bairns, and then I shall go to Will. He needs me. He's been taken to 'Infirmary. He's a cripple!' As the words tumbled out she started to cry, the tension and emotion of the last few hours finally erupting into floods of tears.

Annie stopped her wailing and stared at Maria. 'Oh,

I'm sorry, love. I'd forgot' poor Will, and thee – tha must go home and rest a while, think on thy 'babby.' Conscience stricken, she put her arms around Maria and Mrs Bewley, and together the three women walked out into the bright morning sunshine.

Maria left Annie and Mrs Bewley in the Market Place. There was a crush of people for it was Tuesday and market day. The long thoroughfare was filled with shops and trades of all description. Shoemakers, bakers, grocers and tea-dealers traded side by side with saddlers and pawnbrokers, sailmakers and tallow chandlers.

Outside the draper's shop, rolls of cloth were propped up against the window. Irish linen, soft silks and velvets, were fingered fastidiously by ladies of quality whilst the draper fawned obsequiously and arranged folds of material about his person.

Miss Rebecca Brown the milliner was placing the latest fashionable hats on to tall stands in her window, and trying to ignore the jeers and grimaces of the dishevelled urchins who pressed their dirty hands and faces to the glass as they watched her.

Maria walked on towards the towering Holy Trinity Church. There was a confusion of canvas-covered stalls clustered around the church side and spilling out into the wide road. Vendors selling cereals, country cheeses, eggs and vegetables shouted out their wares. There were live chickens and ducks squawking and quacking in wicker baskets, goats bleating, and horses and carts trying to get through the multitude of people milling there. The sun shone warmly and the heat increased the smells of the town. The aroma of ripe fruit, fish, animals and their excrement mingled with that of unwashed bodies and the heavy stench of processing blubber and seed oil.

She pushed her way through the crowd towards the front of one of the stalls and elbowed out of the way the unruly, grimy children who always hung around waiting for their chance to steal an apple or a pie, or even a purse from the unsuspecting. She bought a bag of barley for making broth, and today because she was weary she paid the market price without haggling, as she would normally have done. Then she went to the next stall for a sack of potatoes and turnips and a bunch of marjoram and rosemary which the stallkeeper, a country man, had brought in with him, and hoisting the sack over her shoulder she set off back through the town towards home.

'What news of Will, Maria?' a voice called to her as she crossed the long row of shops in the Butchery. Will Foster was well known to the tradesmen as an honest customer who always paid his bills, and in this close-knit community word was already out of the *Polar Star*'s return.

'He's in 'Infirmary,' she paused to reply. 'Mr Masterson has sent him. He told me not to worry, but I can't help it. He won't be whaling any more.'

'They'll look after him all right.' The butcher nodded sympathetically. 'They'll be behodden to him, 'account of what he did. I hear tell he saved 'master's nephew. Would that be right?' He waited for confirmation of the morning's news, his cleaver poised in his hand.

Maria shuddered. 'Aye, summat like that,' she agreed. Will wouldn't want people talking about him, even if it was complimentary. 'I'll take a bit of scrag end o' mutton while I'm here,' she added, 'and make Will a drop of broth.'

When she lifted the sneck of the door to her home in Wyke Entry she found a small bright fire burning in the grate, and yet the room felt cold and damp in contrast to the warmth outside.

Tom was sitting on the bed with his arms around his sister, gently rocking her. 'She's badly, Ma, she's got a cough.'

Alice was flushed, her eyes bright and feverish and her dark hair damp on her forehead.

'Mrs Morton lit 'fire. I found wood down by 'river,'

23

Tom went on eagerly, 'and I've drawn 'water, but I couldn't lift 'pot on to 'fire.'

Mrs Morton lived in the room upstairs, with her husband when he was home from the sea, her aged parents, and a large brood of children which increased yearly, and Maria was grateful that she would take the trouble to keep an eye on her own children.

'Tha's a good lad,' she said. 'Now fetch me some more wood and I'll put 'broth on to boil.'

She put the fatty meat, a handful of barley, the vegetables and the bunch of pot herbs into a large iron cauldron and lifted it on to the fire. The potatoes she put at the side of the grate where they would cook in the hot ash, and then sat down wearily on the bed, drawing Alice to her.

When Tom returned with another armful of kindling, Maria explained what she knew about the *Polar Star* and its disastrous voyage, how it had been in great danger of being crushed as the ice closed in and of their father's accident.

'Shall I go to work now, Ma, if Fayther can't go whaling?' Tom was very anxious to start work and become a man like some of his friends, but Will and Maria had always insisted that he wouldn't until he was at least ten, which was still two years away, and Will was adamant that he wouldn't be allowed to go whaling, that he would find him a job in the shipyards when the time was right.

Maria sighed. 'I hope not, but we'll have to wait and see. Now, Tom, listen, tha must come with me to see thy fayther, but first I want thee to go to 'apothecary in 'Market Place and ask for summat for Alice's cough. Tell Mr Dobson I sent thee.'

She gave him a coin from her pocket. 'Be quick now and don't dally.' Holding Alice close, she lay down on the bed, drawing the thin blanket over them. There would be no work at the staith side for her today, even though she would lose a day's wages.

'Try to rest now,' she said to the child. 'Tha'll

feel better when tha wakes,' and she too closed her eyes as a great tiredness and exhaustion came over her. With their arms around each other for comfort, they slept.

2

A large section of the ancient crumbling gates and walls of Hull had come tumbling down in 1775 as work commenced on the building of the New Dock. The medieval walls, which were constructed of local brick and stone, had been built to repel invaders and to keep the waters of the Humber from drowning the low-lying town. In centuries past the town had opened its gates in welcome to kings and noblemen, and closed them in defiance as well.

Maria had lived and played beneath the shadow of those town walls. Broken, dilapidated and overgrown as they were when she was a child, they had been a refuge from the stinking alley which was home. She used to stand with her brothers on the top of the old Humber wall, her hand shielding her eyes against the brightness of the sun on the water below, watching the great ships of the world coming in to the crowded port, their huge canvas sails creaking and billowing in the east wind.

The shimmering brightness, though, was an illusion, for beneath the turbulent surface lay the glacial deposits of sand and gravel, while silt and clay held the rotting corpses of mangy dogs and the refuse of humanity. Infection lay in perilous wait for the people of the town as they took the river water for their drinking, washing and cooking.

There was good spring water coming into the town from the country district of Spring Head, but for the destitute people living down by the old walls, this was their river, the waters which brought them their scanty livelihood and where some of them ended their days. Here too at the old South End sat the ducking stool, a grim reminder of what would happen to scolding, shrewish wives who didn't keep their place.

On 19 October 1775, Maria had been taken by her father to watch the first stone of the dock ceremonially laid by the Mayor, Mr Joseph Outram, and within four short years the work was finished. With an air of great festivity the first fishing vessel, the *Manchester*, entered the dock. The bands played and the flags and banners flew and the townspeople cheered enthusiastically and proudly.

Maria had stood in awe watching as the shipping merchants, local aristocracy, and members of the Dock Company arrived for the occasion, alighting from their fine carriages with their handsome wives whose feet were clad in softest leather, and whose elegant dresses were of the finest fabrics that money could buy. She could recall too her father saying with great emotion that this dock, the largest in the kingdom, and this historic day would be a great turning point for Hull and its shipping industry.

His words were true, for the shipping and fishing trades increased and the merchants grew rich. They became discontented with their homes which were cheek by jowl with the insanitary hovels of their workforce and, repulsed by the foul smells of the industry which had brought them their wealth, they moved out of the town in their hundreds leaving the poverty-stricken unfortunates to fend as best they could for shelter, fire and food.

The town, so long insulated against its enemies by the ancient enclosure of fortifications, battlements and moats, started to spread and open up, and within a few years, wide streets of grand houses and fine buildings for commerce and trade stretched like slender fingers northwards from the old town into the countryside beyond.

As Maria grew into womanhood and then became a wife, she rarely ventured out into the country, and then only when Will escorted her. She was a town woman and felt uneasy when she was outside her boundary, vulnerable and fearful. She had no fear of being alone in the town, nor even traversing the dark unlit alleys and wharves which bounded the great River Humber.

She was glad therefore of the company of young Tom as they set off out of the town towards the Infirmary, having left Alice in the charge of Mrs Morton. She had fed the children with the steaming broth and potatoes and put the remaining broth into a jug to take to Will.

She wiped Tom's dirty face and tied her own long thick hair into a plait, and then, because she wanted to look her best for Will, she searched around in a cupboard and brought out a clean white collar, which was kept for special occasions, and placed it neatly around the neck of her dress.

The bright morning sunshine had disappeared and low, dark cloud hung menacingly above them as they made their way out of town. They approached Charity Hall, where poor children of the town were given shelter and work, and where Maria as she went by gave silent prayers of thanks that Tom and Alice were more fortunate than some. They passed the courtyard of the Seamen's Hospital where Mrs Bewley would make her home, and out through the boundary where once stood the Beverley Gate, the ancient gate which had guarded the town for centuries and which now was overgrown with elder and nettles, and a tangled mass of bramble and dog rose.

Tom ran ahead of her, his young body leaping and jumping, skipping and bounding with the sheer joy of freedom, exulting in the span of unconfined space.

'Come here, Tom,' she said at last, 'Come and walk by me, we'll soon be there.'

She could see the outline of the Infirmary less than a mile away. It was a large imposing building and stood alone in a quiet green meadow, surrounded by tall trees and with the waters of the Spring Ditch running nearby. She began to shiver with anticipation at the thought of seeing Will and anxiety at how she would find him.

The rain was just starting to fall as they walked

through the huge iron gates and into the entrance porch. Tom stood on tiptoe and pulled the bell rope at the side of the wooden door. They heard the peal jangling and echoing down the corridors and presently the sound of heavy footsteps approached and the door opened. A uniformed porter stood there, smart and imperious in his navy coat and shining buttons.

'Yes,' he asked with an air of authority. 'What is it?'

'I've come to see my husband, sir,' Maria explained. 'Will Foster. Mr Masterson sent him in.'

The porter, with some sniffing and complaining that this wasn't the right hour for visiting, reluctantly let them inside. They stepped into a wide entrance hall and Maria marvelled at the size of the place as she gazed at the great staircase and marble columns. A fire was burning in a grate with a large wooden chimneypiece, and Tom left his mother's side and went to warm his hands.

'Come with me.' The porter crossed the hall and they followed him up the staircase and down a long corridor and through several doors until Maria was sure that they would never find their way out again. Finally he opened a door and said, 'There he is, missus, in there.'

Slowly she walked past the row of beds, anxiously looking at the faces of the patients lying there, then to her joy heard a familiar voice saying, 'Now then, lass, doesn't tha know me?'

And there was Will, his face pale and creased with pain, but alive and with a loving smile on his lips.

Will's emotions were mixed as he surveyed his wife and son at his bedside. He was thankful to see them again but felt a helpless despair that fate had dealt him such a blow. How would he support them? How could a man with such a disability hope to get work and earn enough money to pay the rent and feed his family?

Maria looked pale and tired, he thought. The work at the staith side was hard with long hours and he had planned that with enough money from this voyage she could have taken on less arduous work. Now it would seem that she would have to support them all. Tom too would have to start work soon: Will sighed, for he had wanted a different life for his son from the one he had had himself.

'Will?' Maria's soft voice interrupted his thoughts and she gently stroked his hand. 'Mr Masterson told me he had thee sent here, and that we wouldn't have to pay.' Her voice faltered. 'Not for 'surgeon or medicine or owt like that.'

'I know that,' he answered. 'Masterson is a benefactor of 'hospital. He's rich enough to pay a subscription. Ten guineas it cost him, 'nurse told me when I asked who was paying.' He nodded towards the beds opposite. 'All o' them, they've all been recommended by some-body, except that poor devil over there. He was crushed under some carriage wheels and was brought in this morning, but I doubt he'll last 'night. Rob Hardwick went home today,' he added. 'He lost two fingers with 'frost.'

He shuddered. 'It's been a terrible voyage, this one, Maria. We must thank God that we got home at all.'

'Just get well, love,' said Maria, her grey eyes swim-ming with tears. 'We'll manage somehow and I know how worried tha'll be, but I'll work until my time.'

She bit her lip. She hadn't intended telling him yet about the expected child. She had been going to wait until he was home, for she knew that the pleasure which she had first anticipated in telling him would now be another blow, bringing with it the hardship of another mouth to feed.

Will groaned. 'Oh God – how shall we manage? Another child! I'm sorry, Maria, I know how tha's longed for another bairn. Pray God it will be a boy and can soon fend for hissen.'

'Fayther,' interrupted Tom, 'did tha save somebody's life, like Ma was told?'

Will brushed aside the boy's question. 'I'll tell thee about it some time, Tom, not now.'

'Tha fayther's tired now, Tom, and must get his rest, and we must be getting back to Alice,' said Maria, rising from the chair as she saw fatigue in Will's face.

A nurse came in with a rush light in each hand and placed them in iron brackets on the wall where they gave out a smoky glow.

'Is it night?' asked Will. 'I seem to have mixed up days and nights.'

Maria bent to kiss him, and stroked his thick red beard. 'Nay, it's still day, but so black and stormy it could be midnight.'

Will saw them go, his wife and son, and with warnings for them to take care as the road into the town was a lonely one, he settled down as he was bid by the nurse to try and rest, but he had no sooner dozed off to sleep when he was roused again, this time by the nurse who gently shook him by the shoulder.

'Wake up, Mr Foster. Here's a gentleman for thee.'

This information was conveyed in a more respectful manner than was usual, and she departed, giving a polite curtsey to the visitor standing by the bed.

That he was a gentleman was obvious from his appearance; fresh complexioned, he was perhaps sixteen or seventeen years of age. None of Will's acquaintances wore smooth silk stockings or carried clean white gloves as did this young man who smiled down at him, and he was perplexed.

'Mr Foster – Will, it's good to see you! I have been extremely anxious about you.' His voice was cultured.

'I'm sorry, sir, but I'm afraid tha has me at a disadvantage.' Will thought the face and voice seemed familiar and yet he had no recollection of having ever met him.

The young man's smile broadened and he gave a mock bow. 'John Rayner at your service, Mr Foster, lately of the good ship *Polar Star*!'

His smile disappeared and he became serious. 'Surely you remember the man whose life you saved? But for you, I would now be sleeping in a watery grave with only the creatures of the ocean for company!'

'Young John!' exclaimed Will with a grin and pulled

31

himself up in the bed. 'I didn't recognize thee, sir,' he added as realization told him that this was no ordinary shipmate.

The crew of the whaler had known that the youth assigned to them was of a different class by his manner and speech, but he had not assumed a superior attitude towards them. They were familiar with the sons of merchants coming on board the whalers for a voyage, but they usually shared the master's cabin, unlike 'Young John', as they had called him, who had taken his food with the men and shared their accommodation.

'Mr Foster – Will, I have come to thank you yet again, as I fear that you were in no fit state to listen to my thanks whilst on board. We were fearful that you would not make the voyage home, and I was grieved to think that it was due to my carelessness.'

'Nay, tha was inexperienced, that's all, we all learn by our mistakes,' answered Will, 'and from what I recall it wasn't just thee who should tek 'blame.' He lay back on his pillow and looked at John Rayner. He remembered it all so clearly now.

They'd lowered their boat into the water with five men on board, rather than wait for a replacement for the sixth who was sick, for the whales were there and they didn't want to miss out on a kill. Alan Swinburn was the boatsteerer and linesman, Richard Bewley, Rob Hardwick and himself were harpooners and young John was there to assist.

Three other boats had put off from the *Polar Star* and others could be seen from the *Greenland Star* which had anchored nearby. There had been good fishing that day and the men were jubilant: there would be a handsome bonus on their return home.

They'd secured two whales with the help of two of the other boats and were returning to the whaler, when a third whale appeared alongside them. It was obviously in great distress and a gaping hole could be seen in its side where a harpoon had hit but the line severed. The whale, on seeing them so close, plunged suddenly below them, causing the sea to erupt and tossing the boat about wildly. It emerged again, staining the turbulent water with its blood, its great body threshing in convulsive spasms.

Rob Hardwick threw a harpoon and secured a hit, paying out the line to secure it, but the whale dived again and drew them closer to the ice.

It was as it rose again from the depths of the seething sea that Richard Bewley threw his harpoon with all his force, but the boat at the same time was pulled with such speed by the frantic creature that he overbalanced and disappeared over the side.

Now there was a great commotion as the other boats drew around, trying to secure the stricken whale, while the men in Will's boat searched the icy sea in vain for Bewley. It proved an impossible task for the weight of the whale drew them away from the area in which he had fallen.

'Are you in much pain?' John Rayner's question disturbed Will's meditation.

'Not so much as I was,' he answered. 'Only I could swear that my leg is still there, it throbs that much.' He could still feel, or thought he could, the ever increasing tightness of the line around his leg.

Alan Swinburn had handed over the task of linesman to John whilst he concentrated on keeping the boat steady as they were pulled faster and faster through the water towards the ice. But John, though willing, was inexperienced in the work and though he worked fast, throwing water over the lines to stop them from burning with friction, he somehow entangled himself in the uncoiling rope and with a terrified shout toppled overboard.

Will had moved swiftly, and leaning perilously over the side managed to grab hold of the drowning boy by his hair, holding fast as the boat plunged violently. It was then that he'd felt the lash of the line, for with no-one to feed it out it ran uncontrollably faster and faster, until finally it whiplashed with great speed and ferocity around his leg.

He recalled the agonizing burning and yet his grip had tightened on the boy and he didn't let go. Rob Hardwick without hesitation swung his axe and severed the line which held Will fast and would have dragged him out of the boat. Together they had managed to pull the half-drowned boy out of the water. Now, piece by piece, Will and John Rayner put together the memories of that terrible day. Other boats were put off from the *Polar Star* when it was seen that they were in difficulties, and the whale with a final frenzied struggle was slaughtered and the blood-stained corpse towed back to the whaler.

'We were given rum and blankets when we got back on board,' John said. 'I swear I shall never feel so cold again as I did that day.'

It was some hours later that the surgeon, Mr Ambrose, was sent for to attend Will's leg, for the flesh had ballooned up around the circle of line below his knee and the men couldn't cut it free. The surgeon painstakingly picked with his scalpel until the line fell away, but by now the wound was bleeding and raw and Will couldn't stand. He was given another tot of rum and put to bed in the surgeon's cabin.

'I don't recall what else happened,' Will frowned, 'but perhaps it's just as well.'

'You were very ill and delirious for days,' John replied, 'and we thought that you would die, for your leg became gangrenous. Mr Ambrose took the decision with the captain's consent, that the only chance you had was if he amputated.'

John shuddered. He remembered the nausea he had felt when the surgeon opened up his wooden case and he had seen the array of knives and instruments designed, so Mr Ambrose explained to him, to cut quickly through flesh and sinew, before the patient went into shock. 'I felt that it was because of me you were in such a perilous state, and I should volunteer to assist him. I might say that I hope in God's name I never ever have to do it again.'

'Don't think on it now,' replied Will calmly to alleviate his distress, for he realized that the young man was troubled by the incident. Over the years at sea Will had seen many accidents with flensing knives and drownings, and knew that it took years to become hardened.

'But I am in your debt, Will, and you must let me help you in any way that I can. I am not yet of age of course and cannot help with finance, but I have told my uncle, Isaac Masterson, who is also my guardian, of the circumstances and that I wish to be of service to you.'

Will's eyebrows rose: he had had no idea who this young man's family was and he was surprised that he was a nephew of the shipowner. And yet his words also angered him, for he was a proud man and not prepared to accept charity from anyone. He replied civilly but curtly, 'I thank thee most kindly, Mr Rayner, but I have no need of thy charity. I only did what I would do for any man, no matter what his station, and as soon as I am out of this hospital bed I'll find work of some kind.'

John Rayner flushed. 'I beg your pardon, Will, I didn't intend to sound condescending.' He put out his hand. 'Come, let's shake hands, I came only with good intentions and to offer my grateful thanks.'

Will's good nature was restored. He saw that his former shipmate was genuinely concerned and put out his hand. 'If tha has a mind to help, Mr John, there is summat tha could do. I don't want owt for myself but I'm worried about my Maria. She's expecting another bairn, and our young 'un is sick. If tha could see that she gets my benefit, I would appreciate it, just till I get out of here.'

With the promise that he would do all he could John Rayner left, leaving Will to ponder once more on what the future held for him.

A dark mass of cloud hung low over them as Maria and Tom made their way back from the Infirmary along the road into the town. She turned to look back just once, but all she could see of the building was a dim light shining through the windows; the rest of the building was shrouded by the sleeting rain which was coming down in torrents, drenching their thin clothes and making them cling coldly round their bodies.

'Oh, Tom, I must stop and rest a bit, or I fear 'worst, I'm fair wore out.'

They were within sight of the town's perimeter and could see the square tower of the new church of St John, the wooden scaffolding still surrounding the unfinished building.

'Let's shelter in 'church, Ma,' said Tom, his teeth chattering with cold. His cap pulled down around his ears, he took hold of her hand and hurried her towards the red brick walls.

They sat on the stone floor beneath the raised arches, watching as the rain splashed and cascaded on the road outside, until Maria felt that she could continue. Still the rain persisted, and now she began to feel uneasy. She knew that if it did not abate, then at high tide the river might well break over the banks and flood the streets as it had done so often before, oozing thick mud and slime down the alleys and entries and into the houses.

'We must get back, Tom, I'm bothered about our Alice,' she said, picking herself up from the stone floor, her bones aching with cold. She wondered if God's presence was yet in the unconsecrated church, for although she wouldn't have described herself as religious she had a simple trust in His mercy.

She peered through the door into the empty building, which was littered with bricks and stone and workmen's materials, and gazed up at the tiers of unglazed windows, searching for a sign of spiritual existence, then offered up a silent prayer asking Him to look kindly on them in their need.

As they scurried through the entry, their heads bent against the wind which was now blowing hard, they felt the coldness of water around their ankles, and slippery mud beneath the thin soles of their boots, which were now wet and useless against the weather. The water hadn't yet reached their door but was almost up to the step.

The fire was out and the room in darkness and Maria called upstairs, 'We're back, Mrs Morton, I'll take Alice now.'

'Come on up, Maria, and have a warm by 'fire, tha must be half starved.'

Mrs Morton was sitting by a blazing fire, with Alice on one knee and her own youngest suckling at her breast, her skirts pulled up around her fat thighs which were toasting from the heat of the fire.

'Don't ask where we got 'fuel,' she said with a sly grin when she saw the look of amazement on Maria's face. 'Our Francis brought it home and it doesn't do to ask too many questions.' She leaned forward and stirred a pot of stew that was bubbling on the flames.

'He brought back a nice piece o' meat as well that somebody give him.' She sighed contentedly, 'There's some grand folk about, Maria, always willing to part company with summat for a few favours.'

Maria didn't ask any questions, but she and Tom moved nearer to the heat of the fire. It was well known by the local community that the Mortons' eldest son was a rogue and a thief. How he had kept out of the county jail and avoided transportation no-one could understand, except that he was a happy-go-lucky charmer who had probably bribed officials with the promise of favours to follow.

'Tek off tha shawl and tha skirt, Maria, tha's soaked through.' Mrs Morton moved back to make more room. 'Come on, and thee, young Tom, tek off tha boots and dry thissen.'

They sat by the blazing fire, their wet clothes steaming, and accepted Mrs Morton's offer of supper, which Maria thought tasted wonderful as she supped the hot greasy stew.

'By, that was grand, Mrs Morton, 'best I've ever tasted,' said Tom enthusiastically as he drained his bowl. Mrs Morton gave him a cuff around the ear and took the bowl from him, refilling it from the cauldron.

'Plenty more where that came from,' she laughed cheerfully. 'Anything tha wants, our Frank can get.' She winked knowingly at Maria. 'Tha only has to ask.'

' 'Only thing that I want is for Will to get better. And there's nothing nor nobody can give him back his leg. Nor have we anything to offer in return for a favour,' Maria added so as not to offend Mrs Morton who had been both kind and generous towards them.

She was interrupted in mid sentence by a sudden rattle at the outer door and the sound of rushing footsteps up the stairs. Mrs Morton sat stockstill, looking tensely towards the door, and then relaxed as Francis Morton came bounding in, in a great hurry, followed closely by a dishevelled-looking man with a rough beard.

Maria picked up her shawl from the hearth where it was drying and put it around her shoulders, for she had taken off her wet blouse and was sitting in just her shift.

But the sharp-eyed Francis had already seen the glimpse of her bare shoulders. He put down his bag and, dropping his wet coat to the floor, came across to her by the fire.

'How do, Maria, tha looks well; 'fire has put 'roses in tha cheeks.' He touched her still damp hair and delicately wound a lock of it round his fingers, an amiable smile on his handsome face. Nervously she moved away from him. He was well known as a womanizer. His smile grew broader as he saw her embarrassment and he drew closer, whispering in her ear, his warm breath fanning her cheek.

'I was going to ask thee for help, for tha to say we'd been together all afternoon!'

He laughed as he saw the shocked look on her face. 'But as we're both wet and our boots soaked through, perhaps we'd better not or we'll both be shipped off to Botany Bay. Though if we'd been together all afternoon, Maria, we wouldn't have been out in 'rain, we'd have found somewhere warm and cosy!'

He drew away and roared with laughter and his companion joined in until with a rough edge to her voice Mrs Morton ordered them to stop at once or she would throw them both out.

'Don't lead Maria into thy mad schemes,' she said angrily, 'she's got enough trouble of her own without sharing thine.'

'Trouble! Who's got trouble?' Francis answered jubilantly. 'Not me,' and he picked up the bag that he'd dropped and shook it. There was a soft clank as if metal was wrapped in cloth. 'We shall celebrate. My troubles are over!'

'Or only just beginning,' said Mrs Morton looking anxiously at Maria.

Maria stood up and hurriedly gathered up their things. 'We must go, Mrs Morton, we've taken up too much of tha time, tha's been very kind, looking after Alice and everything.'

Her thanks tumbled out as she picked up Alice and took hold of Tom, who was gazing with admiration at Francis, who had stripped off his wet shirt and was standing bare chested, his blue eyes dancing with mischief. She pushed the boy towards the stairs. She had no wish to get involved with the Morton intrigues for she suspected that sooner or later the law would come bursting through the door, rounding up all who had been in contact with Francis Morton.

Downstairs, she put the children into bed and gave them a tot of the rum which she kept for emergencies, and then, climbing in beside them swallowed a large mouthful herself, grimacing as the rough spirit set her throat on fire. 'It's medicine,' she explained to Alice in reply to the child's questioning. 'It'll keep us warm and help us to sleep.'

But in spite of the rum they spent a restless night listening to the howl of the wind and the sound of the relentless rain. Maria tossed and turned, imagining that she could hear footsteps on the stairs above her head, for their bed was under the stairwell and every sound could be heard. In the past she had often been awakened by the creaking of the treads as someone crept upstairs to the room above, and this night, her senses disturbed by the day's events and Francis Morton's demeanour, she imagined constantly that she could hear whispering and grim laughter above her.

I must get another lock for 'door, she thought the next morning as she rose heavy-eyed from lack of sleep. She put her feet to the floor and with a shudder drew them back instantly. The rain which had beaten down constantly all night had risen above the doorstep, seeping into the entrance and down into their room leaving an inch of muddy water over the floor.

Maria wept as she swept the water out of the door, her skirts tied up about her knees, only to find that the entry was flooded and there was nowhere for the water to go. The old gutters were already choked by the silt from the river and completely blocked.

Dejectedly she went off to work at the staith side. She couldn't afford to lose another day's wages, and felt wretched and dispirited as she worked amongst the mass of cold, wet fish, which seemed to stare at her accusingly with their pale eyes as if she was responsible for their predicament as well as her own.

In the midst of her misery she was worrying too about Annie. She hadn't come in to work and Maria asked some of the other women if they had seen her. They shook their heads and one of them laughed cynically. ' 'Reckon she's spending 'bonus already. She's well shut of Alan anyway.'

They sounded hard-hearted, these women, but some of them knew from their own experience what it was like to have a bully for a husband.

I must go round to see her, she thought. Poor lass, she must be in a state.

But as she made her way home after her shift had ended she heard a familiar voice calling to her.

'Hey, Maria, Maria! Come here, I want thee.'

Annie was leaning against the doorway of the Swan

Inn. Her face was flushed and she was slightly unsteady on her feet.

Maria went across to her. 'Annie, tha shouldn't be here.' The inn was notorious, serving sailors and foreign seamen who came into the port, and wasn't a place for decent women. 'Where are thy bairns?'

Annie laughed wildly; plainly she had had too much to drink. 'They're all right, tucked up in bed where I left 'em. Come on in and have a drink. Drown thy sorrows, that's what I'm doing.'

She leaned forward and Maria could smell the gin on her breath. 'I've found a friend,' she whispered confidentially. 'He's paying.'

'Oh, Annie, tha'll pay, tha knows that. Come on home,' Maria begged her friend. Her pleas were without success, and reluctantly she left her there, Annie's raucous laughter echoing after her.

'Tha's had a visitor, Maria.' Mrs Morton called from the upstairs window. 'Gentry by 'look of him.' She added curiously, 'He wouldn't say what he wanted. Said he'd come back later.'

'It can only be somebody from 'company. There's nobody else.'

Maria went indoors and wearily started to clean up the room. She took a broom and swept the water out. The water in the entry had subsided, leaving a thick layer of slimy silt, treacherous to walk on. Then she washed her hands and face and tidied her hair and prepared to wait for her visitor.

Maria knew that some of the other fish wives laughed at her for keeping herself and her children clean and their clothes mended, and even called her derisive names and said she was too proud. If John Rayner, when he returned to Wyke Entry with its stinking layer of mud and other unmentionable deposits, expected anyone other than a female drudge to greet him, then he showed no surprise on his pleasant face save for a raised eyebrow and a quick smile.

41

'Mrs Foster? I called earlier – your neighbour—!' He pointed upstairs.

'Yes, please come in, sir. Tha'll be from 'company?' asked Maria as she showed him inside.

She saw his expression change as he gazed around the dark, gloomy room, at the floor still covered in mud, and a flush came to her cheeks. 'We – we've had a flood,' she stammered. 'Once the mud's dried out, I shall be able to sweep it through.'

'I'm so sorry, Mrs Foster. For you to have to deal with this on top of all the worry about your husband. I had no idea—' He started to say something more and then stopped in confusion.

'Will asked me to collect his wages, which I have here.' He brought out a small bag from his pocket which he gave to her. 'But the bonus is not yet settled, there is some dispute as to whether or not it is due, as the ship returned early. There will have to be a customs enquiry before it is paid.'

He saw the anxious look on her face and was quick to reassure. 'Please don't worry, Mrs Foster. My uncle, Mr Masterson, is confident that it will be settled satisfactorily.' He turned to make his departure. 'My name is John Rayner and I am for ever in your husband's debt, Mrs Foster. I will do whatever I can to help you, you only need to ask.'

Maria reflected that this was the second time today that she had been offered help and considered that, of the two, if she was in need she would unhesitatingly choose John Rayner's assistance. She recognized in the young man someone who would resolutely give help without asking a favour in return.

'He'll need work when he's well, Mr Rayner,' she answered. 'If tha should hear of owt?' She hesitated, knowing that she was asking the impossible. Will knew no other life than that of the sea and yet as she smiled shyly at the young man standing in front of her she felt for the first time a ray of hope, an uplifting of her spirits as warmly he returned the smile.

42

3

'I had no conception of the conditions these people are living in, Uncle. How could I have been so ignorant of the poverty and squalor that exists in places like that hell hole of an alley?'

John paced the floor in the elegant drawing room of his uncle's High Street home. His face was flushed with anger and his fair hair was dishevelled as in his concern he ran his fingers through it.

Isaac Masterson smiled. He liked to see a sign of passion in a young man, and until John had asked to go on the first voyage of the *Polar Star* he had thought him a trifle too gentle and mild for someone so young. But from all the reports that had come through from his captain and mate – and Isaac Masterson always made sure that he knew all that happened on board his vessels – John had done exceptionally well.

'It is a fact that conditions are not always very good,' he answered calmly as he stood with his back to the fire which was burning in the marble fireplace. 'But I think that perhaps you chose a bad time. Everything looks worse when it's so cold and wet. This has been a terrible summer.' He lifted the tails of his coat and moved nearer to the fire.

'But, Uncle, think then how it will be in the winter, when it freezes and the snow comes. How do they manage?' exclaimed John, adding bitterly, 'There is no wonder that so many bodies are fished out of the river. Death must be the only comfort and certainty that the poor wretches have to look forward to.'

'John, my dear boy, don't get yourself into such a state, I'm sure they wouldn't thank you for it.' His aunt interrupted him from where she was lying on a small

43

sofa. Her face was pale from lack of sunshine, for she was in the fifth month of pregnancy and refrained from any exercise, save for an occasional carriage drive to visit friends. She adjusted the shawl which covered her. 'From what I understand of it, most of them prefer to live like that or else they would move, wouldn't they?'

John controlled the outburst which came to his lips. Isobel wasn't knowingly unkind or unfeeling, simply ignorant and unconcerned about anything which didn't affect her or her family and their comforts. She had been most upset when he had announced his intention to go whaling, and couldn't comprehend at all why he desired to risk the dangers of the voyage when he could have stayed comfortably at home and kept her company.

He was grateful to his aunt and uncle, who had taken him into their care when both his parents had died of smallpox ten years before. Isobel was just a young bride then with expectations of starting a family of her own, and yet she had welcomed the young orphan warmly and embraced him as her own. As the years went by and there was no sign of children of their own, John became her constant companion until he was sent to school. Isobel had declared that she wasn't too distressed at her childlessness, for she had heard that it was quite a distasteful business, but now at the age of thirty she had become pregnant, to her dismay and her husband's delight.

'Aunt, they have nowhere to move to,' John explained gently now. 'They have to stay where the work is and for most of these people it's here by the river.' He waved his arm in the direction of the Old Harbour which ran along the bottom of the garden to the rear of the house.

'Just like us then,' she declared, dismissing the subject and picking up her needlework which was lying on the cushion beside her.

John didn't intend to let the matter drop. 'If you had seen this young woman,' he said, 'you would have seen that they don't all like to live in these hovels. I could see

44

by her manner that she was downcast by her circumstances, and yet she made no complaint.'

'I hope, John, that you didn't go inside the dwelling, there might well be all kinds of loathesome diseases lurking there,' exclaimed his aunt.

He laughed at her expression of horror. 'Don't worry, Aunt, I haven't brought anything mortal home. As a matter of fact,' he added, 'Mrs Foster is very neat and presentable, unlike her frowzy neighbour who looked as if she would steal the coat from my back, and who expected a reward for delivering a simple message.'

He turned to his uncle. 'Seriously, sir, I would like to help them if it is at all possible; to make some kind of amends for what happened on the voyage.'

Isaac agreed to think about it. Will Foster had been a good and honest worker for many years, though he didn't hold out a lot of hope of finding him work in an industry that needed only fit and able-bodied men.

John remained sick at heart, and angry with himself for being unable to dismiss the picture of poverty which he had encountered that afternoon. He felt shame that he couldn't wait to get out of the dirty, narrow alley, and yet as he entered the doorway of his own home the contrast had hit him like a blow.

His uncle's house was large and elegant, with an imposing entrance and staircase, with light airy rooms and fine furnishings. True, they couldn't escape the odour of blubber and seed oil, and the servants were instructed by Isobel that on no account should they open any windows lest the furniture and draperies be contaminated by the stench.

He glanced now at his handsome aunt as she sat serenely on her sofa, her golden curls piled elaborately on top of her head and her blue silk dress falling in elegant folds around her feet, and thought again of the raven-haired woman with the large grey eyes in the shabby, mud-spattered dress, who had smiled so sweetly at him and who had asked for nothing but the chance of earning an honest living.

Isaac Masterton sat down thoughtfully in a comfortable chair by the fire. He knew that all his nephew said was true, that the people down by the river lived in abject conditions in mean, damp houses without sanitation; and the situation was getting worse as more people poured into the town looking for work and housing, trying to escape the poverty of the countryside.

He did the best he could for his own men, he reflected. They received good rates of pay, and ample food and provisions were provided on board his ships. His vessels were sound – they had to be to withstand the battering they received from the gales and the ice. But he was disappointed with the *Polar Star*. She was Plymouth built, three hundred tons, and he had had her specially strengthened and fortified to resist the pressure of the ice. He had expected this last voyage to be a long and successful one, but the vessel had been beset by problems from the time she had reached the northern seas.

He sighed. He'd lost three good men, two dead and one maimed, and at least four others had lost fingers to the frost. He looked down at his own hands, at the stump of the little finger on his left hand, where he too had been the victim of the deadly cold and at which his sensitive wife shuddered.

Still, he thought, they had caught four whales, all good sized, and a number of seals, so the voyage should break even as far as profit was concerned, and the damage to the *Polar Star* wasn't irreparable. The ship's carpenters had done some good work on repairing the damaged timbers when the ice had hit and she should be sound again, ready in time for the next voyage.

He only hoped that the *Greenland Star* would come safely home, for the last news he had received was that conditions were bad and that she was fast in the ice and unable to move. Captain de Raad of the *Polar Star* had taken the right decision to head for home rather than risk the ship breaking up.

'Come and sit down, John, there are a few things that

I'd like to discuss with you.' He indicated the chair opposite. 'I would like your opinion on a venture that I am planning. And you, Isobel, my dear, I would like you to attend if you would.' He paused for a moment. 'I have in mind the notion of purchasing a country estate. There is a property on the market which I am very taken with; a fine house with good land overlooking the sea.'

His wife looked at him in astonishment. 'A house in the country! But whatever would we do? Who should we see?'

'You would do whatever it is you do now,' he answered rather testily. 'You will have your coach and you could visit, and have people to visit you. Much as you do now – but the air will be better.' He smiled. 'And there will be no noxious odours to complain of, only the smell of the sea and the scent of the flowers which you will grow in your garden.'

John cut in enthusiastically. 'It sounds a capital idea, Uncle, and presumably you would keep this house for offices and storage?'

'That's it exactly. We're getting very short of warehouse accommodation, and this will be convenient with the garden running down to the harbour edge. The clerks and tallymen will work from here and that means a saving of time and money.'

He rose from his chair as a servant came in to announce supper. 'But more of that later, for I have other things that I wish to discuss with you on the same matter.' He turned to his wife. 'If you are agreeable, my dear, and the weather is clement, I suggest that we take a drive over to see the house on Saturday. I will make the necessary arrangements with the agent.'

During supper, which was a plain, well-cooked meal since Isaac Masterson was an unpretentious man with no inclination for what he called fancy food, Isobel asked with a sudden burst of enthusiasm if they would have new furnishings and carpets if they should remove to the country – the embellishments of a town house would be quite unsuitable for country living.

'Yes, yes, I expect so,' replied her husband benevolently. 'The house will be considerably larger and I suppose that nothing will fit. The air will be very good for you out there, my love, and for our child.'

He didn't add that the sooner they could get away the better, for the doctor had warned him that Isobel's confinement was sure to be difficult and possibly dangerous as she was at such a mature age for a first child. In a larger house they would have room for a nurse to live in as well as the midwife. Isaac was determined that his wife and child would want for nothing.

'So, Uncle, will you try your hand at farming as well as shipping?' John asked later as he and Isaac sat alone together, Isobel having retired to rest in her room.

'I will,' he answered, holding a glass of brandy towards the fire to warm it. 'And I hope to be as successful in that as I have been in shipping. But I must confess that I am looking towards the future and the time when I can safely leave the running of the business in other hands, to someone I can trust.'

He looked keenly at John and sipped the amber liquid. 'I would like to take on a partner, but the man I have in mind is not yet ready, being rather young and inexperienced.'

John raised his eyes from the fire into which he had been gazing reflectively. 'A partner, sir?'

'Aye,' replied his uncle. 'Do you think that you could contemplate it? I have had the plan in mind for some time. You will need more instruction, of course, and practical knowledge. If the men know that their employer has had experience of the hazards out on the ice and the working conditions, then they will respect him; not just as someone who pays their wages, but as someone who understands their needs.'

He finished his brandy and went on, 'I do believe that this is the reason why this company has been so successful. But whaling isn't something to be undertaken lightly. As you have already discovered, it is a perilous and hazardous life and you will need to think seriously about it.'

'It's what I have dreamed of, Uncle, and more than I could ever have hoped for. I can't thank you enough for what you and Aunt Isobel have done for me and for the affection you have given me. If by becoming your partner I can in some way repay your generosity then I shall be more than happy.'

Isaac nodded. It was the reply he expected from his sister's child. John was always courteous and very warm hearted, just as his mother had been. He had planned for some years that when the boy came of age and if he came up to expectations, then he would offer him a partnership. If his own child lived and was a son, it would of course make some difference, but as he was now in his middle forties he couldn't envisage that he would live to see a son take over the running of the business.

'I would very much like to go whaling again, sir,' John added. 'As this last voyage was so short, I don't feel that I acquired much experience.' He smiled grimly. 'That is, apart from assisting the surgeon to amputate that poor devil's leg.'

'Very well. If you're sure, then we'll work towards a future partnership.'

John was very sure. He wanted to explain, but hesitated in case his uncle thought him a fool, that in spite of the danger and the risks which existed, the excitement that he had felt on his first voyage and the soul-stirring exhilaration on seeing the ice for the first time had filled him with wonder. The field of ice spreading before them, with its curious white light hovering above it, had given him an extraordinary sensation of entering a mysterious new world.

For three weeks Maria walked each day down the long road to the Infirmary. She had wanted to bring food to tempt Will's appetite, for she could see how thin he had become, but she was told that this was against hospital rules which were extremely strict. She brought him clean

49

nightshirts which she had washed at home or, if the weather was fine, along with other women, she would wash the soiled linen in the clear water of the Spring Drain which ran alongside the hospital grounds.

Then at the end of the third week she arrived at his bedside to find him sitting in a chair, a nurse at his side and a pair of wooden crutches leaning against the bed.

' 'Doctor says he can go 'ome, missus,' said the nurse. 'He just has to walk 'length of 'ward and he can go. We can't do any more for him in 'ere.'

Maria moved forward to help Will, but he put his hand up to stop her.

'No, I must do this missen. I don't want anybody's help.' And gripping the iron bed rail he pulled himself up and, gingerly balancing, propped a crutch under each arm and slowly and painfully started to move along the ward.

Sweat ran down his face as he concentrated on remaining upright, and with the unaccustomed activity the pain in his body and limbs was excruciating. He was determined to reach the end of the ward unaided and without falling, and yet as he almost reached the far door he overbalanced, falling with a crash to the floor.

Maria rushed towards him.

'Leave me be, woman,' he shouted in a voice that she had never before heard him use. 'I have to do this missen, I won't be a cripple and rely on women's help!'

He saw the look of dismay on Maria's face as she stood back and he was sorry, but he was resolved that from the start he would still be his own man and would look to no-one for help, not even his wife.

'Then I'll go and hire thee a cart,' she said curtly, 'for even thou can't walk all 'way home on a pair of wooden sticks.' With a flounce she turned away and walked out of the door leaving him sprawled on the floor.

His anger evaporated as she disappeared, and he cursed himself out loud for the fool he was with his quick temper. He pulled himself upright again and once more set off to walk down the length of the ward, this time with the encouragement of the other patients, who cheered him on as he passed their beds.

Ten times down the ward and ten times back he went without falling again, until he fell back exhausted on to his bed, his face flushed with effort and his armpits sore where the crutches had rubbed.

It was here that Maria found him later when she cautiously put her head around the door. 'Art thou still in a foul temper, Will Foster? Or is it safe to come in?' she asked.

'Come here, lass.' Oblivious to the grins of the other men, he drew her near to him on the bed. 'Next time I shout at thee, just clout me one with my crutch.' He buried his face in the soft dark cloud of her hair. 'I'm that desperate to get home.'

'Come on then, let's go.' She disentangled herself from his arms. ' 'Doctor says he'll discharge thee,' and with a light laugh she added, 'Thy carriage awaits at 'door, sir.'

'Carriage, what carriage?' he asked suspiciously.

'Well, hardly a carriage,' she answered, her lips trembling a little with apprehension. 'More of a cart, for I just met Francis Morton and he arranged it for us.' She spoke rapidly for she knew that Will didn't approve of the Morton family and she saw his face darken.

'Just this once, Will, accept some help, please – the Mortons have been very good to me, and I'm just about all in.'

He smiled at her then as he saw the tears glisten in her eyes and he took her roughened hands in his. 'It's all right, Maria, don't tek on so. I'll be glad to ride in Frank Morton's carriage, just as long as it isn't going up 'turnpike road to 'gallows.'

Maria smiled back and was relieved to know that she didn't have to explain to Will how she had met Francis on the road outside the hospital, where he had obviously been waiting for her, and on hearing of their need for some kind of transport had offered to help. When she

51

had thanked him he'd laughed softly and told her to think nothing of it.

It was later, as they'd returned to the hospital after collecting the horse and cart and he'd helped her down with a swagger, that he'd kept hold of her longer than was necessary, and pulling her towards him and running his hand over the swelling protuberance of her belly had said smoothly, 'Of course, Maria, don't forget tha's in my debt now, and I might one day come and collect!'

The cool air was like a tonic as Will emerged from the hospital after the weeks of confinement indoors and on board ship, and he took a long, deep breath, filling his lungs. He gazed at the lush green meadows surrounding the Infirmary and thanked God for his recovery. Although he still felt weak and in pain, he experienced a longing to start his life once again after having almost lost it.

'Can we go through 'market, Frank?' he asked, 'I've a mind to see a bit o' life, now that I'm out.'

Francis good-naturedly agreed and they drove along at a cracking pace. They passed the fine new houses which were being built on the outskirts of the town, some of them already occupied, and Francis, who seemed to be very knowledgeable, told them who lived where, and which rich merchant owned what.

'Tha should see some of 'fine silver, Maria,' he said cynically. 'It fair makes tha mouth water. Doesn't seem right, does it, that some should have so much and others have nowt?'

'I reckon they've earned it, some of 'em,' answered Will sharply. 'I don't begrudge them it.'

They turned into the narrow Posterngate and jostled with other carts as they moved down towards Holy Trinity Church, and into the Market Place which was congested with stalls. Crowds were gathering in groups to meet and talk and drive a bargain with the stallholders.

'Will, Will Foster!' a voice called to them, and Francis pulled the old horse to a stop as they saw the tall figure of John Rayner striding towards them.

He held out his hand to Will. 'It's good to see you out again,' and turning towards Maria, he touched his hat, 'and you too, Mrs Foster.'

They talked for a few minutes before he took his leave, and as he turned away Will said hesitatingly but still with a touch of pride, 'If tha does hear of owt in 'way of work, I'd be glad if tha'd put in a word.' He glanced towards Maria who was sitting in the back of the cart, her shawl covering her swelling figure, and muttered, 'Matters are rather pressing, as tha'll realize.'

'I'll keep my ears open,' John answered as he turned away. 'Rest assured.'

'Mixing with quality now, are we?' asked Francis with a sneer as he shook the reins. 'Aye well, it's just as well to keep in with folks who have plenty, tha never knows when they might be useful.'

Will didn't answer though he could feel his temper rising, the more so as he realized that Francis's voice had carried and that John Rayner must have heard him.

Their progress towards home was slow as many of Will's acquaintances stopped them to enquire about his health and to ask curiously how the accident had happened, tutting sympathetically as they regarded the stump of his leg.

Will was reticent and sometimes abrupt. He hadn't as yet come to terms with the disability or how to cope with it, and for those unfamiliar with the whaling life there was no possibility of them envisaging the dangers, privations and sufferings encountered in the arctic regions. And as for the men of the whaling fraternity who greeted him, his comrades in adversity, there was no need for words of explanation, for they shared an alliance with an unspoken bond of understanding between them.

Saturday morning was fine but cloudy as Isaac and Isobel Masterson stepped into their carriage to start the journey towards the village of Monkston to view Garston Hall. It was ten o'clock and the street was crowded with people. Some of the women had bunched together in small groups when they saw the carriage waiting outside the house. Mrs Masterson was well known for her fashionable dress, and spectators often gathered if word got out that the Mastersons were going out to dine or visit the theatre.

However, if they expected high fashion today they were somewhat disappointed, for Isobel had dressed in a simple dark green gown, which was comfortable for travelling as her figure enlarged. As her maid Ellie had helped her to dress she had told the girl to leave the lower buttons of her jacket undone for comfort. Over the top she wore a long wool cloak, and perched on top of her fair ringlets was a green felt hat with feathers.

Isaac put a blanket around her. 'Keep well wrapped up, my dear,' he said. 'It will be perhaps a two-hour journey to reach the house, but I fancy the drive will be pleasant. It is a straight enough road, though perhaps a little rough in places.'

He called to the coachman that they were ready before closing the window and the pair of greys responded to the flick of the reins, the crowds moving back against the walls of the houses to make room in the narrow thoroughfare.

The coachman slowed the horses as they approached the east end of the dock, and Isaac looked out of the carriage window to view the shipping. They then turned to cross over the River Hull, rattling over the ancient, rickety North Bridge, passing over the crowded shipyards which stretched on either side, and headed out of town along the turnpike road towards the plain of Holderness and the sea.

Except for tradesmen and farmers coming into the town for the market, they saw little traffic as they moved swiftly along through the villages of Witham and Drypool and out into the open countryside. Isobel viewed with some misgivings the lack of houses and population as they left the busy streets behind them for the vastness of the empty countryside, interspersed only with a scattering of village houses and isolated farmhouses.

'I don't know if I shall like it so well, Isaac,' she said petulantly. 'What shall I do for company when you are at your business?'

Isaac sighed. The problems of females were quite beyond him. He led such an active, busy life that he couldn't imagine what it would be like to have nothing to do but yearn for other people's company.

'You will find with a child to take care of, a large house to run and servants to organize that your time will be very full,' he said patiently, patting her hand, 'and,' he added, 'there will be plenty of people anxious to make your acquaintance. I am not entirely unknown, you know.'

Isobel sulked, a frown wrinkling her smooth forehead. 'But we have so many people coming and going all day in our town house that I shall feel very cut off out in the country.'

'Then what we will do,' replied her husband in a conciliatory tone, 'is keep a small suite of rooms in the house in High Street, and then if you wish to visit the theatre or friends, you may do so without the inconvenience of a long drive home again. But mark my words, you will be glad to get back to the fresh air and open space.'

'If only we could go to the other side of town,' she said, determined not to give in without a struggle. 'That's where everyone else is going.'

And that, thought Isaac, is precisely why we are not. Wisely, however, he said nothing.

Garston Hall had been built in 1780 on the site of an old castle, and as the agent, Mr James, was at pains to point out was set in one of the few landscaped parks along the Holderness coast. It lay quite close to the sea, but not so close as to feel the full effects of the east wind, which blew only moderately that day.

Isobel was transfixed: she had had no idea that it would be so large or so grand, and her gaze followed the agent's hand as he pointed out the round towers and battlements which embellished the house, and the fine mature trees which surrounded it, hiding it from view and protecting it from the elements.

'I have arranged for Mrs Scryven, the present housekeeper, to show Mrs Masterson the house, if that is agreeable to you,' said Mr James, turning with a smile and a bow towards Isobel at the main door. 'And I will conduct you around the grounds, sir.'

Mrs Scryven curtsied, her weather-tanned face inscrutable as Isobel entered the hall. 'If tha'll come this road, ma'am, I'll show thee round.'

Isobel hid a smile. The woman had a rough country accent and although she was neat in appearance, with a clean white apron and bonnet, she was very small and very stout with roughened, red hands and had no grace.

She imagined her friends' astonishment if they should be greeted by such a person when visiting, and the delight they would find in tittle tattling to all and sundry the news that the Mastersons had a rustic bumpkin for a servant. No, that would never do, she decided. If they took the house, and with it new status, the woman would have to go, or else be relegated to the kitchen where she wouldn't be seen.

Mentally Isobel began to plan which of her servants she would bring with her and the roles they would play. Fortunately her own maids knew how to behave. She insisted that they spoke clearly without mumbling and she brooked no slovenly behaviour or dress. She was certain that they were grateful to her for training them so well, and that they would relish the opportunity of being part of such a splendid household.

She was quite won over as Mrs Scryven showed her around the house, although no sign of pleasure appeared on her face. It didn't do to let servants know one's feelings, unless of course it was annoyance.

She was delighted with the spaciousness of the house, with the living rooms and dining room situated quite separately from the servants' quarters, which were at the rear of the house. She came down the central staircase from the bedrooms and across the wide hall into the drawing room, and saw out of the long windows lush green lawns, newly mown, and a long rosewalk which was covered in a profusion of climbing, scented roses which sent their perfume drifting towards the house.

'Well, what do you think of it, my dear?' asked Isaac when he returned from his tour of the grounds and had viewed the extent of the farmland and the cottages with it. The estate stretched to the cliff edge and although he didn't walk so far, he was assured by the agent that there was a good path down to the sea and a safe anchorage if he should want to keep a small boat for fishing.

'I like it very well, or will do after a few necessary alterations,' she conceded. 'There is a good dining room for entertaining, and a splendid withdrawing room, and ample provision for servants' quarters, and on the second floor there is a small room which will be suitable for a nursery, with an adjoining one for a nurse.' Isobel chattered on about the decoration required and the furniture and curtains that they would need, and quite forgot her earlier concern of being cut off from her friends.

Isaac nodded. He knew he had won. His pocket would be dented, but he didn't mind. His finances were healthy in spite of the losses on the *Polar Star*, and he had this morning heard the good news that the *Greenland Star* had been sighted off the coast of the Orkneys. He was well thought of in business circles and if the Dock Company opened up another dock, as he knew they were planning to do, with John to help him now he would buy another vessel and the future should be even brighter.

He glanced around the spacious hall. The sun was breaking through the clouds, emitting a clear radiant light through the open door. There was a sharp salty smell of the sea in the air. He felt a glow of satisfaction, it seemed almost an omen. He smiled fondly at Isobel. If all went to plan he hoped that one day he would be able to leave, as well as a prosperous shipping company, a successful country estate to his son and heir.

4

'What shall we do, Will?' Maria observed her husband
keenly as she sat across from him in front of the small
smoky fire. The children sat on the floor by their feet
playing with a pile of sticks, building them up into a
pyramid and shrieking and laughing as they knocked
them down again.

She was concerned about Will. He was well physically,
his arms and shoulders getting more muscular as they
took the weight of his body, and he moved swiftly and
expertly on his crutches. But he was morose and dejected
and often when she came home, tired from work, she
would find him sitting in front of a dead fire with his
head in his hands, or gazing into space and so pre-
occupied that he didn't even hear her come in.

'Do? About what?' Will looked at Maria vacantly. He
had been daydreaming, miles away, out on the ice,
re-living the dangers of his life at sea. He came back to
reality slowly, and as he did so felt again the weight of
depression which had been with him for so many weeks
settle on him again like a black shadow. His delight at
coming home had very soon been dissipated as he came
to realize that there was no work for him and therefore
no money, apart from his dues from the Seamen's
Sixpence, which wasn't anything like enough to feed
them all and pay the rent. His bonus still hadn't been
paid because of the dispute and he was beginning to feel
desperate.

'I know it's difficult for thee, love,' said Maria, 'but
tha'll find work soon, I'm sure. But we have to talk about
it.' She leaned across and took hold of his hand. 'We
have to think of what else tha can do.'

Will groaned and took his hand away. 'I'm a seaman,

Maria, what else can I do? I've been down to 'dock and to 'blubber yards, but there's nowt for me. There's plenty of able men looking for work as well as folk coming in from 'country districts, so why should anybody tek me?'

He got up from his chair. 'I'm off down to 'George for a bit, see if there's owt happening. I thought I might see Rob Hardwick and have a dram or two.' He put on his old coat and picked up his crutches. 'I might be late back so don't worry.'

'Will!' Maria hesitated, 'Please – be careful.'

Will laughed harshly. 'Tha needn't think that 'press gang will come after me. Even *they* wouldn't want me!' He went out of the door banging it behind him, leaving Maria miserable and unhappy.

She hadn't given a thought to the press gangs who roamed the streets of the town, coercing and threatening and carrying off any man or boy that they might find. Drunk or sober, the unwary might easily find themselves on board a naval ship. Even those seamen with a protection ticket were sometimes captured, and to avoid confrontation and sometimes pitched battles with the press gangs, the whalers' crews devised ruses to avoid them.

Maria had one night some years ago opened the door to find a strange looking woman standing there, who had asked in a quavering voice to be given food. Maria had invited her in, and to her astonishment the woman started stripping off her clothes to reveal, not a woman at all, but Will, who roared with laughter at having tricked her! He'd picked her up and swung her round and round until she was breathless, saying, 'Now let that be a lesson to thee, letting strangers into 'house.'

Now she smiled wistfully as she thought of those times. Her lively, vigorous husband, with a wit and temper to match his red hair, had disappeared and left behind a saddened, disillusioned man.

No, it wasn't the notion of the press gangs which worried her, but the assembly of drunkards and ruffians who gathered around the public houses and dram shops, looking for trouble or potential criminal activity. She hated the thought of Will becoming involved with such people, and in his present state of misery she feared that he might well succumb to temptation.

'Over here, Will!' Rob Hardwick was beckoning from the other side of the crowded room. Will had deliberately chosen to come to the George Inn close by the river in the hope that he would find some of his old shipmates. He pushed his way across towards Rob, elbowing out of the way the foreign seamen and the flock of painted women who were hanging around them.

Rob pushed a small glass of rum towards Will and waved away his offer of payment. 'Have this on me. I've had some good news today. Masterson has taken me on stand-by till 'next trip.' He looked down at his left hand with two fingers missing. 'I seem to manage all right without these.'

Will nodded, he was glad for Rob's sake about the news. But for his own accident he too would have expected to have been put on stand-by. The ship owners paid a remittance to their regular, reliable men during the time the ship was in port in order to ensure that they didn't take work with another company.

'Have you tried for work down at 'Greenland Yards?' asked Rob as he bought two more rums. Will tossed back the harsh liquid in one swallow and felt the satisfying warmth searing his throat. He was about to answer when he felt a sharp slap on his back and he turned to see Francis Morton standing behind him.

'Three more rums,' called out Francis above the hubbub of noise. 'Only make them doubles.'

Will started to protest but Francis would have none of it. 'I've just concluded a nice piece of business,' he said, winking slyly. 'So I'm not short of a bit o' brass.'

Will sighed as he drank; everybody seemed to be in luck but him. But, as the rum took effect, he began to

60

feel less depressed and hoped that perhaps the luck would rub off on him.

'Hello, Will, how's tha doing?'

He stared down at the woman who stood in front of him smiling boldly. It was Annie, but an Annie so changed he barely recognized her. Her hair was a brassy yellow and her face was white with powder. Her large blue eyes stared out of deep sockets and her lips were two bright uneven slashes of scarlet.

She giggled up at him playfully. 'Didn't tha know me, Will, Maria's best friend?'

Francis leaned forward and roughly drew her towards him. He ran his hand around the back of her neck and across her bare shoulders, his fingers probing the low neck of her shabby satin dress.

'Course he knows thee, Annie, doesn't everybody?' He bent over her and buried his face into the curve of her neck. As he laughingly pulled away there was a reddening mark on her flesh that his teeth had made. He drew up a stool and sat down drawing her on to his knee, his arms wrapped tightly around her, pulling her body close to his.

'I'll be moving off now.' Rob turned to go, and Will was about to do the same, but Francis protested loudly. 'Stay and have another drink, Will, I have summat in mind for thee.'

Will viewed this with suspicion but decided to hear him out. There was always the chance after all, small though it was, that Francis did have a legitimate proposition and he decided to give him the benefit of the doubt. He said good night to Rob and sat down reluctantly, avoiding Annie's eye as she wriggled and squirmed on Francis's knee.

'All it is,' said Francis, 'I've borrowed a cart and a lively little hoss and I've a mind to go for a jaunt into 'country.' He smiled benevolently. 'I thought perhaps tha might like to come along for a ride?'

Annie squealed with pleasure. 'Oh, Frankie, can I come?'

61

He pushed her off his knee and slapped her behind. 'Fetch us another drink and then I'll see.'

Carelessly he put his feet up on a table and asked Will. 'Well, what about it, does tha fancy a bit of fresh air?'

'Aye, I reckon I do,' said Will slowly. 'I could do with a change of scenery.'

The two men eyed each other narrowly, there was no love lost between them. Then, as Annie returned with his drink, Francis took his boots off the table. 'Right then. Tomorrow. I'll pick thee up mid morning. I reckon tha'll enjoy it.'

Will nodded and looked away; he felt he'd been dismissed and rose to leave. Francis Morton was the last person that he would have chosen for a confidant. He was a town tyke born and bred, who earned his living on the streets and alleyways of the town, and wouldn't have known what Will was talking about had he attempted to explain the terrible feeling of confinement that he felt, like an animal or bird in captivity. To be restrained by his disability to the boundary of the town streets, when he was within sight and sound of the River Humber which led down towards the vast, powerful sea, the sea which had been his livelihood and destination since he was a mere boy, not much older than his own son, and from which he was now banished for ever.

'What do you mean, you don't want to come?' Isobel bristled with anger as she stared at Ellie standing in front of her, her head bowed so that all she could see was the top of her white cap.

Ellie fiddled with a corner of her apron. 'I don't want to come, that's all, ma'am.'

The girl was sullen, she shifted from one foot to the other. 'There's nowt – nothing to do in 'country and besides, the others don't want to go either.'

Isobel's mouth dropped open and then she quickly shut it again. This was something she hadn't foreseen. She had been quite sure that her staff would have been willing to accompany her to the new house.

'What, none of them?'

'Only Mrs Harris, but then she wouldn't be able to get another position at her age.' Ellie stopped as if wondering if she had gone too far.

'If I don't recommend you, then none of you will get another position.'

Isobel was angry and she knew that the statement she had made wasn't true, for with the increase in trade and the number of new houses being built on the periphery of the town, there was now a shortage of good servants. Everyone knew how well trained her staff were, they would obtain a position without her recommendation.

She tried wheedling. 'There will be more time off, of course, and perhaps more money.'

Ellie shook her head. 'There's no entertainment in 'country, ma'am, and besides folks are a bit slow out there.' She tossed her head and added, 'And all the men are leaving and coming into town, it's much more lively here, what with 'fair and theatre and that. I'm sorry ma'am.'

Not as sorry as I am, thought Isobel as she curtly dismissed the girl from the room. She sat by the window of her first-floor sitting-room and looked down at the busy street below. They were a motley looking crowd, she mused, how would she ever find servants from among that seething mass of humanity?

From her vantage point she saw the tall figure of John as he strode along the street on return from his work with the tallymen. He was making a point of finding out every facet of the business and had already established a good reputation with the staff and tradespeople.

She moved aside the curtains and waved to him, indicating that she wanted to speak to him. He smiled up at her. How handsome he was becoming, she thought, I shall soon have to be looking out for a suitable wife. And how well he carried his clothes. He was not a dandy by any means, like some of the young men they knew, but always dressed with good taste, his coat of a fine cloth and his hussar boots of soft leather. Neither did he powder his thick fair hair but wore it brushed back from his forehead and tied loosely behind.

She heard him run up the stairs and sat back with a sigh. She would get a sympathetic hearing from him, she knew, unlike Isaac who would expect her to deal with the servant problem herself without any help from him.

'I can't stay long, I'm afraid.' John put his head around the door. 'I'm wanted down at the dockside.'

'Just have a cup of tea with me, John, I really need to talk to you.' Isobel reached for the bell, but he forestalled her.

'No, no tea, thank you, but tell me what is the trouble.' He was anxious to be off and was sure that the concerned look on her face was probably over something quite frivolous that could soon be allayed. Nevertheless he listened patiently as she finished her worrying account of staffing the new house.

'Well, you'll have to use local labour, Aunt. I don't see that there is a major problem.'

'But don't you see, John,' she exclaimed, glad for once to be able to impart knowledge to him. 'All the country girls are coming to town to look for work, the wages are better and so are their marriage prospects.' She threw up her hands and wailed, 'The only ones left will be the country bumpkins like Mrs Scryven, or the ones who are unemployable.'

He got up to leave. 'I'll try to think of something,' he said, 'but finding servants isn't something I'm familiar with, I'm afraid.'

He laughed and with a contrived flourish drew back his arm as if to aim. 'Now if it's a harpooner that you require, ma'am, then I can supply you with several.' He crouched down and brought out an imaginary knife from the top of his boot, 'Or how about a flenser, skilled in his trade?' He shook his head and piped humorously, dropping a mock curtsey, 'But little maids I know none.'

'Get off with you,' Isobel laughed at him. At least she felt a little better for his cheerful company, and I dare say, she thought philosophically, somebody will find a solution.

'You're late, John, what kept you?' Isaac looked up irritably from his desk as John knocked and entered his office.

'I'm sorry, Uncle, but I was waylaid.'

He didn't want to blame Isobel, but Isaac replied sharply. 'By whom? I trust it was on business matters?'

'Well, not exactly, sir. But seemingly you have a problem. Aunt Isobel can't persuade the servants to go out to Garston Hall. They don't want to move to the idyllic charm of the country, but prefer to stay for the delights of this merry town, smells and all.'

Isaac swore softly. 'I had an idea that this might happen, and unfortunately the country people are moving to town. They are losing their common lands with this enclosure legislation and can't make a living.'

He brushed his hands over the pile of papers that littered his desk. 'As you see, I'm extremely busy and I haven't the time to attend to it. Perhaps you will see to it, John, I don't want Isobel to be bothered about something like this, it's not good for her to have any worries at this time.'

He waved his arm towards the window. 'There must be somebody out there who would like to exchange an existence in the town for a living in the country.'

John felt the germ of an unformulated idea growing in the recesses of his mind. 'You would need a housekeeper perhaps, if Aunt Isobel is set against Mrs Scryven? Perhaps if I find a suitable woman, then she could find the maidservants?'

He paused to see the effect on his uncle and, finding it favourable, went on, 'And it might be an idea for you to have a man about the place, for you will be here in Hull quite often. Someone who could keep an eye on the estate and do jobs about the house, bringing in wood, that sort of thing.'

'If you can think of someone who will suit Isobel then

arrange it, but don't worry me about it until it's decided,' said Isaac briskly. 'But it must be someone completely trustworthy. And in the meantime,' he dismissed the matter, 'you will be pleased to know that I've heard from the Customs Office. The Commissioner has ordered that the bounty can be paid after all. They are satisfied that we have followed all the legal requirements and that the ship was bound to return early because of the damage.'

He sat back in his chair. 'That's the reason I wanted to see you. I've told the clerks to go ahead with the paper work and I would like you to see that it is paid out immediately.'

John smiled as he left the office. He speculated that with a little diplomacy he might well be able to repay a debt, help a family in need and solve his aunt's domestic problem at one and the same time.

Tom hurtled breathlessly through the door. 'Fayther, Francis is here with the hoss and cart, can I come with thee?'

'No, not this time, son, maybe another day.' Will knew that if there was any business to discuss, Francis wouldn't divulge it with the flapping ears of young Tom within hearing.

'Ooh, why not?' Tom's face puckered in disappointment. 'Annie's going, why can't I?' He'd seen Annie sitting at the side of Francis as the cart trundled towards the entry. She'd waved to him graciously as if she was in a carriage instead of a battered old cart, and he longed to do the same to his own friends.

Will spoke to him sharply as he eased himself out of the wooden chair and on to his crutch. He was finding it easier to move around now and had decided to discard one crutch altogether, and although he still sometimes had terrible pain in the stump of his leg, his arms and shoulders were stronger than ever before.

'Go on, clear off!' Francis gestured to Annie as Will approached them.

'I thought I was coming with thee?' said Annie in dismay. 'Tha promised me!'

'Well, tha thought wrong. Don't go getting any fancy ideas.'

'Go and see Maria,' suggested Will sympathetically, feeling sorry for the girl as she stood forlornly in the road in her cheap finery. 'She could do with some cheerful company.'

He hoisted himself into the cart and reflected that he was a poor companion for Maria these days, beset as he was with his own problems.

'Women!' Francis cursed as he urged the horse on. 'They're nowt but trouble. Tha won't catch me getting tied down to 'em.'

'Come on inside, Annie, it's grand to see thee.' Maria hid her astonishment at her friend's appearance. Annie had never before had any spare money for anything but the bare necessities of life, and certainly not for the sort of clothes she was wearing now.

She was aping the fashionable with her low-cut satin gown, but the colour was garish and the frilly petticoats peeping below the hem were torn and none too clean. She had draped herself with a black lace shawl and adorned her hair with flowers and feathers.

She twirled around now to show off her finery. 'Does tha like it, Maria?' she asked dreamily, 'Frankie bought it for me.'

Stole it more likely, thought Maria privately, from some other poor woman that he'd discarded.

'He's so generous, Maria, I've never had anybody give me owt before.' Annie's face creased sadly. ' 'Course, Alan would have, but he never had any money to spare.' She wiped away a tear which left a streak down her powdered cheek. 'I do miss him, Maria. I know he was a bad 'un, and he knocked me about when he was in drink, but he didn't mean to. He loved me really, I know he did.'

She sniffed loudly and wiped her nose on her shawl.

Then she lifted her chin and tossed her head defiantly. 'Anyway,' she smiled, 'now I've got Frankie and he'll look after me. He said he would.'

Maria wanted to warn her, to caution her against the ruthless Francis Morton who would use Annie or any woman for his own ends. She could understand them falling for him, for he had a beguiling charm, but it hid a cruel streak which, once displayed, could spell calamity and disgrace to a woman unlucky enough to be involved with him. She remained silent now, though, for she knew intuitively that for Annie it was already too late.

John cleared up his work as fast as he could. If he was to implement his plan then he must put it in motion straight away. He knew his uncle wanted to make the move to Garston Hall quickly so that Isobel was settled in before her confinement and, although he knew nothing about babies and their delivery, it occurred to him that Maria Foster's pregnancy was probably at the same stage as his aunt's.

'I'll be off,' he said to the clerk, and picked up the papers and small bags of money which he placed beneath his greatcoat. 'I'll deliver as many of these as I can, and where I can't, then they must collect it themselves. The men will be glad enough to receive it.'

The clerk grimaced disdainfully, 'I reckon 'innkeeper will be even more pleased, sir. That's where 'bonus will end up, in his pocket and down 'seamen's throats.'

John strode purposefully across the town and towards the river and the houses on its banks. He would make the Foster home his first call, to deliver the long-awaited bonus and to sound out their reaction to his proposal. He had a romantic notion of delivering his hero and his lovely wife from the servitude and despair of the hovel in which they lived.

He was therefore somewhat taken aback when in answer to his knock the door was opened immediately, not by the gentle Maria, but by a young woman dressed in a most bizarre fashion, with flowers, feathers and lace

68

bedecked about her person, who gave him a coquettish glance as she stood aside to let him in.

He swallowed hard and politely gave a small bow. He wondered curiously if she was a woman of easy virtue, for by her painted appearance she might well be; but if that was the case then what was she doing here?

'I wondered if Will was at home, Mrs Foster?' he asked as Maria appeared. 'Or if you expect him back shortly?'

'He's gone for a drive into 'country, Mr Rayner. I don't know what time he'll be back.' She added by way of explanation. 'He gets very downcast if he spends too much time inside. He's so used to being outdoors.'

She hesitated before saying, 'You'll pardon me for asking, sir, but did you come about 'bonus? Word is out that it's going to be paid.'

John marvelled at the speed in which news travelled in this community. It was only a few hours since he had been given the report himself. 'Yes, that's it exactly, but I also wanted a word with him about another matter.'

He was interrupted by Annie who with a shrill exclamation on hearing this information, gathered up her shawl and prepared to depart.

'I must get down to 'docks and collect my dues,' she said excitedly. 'There's sure to be summat for me.'

'It's Mrs Swinburn,' said Maria as Annie disappeared out of the door and she saw the questioning look on John's face. 'Her husband was killed on 'Polar Star and she's badly in need of money.'

'So how does she manage?' asked John curiously. 'She appears to have money for clothes.'

Maria thought he was sneering and she answered sharply. 'When we have no money at all, sometimes we have to sell our precious possessions.' She indicated the bare and gloomy room, devoid of any ornaments or embellishments. 'And God knows we have few enough of those. Annie only sells what is hers, and hurts nobody, only herself.'

'I wasn't criticizing or passing judgement, Mrs Foster,' John said quietly. 'I do apologize if I gave you that impression.' Clearly the tender Maria wasn't as timid and reserved as she first appeared to be, and he admired the spirited way in which she defended her friend.

She was immediately penitent. 'No, it's me that should be sorry, I don't know what comes over me sometimes.' Her eyes filled with tears and she brushed them away with the back of her hand. 'But we folks have to help each other, there's no-one else who will.'

He wanted to take her hand, to comfort her, as he would have done with Isobel, but he knew that the action would be misconstrued, that she would shy away from him in distrust. Instead he gave a small bow and said that he would call again the next day. In spite of her rough upbringing, this was a modest, gentle woman who would recoil with dismay if he should commit the unpardonable sin of bridging the social barrier which divided them.

Will relaxed for the first time in weeks. They'd cleared the town and were heading out on the Beverley road. He took a deep breath. It was good to be away from the confines of the town and to smell the sweetness of the country air. They'd passed the Infirmary, and were now bowling swiftly along the main coach road. It was a good surface and the young mare kicked up her heels and trotted briskly along.

'Would tha like to take a turn with 'reins?' Francis asked presently, and obligingly pulled over and swapped places.

Will took the reins diffidently. 'I'm a seaman,' he said cautiously. 'I'm not used to hosses.'

'Just let her have her head for a bit until tha gets used to 'feel of 'rein. She's a good hoss and won't go wild.'

Will shook the reins and felt the strength of the animal as she responded to his signal. He smiled to himself and straightened his shoulders. This was akin to being at sea. To feel the power beneath his fingers, the breeze blowing in his hair, and the surging movement beneath him as they were carried along.

He laughed out loud, a resounding cry to which the horse reacted as, startled, she broke into a canter which tipped Francis unceremoniously backwards into the cart, making the two men roar with laughter.

'Where are we heading?'

They'd been on the road for an hour, there was little habitation apart from an occasional farmhouse or country estate and he didn't think for a moment that Francis had brought him out this far just for his pleasure, there had to be some other reason. They were coming towards a wooded area and ahead he could see a small crossroad.

'Turn left here,' Francis said abruptly. 'There's a property I want to look at. Just curious like,' he added as Will looked questioningly at him.

He followed his instructions and slowed the horse down to a steady walk as they turned into a narrow rutted lane, the banked up sides overgrown with blackthorn and bramble.

'Just stop here a minute.' Francis spoke softly. 'I want to take a look over yonder.' He jumped down lightly from the cart and, grabbing hold of the long grasses and scrubby branches as support, pulled himself up the bank.

On reaching the top he dropped to his knees, and with his hand shielding his eyes looked out into the distance. From where he was sitting in the cart, Will could see a cluster of tall chimneys.

'What's up?' he asked quietly, but Francis put up his hand in warning and scrambled back down the bank.

'There are some dogs about.' He took hold of the mare's head to turn her around. 'If they get wind of us, they'll make a devil of a row.'

Will wondered why that would matter if the reason for them being there was innocent, but, knowing Francis, said nothing.

They had turned out of the lane back on to the road when Will was suddenly conscious of a rustling movement and cracking of twigs, and turning saw a man half hidden in the undergrowth, who on realizing that he had been observed, quickly covered his mouth with the scarf he had around his neck.

'Where did he come from?' Will turned towards Francis beside him, in time to see him make a quick nodding motion towards the man.

'What?' said Francis cheerfully. 'I don't know what tha's talking about. Come on, let's get moving.'

'So what's thy interest in yon mansion?' Will urged the horse into a brisk trot.

'Tha's a bit sharp, Will!'

Will said nothing but kept his eyes to the front and waited.

Francis pursed his lips and whistled quietly and tunelessly. 'All right I'll tell thee. House yonder—' With a toss of his head he indicated back to the crossroad. 'It's laden with stuff – silver, brass, clocks – all good stuff that would fetch a fortune. 'Owners are away and there's only a housekeeper and a gardener there and they're both old and deaf as stone.'

'How does tha know all this?'

Francis grinned. 'There's always ways of finding out, but I happen to know somebody who used to work there. He was dismissed – a bit light-fingered he was, and 'fool got caught!'

'So what happened to him?' Will thought of the man hidden in the undergrowth, and of the penalties for theft.

'Well, he didn't get transported. He pleaded poverty, that his wife was dying, and he couldn't resist temptation, all that sort of thing.'

He laughed contemptuously. 'And 'magistrate believed him. He was sentenced to six years hard labour – and he escaped after six months!'

'So what's thy intent?' Will was curious, and yet felt misgivings as if fate was drawing him into some misadventure.

'Well, it's obvious, isn't it, but don't think I'm going to let thee in on my plans,' Francis answered harshly. 'Not unless I can be sure that tha's with me.'

'Me?' Will scoffed. 'How could I come in with thee, even supposing I wanted to?'

He had always been able to turn away from temptation or trickery. He had made a virtue of his pride in earning an honest living by his own endeavour, without having to resort to borrowing or stealing, and felt no sympathy for common thieves like Francis and his associates. But he was beginning to feel some compassion for the poor wretches who were dragged off to transportation to pay the price for stealing food for their children's bellies.

'I need a waggoner, somebody who can be ready with 'hoss and cart, ready for a quick departure – just in case there's any trouble.'

'I'd never thought of being a waggoner,' said Will thoughtfully. 'That hadn't occurred to me.'

'Well, there tha has it. With a bit of practice, tha can be a coachie! But if tha comes in with me there'll be no need, for there's enough riches back there to set us up for life.'

'But it isn't right,' Will muttered uneasily. 'Who are these people? They've probably worked hard for what they've got.'

' 'Beaumonts!' Francis was scathing in his contempt. 'Not them. They're bankers. Up to their ears in money – rolling in it – and I'll tell thee summat, that place is so stuffed with goods they won't even notice that owt's missing.'

'Nay, I can't.' Will felt the twin emotions of morality and need battling for supremacy. 'I need 'money, God knows, but it goes against 'grain.'

Francis cursed angrily. 'Does tha think that anybody will think 'better of thee for thy scruples? Who's going to pull thee out of 'gutter when tha's lying there? Who's going to feed thy wife and bairns? Nobody, that's who. Nobody will give a hang for thy virtuous reputation!'

In his anger Francis wrenched the reins from Will's grasp and, lashing out, drove the horse into a gallop, the cart careering wildly about the road.

Presently he calmed down and, slowing the horse to

73

a trot said, tersely, 'Just think on what I say. Tha might have only one leg, but tha has a pair of hands to help thyself. This job will be easy. My mate back there will take care of 'dogs, I'll do 'house, and all tha has to do is make sure 'hoss and cart are turned round ready for off, and give warning if anybody's about.'

He added persuasively, 'Tha doesn't have to do another job. This can be 'first and last, but it'll give thee a taste of excitement and buy thee a roof and vittals.'

They had approached the outskirts of the town and Will felt again the hopelessness of his situation returning, sending him down into a trough of despair.

'I'll let thee know. I'll think on it.'

'It's got to be tonight.' Francis skilfully manoeuvred the horse and cart through the narrow streets. ' 'Beaumonts will be back soon and 'goods must be got away before they realize that owt's missing.'

Will looked at him sharply. 'I can't make up my mind so soon.'

Francis reined in by the entry, 'I'll give thee till six o' clock to make up thy mind. But if 'answer is no – just remember—' He put a finger to his lips and then made a sharp slicing movement across his throat. Then he smiled. 'Only fooling of course, Will – only fooling!'

He shook the reins and the mare skittered across the cobbles, the cart wheels clattering noisily, and waved his hand in farewell.

Will stood watching for a few minutes and then turned towards home. He knew beyond question of doubt that Francis Morton never, ever fooled.

Maria was sitting on the bed with Alice on her knee as Will came in, ducking his head through the low doorway into the house.

'Dost feel better for thy airing?'

'Aye, I reckon so. We went a good way into 'country and I breathed in some good clean air.'

He picked Alice up from her mother's knee and lifted

her high to touch the low ceiling. 'Now then, my little recklin, what's up?'

Maria frowned, she didn't like him to use that expression to describe Alice's frailty, even though she knew he used it only as a term of endearment. 'She's not well again. She could do with some fresh air too, and she needs more medicine for her cough.'

Then with a sudden swift smile which lit up her pale face, she drew out the money bag from her pocket and shook it tantalizingly in front of him. 'Guess what? We've had a visitor. Tha bonus has come!'

'Praise be!' he said with relief. 'Let's count it.'

They poured the coins on to the floor and then placed them into small piles. Will pushed several towards Maria. 'Take these for food, and medicine for Alice. Then get Tom some boots, he'll need to start work.'

He sat back in the chair, the elation of the moment draining from him. The few remaining coins would last only a week or two, a month if they were careful, and then they would be back in poverty again.

Alice started to cough, a harsh wracking sound that made him wince. She put her head against her father's chest for comfort and he stroked her hair, rocking her gently.

'John Rayner brought 'bonus himself.' Maria got up, stretching her back as she reached for the potatoes to scrub for their supper. 'He was disappointed that tha wasn't here, he wanted to discuss a matter with thee – with us both.' Curiously she asked. 'What could it be about?'

Will was deep in thought and he shook his head in reply.

'Anyway, he said he would come back.'

Will looked up. 'I hope tha didn't tell him to come back tonight,' he said decisively. 'Tonight I shall be out.'

5

They'd made their way separately to a meeting at the derelict Beverley Gate, as Francis insisted that they shouldn't be seen together.

The sky was light in spite of the hour being close on midnight, and the crumbling ancient remains of the town entrance were silhouetted against the night sky.

As Will waited for Francis to appear he kept thinking of Maria. He'd told her that he would be late and not to wait up. She was apprehensive and suspicious and filled with foreboding and had implored him not to go out.

'Stay in tonight, Will – please, I beg thee. Summat's wrong, I can feel it.'

He'd teased her, although he felt not in the least jovial, and told her she was a witch and would have to be careful or she'd get a ducking. But she'd turned away from him and didn't speak to him again.

He'd gone out early in the evening and spent his time going from inn to inn, making sure that he was seen by several of his acquaintances, but refusing any grog from them. The inns and taverns were teeming with sailors and fishermen. Two whalers had arrived in port that morning with full ships, fifteen whales between them and four hundred seals. The men were in celebratory mood and spent money freely in anticipation of the bonus they would receive. The whole town had a jubilant air, for the arrival of such a harvest of oil, blubber and whale-bone meant industry for the whole community.

Will had stood apart from the talk and the laughter. He was finished with all of that now, it was part of his past. He would never again experience that strange thrill of pleasure as they sighted the ice, or watch the mysterious lights of the aurora borealis. Never again would he be tossed on the angry seas during the hunt. That was a different world, a world of bravery and danger, of bloodstained men and sobbing whales staining the seas with their life blood.

'Put this round thee,' Francis whispered as Will climbed up beside him now. 'That leg's too easily remembered.' He fished around in the back of the cart where there was a heap of sacks and bits of rag and passed a piece of sacking to Will to use as a coachman's apron.

'We'll go out on 'old road across country for a few miles. We can't risk anybody recognizing us from town.'

Suddenly Will felt a familiar surge of excitement in the pit of his stomach. The recognition of danger and the thrill of a chase of a different kind was about to begin, only this time there was no exhilaration, only a bitter unease.

They spoke in whispers and carried no light on the cart, the horse picking her way sure-footedly on the uneven surface. They neither saw nor heard any other traffic until, deciding to cross over to the coach road as the old road was now becoming extremely rutted and filled with potholes and the cart was in danger of becoming fast, Francis suddenly hissed, 'Listen!'

Unmistakably in the far-off distance they heard the rhythmic thud of hoofbeats and the rattle of wheels.

Francis jumped down from the cart and guided the mare to the side of the road beneath some overhanging trees. He spoke softly to her, stroking her neck and blowing gently into her nostrils.

The jingle of harness came nearer and a dim light could be seen swaying and bobbing.

' 'Midnight mail!' Will breathed softly, as the coach rattled by and the raised voices of the coachmen could be heard.

'Phew, that was near, I hadn't reckoned on 'mail coach.' Francis climbed back on to the cart once the coach was out of hearing. 'We'll have to move now or we'll be late.'

They travelled on at a cracking pace, trusting in the horse's judgement and their own keen sight to keep to the road, until they were about a mile from the crossroad and Francis, drawing to a halt, handed the reins over to Will. He jumped down again and went to the back of the cart where he took out some pieces of rag.

Swearing softly because he couldn't see, he carefully bound the rags around the mare's hooves so that they were well padded and made no sound. 'Keep her at a walk now,' he commanded, 'so that she won't feel fettered by 'bindings.'

As he watched him, Will conjectured wryly on the duplicity of thought and action which was required in order to rob or defraud one's fellow man.

As they neared the crossroad Francis silently indicated that they should stop. Quietly they sat, hearing only the rustling of the trees and the snuffling and scratchings of nocturnal animals. Francis gave a long, low whistle, paused, and then another. They waited a few minutes until from the direction of the crossroad came an answering call.

He replied with two short, sharp whistles and they saw in front of them the light of a lamp swinging from side to side.

'Come on.' Francis walked at the horse's flank. 'That's Jack Crawford, let's get on with it.'

Will felt his throat tighten. He wasn't afraid of danger, he'd proved that many times out on the ice, but he was full of misgiving that he had allowed himself to be drawn into such a business. It was too late now to think of backing out: not only would he be branded as a coward, he knew also that Francis would take revenge, and had many dubious acquaintances who would be quite willing to see his own swift departure to the bottom of the river to make sure that he held his tongue.

'Keep 'hoss quiet and turn 'cart round in 'clearing yonder.' Jack's dialect showed that he was a local inhabitant. 'Don't show a light and we'll give 'signal when 'job is finished.'

He seemed to be taking charge, giving orders to Will and talking in whispers to Francis and pointing towards the house.

They disappeared over the bank, taking two sacks each with them, and Will saw to his alarm that they were each carrying a heavy stick.

He climbed down from his seat and leaning awkwardly against the mare's side moved her up the lane into the clearing to turn the cart about. The ground was soft under the trees and for a moment a tremendous effort was needed to push on the cart when the wheels stuck fast. His crutch he'd left on the seat for he knew it would be of no use to him here. The mare munched contentedly on the overhanging branches as he struggled, and ignored his whispered commands. Finally in exasperation he hauled himself on to her back and, digging in hard with his good leg, he gave her a sharp thwack with a green stick, and managed to pull her and the cart round ready for a swift departure.

He had sat for perhaps an hour, his head sunk deep into the collar of his coat, his ears attuned to the night sounds and the scurryings of small creatures in the undergrowth, when suddenly he was startled by a long wild screeching which broke into his reverie. He caught his breath, but as he looked up he saw the ghostly form of a barn owl against the sky as it flew in silent winged flight above him.

The mare was becoming impatient and starting to stamp and shuffle her hooves restlessly. Will clicked his tongue at her soothingly, when out of the darkness came the noise of dogs barking and voices shouting. The horse whinnied and moved nervously and Will took tight hold of the reins to steady her.

Then he heard them, the sound of feet crashing through the copse and the sharp snapping of dry twigs as heavy boots trod carelessly on them. Then came a sharp piercing whistle to which Will answered and within a minute the two men came stumbling and slipping down the bank, their speed hampered by the laden sacks which they carried.

'Move – quick!' They threw the sacks into the back of the cart and jumped in as the sound of the dogs came nearer.

'What happened?' said Will hoarsely as he shook the reins and they rumbled down the narrow lane towards the crossroad.

'They've got a new dog.' Jack cursed. 'It didn't know me and as soon as it got wind of us it set all 'others off. Just our rotten luck that 'old fella was still awake.'

'Tha shouldn't have hit him so hard.' Francis was sharp. 'He hadn't seen thee. If he snuffs it, it's murder, and we'll swing.'

Will was blazing with anger. With them for the violence committed on some unknown old man, and with himself for being so stupid and weak as to get involved. He knew the law would find him just as guilty as the other two, and he urged the horse on faster until they reached the crossroad.

'Let me off here,' said Jack, 'and keep going straight on, don't tek 'main road in case tha's seen.' He jumped down, not waiting for them to stop, and ran off, disappearing into the darkness.

Will urged the horse on and the animal, sensing the urgency, put back her ears and moved swiftly down the smaller roads across country, the cart swaying precariously on the uneven surface.

They heard the chimes of three o'clock striking as they reached the town boundary. 'We'll leave 'cart here.' Francis guided Will towards a disused building with a yard behind it, one of many in the town that were being demolished to make room for new buildings. 'It'll be picked up when 'tumult's died down.' He removed the rags from the mare's hooves, surprisingly still intact in spite of the hard going.

'What about 'hoss?' Will uncoupled the harness.

In reply Francis slapped the mare on the rump and

she cantered off down the quiet street. 'She'll find her own way home, she always does,' he replied with a grin. 'She's a good 'un.'

There were four sacks to carry and they were heavy and awkward. Will found a piece of twine in his pocket and tied the necks of two of the sacks together and slung them around his neck, distributing the weight across his back.

'I want thee to take all 'four sacks and hide them,' Francis said as they neared the entry. 'If 'law comes looking they won't suspect thee.'

'No,' said Will bluntly. 'I've changed my mind. I've come along with thee so far, but I'm finished with it now, I want no part of it. Tha can trust me to say nowt about it, but I don't want a share. Divide it up two ways.'

'It's too late for that.' Francis turned menacingly towards Will, his voice low and threatening. 'Tha's in it now, and if I'm caught so's thee, so don't try and back out. Don't forget Maria and thy bairns. If owt happens to thee, who'll look after them?'

Will slid the sacks down to the ground and leant heavily on his crutch. 'I'm not a fighting man, Frank Morton, but it wouldn't take much for me to give thee a thumping.'

Francis laughed softly. 'Tha's forgetting summat. I'm younger than thee, and I've got two legs to stand on – tha wouldn't stand a chance.'

Inwardly Will raged as he fought to keep his temper. He recognized the threat to his family was real, and so dismissively he shrugged his shoulders. 'Give us a hand then – let's get them inside.'

He opened the door quietly. The room was in darkness and he could hear only the mutterings of Tom who sometimes talked in his sleep.

Together they slid the sacks across the floor and then Will signalled to Francis to go. He waited until his footsteps reached the top of the stairs and he heard the creaking of the door above, then lying down on the floor

81

he shuffled and pushed the sacks towards the bed where Maria and the children were sleeping.

He'd safely deposited three of them under the bed when Maria stirred.

'Will, is that thee?' Her voice was anxious and husky with sleep.

'Aye, it is. Go back to sleep.'

'What's tha doing? Stir the fire so we have some light, I can't see thee.'

'No, hush, I'm coming to bed. I'm just stowing some stuff away.'

The bed creaked as she sat up and he prayed she wouldn't get out and fall over him or the sack as they lay on the floor.

'Will Foster, I do believe tha's drunk or up to summat.'

He hauled himself up on to the bed and put his arms around her. 'I'm certainly not drunk.' He kissed her tenderly. 'But I might well get up to summat, given some encouragement.'

Beneath his fingers he felt her face crease into a smile.

'Come to bed,' she said, 'it must be very late and I have to be up for work in 'morning.'

He felt the softness and warmth of her as he held her close and the stirring of the life moving within her, and silently vowed that regardless of any threat or humiliation by Frank Morton and his cronies, he would make amends for the mistake he had made. Never again would he be dragged down to the level of thieves and ruffians. He swore an oath on the head of his unborn child that whatever came in the way of poverty or hunger he would know again the freedom of spirit that accompanies a clear conscience and peace of mind.

6

'I'm sorry to come so early.' John Rayner stood at the door. 'But it is imperative that I speak to you today.'

'Maria said that tha'd called before. I'm just off for a walk down by 'river, to see what's going on and to try for work.'

'So you haven't got fixed up yet? Can I walk with you and then we can talk?'

They walked slowly down to the mouth of the Humber, their strides not quite matching as Will swung along on his crutch, but their height equal. They passed the Ropery where the long strands of rope stretched the length of the street, and there were a few curious stares as they approached groups of men working at the warehouses. Some doffed their caps to John whilst others looked sullenly away.

They stood silently watching the river traffic, the breeze ruffling their hair.

'I can't tell you how I'm longing to sail away again,' John said suddenly.

Will flinched and turned away and John, realizing his error, gasped, 'Oh, I'm so sorry. What a crass idiot I am. You must think me so unfeeling!'

Will laughed regretfully but without rancour. 'I have at last accepted that I won't be sailing again, and I must thank heaven that I am at least alive and not in a cold foreign grave. If I could only get work, I would count myself a very lucky man. I'm glad to hear that tha's taken to whaling, though. It's a fine life for a man – adventure, excitement, danger. Although not one that I'd recommend for my own son.'

'Would you leave this town, Will, if you could find work elsewhere?'

Will considered. 'Aye, I reckon so. It seems to me that Hull has no more use for me, and I must confess that I feel oppressed now that I can no longer sail away from its shores. I'm not used to being shut in by walls and boundaries.'

'Then I have a proposition for you. I can't make the final decision, but I think I can safely say that I can be instrumental in recommending your name and reputation.'

'I'll consider owt.' Will was eager. 'I'm as strong as most men, and more than some, and I'm not afraid of hard work.'

John outlined the Mastersons' requirements for staff at Garston Hall. 'They need a good man for general work, although I expect they will employ a farm bailiff, and servants for in the house.'

He hesitated. 'I know that Mrs Foster is in delicate health at the moment, but perhaps later on she could take on some duties in the house or even help with Mrs Masterson's child when it is born.'

Will put back his head and roared with laughter. 'Maria in delicate health! Having a babby, tha means? She's as sound as a roach! Listen, my young friend, should tha care to take a walk by 'staith side tha'll see plenty of women in "delicate health" as tha puts it, shifting barrels of fish that would make many a young dandy flinch.'

John joined in the laughter without any embarrassment, and commented wryly, 'You must realize, Will, that I have had a very sheltered upbringing. It just isn't the done thing to speak of such things.'

'Tha's brightened up my day, no doubt about it.' Will became serious again. 'I'm very grateful that tha thought of us. A life in 'country – it sounds good to me, but I'm not sure how Maria will take to it. She's lived all of her life here by 'river, never been anywhere else.'

'Think about it for a day or two, but we must know soon. My uncle wants to get his wife away before—' he smiled, 'before her confinement! I did tell him that I would find someone honest and trustworthy and I know that that is what you are.'

He looked anxiously at Will as he saw him recoil and his face pale. 'Are you unwell?'

Will leaned on the river wall, his head in his hands. The relief he had felt as he viewed the prospect of work was slipping away. He had momentarily forgotten the escapade of the previous evening and his own vow to put matters right. He was still guilty of aiding a theft, even though he hadn't physically stolen the goods with his own hands. Until he had rid himself of that problem, how could he with his hand on his heart say that he was honest and trustworthy?

With a start he realized that the sacks were still lying under the bed. What more proof of his guilt would be needed if the law came looking, or if Maria or the children found them and became involved themselves in his predicament?

'Are you sick?' John repeated, putting his hand on Will's shoulder.

'Aye, I'm sick all right – sick at heart, not in body. I'll tell thee, young John,' he said as he straightened up with a deep sigh, ' 'pain I felt on losing my leg is nothing to 'pain and shame that I'm feeling now.'

'Then let me help you. If there's anything I can do, then name it and I'll do my utmost to see that it is done.'

Will shook his head. 'It's not possible, I wouldn't want to involve thee – and besides, tha wouldn't understand 'circumstances, being too young for one thing and 'wrong class for another.'

John considered for a moment, then said seriously, 'My youth and social position I am unable to alter, although I'm told by my elders that youth is but fleeting; and my social standing does not mean that I am devoid of understanding or sensibilities. Come, Will, you need to talk to someone and I'm as good a listener and confidant as any man.'

Will studied the younger man's face. He had an open, honest countenance, too young yet for life to have etched

85

its shadow upon it, and he supposed that if John was to be enlightened as to the realities of life outside his own comfortable existence then he might as well learn from him. In addition, he was desperate to speak out to someone, in the vain hope that by so doing he might perhaps find a solution to his dilemma.

'Tha might well walk away in disgust if I should tell thee; and if 'law should come after, then I won't blame thee.'

As they paced up and down by the river side, Will felt that he was locked in by an invisible prison as he talked and explained the circumstances of his lapse, whilst out on the wide Humber ships with full canvas sailed away towards the open sea as if they belonged to another time and another world.

'Tha thinks me honest – well, I'll tell thee, until yesterday there was no-one more honest or trustworthy, but poverty and hunger can do strange things to a man's mind as well as his belly. Tha must look for someone else – but I would defy thee to find anyone in this town who hasn't given in to temptation at some time or other. If I could only stop Father Time and go back and undo what's been done,' he said finally, 'then I would accept poverty and hardship as my lot in life, rather than live with my wretched conscience – even though it's hard to see my wife and bairns going hungry.'

'Then that is what must be done.' John had listened in silence to Will's outpourings, asking only an occasional question.

'What must be done?' The other was only half listening.

'We'll undo what is already done.' John spoke quickly as the idea formed. 'We'll take back the stolen goods to where they belong, if you still have them, that is?'

'We? There'll be no "we". I said I wouldn't involve thee!'

'But – don't you see, if I help you it will be easier. I can get a horse and waggon without suspicion, and I know the house, I've been several times on visits with my aunt. We can leave the sacks near to the house where they will be found.' He smiled grimly. 'And my social influence could come in useful should we by some mischance be caught, for there is no doubt that my word as a gentleman would be believed when I explained the sorry circumstances, whereas, my friend, I'm sorry to say, yours would not!'

Maria had viewed Will suspiciously when he had tried to persuade her to run some paltry errand for him and take the children with her.

'I know tha's up to summat, Will Foster, I can sense it and I don't like it. Tha's been acting very strange for 'last few days.'

'Just go, love, trust me, and I might have some good news for thee soon.' He put his arms around her and she felt the stirrings of hope and the awareness of his returning confidence.

'Be careful, Will.' Again she warned him and looked anxiously back at him as she gathered up Alice and Tom and went out into the descending dusk.

He was concerned that he shouldn't be noticed as he moved the sacks outside into the entry. Francis hadn't been seen, he was obviously keeping out of sight for a few days, but his mother, Mrs Morton, never missed a trick, and Will could hear her moving about upstairs.

The entry was narrow with six houses in it, three on either side facing each other. Should the occupants lean out from the topmost rooms then they could shake each other by the hand quite easily. At the widest end of the entry was the opening leading out into the busy thoroughfare of Blanket Row and the direction of the Market Place, and at the opposite end, where the house walls tapered together, was a thin slit, just big enough for a man to get through. Why this entrance was there no-one knew, but it was assumed that it had been used at some time by smugglers, for it led through into the Ropery and down to the river.

It was here that Will piled the sacks and slipped quietly

through the gap, his hands on the walls for support. He peered cautiously out and saw John pacing about in the now quiet street, a horse and waggon tethered nearby.

He gave a low whistle and John turned round, startled.

'Where did you come from?' He had been unaware of the hidden entrance and wondered why Will had chosen this meeting place. The scheme was already assuming a suggestion of intrigue. When he had asked the foreman for the use of a waggon for a few hours, the man had looked at him questioningly. 'A waggon, Mr John, doesn't tha want a driver?' John in a flash of inspiration had winked impudently, and the storeman, as he had intended, misconstrued his intentions and surmised that young Mr John was at last becoming a man of the world and wanted the vehicle for some night-time jollifications, and had nodded approvingly.

Together they placed the sacks into the high-sided waggon and Will climbed in with them and stretched out on the floor.

'Take 'side roads,' he said. 'And don't drive too fast, we don't want to be noticed.'

He guessed, rightly, that John was beginning to enjoy the escapade and though he was well intentioned, any rash move could spell disaster for them both.

They left the town and once out on the country road Will slid out of the back of the waggon and up on to the seat at the side of John.

'Shall I take 'reins for a bit? If there's a chance of my becoming a country man then I need to show thee my skills with a hoss and waggon!'

This time the driving was more hazardous. The road was muddy and in parts little more than a track. The ruts were deep and waterlogged as there had been steady rain during the afternoon, while the waggon was much heavier than the cart had been. Will found that he had to use the whip increasingly to keep the horse moving.

'We can't risk taking hoss and 'waggon down that lane. If we get stuck we'll never get out again. We'll have to leave them on 'road and hope that no-one sees them.'

'Let's hope that the clouds don't lift for there's a full moon due tonight and that will give the game away.' They whispered now as they manoeuvred the horse and waggon under the trees. 'I'm wondering whether it would be a good idea to take the horse with us. We could get there in half the time if you rode him and carried some of the sacks, and I'll carry the others?'

Will agreed, and after uncoupling the horse from the traces John cupped his hands to help Will mount. He found that he could manage three sacks and John took the other and walked alongside.

'Poor old Prince, what an indignity,' John laughed. 'He's never been used as a pack horse before. Just as well he can't carry tales.'

'Shh, don't tempt providence, and keep tha voice down. Sounds carry a long way!'

They continued their journey in silence until they reached the same spot by the bank where Will had waited previously.

'I'll have to go alone now, Will. I can move faster. I'll take two sacks and then come back for the others.'

He threw the sacks up to the top of the bank and scrambled up after them. 'Wish me luck,' he said in a hoarse whisper and disappeared out of sight.

Will started to count. He reckoned it would take John no more than ten minutes to get across the estate, find a suitable place to leave the sacks and five minutes to run back and collect the remaining ones. With luck we could be out of here in half an hour and home before midnight, he mused, and then all I have to do is deal with Francis Morton!

John arrived back breathless. 'So far, so good,' he gasped. 'They're having a house party, so the Beaumonts are obviously home again. I hope they'll be too engrossed to notice any noise from outside, and there's no sign of the dogs that you mentioned.'

As John ran once more across the Beaumont field, the sacks buffeted painfully against his legs. He had never before thought of himself as adventurous, and yet danger seemed to seek him out. After being half drowned in the icy seas, he was now risking incarceration, or worse, transportation, for handling stolen merchandise. Although he had spoken confidently of the magistrates believing in his honesty and integrity, he only half believed it himself, being inclined to think that should they be caught, the law would believe that he was involved with a den of thieves.

The Beaumonts' house was double-fronted with central steps leading to the entrance, and on either side were windows with shutters not yet closed against the night. Through those on the left he could see a small gathering of people, including some military officers in uniform, and on the right, servants were putting the finishing touches to the dining table. There was a splendid array of silver and glassware, and unconsciously he echoed Francis Morton's views that the stolen goods would barely be missed.

He had placed the first two sacks at the side of the entrance and had just done the same with the second two, and was preparing to run once more across the wide lawn, when he heard the rattle of wheels and a coach turned into the drive and rolled up to the steps.

He crouched back against the wall but, his curiosity getting the better of him, he peered over the steps to see who was arriving. As he did so he leaned rather too heavily against the sacks and with a slithering sound they toppled over. It was not a loud noise but unfortunate that as they fell, the occupants of the coach descended and turned towards the sound. The front door was opened at the same instant and a gentleman from the coach called out in some surprise, 'I say, I believe that somebody is skulking about down here!'

John waited no longer, now wasn't the time for formal introductions or explanations, and keeping his face averted and his head down he ran as fast as his legs would take him across the lawn and through into a small copse before the people at the door had recovered from the shock of seeing him there.

As he ran the moon appeared from behind the clouds, its brightness highlighting the lawn into pale silver and etching his shadow long and thin behind him. He could hear the sound of raised voices and knew that it would only be a matter of minutes before the alarm was raised and someone would be after him. His saving grace, he thought, would be the discovery of the sacks with the stolen goods. Someone would be sure to want to examine them. However, he was bothered about the officers, who would almost certainly have arrived on horseback, and who would very soon be saddled up and into the chase.

He slithered down the bank, landing in a heap almost under the hooves of Prince who shied away, startled. 'Give me a hand up quickly.'

Will put out his hand and with a great leap John was hoisted up on to the horse's back behind him.

'Let's go as sharp as we can, or we are in real trouble.'

As they galloped back down the lane, John was thankful that they hadn't brought the waggon, for the ground was soft and muddy and they would surely have been bogged down. He felt also that if the soldiers came after them, the likelihood was that they wouldn't know the area or of the existence of this little lane which was nothing more than a narrow cart track, and would go the long way round, meeting up with the other road at a point nearly a mile from where they had hidden the waggon.

'Are you willing to take another chance, Will, I think with some degree of success?' They were feverishly coupling up the waggon, their fingers fumbling clumsily in the dark in their haste.

'Huh, one more won't make a lot of difference. What has tha in mind?'

'I would like to risk driving along the coach road if we reach it in time. If anyone should see us they're not likely to suspect that we're on the run if we are driving on the main highway, but will more probably think that we are on legitimate business.'

Will laughed, 'I'd say tha's wasted in whaling, John. I reckon tha should join 'French Revolution, they need clever people like thee!'

'In all seriousness I have already considered it,' John replied with a grim note in his voice as they moved off. 'But my problem lies in choosing sides. Although I abhor all the violence that is being committed by the Paris mob, my sympathies still lie with the common people, who in my opinion have suffered for far too long.'

They had been on the highway no more than ten minutes when they heard the sound of hoofbeats coming up fast behind them. Will turned to look, and in the moonlight saw two riders bearing down swiftly upon them. He pulled on the reins as they drew alongside and called out in mock anger, 'Go steady there. What's tha hurry?'

The two officers sat high on their mounts, one on each side of Prince.

'What's your business out here?' one of them asked.

John leaned forward. 'What seems to be the trouble, sir. Can I help you?'

'Oh – sorry to bother you, sir, but we are on the lookout for a thief.' The soldier was obviously non-plussed by John's manner and accent.

'I see, and you thought that you had found him? Well, I'm sure that the driver won't mind if you look in the back of his waggon.'

Will shrugged his shoulders and feigned indifference.

'That won't be necessary, sir. I can see that there is no-one there.' He looked more closely at John. 'Could I ask what brings you out on the road tonight?'

'Certainly,' John replied cheerfully. 'My horse went lame on the other side of Beverley and this good fellow here offered me a ride home.'

He leaned towards the officer confidentially and lowered his voice to a whisper. 'It will cost me something, I expect, but I didn't want to wait for the coach. I need to be home before midnight.'

'I understand, sir, I am a family man myself.'

The other officer had been observing Will closely and beckoning to him said sharply, 'You. Step down a minute.'

Will turned in surprise towards him and shuffled along to the edge of the seat. He took off the sack which had been covering his legs. 'Aye, I will, but tha'll have to give me a hand to get up again.'

The soldier saw then his disability. 'Your pardon. I didn't realize. It's just that the man we were looking for is seemingly quite tall, and I thought that you fitted the description. But obviously it couldn't possibly be you.'

Will took up the reins again and prepared to move off. 'If there's nowt else?' he said sullenly.

'By the way,' John asked, 'what has this villain stolen?'

The officers shifted uneasily. 'Well,' said one, 'he hasn't exactly stolen anything. As a matter of fact, he brought something back.'

John sat silently, gazing at the two officers, then slowly he nodded his head and smiled quizzically. 'What kind of a thief would bring something back? Some kind of jape, is it? Or perhaps he's diverting you whilst he's up to some other mischief?'

'I don't know, sir, but I regret having bothered you. I trust you won't be too late home.'

They were anxious to be off, back to the delights of food and wine and feminine company, and with more apologies they wheeled about and galloped back the way they had come.

Maria was uneasy. Something was happening that Will didn't want her to know about. He had wanted her out of the way at all costs. He had been irritable and tense all the evening, constantly going to the window and looking up at the small patch of sky which could be seen above the houses at the opposite side of the entry. She knew better than to harass him with questions. To choose an ill-timed moment might unleash a sudden explosion of exasperation, a thunderous flashpoint which once set free would then melt away as instantly as it had appeared, leaving him as penitent as a rebuked child.

She took Alice by the hand and Tom ran in front of her as they made their way towards the apothecary's shop in the market place.

'Will needs something for 'soreness on his leg, Mr Dobson. It's still giving him a lot of pain and it hasn't healed properly.'

'Try to get fresh comfrey leaves, they're the finest poultice of all,' said the man. 'They reduce the swelling and help the wound to knit, but I'm afraid that I haven't any in stock.'

He reached up to the shelves which lined the walls of his tiny shop, and from amongst the coloured bottles and stone jars there, took down a large bottle and poured some of the contents into a smaller one.

'Try this rosemary oil and see if it helps, but tell him he must keep the wound clean or it will become infected again.'

He sighed, shook his head morosely, and patted Alice on the head. 'Let's hope this poor child gets through the winter safely. I do believe we shall have a cold one; and you'll have to take care, you ought not to be lifting those heavy fish barrels.'

'I'm very fit,' Maria reassured him, 'and we don't lift them, we roll them, there's a knack to it.'

Nevertheless, in spite of her cheerfulness in the face of his gloom, she felt perturbed, especially by his concern over Alice who, although she didn't want to admit it, seemed to be growing paler day by day.

'Come on,' she said as they stood outside the shop. 'Let's go and visit Annie and her bairns, we haven't seen them for a long while.'

The small house in the dim square was in darkness as Maria knocked on the door and tried the sneck. 'Annie, it's me,' she called.

She could hear a soft shuffling sound inside and then silence as though someone was listening behind the door. She called again. 'It's Maria, Annie.'

There came the rattle of the bolt being drawn, the

door slowly opened and through the crack a pair of wide blue eyes in a small pallid face stared up at her.

'It's only me, Lizzie, is tha ma at home?'

The child opened the door a little wider and shook her head without speaking.

'Can we come in then?' Maria stepped inside. The room was cold and bare with a stale, damp smell. There was no fire in the grate, nor had there been for some time, Maria observed, for the ashes were grey and lifeless.

'Has tha no light?' she asked.

Lizzie shook her head again but remained silent.

Maria took her by the hand and led her over to the window where she could see her better. She drew the child towards her and said softly, 'What's 'matter, Lizzie, come on, tha can tell me. Is't afeard of 'dark?'

The little girl shook her head again and started to tremble, first her hands and then her thin slight body, until she was shaking uncontrollably.

Maria bent down and put both arms around her, holding her close to her, and gently rocked her to and fro.

'It's all right. Tha's quite safe, just tell me what's wrong. Where's thy ma?'

'She – she's gone out to look for – to look for Frankie.' Lizzie started to tremble again as she uttered Francis Morton's name.

'He hasn't hit thee?' Maria demanded.

'No, no – he never hit me,' she whispered, her eyes wide and frightened. 'He said he wouldn't hit me—'

Maria stood up straight and stared down at Lizzie. 'Unless what?'

Lizzie bent her head and refused to be drawn any further. Maria could see that she was too afraid or ashamed to say any more. She took her gently to one side, away from Tom and Alice and very quietly said, 'Listen to me, Lizzie. If anyone tries to hurt thee or tries to make thee do summat against thy will, come to me – come to my house and I'll take care of thee.

95

Understand?' She shook her gently to impress what she was saying.

They stayed with her, waiting for Annie's return. Maria sent Tom to look for kindling and they lit a small fire which sent dark shadows dancing around the room, accentuating the bareness but giving a little warmth and comfort, but still Annie didn't come.

'I'll go and look for thy ma, Lizzie,' Maria said at last, 'and send her home. Now don't forget what I said.'

Lizzie nodded tearfully and on Maria's instructions she bolted the door after them, promising to open it only to her mother or her brothers.

Maria hurried through the town. She guessed that Annie would be in one of the inns or alehouses, but which one she frequented she had no idea. Fruitlessly she searched in the dram shops by the river, peering through the steamy windows, and enquiring of other women who were listlessly hanging around outside several establishments, some about their own business, and others who with young children clinging to their skirts were waiting patiently for their men to appear, but no-one had seen Annie or Francis.

Wearily she decided to go home. It was very late and Alice had started to cry fretfully with tiredness. She hoped that by now perhaps Will would be back from wherever he had been. She wanted to discuss the matter with him, to ask if he thought she was imagining things. She felt a gnawing concern about Lizzie, a feeling deep in her mind that all was not right.

Surely, she thought, not even Francis Morton would harm a child, not a gentle, docile little girl like Lizzie, who had suffered bruises already at the hands of her bully of a father. She was bewildered too by Annie's apparent lack of concern over her children, though she excused her, for she guessed how difficult it would be for Annie to manage on her own.

As they reached home, Tom charged in through the door in front of her but stopped so abruptly in his tracks that she almost fell over him. The glow from the fire highlighted the corners of the room and they stared in amazement at the sight of Francis Morton rising from a crouching position on the floor by the bed, where they had obviously disturbed him.

Maria, recovering from the shock of seeing him there, and with a growing anger at seeing him uninvited in her home, demanded, 'What's tha doing in here, how did tha get in?'

He smiled slowly at her. 'Tha needs a new lock, Maria, tha'll have to persuade Will to fix one. There's a lot of villains about, tha can't be too careful.'

'Tha didn't answer my question. What's tha doing in here?' Her voice was sharp.

His face flushed with anger and brusquely he answered, 'I'm only looking for what's mine.'

'There's nowt of thine in here, Francis Morton, so I'll thank thee to leave now before Will gets back.'

Francis laughed savagely. 'Dost think I'm afeard of that cripple? It'll take more than him to scare me off.'

He took hold of her arm roughly. 'Now then, what's he done with 'sacks? Tha'd better tell me or it'll be 'worst for thee.'

Angrily she shook him off. 'I don't know what tha's on about. There's no sacks in here, nor has there been.' She stopped suddenly, drawing in her breath, as recollection came to her. What was it that Will had been doing last night when he was so late home, when she'd woken to find him moving something? He'd said something about stowing some stuff away, but in her sleepy state she'd thought that she was dreaming.

Francis caught her look of uncertainty and smiled again sardonically. 'So – little innocent Maria, so chaste and virtuous, tha does know summat after all!'

'I know nowt,' she said, backing away from him.

'Come on, Maria, tell me where he's hidden them.'

He lifted her chin with his finger so that she was forced to look into his eyes. Blue, penetrating eyes, that sparkled like splinters of ice, cold and cruel.

Frantically she signalled to Tom and Alice to run, for

the two children were standing in stark terror at the sight of their mother in Francis's grasp. Eventually Tom understood her gestures and with a backward glance he slid quietly out of the room.

'Thee and me could have a good time together.' He ran his fingers down the front of her dress. 'Tell me where he's put 'sacks and we could go off together, just 'two of us.'

Slowly and deliberately he started to unfasten the buttons on her dress. 'Tha knows I've always wanted thee, Maria,' he muttered huskily. 'That look of purity hides fire – I know it.'

Her dress fell to the floor in a heap about her feet and she shook her head and banged her fists against his chest.

'No – don't, please. I'll lose my babby.'

He stroked her neck and breasts. 'I won't hurt thee. I promise,' he murmured. 'I just want to hold thee and touch thee.'

With a sudden spurt of fury she pushed him from her. 'Is that what tha told 'bairn? Did tha say that to young Lizzie?'

'Who's been telling thee that?' The viciousness in his voice frightened her and she shrank from him. 'Just keep thy mouth shut or tha'll feel my fist in it,' he shouted and raised his hand towards her.

The next instant he was lying spreadeagled and groaning on the floor as the force of Will's crutch caught him on the back of his head and sent him reeling.

Unbridled rage had given Will mercurial speed when he saw his son hurtle out of the dark entry, and Tom had blurted out to him to come quickly for Francis Morton was hurting his mother.

With all the strength he could muster, he grasped him now by his hair and coat collar and dragged him towards the door.

Maria cried out in fear, 'Don't hit him again, Will, tha'll kill him.'

'Killing's far too good for 'likes of him.' Will replied and with a great heave threw him outside into the entry.

The oil lamp was sending thin spirals of smoke twisting and curling up to the ceiling as Will and Maria talked quietly. The children were both asleep, worn out by the late hour and the turmoil of the evening.

Maria had attempted to tell Will some of her fears about Lizzie, and he said bitterly that he wished he'd hit Francis Morton harder and made a better job of it.

'Could tha face moving away from here, love?' he started to say when he stopped and they both listened intently to a sound coming from outside the door.

Will reached for his crutch and moved quietly across the room, then stopped as he heard a soft tapping on the door.

'It's only me, Maria – Will. Can I come in?'

Annie stood there with Lizzie in front of her. The child looked tired and white-faced, but Annie was flushed and her eyes were bright and feverish. When she spoke there was a tremble in her voice. 'Hast tha seen him? Is he upstairs? Francis, I mean!'

Will took her arm gently to bring her into the room, but she shook him away fretfully.

'I need to find him, tonight. I've a score to settle.'

'He's out somewhere licking his wounds,' Will said with grim satisfaction. 'He'll have found some hole to crawl into.'

'Then I'll go and look in all 'holes.' Annie answered bitterly. 'I'm familiar wi' most of 'em.'

She turned towards Maria. 'Can I leave Lizzie here with thee for a bit? And if owt should happen to me, or if by any chance I don't get back, will tha take care of her for me?'

She looked intently at Will who was watching her anxiously. 'I know I can trust thee both to be good to her. I've taken care of 'lads already – they're in Seamen's Hospital, just for a bit like. They'll look after them, till I – till I get back.' Her voice broke and she bit back tears.

Maria put her arms around her. 'What's happening,

99

Annie, where's tha going? Tell us, we'll help thee!'

Annie released herself from Maria's embrace. 'No, don't make it worse for me, Maria. Don't give me tha pity or I'll weaken, like I always do. It's time now for me to stand on my own two feet.'

She shook her head sadly. 'All my life I've been ill-treated by men. My fayther, my husband and now by Francis. But I've put up with it, I've always thought that that's what women had to do.'

She drew Lizzie towards her and the little girl buried her head in her mother's skirts. Annie's face hardened. 'But when it comes to my bairns, then it's a different matter. I'll not let it happen to Lizzie. Nobody will harm her without answering to me!'

She smiled wistfully. 'If I'd been lucky enough to have met somebody like thee, Will, things might have been different, but I was always attracted to 'wrong sort. So I'm begging thee to look after her, make sure she doesn't make 'same mistakes as me.'

'But where's tha going, Annie?' Will asked. 'Don't go looking for Francis, he'll be in a foul temper after what's happened here, and he'll be looking for someone to pay for his sore head.'

Annie didn't answer, she turned to kiss Maria on her cheek. 'Tha's been a good friend to me, Maria, be a friend to Lizzie too.' She turned towards Will and he bent and kissed her tenderly on her upturned face.

'Those are 'first loving kisses I've ever had,' she said, her eyes brimming with tears, 'except from my bairns. I know folk think I've neglected them, but nobody loves them more than I do.'

She flung her arms around Lizzie, then with a soft cry pushed her towards Maria and ran out of the room.

Will called after her as she ran swiftly out of the entry. 'Wait, Annie – I'll come with thee.' But she was gone, disappearing into the shadows.

They both lay awake most of the night, staring into the darkness, their minds too unsettled for sleeping, Maria between Alice and Lizzie, her arms around both girls, consumed with a black foreboding about Annie, and Will at the bottom of the bed next to Tom, wondering what the morning would bring.

As dawn broke and Maria rose wearily to get ready for work, her body aching with fatigue, Will reached across and took hold of her hand.

'Come back to bed, love, try to sleep for a bit longer.'

She sighed deeply but protested. 'We need 'money Will, there's nowt left.'

'Come back to bed and get some rest. Tha must look tha best today.' He smiled at the puzzled expression on her face. 'I didn't want to tell thee before, in case nowt came of it. We've got to see 'Mastersons this morning. We're about to start a new life.'

Annie ran swiftly, her bare feet not heeding the sharp grit and the hard cobbles. She had to find Francis tonight whilst she still felt the angry fire and pain inside her. By the morning her rage would have vanished and he would once more be able to manipulate her with his sweet talk and his sexuality.

She knew that he met his cronies in the dram shops down by the river at the South End. It was not a place to be in after dark. In the old days the area was used by smugglers who brought in goods by boat to the wharf side. Now it was a haunt of rogues and thieves, and the mariners who had no conscience about selling their masters' wares for their own profit. Under cover of darkness rolls of silk, cases of spirit and any other easily disposable goods were brought ashore and exchanged for money or for the return of a favour.

Annie kept to the shadow of the walls as she peered into the dimly lit windows of the taverns. If she was found nosing around, chances were that she would be given a cut lip and a black eye, or worse.

There was no sign of Francis as she crept quietly from one place to another, and she was beginning to feel cold. A chill wind was blowing off the river, and she wished that she could have a drop of rum or gin to warm her.

Her anger was slowly melting as discomfort took hold when she heard the sound of his laughter.

Immediately it provoked her resentment, for it was the laughter of a man without a care or a worry in his being, and she watched him as he emerged from a gin shop just a few yards from where she was standing.

He waved a cheerful goodbye to someone inside and made a sly remark to which there was an answering guffaw of male laughter, and then turned to walk towards Annie where she stood, pressed close to the wall, hardly daring to breathe.

She watched as he passed within inches of her, so close that she could have stretched out a finger to touch him. But she let him go. She could see his handsome face with a smile still lingering on it, and for a moment she experienced a yearning to hold him close just once more.

But the thought of the miseries and hurt that she had endured, and the fear that Lizzie would follow the same path unless she stopped it here and now, gave her courage. She put aside her own longings and hardened herself against Francis, whose concern, she knew, was only with his own bodily needs.

She draped her shawl over her head and covered her face, so that only her eyes were showing, and stepped out of the shadows behind him.

'Hello, mister,' she crooned. 'Does tha fancy a bit of entertainment?'

Francis swung round. He obviously had not heard her behind him and knew that that was dangerous in a place like this, where the unwary could so easily find themselves in trouble.

'Who is it?' His voice was cautious.

'Does that matter?' she answered softly. 'There's no need for names when tha's taking thy pleasure.' She was close to him now and could sense his awakened interest. She could hear the smile in his voice as he answered her.

'I need to call thee summat – if we're to know each other!'

She kept her voice demure, for she knew that timidity excited him, while vulgarity in women offended and angered him. 'Then call me Angel, and I'll take thee to Heaven!'

He took hold of her arm firmly. 'I'd like to see 'angel's face before we go to Paradise!'

She simmered with fury as she listened to his honeyed words and knew that this was all sport to him. She determined that this was one game that he would lose.

'Come with me then,' she said as gently as she could, keeping her emotions in check, but with a quaver in her voice. 'I know a quiet place where we can be comfortable, and then tha can look at me – all tha wants!'

As she took his hand in hers she could feel the throbbing of his pulse, and his anticipation. He moved closer towards her as she led him down towards the river.

'Hey, wait a minute.' He stumbled as he followed her down beneath the old wooden wharf. 'Where's tha taking me? I can't see, it's as black as Hell down here. We'll slip into 'water and I can't swim.' Panic showed in his voice and Annie felt the satisfaction of power.

'It's all right,' she said soothingly. 'Tha'll be able to see in a minute. We're underneath 'wharf, but don't worry, it's quite safe, 'tide is out and there's only soft mud below. There's a walkway under here where we'll be able to sit down.'

She led him, his hand gripping hers, until they reached a stretch of wide planking, where he sat down in some relief.

'Well, that's taken 'passion out of me,' he said roughly. 'Tha'll have to work hard for thy reward now. Is this thy regular patch?'

He peered curiously at her. There were some small chinks of night sky coming through the planking above them and as his eyes adjusted to the darkness, he reached out for her shawl. 'I know thee, I know that voice!'

'And so tha should,' said Annie, her voice bright and merry, as he pulled the shawl away from her face. 'What a lark, eh, Frankie, tha didn't guess?'

'What's thy game, Annie?' He took hold of her roughly. 'Has tha been following me? For if tha has!'

She was on dangerous ground, she heard the threat in his voice, but it only served to harden her resolve.

'No, no, not following thee, Frankie – just looking for thee. I missed thee – didn't tha miss me?' She put her head on his shoulder and stroked his thigh with long sensuous movements, feeling the muscles tense beneath his breeches.

He didn't answer but she could hear the quickening of his breath as desire returned.

Gently she traced the outline of his mouth with her fingers, then slowly slid her hand down his throat and chest, until it came to rest at the belt on his breeches. She fumbled as she tried to undo the heavy buckle, until with a grunt he came to her assistance, and with clumsy haste tore off the belt, throwing it to one side.

'Lie down!' he commanded roughly as he knelt above her, and as she turned to obey she slipped her hand under the folds of her skirts to find the object she had concealed there.

His breath rattled in his throat as the thin steel blade found its mark in the softness of the flesh below his ribs and brought him to his feet.

'Bitch!' he gasped as oblivion started to cloud his comprehension. 'Bitch. Curse thee!' He fell again to his knees, his hand clutching the wooden shaft of the knife, and as he sprawled, his other hand touched the belt as it lay on the planking. With a sudden spasm he grasped it and lashed out at Annie, the buckle catching her on her cheek, drawing blood.

In cold fury she raised her knees to her chest and with an explosive force kicked out with both feet, knocking him off the walkway down to the mud below.

In unhurried calm and without looking down, she made her way back, feeling her way as surefootedly as she used to when as a child she had played beneath the wharf, scrambling and swinging from the creaking beams above the muddy water, daring and being dared by the other children. The 'River Rats,' they were named, for some of them, without a roof to call their own, made their homes there.

She ran, her feet making no sound, back to her room where she bundled bread into a cloth. The few remaining coins which she had left from Alan's bonus she wrapped in a piece of rag and attached under her skirt. Taking more rags, she carefully wound them around her feet before putting on her boots.

She took one last look around the bare room before she opened the door, and caught sight of Alan's bag in the corner where she had left it. It had been lying there ever since she had brought it home on the day she learned of his death, how in a drunken stupor he had got in the way of a careering barrel of blubber.

She'd found the sharp flenser's blade quite by chance as she had searched the bag one day, desperately hoping to find either money or something to sell, so that she could feed the children and buy some comfort for herself. She knew that she should have returned the knife to the company, for the men were forbidden to bring implements ashore. She always meant to but never did, and kept it hidden away.

She shuddered now as she realized the enormity of her action, but she steeled herself to think only of Lizzie. Her sons she knew would one day be able to take care of themselves.

She drew her shawls around her. She was wearing all the clothes that she possessed, and quietly closing the door behind her she stepped out into the night.

She had no clear idea of where she was going, but she headed off towards the Humber once more, feeling comfort in its familiarity, and knowing that if she kept to its shores she would eventually reach the riverside villages of Hessle and North Ferriby. Following the river's course to the town of Selby, where no-one would know her, she would try to get a ride to York or even London.

With this in mind she strode purposefully away from the town, glancing only briefly towards the area where she knew Lizzie would be sleeping safely in the custody of Maria and Will, and out through the old town walls.

She reached the river bank as the day lightened and the fog from the river shifted and eddied, and in a few minutes, as protectively it drew a curtain about her, she was lost from view.

7

Maria put on her white collar and smoothed out her dress. It was very tight, and she draped her shawl about her to cover her body.

'I've heard that some society ladies don't care to see pregnant women,' she said nervously to Will as they prepared to go out. The children were clean and tidy, and Tom was hopping from one foot to the other in his impatience to be off. 'I hope Mrs Masterson isn't one of them. Annie says that they pretend it isn't happening to them.'

She looked anxiously at Lizzie as she mentioned Annie's name, but the girl appeared not to notice as she was busily engrossed in fastening on a clean apron which Maria had given her.

'Don't believe everything tha hears.' Will laughed at her. 'I happen to know that Mrs Masterson is in 'same delicate situation as thyself.'

'Delicate situation! What is tha talking about, Will Foster?'

'Never mind, tha'll find out soon enough. Come on, we mustn't be late or it'll look bad.'

As they walked, Maria was consumed with apprehension. She had heard that Mrs Masterson was a great beauty, but very imperious and fastidious, and she wondered if she would come up to her exacting standards.

'Don't be scared, Maria, she won't eat thee.' As if he had been reading her mind, Will took her hand comfortingly.

'What does tha think I'll have to do, Will? Shall I have to clean 'house and wash 'china and glass? And what if I break owt, will I have to pay?'

He squeezed her hand. 'It can't be worse than working on 'staith side, can it? There's no worse taskmaster than old Johnson.'

He was right, of course. Johnson, who was in charge of the women, was hated for his meanness and foul tongue, and would cut the women's wages on a mere whim.

But how will we ever manage, she thought, living in a quiet country district amongst strangers, with their different customs and strange talk? She smiled to herself, the townspeople used to mock the country folk for their slow ways when they came into town to sell their produce, but oddly enough, when a bargain was struck, the country folk were not often the losers.

As she looked back down the Market Place she saw the bronze statue of William III glinting in the morning sunlight. King Billy, as he was affectionately called by the Hull residents, sat proudly on his steed in splendid isolation in the midst of the bustle of the crowded street.

'Is this what tha wants, Will, does tha want to move away from all of this?' Her voice broke and she could barely hold back her tears.

'I know tha'll miss it, lass. It's home, I know, in spite of everything. But it's our only chance. If we stay, things will only get worse, we'll have to move to a smaller place with less rent, or else we don't eat!'

Maria nodded sadly. If she ate any less than she was doing, and there were times when she gave the children her share of food, then she wouldn't have any milk for the baby and the baby would die. She wanted desperately for it to live, and to grow strong and healthy, for this was a special baby. She could sense it. As it moved within her she could feel the strength of its being and was comforted.

'Mrs Masterson said for you to come up.' The maid, Ellie, looked curiously at Maria as she waited by the kitchen door, Lizzie and Alice close by her and Tom gazing inquisitively about him.

'Is tha going to 'country?' she asked, her curiosity getting the better of her, as she led them up the stairs.

'Perhaps,' Maria replied with caution. 'It's not settled yet.'

'Watch your thee's and thou's then,' Ellie whispered as a parting shot as she knocked on the sitting-room door and ushered them in to Mrs Masterson's presence.

What does she mean? thought Maria in a sudden panic. I wish Will was here. Will had gone alone to meet Isaac Masterson in his office down at the docks, leaving Maria and the children to their interview with Mrs Masterson.

'Come over here, please, where I can see you.'

Isobel Masterson was sitting in a chair by the window, her feet raised on an embroidered footstool.

Maria obeyed, her eyes lowered, and she saw then that Mrs Masterson's dainty little feet were swollen and shoeless. As she raised her eyes she realized the meaning of Will's words.

Delicate indeed, I'll give him delicate! she thought to herself, and found herself smiling sympathetically at the gentlewoman before her who was obviously in some discomfort.

'I am not at all well today, Mrs Foster, so I will ask you as few questions as I think necessary, and the first one – so that we don't waste time – is would you be willing, provided, that is, that I find you suitable, to come out to Monkston, to Garston Hall, to work in service for me?'

'I'll gladly come and work for thee, ma-am, if Will says that it's all right. As for Monkston, well, I don't rightly know where it is, as I've never been anywhere but here. But I'm sure that it will do as well as anywhere, if there's work for us.'

She became bolder. 'I would like to say, ma-am, though I've never been in service before, and am very ignorant of what should be done right, tha'll – you – will only have to tell me once and I shall remember.'

Isobel breathed a sigh of relief. 'Then I think we shall

get along very well, for if there is one thing I cannot abide, it is having to repeat myself.' She looked at the three children standing quietly behind Maria.

'Will your eldest girl be able to help? Is she useful in the house?'

'Lizzie isn't my own,' said Maria, drawing her in front of her so that Mrs Masterson could see her clearly.

Lizzie looked pleadingly up at Maria before turning her eyes towards Mrs Masterson.

'But we take care of her, for her mother. She's part of our family now,' she added firmly. 'And she's very good with 'childre', she can help with 'bairns when they come, ma-am.'

She thought that perhaps she had gone too far, that she had overstepped the boundaries of etiquette as Mrs Masterson frowned.

'The bairns? I don't understand what you mean.'

Maria blushed. Now she knew that she had gone too far. Annie was right, these ladies did pretend that pregnancy and all that went before didn't happen to them.

'I only meant, ma-am, that when my babby comes, she can help to look after it, so that I can work for you.' She also wanted to say that Lizzie could look after the Masterson baby too, but she hesitated in case she was being too forward.

Isobel's face cleared. 'Oh – I see – you mean children! I shall of course expect you to speak clearly and correctly if you come to work for me.'

This wasn't conveyed unkindly and Maria didn't take offence, but she was surprised when Mrs Masterson added, 'I hadn't realized that you were expecting a child, when is it due?'

'In about four weeks, ma-am. If it's on time.'

'Four weeks! Then how are we to manage? When will you be able to start work again?'

Maria smiled. 'I'll only need a couple of days, ma-am, just until my milk comes through.'

It was Isobel Masterson's turn to blush and she turned

towards the window to hide her embarrassment.

'I'm sorry, ma-am. I didn't mean—' Maria was lost for words.

'No, don't be sorry.' Isobel turned to face her with an impatient shake of her head. 'It's just so silly that a woman of my age doesn't understand the normal facts of pregnancy. But who to ask, that's the problem?' she added softly.

Maria remained discreetly silent, but her heart went out to the grand lady who was obviously so bewildered over a natural event.

Isobel leaned forward and then glancing towards the children said, 'If the children would just step down to the kitchen for a moment, I'm sure Cook will find them some cake.'

They needed no second bidding. Lizzie gave a small curtsey to Mrs Masterson and led the way out.

'I hope you don't mind my asking, Mrs Foster.' Isobel hesitated for a moment and then took the plunge. 'But you have been through childbirth before. Is it very painful? Does it hurt very much?'

'Sometimes it does, ma-am,' Maria admitted. She felt that Mrs Masterson would want the truth and it would be wrong to mislead her. 'Especially with 'first, but with Alice my mother showed me what to do, and then it became easier. But you soon forget 'pain when 'babby's in your arms.'

She smiled at the recollection, but Mrs Masterson, with no preconceived notion of motherhood, was unimpressed, and the thought of her own mother dispensing wisdom was ludicrous, as that lady finished with childbearing once and for all, after her only child, Isobel, was born.

'Very well, Mrs Foster,' she said as she concluded the interview. 'Mr Masterson will make the final arrangements, but I hope that we shall be able to remove to Garston Hall within the next two or three weeks, and I would like to think that you will be there already to help with the arrangements.'

'Yes ma-am, we can go any time, we've nowt – nothing to keep us here any more.'

She walked outside into the High Street to find Will waiting for her, a jubilant grin on his face.

'Well, that's it, 'job is ours. We go tomorrow!'

'Tomorrow? So soon?' She hadn't thought that they would go immediately. Now there would be no time for lingering goodbyes to all the familiar faces and places.

'And guess what?' Will almost crowed with delight. 'Garston Hall is in Monkston – and Monkston is on 'coast.' He flung his arms around her and the children laughed aloud to see him in such high spirits.

'Maria, we're going to live by 'sea. The magnificent, rolling, deep, deep sea!'

Will rose early. It was still quite dark and as he peered out of the window he saw that there was a light drizzle falling.

'I'd hoped it would be fine this morning, we've a long journey ahead of us. I'll go off now, and see if we can get a lift with 'carrier. Today's his day for going to Hornsea, and happen he'll drop us off on 'road.'

The carrier travelled twice a week to the east coast town carrying a variety of goods and provisions, and sometimes, if he had the room, would take passengers also.

'Otherwise I'll have to hire a cart from 'yard. Mr Masterson said I could, and he would take it out of my wages.'

He left Maria and the children sorting out their few possessions. He swung along easily and swiftly now on his crutch, and indeed didn't use it at all when he was inside, but jumped with a short rapid motion. His uncanny balance was due, he said, to his years of sailing, when surefootedness meant the difference between life and death as a ship tossed and pitched in mountainous seas.

He was about to turn towards the Market Place and

the Blue Bell inn, where the carriers came in with their carts and waggons, when he heard the sound of shouting, and saw in the distance a small crowd of men running towards the jetty at the old South End. Curiously he turned that way. It would be either the wreckage of some small boat or some poor devil's body, he thought, brought in on the tide.

They'd already turned him over when he got there, the men hanging precariously from the lower beams to pull the body clear of the broken crates and tattered canvas which littered the mud, just above the high-water mark. The thick brown mud had filled his eyes and nostrils, and a dark stain covered his shirt front.

There was muttering from the crowd: some of them knew him and with raised eyebrows and pursed lips signalled their confirmation that they had always known he would come to this.

'River didn't tek 'im,' said one. 'He was no water rat.'

Will turned away. There was a superstition that the waters of the Humber would only take their own kind, and Francis Morton was a town rat, who made his living scavenging in the streets and alleys. The river didn't want him, and had cast him off, discarded and unwanted with all the other flotsam and jetsam that lay in the mud beneath the ancient wharf.

Hurriedly, he made his way towards Annie's house. He wanted to be the one to tell her, the first to break the news. Or did he want to warn her? He was unsure in his own mind. She'd been in distress two nights ago when she had gone looking for Francis, but surely not enough to kill him? He dismissed the thought as fanciful. He'd seen the wooden shaft of the knife. No woman would have the strength to plunge it so deep into a man as physically powerful as Francis Morton.

He felt disturbed and conscience-stricken. He knew that he too had been in the right frame of mind to do serious injury to the dead man. He had always disliked him and he never had trusted him with Maria, having seen the way his lustful eyes followed her. But he wouldn't in honesty have seen any man finish his days the way Francis had, reprobate though he was.

Telling himself that he was getting soft in the head, he turned into the square where Annie lived. He hammered loudly on the door several times, but on getting no reply turned away. A scrawny old woman leaned out of a window across the square and gave him a wide toothless grin.

'If tha's looking for Annie, tha's too late, she's gone – flitted.' She cackled with laughter at her own wit.

'Where's she gone?'

The woman's smile disappeared. 'Can't say. Who wants to know?'

'I'm a friend. Lizzie is staying with us.'

The woman leaned further out of the window and dropped her voice to a whisper. 'She left yesterday morning, 'fore it was light. I saw her go. I reckon she won't be back!' She drew her head back inside and disappeared.

Will was dismayed. If Annie had gone, it would look very suspicious should the constables come enquiring into Francis's death. And yet he knew that no-one here or at her workplace would give her away. An impenetrable wall of silence would descend, impossible to pass or scale.

The carriers' notices were posted up outside the inn, and although Will didn't read well, he managed to make out the times and days that they set out. The Hornsea carrier, William Mires, didn't move off until the afternoon, making it very late for them to travel if they had to walk some of the way.

I'll go across to Mr Masterson's yard and hire a cart, he thought, he did offer after all. It just means I'll be a bit short in my wages, and they're little enough as it is. He was grateful to Isaac Masterson for giving him employment, but astute enough to realize that the wage he would be earning at Garston Hall was a mere pittance compared with what he had once earned as a whaling man.

He had turned the corner from the High Street to cut down one of the alleyways leading to the Old Harbour and Masterson's yard when he realized that he was being followed, that the sound of footsteps had been behind him since leaving the Blue Bell. He stopped abruptly and swung around.

A vice-like grip clutched his throat, knocking him back against the wall of the alley, his crutch slithering from under his armpit to the ground, and he found himself staring into the threatening eyes of Jack Crawford, Francis Morton's crony.

He held him so close that Will could see his own eyes reflected in the dark pupils of the man's jaundiced eyes, and smell his warm, rancid breath as he spoke.

'I've been looking for thee, Will Foster.'

With a great heave from his muscular arms, Will shoved him away and the two men stood in the gloomy alleyway glaring at each other, their arms raised for attack. People on their way to work glanced down the alley and some made as if to come down it, but on seeing an obvious confrontation backed away.

'So, now tha's found me – what now?'

Crawford drew nearer menacingly, his busy eyebrows drawn together to meet above his flattened nose.

''Sacks – where are they? I want my share. That swine Frank Morton has disappeared. His ma says she doesn't know where he is – but I reckon she knows all right. And if either of thee thinks tha can deceive me, then tha's mistaken.'

Will hid a grim smile. Obviously the word of Francis's untimely end hadn't reached Crawford's ears.

' 'Sacks have gone back – back to where they belong,' he said dispassionately. 'What about that old man? Has he recovered?'

Crawford looked sharply down the alley. 'Keep thy voice down. Aye, he's all right, just got a sore head, that's all.'

'Tha might have killed him.' Will's voice was caustic.

'Well, I didn't, did I? Never mind about that, what

115

about all that stuff? Who would be so daft as to take it back? Dost take me for 'village idiot?'

Will shrugged and bent awkwardly to pick up his crutch, keeping a wary eye on Crawford as he did so. 'I said they've gone back – I took them.'

Crawford took a step forward. 'Tha crazy fool. I told Frank Morton not to tek thee on, that tha wasn't up to it.' He shook his fist in Will's face. 'Don't think that I'm taking risks for nowt. How do I know they've gone back? How do I know that it hasn't been shared out between 'pair of thee?'

'Tha doesn't know. Tha just has to take my word for it. This is one time when tha has to trust somebody.'

Crawford fumed, his dark skin flushing, the veins standing out on his temples. 'Frank Morton'll answer for this. Don't think this is 'end of it. He'll not hide from me – I'll find him, don't worry about that!'

Will watched him as he blustered, his thick fingers clasping and unclasping impotently.

'Tha hasn't heard about Frank then?'

Jack Crawford looked blankly at Will, his eyes narrowing suspiciously.

'Tha didn't hear all 'commotion down at 'South End?' Will spoke slowly and deliberately.

'I don't know what tha's talking about. If tha's got summat to say, spit it out!'

Will gave a thin smile. 'They've just pulled him out of 'river – with a knife in his guts.'

He waited a moment for the information to take effect. 'I dare say 'constables are asking questions already, looking for somebody with a grudge!'

A muscle twitched in Jack Crawford's cheek and he glanced up and down the alley.

'It's got nowt to do with me, I haven't seen him.'

'But tha's been looking for him,' said Will softly. 'How many folk did tha ask? Who knows that tha had a reason for finding him?'

Crawford backed away, edging his way down the alley. 'I said, it's nowt to do with me, and it hasn't!'

116

'But nobody will believe thee, thy reputation will see to that. If I were in thy breeches,' Will's voice was persuasive, 'I wouldn't wait about till they came for me.'

Jack Crawford hesitated, then snarled, 'If I hear so much as a whisper that tha's been spreading rumour about me, Foster, then make no mistake I shall be after thy blood.'

'Threats?' said Will coldly. 'And me just a poor cripple! Tha'd best be careful for fear somebody hears thee.'

With a final shake of his fist, Crawford turned his back and headed out of the alley towards the river, and when Will emerged a minute later he was gone, hidden by the mass of merchandise piled high in crates and barrels at the staith side.

Tom couldn't contain his excitement as he saw his father driving the cart down the road towards the entry. He'd been chasing in and out for the last hour, anxiously looking for him to tell him the news about Francis, and his disappointment was keen when he discovered that he already knew and had even seen the body.

'What did it look like? Did tha see 'blood? What was—?'

His father interrupted him sharply. 'That's enough, Tom. Don't forget that it's a man's life tha's talking about.'

'Ma's with Mrs Morton. She's wailing and roaring.'

'Who is?' Will frowned.

'Mrs Morton,' answered Tom enthusiastically. 'She says she'll find out who did it, and have 'em strung up on 'gibbet.'

Will groaned. He should have expected that Mrs Morton would want to wreak vengeance on her son's killer. Francis had been her favourite, the eldest son who in her eyes could do no wrong, and who kept her in comfort and small luxuries.

*   *   *

'I'm sorry about thy trouble, Mrs Morton.' He could hardly make himself heard above the hubbub of women and children who had crowded into the small, hot, upstairs room, out of curiosity or to give support to the grieving woman.

Mrs Morton took a deep breath and for a moment Will thought she was going to start wailing again, but instead she blew her nose vigorously on the end of her shawl and said, 'Aye, it's a bad day, Will, but I'll get through it with the help of my friends. Thy Maria's been a great support and it's grand to know that she's here to lean on.'

Will glanced across at Maria, as she sat gently rocking the Morton's baby, a questioning look on his face. She shook her head slightly in answer to his unspoken question.

'Aye, and I'm only sorry that we can't stay. Maria won't have had 'chance to tell thee that we're moving on.' He added firmly, 'I've 'chance of a job, but we've got to go now. 'Cart's here, Maria, we must get loaded up.'

Mrs Morton looked askance, first at Will and then at Maria, who whispered quietly, 'I'm so sorry, we would have stayed if we could.'

Mrs Morton sniffed. ' 'Course if tha has to go, I expect I shall manage.' She looked at Will for a moment and then said malevolently, 'I heard thee and our Francis having a fight 'other night.'

There was a sudden hush as everyone in the room stopped their talking to listen.

'Aye, we did have a scrap. He was bothering Maria and I threw him out. But that was 'end of it.' He looked her in the eyes. 'He's crossed plenty of folk, has Francis, there's a few who wanted him out of 'way – only I'm not one of them.'

The women in the room nodded their heads in agreement, and some tut-tutted sympathetically at the thought of Will, with his disability, having to protect his pregnant wife from the lecherous Francis.

'I didn't mean owt,' Mrs Morton was quick to reply as she sensed she was losing her audience's support. 'I know he had some enemies, and I knew—' she nodded her head significantly. 'I knew when he didn't come home 'other night, that summat was up. He's stayed away before, but I've always known where to find him.' She spat out her words maliciously. 'Especially when he's been with that whore, Annie Swinburn. Mark my words, she's not blameless, she'll know summat about this!'

Maria got up from the chair and handed the baby back to Mrs Morton. 'Take 'bairn, Mrs Morton, he'll be some comfort to thee. And don't think badly of Annie. She's had a hard life, but she's not wicked.'

She put her arm around Lizzie who had been sitting pale and quiet in a corner with Alice on her knee. 'There's some folk who take a lot of knocks, and there's no point in our adding to them.'

She turned to the women in the room as she prepared to leave. Some of them were her age, some older; most of them looked shabby and worn, but one or two others had the shrewd look of those who lived by their wits, as the Mortons did. All of them she had known the whole of her life.

'I'm right sorry to leave thee,' she said, her voice catching. 'I don't know if I'll ever see any of thee again, but I'll think on thee often.'

Some of the women came across to her then and kissed her on her cheek and hugged Alice and Lizzie, whilst Tom, in alarm that they might want to embrace him, slipped hastily down the stairs, followed as swiftly as he could by his father.

'Anybody would think we were going off to 'North Pole, fuss they're making in there,' Will grumbled as he and Tom loaded up the cart. They had just one long bench and a table, two chairs, a few iron pans, plates and cups and a couple of blankets. The wooden bed which Will had made many years before they had to leave behind as it wouldn't fit on the cart, but they took the feather bed and bolster which Maria and her mother had stuffed laboriously before she and Will were married.

'It looks as if we are going there,' said Tom as he tried to heave Will's seaman's bag on to the cart. It was the largest sack on the cart, for Will had always been well catered for with warm shirts and breeches, a thick jacket to keep out the arctic cold and heavy boots and shoes.

'Aye, well, these might come in useful, 'east wind can be a bit sharp out on 'coast.'

He shouted through the door, 'Come on, Maria, let's be off.' Will wanted to be at Monkston before nightfall, the nights were drawing in now that autumn had arrived, and the evenings were damp and chill. The lamps had to be lit early and he had no desire to be unloading in the dark.

Maria emerged reluctantly from the house and took one last look back as she closed the door behind her.

'My poor, sad Mary,' said Will as he helped her into the cart. 'We're not going to 'end of world, lass, we're less than twenty miles away.' He squeezed her hand. 'Tha'll be able to come back, see thy friends, go to 'market, or even—' he added, trying to engender some enthusiasm – 'come back for 'Fair.'

Maria choked back her tears. 'It might just as well be 'end of world, as far as I'm concerned,' she answered, trying to smile, her eyes wet and bright, 'but tha doesn't have to worry. I'm happy to come with thee, Will, and so are 'bairns. We'll start a fresh life, and our babby will begin a brand new line of Foster country folk.'

They set out, a small cavalcade journeying to an unknown destination, Will and Maria riding in the cart with Alice between them, and Tom and Lizzie alternately running in front or lagging behind as they stopped to brag about their journey to the curious children who enquired.

'They'll be worn out before we're halfway there,' said Maria as she looked back and waved to them to hurry.

'Wait, wait.' Tom and Lizzie ran to catch up as they approached the river and North Bridge.

'Get into 'back of 'cart for a minute,' said Will, 'and we'll all travel out of town together.'

They scrambled in and the cart tipped precariously with the extra weight. The horse strained as Will shook the reins and they crossed the rickety old bridge. Tom, Lizzie, and Alice, who stood on her mother's knee to see down into the water, all waved and shouted goodbye to anyone who was watching from the ships below.

The first few miles were long and arduous, especially for Tom and Lizzie, who after the initial excitement of setting out on what they thought would be a great adventure, became bored and weary and were increasingly admonished to look sharp or they would be left behind. Lizzie would then run breathlessly after them as if terrified of being abandoned, whilst Tom defiantly slowed down, dragging his boots through the pools of muddy water. They decided to stop to give the children a rest and to take a drink from a stream running just beyond the roadside.

'It's good fresh water in Holderness,' said Will. 'Mr Masterson told me – and plenty of it. That's one thing we shan't be short of.'

'Perhaps we could sell it then,' said Tom as he cupped his hand and drank the clear sparkling liquid greedily.

Will and Maria both laughed. 'Tha'll make a business man yet, Tom,' said his father. 'But tha'll have to find summat else to sell apart from water.'

Lizzie took off her boots and tenderly rubbed her feet, then with a grimace dabbled them in the cold running water. Maria saw that she had two broken blisters, red and raw, one on each heel.

'They're not my boots,' she said in an apologetic tone in answer to Maria's questioning. 'Somebody gave them to my ma. They were too small for her, but they're too big for me.'

Maria threw the boots into the back of the cart. 'We'll keep them until tha's grown a bit. Tha's better off without them. Climb up into 'cart, and thee, Tom. Tha can both have a ride, and Alice and me will walk for a bit.'

Will looked at her anxiously. 'Is tha sure that tha can manage?'

'Aye, I can do with a walk after all that jolting. But don't get too far ahead,' she added hastily. 'We don't want to get lost.'

He laughed. 'Tha'll not get lost out here. Tha can practically see 'coast from here.' And whilst he was exaggerating, Maria saw what he meant, for the road stretched forever onward over the hummocky plain of Holderness, and though it dipped and curved, so wide and flat was the landscape it could still be seen in the far distance as it twisted and snaked on towards the horizon.

'When will we be there?' Alice was plaintive as they trudged hand in hand, and her father, horse and cart and passengers were becoming blurred shapes in the distance.

'Shh, be patient. Soon!' Maria answered her daughter with a conviction that she didn't feel.

At the top of a shallow incline they came to a hamlet of a few scattered timber-framed houses, an old church and an inn, and took a drink from the pump. There were no people around, just a stray dog who barked at them from the safety of one of the buildings. Then a woman came out of one of the houses and watched them curiously for a few minutes before disappearing again inside.

Maria looked down the hill. To their right grew a dense cover of trees, dark against the skyline, whilst below and as far as she could see, the harvested stubble of gathered wheat glowed the colour of warm sand in the afternoon light, the muddy road running between like a sluggish, meandering river. The sky had lightened after the rain, the breeze whipping up the mantle of grey into a froth of soft rolling clouds, sending them scudding rapidly inland towards the shelter of the Wolds and leaving behind a wide sky streaked with long shafts of white and gold from the hidden sunlight.

She was overawed by the immensity of the broad landscape, used as she was to the limiting vision and confines of town walls, and dismayed by the loneliness and isolation. As she paused, trying to find the determination to go on, she heard a sound behind them. A man was coming towards them leading a thin, scrawny-looking old horse. He had plainly come from out of one of the village buildings behind them, for he turned to speak in answer to the woman who had marked them previously, and who now stood in the middle of the road, her arms folded in front of her and calling out instructions to him.

He nodded to Maria, his head kept low so that he was looking at her from under his faded old hat. 'Missus said to give thee this.' He handed her a hunk of bread, crusty and warm.

Maria took it gratefully and turned to thank the woman, but she had gone again into the darkness of her doorway.

'Would 'little lass tek a ride on owd hoss?' His dialect was thick but he gestured Alice towards the horse so that there was no mistaking his meaning.

They made better progress as Alice sat contentedly on the horse's back, munching on a piece of bread, and Maria, easier in her mind for the addition of company, however taciturn, strode out more briskly down the hill.

'There's Will!' she exclaimed in relief as she saw the cart coming back towards them.

'I've dropped 'bairns off,' he said. 'I was getting worried about thee, tha took so long.'

He turned to the man with the horse. 'I thank thee kindly. It's right neighbourly of thee to help my wife.'

'Don't thee worry about that,' the man replied. 'We have to help each other out here, or we don't get by.'

He looked at the bits of furniture in the back of the

123

cart. 'I reckon tha's going to Monkston, to work at Garston Hall?'

Will and Maria looked at each other. News travelled fast, it seemed.

The man caught the look and smiled knowingly. 'There's nowt much happens around here that folk don't get to know about. Trouble is,' he went on, suddenly finding his tongue, 'nowt much happens, so if somebody dies or has a babby,' he looked significantly at Maria, 'or flits and moves on, then 'news keeps 'women's jaws moving for weeks.'

He helped Maria into the cart. 'I'll go with thee as far as Ol'bro',' he pointed up the road with his stick, 'and give 'other childre a ride. Monkston's not so far from there. Tha should be there afore nightfall.'

By degrees they finally arrived in the old village of Aldbrough, where their companion, who didn't offer his name, or ask theirs, left them.

'Keep going 'till tha gets to Tillington,' he called as he moved off towards the inn. 'Then go down 'road towards 'sea. It's a bit rough and snaggy in places, but tha'll get there alreet.'

They could see the square tower of the grey stone church of Tillington at the top of a hill as they approached from the winding road, a scattering of houses and barns surrounding it.

Maria got out of the cart to stretch her legs and walked up towards the church. It looked to her very ancient, and here and there the crumbling stonework was supported by rocks and boulders. It had a trim, neat churchyard and the small number of graves reflected the size and population of the hamlet.

As she stood quietly reflecting and looking down at the earthy mounds, she became aware of a strange sensation creeping over her. An image of her dead mother came to mind; her mother who, it had been whispered, was 'fey', and could see what others could not. A muffled roaring filled her ears and her body seemed to be getting lighter. She felt a great wind buffeting and lifting her off her feet and with a sudden cry she bent double as if to protect her unborn child.

'Maria – Maria! What is it? It's not thy time, is it?'

From far off through a mist she could see Will's anxious face and felt the support of his arms. She gave a sudden shudder and shook her head. 'I'm all right,' she answered weakly. 'I just felt a bit strange, and I heard a roaring in my head. A ghost walking over my grave, that's all.'

'Don't talk like that, Maria.' Will's voice was sharp. 'Tha knows I don't like it. It's been too much for thee, travelling all this way. I should have sent thee on 'carrier's waggon, it would have been more comfortable than in this old crate. Or if we could have afforded 'coach—!'

'Well, we can't, it's not for 'likes of us. Let's get on, I shall be all right now.'

They helped her back into the cart and Lizzie solicitously padded the blankets behind her so that she could rest more easily. They moved off on the last lap of their journey down the narrow track into the village of Monkston.

Garston Hall was set back from the village and approached by a long winding drive, and heavy iron entrance gates loomed large above them as they approached. The village meandered down a rutted road towards the sea and had, in some time past, enjoyed prosperity, judging by the number of thatched houses and farmsteads. It had an inn, and a fine church close to the sea, but some of the houses were now empty and derelict, their front doors swinging and creaking between the mud and chalk walls.

'There's folk watching us, Fayther,' whispered Tom.

'Well, what of it?' his father replied. 'Wouldn't tha do 'same if tha saw strangers coming?' He too had seen the shadows of faces looking out from some of the doors and windows as they passed by.

As they drew up by the gates, hesitating as to which

way to enter, a man came down the road from the sea leading a cow on a long rope.

He stopped and looked at them. 'Tha'll be new folk for Garston?'

'That's right,' said Will. 'Is this 'road we should take?'

'Aye, it is, but tha's not expected yet. Ma Scryven said tha was due tomorrow.'

'Who's Ma Scryven?' Will was perplexed. 'We were told to come today.'

'She's looking after 'house for 'time being. She'd find thee somewhere to stay, only she's over at Tillington, tending to somebody what's sick.'

'Is there somewhere to rest now? 'Bairns are weary,' Maria interrupted. 'They've walked from Hull.'

The man stared at the children. 'That's a good walk,' he said. 'Tha needs a pair o' strong legs for that. I went to Hull once.' He leant on the back of the cow. 'Didn't like it, though. It were full of villains and drunkards, and somebody stole what bit o' money I had.' He stood silently shaking his head. 'I nivver went back. Nor shall I.'

He stared at them thoughtfully as if assessing which category they fell into. 'Tha could stay in 'old barn that's on Garston land – just for tonight. It's dry and warm, then Ma Scryven will fix thee up tomorrow.'

The stone barn was set in a sheltered corner of a field and was warm and welcoming, with a rich smell of ripe apples and hay. Maria flopped down in exhaustion, her body aching from the jarring and shaking of the cart.

'I couldn't go another step, Will. My legs wouldn't carry me.' She made herself a hollow in a pile of hay and stretched out. 'I'm sorry, but tha'll all have to fend for tha selves. There's bread in a basket and there must be water nearby.'

Lizzie came up with a blanket and covered her over. 'I'll see to things, Maria. Don't worry. Try to get some rest now.'

Maria smiled at the earnest child as she gazed at her.

126

She was a good girl, shy and nervous except when she was doing something for someone else.

'We must all try and get some rest, Lizzie, so that we're ready for what the morning brings.'

Will came and sat by her. The children forgot their aching feet and tiredness, and were soon exploring the far corners of the barn, rolling in the mound of straw that was stacked almost up to the beams at the back of it.

'Well, we're here, Maria.' He looked down at her, elation growing inside him.

'Aye.' She turned her head away.

'What's up, lass?'

She shook her head. 'I'm that scared, Will.' She stared up at him anxiously. 'It's that bleak and desolate. I'm not used to so much space.' She shivered. 'It's all that much bigger than me.'

'Tha'll soon get used to it.' He smiled down and bent to kiss her. 'Tomorrow it'll all seem better. 'Bairns will grow strong here. We'll maybe never have much, but we'll have good clean air which'll cost us nowt – we'll not get diseased!' He could see that she was still unconvinced, but her eyes were beginning to close with sleep. 'And maybe one day, I'll take thee back.'

Gently he stroked her cheek, and then turned away with a sigh. He had wanted her to share the passion which he felt, the excitement growing inside him as he had watched the vastness of the landscape unroll before him on his journey here, and ending at the foot of the waters of the sea.

Telling the children that he wouldn't be long, he went outside and, carefully manoeuvring his crutch in the short tufted grass, walked in the gathering darkness across the field towards the sea. The salt smell gripped his nostrils, and he laughed aloud at the sound of the surf as it crashed against the cliffs.

He felt the untamed wildness wrap round him, challenging him, and he responded. He wanted to run headlong into the wind; to defy nature; to spurn danger.

127

He wanted to make passionate love to Maria, as he always used to when he came home from the sea, when their joy and desire overwhelmed them. And he felt that, cripple though he was, out here was a challenge he could face. He turned to the sea in defiance, his shock of red hair blowing wildly in the wind, gazing past the mass of grey water which thundered and broke beneath the clay cliffs, throwing up frothy white spume, out to the boundless horizon, and raising his arms up to the sky, his fists clenched in triumph, with a mighty primitive cry answered the call.

8

Mrs Scryven assessed the situation immediately she put her head round the barn door the next morning. Her bright birdlike eyes picked out Maria lying motionless on the hay, with Lizzie anxiously watching her. Tom, covered in dust, had made himself a burrow in the straw, whilst Alice was sitting in a corner, her eyes and nose streaming, coughing and crying quietly to herself.

'This won't do,' she said. 'This won't do at all.' She opened wide the barn door and the bright morning sunlight streamed in, making them blink.

'I'm sorry—' began Maria. 'I don't feel too good. My legs—' She broke off and tried to sit up.

'Stay right there, my lovely, don't thee dare move. Ma Scryven will put thee right.'

She beckoned to Tom. 'Come here, young scallibrat.'

Tom, recognizing the voice of authority when he heard it, obeyed immediately, brushing himself down perfunctorily as he did so.

'First thing tha learns in 'country, is that tha doesn't play games with winter fodder. In 'summer tha can have a grand time sliding down 'stacks, but come rain and snow, when neither we nor beasts have owt to eat, then we're glad of a well kept harvest.'

She picked Alice up from the floor. 'Now, take 'young 'un outside away from 'dust, and go find thy fayther and fetch him to me.'

'He's gone for water,' volunteered Lizzie, afraid that they were all going to get a sound ticking off from this small round body who was enveloped in a crisp white apron with not a hair showing from underneath her bonnet.

Mrs Scryven came across to where Maria was lying.

Gently she placed a hand on her forehead, then with care she put her other hand beneath the blanket and softly pressed Maria's abdomen. She stood for a moment, her eyes closed, breathing deeply, then she opened her eyes and smiled, her wizened brown face warm and sunny, as if deep inside a light was glowing.

'She'll do fine,' she breathed. 'Just rest today and tomorrow, and 'babby will be all right.'

Maria prayed that she was right, for all night she had been racked with pain and cramps in her legs. She'd told Will, when she was unable to sleep, that now she knew something of what he had suffered during his ordeal. He spoke then of the fact that not once had she turned away from him, never ever showing by look or word that his disfigurement repulsed her.

'Tha's still 'same man I married, Will,' she'd whispered in the darkness. 'Still 'same one as I yearned for when I was just a young wench, and thee a grown man and never noticing me.'

'Will tha be all right for a bit, if I tek 'bairns with me?' Mrs Scryven looked down at her. 'Then I'll bring thee some gruel.'

She gathered up Alice and Lizzie, one on each hand, and marched them off across the fields towards Garston Hall, where a short while later Will and Tom found them seated at a long scrubbed table in the kitchen, tucking into a dish of steaming gruel.

The previous owners of Garston Hall had not been mean when they had fitted out the kitchen. A brick-built fireplace with a large iron cooking range with fire bars and spit racks within it, dominated one end of the room, with a complement of fire irons, pans and kettles hanging within easy reach. The heat from the fire burning there and the mouth-watering aroma of game and herbs reached Will and Tom as they hesitated by the door.

'Sit thee down.' Mrs Scryven pointed to the bench. 'Tha can't work on an empty belly.' She poured the thick, glutinous liquid into two bowls and slid them across the table towards them.

'Now I'll go and see to thy missus.' She stared sternly at Will. 'If she's to keep 'babby, she's to stay where she is for 'next few days.'

She sat down on a stool facing him. 'Tha's been given farmstead in East Field – Field House. It's not very grand, but 'roof is sound and 'rent is cheap, leastways that's what I'm told, and I'm only passing 'message on from 'agent. So tha can get moved in and made comfortable afore thy missus is up and about.'

With that pronouncement she heaved herself off the stool and proceeded to heat a pan of milk on the fire, which she poured into the gruel, stirring it until the viscous mass was smooth and creamy. They watched her, the motion of spoon to mouth never wavering as they ate hungrily, as she added some white grains from a jar, mixing them patiently until they were absorbed. She picked up her basket and carefully placed the dish of gruel into it, covering it over with a clean cloth.

'I'm much obliged to thee,' said Will as she turned towards the door. 'If there's owt I can do for thee, tha only has to say.'

'I dare say there'll be plenty of jobs that I'll think on,' she answered. 'I've no man around, and though I can fend for missen, there's time's when a bit of brute strength is needed.'

She left them with instructions not to dally around all the morning, but then poked her head back round the door, her shrewd eyes gleaming, to say to Lizzie to make sure that all the gruel was eaten up as she couldn't abide waste.

It took them two days to sweep out and prepare the farmhouse before Mrs Scryven deemed it fit to live in. The last tenants, she said, had had to move away to seek work in the town, leaving the building empty since last Martinmas.

'It's funny tha's brought thy family here, when most folks are moving out of 'country.' Mrs Scryven watched Will as he carefully jointed some discarded pieces of elm which he had found leaning up against a wall.

'I'll work wherever work is,' he answered her. 'I can't sail any more and though I'm no farmer I like it here. 'Sea's in my blood so I'm happy to be within sight and sound of it.'

Tom and Lizzie ran to them. 'Can I go down to 'sea, Fayther? I want to catch a fish.'

Will laughed. 'Aye, tha can try.'

'Can I go too?' Lizzie was still shy and nervous with Will even though he did his best to put her at her ease. 'Everything's done inside.'

'Go on then, but make sure tha watches for 'tide!'

'Me too, me too,' said Alice. 'I want to catch a fish.'

'No, tha'll fall down 'cliff,' said Mrs Scryven. 'Stay with me and we'll bake some bramble tart.'

Alice took Mrs Scryven's hand and they watched as Tom and Lizzie ran swift as young hares across the field towards the cliffs, and heard their shrieks as they clambered down.

'She's a good bairn, that one. A real worker,' Mrs Scryven acknowledged, having watched the way Lizzie had set to with broom and pail to clear away a year's dust and grime.

Mrs Scryven had been busily occupied plying Maria with nourishment three times a day, her small dumpy figure scurrying across the fields, armed with bowls of soup and tender pieces of meat, to the barn where Maria was propped up on pillows and blankets on her mound of hay.

'I shall be that fat, tha'll be able to render me down,' she protested as Mrs Scryven appeared again through the barn door, holding yet another jug of liquid.

'This isn't broth.' Mrs Scryven poured the pale pink liquid into a cup and handed it to Maria. 'This is to help thee when thy time comes.'

Maria sipped the warm pungent liquid with the faint smell of ripe summer fruit and was instantly reminded of the time she was expecting Tom, when her mother, like Mrs Scryven, would appear with strange potions and liquids for her to consume to ensure a trouble-free labour.

'My mother had all this lore,' she began.

'Aye, and now it's lost!' The old lady nodded her head, her thoughts astray. 'But we'll tell 'bairn, she'll know what to do.'

Maria stared at her. 'Dost tha mean our Alice – or Lizzie?'

Mrs Scryven looked flustered, 'Ah, don't listen to me. I'm just a silly old gawk sometimes, my tongue prattles on afore I'm ready.' She leaned forward. 'Wilt tha be satisfied wi' four bairns?'

'Three,' corrected Maria. 'Lizzie isn't one of ours.'

'Aye, I guessed as much.'

Tom's and Alice's thick dark hair and olive skin, like their mother's, was in sharp contrast to Lizzie's fine fair hair and pale complexion.

Will came in through the door and swept off the old hat he was wearing. 'Would Madam care to inspect 'palace?'

'Oh – at last. Can I get up? Mrs Scryven – tha's been so kind, but I'm not used to this life of idleness. It's all right for grand folk like Mrs Masterson, but I've never spent so much time in bed before.'

'And I doubt that tha ever will again, so it's as well tha hasn't a liking for it. But 'babby's safe enough now. Tha'll go thy full time.'

Will walked Maria slowly across the Masterson land, or Garston land as the locals called it, skirting the prickly hawthorn hedges and clumps of bramble which already were bright with berries proclaiming the end of summer.

'Is it all for us, Will? We don't have to share with anybody else?'

Maria was overwhelmed. The stone- and boulder-built house with the overhanging thatch looked big enough for three families. The door opened into a room much larger than the one in Wyke Entry, and their few sticks of furniture looked sparse, but she didn't mind that if there was room to move.

'But tha's forgotten to bring in 'bedding, Will. It'll look well in that corner, over there by 'fire.'

Will smiled mysteriously and opened a door across the room. To her delight she saw another room, smaller than the first, but taking up most of the space was a rough hewn bed which Will had made, with their own feather mattress already on it.

'And we've got our own water pump out in 'yard. There's a deep well, fed from a spring, so we shan't have to go traipsing around looking for good water.' He put his arms around her. 'We'll do well here, Maria. 'Bairns will grow strong.' He laughed. 'And that old witch Mrs Scryven says she'll get rid of Alice's cough with some of her potions.'

They stood by the door. The wind was blowing strongly now and intermingled with its howling they could hear the plaintive shrieking of gulls as they wheeled overhead.

Maria shuddered as the sound assailed her ears. 'Tom and 'girls—' she said. 'Where are they?'

'What? Oh, Alice is up at 'house baking tarts.' His face suddenly changed colour. 'Oh God – Tom and Lizzie!'

Maria turned to him. 'What is it? Will, what's wrong?'

He reached for his crutch and hurried past her. 'They wanted to go fishing. But 'tide—!'

He started across the field, stumbling in his haste but miraculously not falling, as Maria watched horrorstruck from the doorway.

As he ran he realized that above the sound of the gulls and the wind was another thin cry.

He had been surprised when they had arrived at Monkston at the nearness of the farmhouse and the village houses to the cliff edge, but as he stumbled now over the last few yards and flung himself down at the edge, he was thankful for it.

He peered down over the brink. The sea was already licking the base of the cliff and although the water was not yet deep the tide was coming in fast. There was no sign of Tom or Lizzie and he hollered Tom's name, the wind catching the sound and tossing it away landwards. He got up awkwardly and hurried further along the top of the cliff. So anxious was he to move quickly that he didn't watch where he was going and his crutch caught in one of the deep fissures which ran along the cliff edge and he fell heavily.

As he lay there winded, he heard again a shrill cry, only this time he knew it wasn't the gulls and it was coming from slightly down to the right of him. He leaned over again and below a jutting outcrop he saw the frightened face of Tom, trying desperately not to cry, and below him a pale and terrified Lizzie, clinging frantically to the crumbling cliff surface.

'Come on then, Tom, let's be having thee up here,' he called out in a tone more cheerful than he felt, but nevertheless tinged with relief at having found them in one piece.

'We couldn't find 'steps where we came down.' Tom's voice cracked tearfully. 'And 'sea was coming up that fast.'

'Never mind that now,' said his father. 'Just try to get another foothold further up – but don't let go with thy hands,' he added hurriedly as Tom scrabbled around with his feet. 'Just take it nice and slowly.'

He saw Lizzie shake her head as a flurry of sand and bits of debris fell on top of her as Tom searched for another foothold.

'Lizzie!' he called. 'Try to move over to thy left, there's a bit of a ledge where tha can stand easier.'

Lizzie didn't move but gazed up at him, her blue eyes wide and abstracted.

'Lizzie, can tha hear me? Try to move over.'

She remained motionless, her fingers white where she clutched a clump of marram grass growing out of the cliff.

Tom eased himself slowly up, his confidence returning now that his father was near.

'Now then, Tom, I'm going to put my crutch over, and I want thee to take hold of it, first with one hand and then with t'other,' said Will, still keeping a watchful eye on Lizzie. 'Then I'll take 'weight and tha can walk up.'

Slowly, step by step, Tom came up the side, Will's shoulders and arms taking the strain until he finally reached the top, his face showing signs of jubilation as fear receded.

'Run now as fast as tha can, and fetch help from 'village.'

Will knew that getting Lizzie to the top of the cliff was going to prove more difficult. He had seen that look of terror before, when men he had known, confronted by sudden danger, had seen death facing them and became petrified by fear, unable to move a muscle.

'Somebody's coming already,' cried Tom. 'And Ma, she's here as well.'

He waved to two men who were running towards them, one with a rope over his arm, followed more slowly by Maria.

Will didn't turn round but kept his face towards Lizzie, calling encouragingly down to her.

'We shall soon have thee up, don't worry, Lizzie. There's no need to be afeard.' There was no use in asking her to try to move for if he startled her now, she might in a panic slip down into the sea which had completely covered the sand and was surging and breaking up the base of the cliff.

'I'll have to go down to her.' The younger of the two men spoke. 'She's too scared to catch 'rope, and she might tummel over if she tried.'

He handed one end of the rope to Will, 'If thee and me da will take my weight, I'll go down just beyond her.'

Will turned to the other man and saw that it was the same one who had directed them to the barn on their arrival. They each took hold of the length of rope and Will wrapped the end around his waist, taking up the slack with his hands.

'I'll take 'strain,' Will said, 'I'm a deal heavier than thee.'

The man was not only thinner than Will but also a lot older and Will didn't want him to injure himself.

'He'll get her alreet, will our Martin,' said the other reassuringly. 'He's got feet like a goat.'

Surefootedly, and with barely a pull on the rope Martin eased himself down the cliff, testing each foothold before giving it his weight.

Will realized why he had made his way down beyond where Lizzie was standing, for at each step he took, a cascade of stones and sand slithered down before him, dropping with barely a splash into the surging water below.

As he reached Lizzie a change of expression came over her. Whereas she had stood before in stark terror, her eyes now moved frantically from side to side as she tried to see what was happening behind her.

'It's alreet, little lass, we'll have thee up on top in no time at all.'

She shook at the sound of his voice so near, and her foot slipped as he moved towards her. Swiftly he put out a hand to catch her and she clung frantically to the rough tuft of grass.

'Let go now, lovey, put thy arms around me.'

She shook her head, her eyes wide and frightened. She looked up at the top of the cliff and saw Maria anxiously looking down.

'Do as he says, Lizzie, and tha'll soon be up here.'

Again she shook her head, and then came a faint whisper which barely carried up to where they were waiting, 'I want my ma.'

Not once since she had come to stay with them had Lizzie mentioned her mother, and Will and Maria had assumed that in the excitement of moving and with the constant companionship of Tom and Alice, Lizzie had not felt the loss. Now they looked at each other in dismay.

'Poor little mite,' Maria murmured, 'and she never said.'

'Come on then,' said Martin. 'I'll take thee to thy ma.' He picked her up bodily with one arm whilst he held on to the side of the cliff face with the other and put her thin light body over his shoulder. 'We can't stay here all neet. I want my supper.'

Chatting to her all the while, he carefully made his way back, this time making for the safety of some rough steps hewn into the side of the cliff.

'See these steps?' he said, panting with exertion. 'Well, I made them, when I was just a nipper like thee. So next time tha comes down to 'sea, that's 'way tha should come, or down 'village road.'

Will and Maria took hold of her as they reached the top and pulled her over.

'Tha's safe now,' said Martin as he hauled himself over. 'Here's thy ma!'

Lizzie burst into tears as Maria enveloped her in a smother of hugs and kisses. 'I want to go home,' she sobbed. 'I want my ma.'

'Tha can't go home, Lizzie, tha knows that. Stay with us till thy ma comes for thee. We want thee to stay with us.' Maria looked with concern at the distraught child. 'I'm relying on thee to help with 'babby when it comes.'

Lizzie gave a shaky smile at the prospect and then tearfully nodded her head.

Tom, who had been disdainfully watching this feminine show of emotion, came forward, his hands in the pockets of his soaking wet breeches.

'Here, Lizzie, if tha'll stay I'll give thee my shrimps,' and he pulled out of his bulging pockets a handful of bedraggled grey shrimps.

'I dropped all of mine,' she said tearfully as she put out her hand to take them. 'We were going to bring them home for supper. Tom said we could cook them over 'fire.'

'So tha can,' said Will enthusiastically, 'and maybe tomorrow we'll all go down after we've finished our work, and we'll net some more. We can eat in plenty here, there's cod and dabs and even mackerel – food fit for nobility – and free.'

He looked down at Tom and Lizzie, who had caught his enthusiasm now that their fright was dissipating, and put an arm around them both. 'But tha must learn to respect 'sea and all its moods, so first thing I will teach thee both is how to float and keep thy heads above water.'

Martin had been listening and nodded his head in agreement. 'That's 'best idea,' he said. 'And if tha comes over to see my lads, they'll show thee 'best places for crabs. They know every inch of 'coastline round here and tha'll be safe with them until tha gets used to it.'

Will thanked him for his help.

'That's all right,' he answered gruffly, rather embarrassed. 'There's always somebody gets stuck just once. I did missen when I was just a bairn, that's why me da here made me make them steps.'

He looked over the cliff and then scraped the cracked surface with his boot. 'There's no saying how long they'll last, though. We lost over six feet last winter in 'storms.'

Maria took Tom and Lizzie by the hand, leaving the men talking, and hurried them back to Field House. They were both very wet and beginning to shiver with the cold. She took them inside and rubbed them down briskly with an old blanket and then tucked them both up into the large bed.

'Stay there for a bit,' she said, 'until tha gets warm. We can't have thee getting poorly now. Tomorrow we start at Garston Hall – getting it ready for 'Mastersons and we shall need both of thee to help.'

'What shall I do, Ma?' Tom sat up in excitement – at last he was going to work.

'Tha'll help thy fayther with repair jobs and fetching wood for fires and such like; and thee and me, Lizzie, we'll have to see Mrs Scryven to find out what's to be done, for I'm sure I shan't know where to start.'

Mrs Scryven had it all planned, however, when they arrived in the kitchen of Garston Hall early the next morning.

'I'm glad to see tha's an early riser,' she remarked as they knocked hesitatingly on the door.

Maria's mouth watered as the aroma of freshly baked bread greeted her. Simmering gently on the fire was a large pan, its lid rising and rattling gently and emitting small puffs of steam, from which rose the aromatic smell of ham.

'Sit down and sup.' Mrs Scryven put out three bowls and spoons and poured out thick creamy porridge. She then added a generous helping of honey, stirring it in to leave thin golden trails which dribbled off the spoon.

'Is it all right for us to—?' Maria didn't know where to begin.

'To eat?' Mrs Scryven finished off for her. 'Aye, it is. Servants are always fed here at 'Hall. Always have been anyway, and I don't see that it'll change. Course by rights tha should live in, but seeing as special arrangements have been made! Anyway these are my vittals. Milk from my own coo.' She indicated the bubbling pan. 'Ham from my own pig and wheat from my own land.'

'Tha's a farmer then?' Maria, replete from the porridge, broke off a corner of crusty bread.

'Me fayther was, owned his own parcel of land at Tillington where he was born, and a cottage here at Monkston. He left them to my brother Josh when he died, and as Josh never wed and had no other family but me, he signed it over to me when he took sick, so it's all mine now.'

She sighed. 'I won't say it's easy, for it's not, but I won't give it up if I can help it. It's my only bit of security. I let 'piece out at Tillington and Dick Reedbarrow helps me at harvest time, or if I have a pig for 'market, but otherwise I manage.'

She sat down facing Maria and Lizzie and lifted Alice comfortingly on her knee. 'Now then, I don't know what tha's been told, but this is how I see it. M'lady back in Hull doesn't care for me!' She nodded her head at Maria's look of surprise. 'She hasn't said owt, but I can tell! That lady doesn't look below 'surface of folks. She doesn't like what she considers ugly.'

She put up her hand to silence Maria as she started to protest. 'I know I'm considered plain, always have been.' Her wrinkled face creased into a gappy smile, 'but I don't mind about that. Anyroad, Mrs Masterson won't want me hanging around 'house where her fancy friends might see me, she'll want me out of 'way. What she doesn't know is that I'm 'best cook in Holderness. Ask anybody round here. And once she's tasted my bakin', then she'll nivver want me to go – or her husband won't! I've worked in this house and 'other one that stood afore it for as long as I can remember, and I don't intend leaving, not till I'm carried out in 'wooden box!'

Lizzie got up from the table and walked round to where Mrs Scryven was sitting, put her arms around her and gave her a squeeze. 'I don't think tha's ugly at all, Mrs Scryven. I think tha's lovely, and after my ma and Maria, I think tha's 'kindest person I know.'

Mrs Scryven was so taken aback at this show of admiration that she sat open-mouthed.

'Well, out of 'mouths of babes—' said Maria, blinking a little, 'and Lizzie's right, tha's kindest woman I've ever met.'

Mrs Scryven overcame her confusion and continued with her plan. 'If tha will take charge of 'house – I'll show thee what to do,' she added as she saw the look of dismay on Maria's face. 'And we'll get Martin Reedbarrow's daughter Janey to help thee, she'll live in, and there's a young lass in 'village who'll help me in 'kitchen to do 'vegetables and scrub 'pans. And then when 'fine servants arrive there'll be nowt for them to do, and they'll be off back to Hull as fast as they can!'

'They're not coming,' said Lizzie, jumping up and

down in glee. 'I heard them talking in 'kitchen that day we went to see Mrs Masterson. They said they wouldn't come – except for Mrs Harris, and she's an old woman in 'kitchen, and she hadn't anywhere else to go.'

With this report they gathered together an array of brooms and buckets, for although the Hall looked spanking clean to Maria, Mrs Scryven decreed that it wasn't good enough.

'We must be sure that there's no cause for complaint. So what has been done once must be done again. Lizzie, go to 'stable and fetch clean straw for 'kitchen and back doorway. They'll be fetching 'new furniture in soon and I'll not have men tramping mud all over my clean floor.'

Lizzie went out in the direction of the stable, but returned a few minutes later. 'There's a man – 'she began, 'Dick Reedbarrow – he's at 'back door, asking for thee, Mrs Scryven.'

'So what's pleasing thee, Dick Reedbarrow?' Mrs Scryven scrutinized him as he stood shuffling at the door.

Maria could see no sign of pleasure on his craggy features, but Mrs Scryven was obviously a better judge than she was, for he took off his battered felt hat and turned it round and round in his hands, no smile on his lips but a crinkle forming around his eyes.

'I've got 'job here at Garston! Agent's just been round to see me. Says Mr Masterson's left it to him to find somebody to be in charge like, and I'm 'best man for 'job.'

He looked towards Maria. 'I'll need somebody reliable to help me. Our Martin will manage our bit of land, with help of his lads, but most of 'other young fellas have gone off to Hull to seek work. I can always find some old hands to help with 'ploughing and 'harvest but if thy man is willing—?'

'Tha'll have to ask him thyself, but as far as I know he'll do what's needed. That's the arrangement with Mr Masterson.'

She looked keenly into his lined face. Like Mrs Scryven's it was brown and wrinkled, but the furrows ran so deep that his eyes could hardly be seen. 'We've a son ready to work. Can tha take him on? He's a good lad and willing.'

'Aye, I'll do that, missus. He can start at Martinmas, and if he listens well I'll larn him all I know, and mek him into a farmer!'

9

'Don't pull so hard, Ellie. I have a bad headache.' Isobel watched her reflection in the mirror as Ellie stood behind her brushing out each ringlet and curling it around her fingers.

'Why not have it cut, ma-am, and wear false curls? Seemingly it's becoming very fashionable now.'

'Really, Ellie, where do you get your ideas from?' Isobel read all the modish journals, but she didn't expect her servants to keep up with high fashion.

'I've been talking to Miss Brown the milliner, ma-am. She told me.'

Isobel looked at the smooth young face and slim figure standing behind her, and sighed for her own lost youth. She too had been as lovely as Ellie when she was sixteen. How fast the years went by. She leant forward in order to see herself better in the gilt-framed mirror. She could already see fine lines appearing around her mouth and neck, and her eyes had lost their brightness.

Perhaps when this birth business is over I shall get my looks back, and my figure, she thought. She drew the muslin fichu across her chemise gown and sat back with a delicate yawn.

'Leave it, Ellie, I really can't be bothered now. Bring me my lace cap to wear.'

'Miss Brown has some beautiful caps and bonnets.' Ellie placed the small lace cap on Isobel's curls. 'As good as you'd see anywhere in 'country.'

A small frown appeared on Isobel's face. 'What is this, Ellie? I hope you haven't been wasting time down in the Market Place!'

'Oh – no, ma-am. It's just that when you leave here for 'country, I've decided to come out of service, and

Miss Rebecca Brown has offered me a position.' Her face flushed with pleasure. 'I'm going to help in 'shop to start with, keeping it tidy and such like, and then after a bit I can help with 'customers – I mean – the clients.' She emphasized her words carefully.

'Does Miss Brown not require a reference from me?' Isobel's voice was tart.

'She said she would prefer one, if you were willing; just to say I'm honest and that. But I explained how really you wanted me to go with you as it's so difficult to get good servants out in 'country.' She looked slyly from beneath her lashes at her employer. 'And she said she would understand if you couldn't see your way to giving one.'

Isobel couldn't help but give a wry smile. The little minx would do well in a shop. She wasn't very good at household chores, and Isobel had noticed how she always managed to arrange it that the other girl did the really dirty jobs; but she was undoubtedly very good at arranging her hair and kept her wardrobe of gowns and dresses in perfect condition, sewing on lace edging and trimmings, and replacing the feathers and ribbons on her bonnets when she saw them looking at all worn.

'Very well, Ellie, I will give you a recommendation. There's no doubt that I shall miss you for attending to my hair. Perhaps I *will* have it cut.' She shook her curls and adjusted the cap. 'It will be less bother, I suppose. Unless, of course, Mrs Foster is any good at that sort of thing.'

' 'Shouldn't think she's had much practice, ma-am. She got married to Will Foster when she was a bit older than what I am now, and she's been busy having bairns. No time for dressing hair.' She gave a worldly laugh. 'You won't catch me getting tied down like that.'

She moved around the room, picking up clothes, folding them neatly and placing them in the lavender-scented chests of drawers. 'Although my mother says that Will Foster was 'best looking man in town and a good catch for any girl.'

Isobel's eyebrows rose in amusement at the thought of an ordinary whaling man being a good catch, but she let Ellie prattle on. She had nothing better to do so she might just as well listen to servants' gossip. She had chosen the furniture and curtains for the new house and though that had kept her busy, she was now bored with inactivity.

'Yes, it's a shame, for he's still quite handsome, but with a disability like that!' Ellie shook her head and wrinkled her nose.

Isobel's attention had been elsewhere, contemplating vaguely the handsome men she had once known before she had decided to marry the older but eligible Isaac Masterson, but now she sat forward.

'What do you mean – a disability? I understood he had been injured, but no-one said anything about a disability!'

Ellie flushed. She realized she should not have said so much. She hung her head. 'I suppose some folk wouldn't mind,' she said. 'It's just that it makes me feel queasy.'

'What makes you feel queasy?' Isobel's voice became shrill.

'Seeing his leg – or I mean – seeing him without it!'

She watched in concern as her mistress turned pale and clutched the side of the chair.

'You mean, he's lost a leg?'

The look of horror on her mistress's face startled her. 'It's not as bad as all that, ma-am. Men are always losing arms or legs, or getting injured somehow or other, it's what happens!'

'Be quiet, you silly girl, and get me my smelling salts quickly. I feel quite ill.'

She rose trembling from the chair and crossed to the bed where she lay down, her hand clutched to her forehead.

'Should I get 'doctor, ma-am?'

'Yes,' said Isobel faintly, 'and find Mr Masterson immediately. Tell him he's wanted at once!'

*   *   *

Isaac strode up the stairs two at a time, his breathing rapid. He'd been given a garbled message by his clerk to go home at once, and he had naturally assumed that Isobel had started labour, even though it was not yet her time. And now that fool of a doctor who he had bumped into outside the door had wittered incomprehensibly about somebody losing a leg and that she must rest and not be alarmed in any way.

'Isobel, my dear. What has happened?' he began.

'Isaac – I won't have it. I just will not have it.'

Far from looking ill or in pain, Isobel was sitting up beneath the silk draped hangings of her bed, propped up amongst several white downy pillows, her cheeks a soft pink and her eyes sparkling.

Isaac stopped, confused, at the end of the bed. He had seen that look in Isobel's eyes before. It wasn't fever that was making them sparkle but anger.

'Won't have it? What are you talking about, Isobel?'

He came to her side and sat on the edge of the bed, ruffling the lace counterpane, and took her hand in his. 'It will soon be over, my love, you're not to worry about it. The doctor is an excellent man!'

She snatched her hand away. 'I'm not talking about the baby!' Her voice was shrill and the tone of it left him in no doubt of her views on his mental capacity. 'I'm talking about Will Foster! I will not have that man near me. Not under any circumstances. How could you think of it?'

He looked at her in amazement. Did women in her condition have these strange turns? He had no way of knowing, but he tried to humour her.

'Come now,' he laughed weakly. 'What have you against him? He's a good honest worker, one of the best – and his wife—!'

'I've met her,' she shrieked at him. 'But nobody thought to tell me that he was maimed!' She started to sob. 'You know how I hate that sort of thing!'

'That sort of thing!' he exploded. 'Good God, woman, he almost lost his life trying to save John, and you say you can't stand that sort of thing! How do you think *he* feels?'

He got up and stormed across the room to bang the door, conscious that the servants could hear them.

'Well, give him some money or something,' she wailed. 'I just don't want him working for me!'

'I will not give him money,' he answered sharply. 'A man like that has his pride. He wants to earn a living like anyone else, not accept charity.'

They sat in silence for a while, Isaac trying to control his temper and Isobel stifling her sobs.

'What will people think?' she said at last. 'We've got a wizened old woman for a housekeeper and a man with a terrible disability.' She couldn't bring herself to mention his loss of a leg and started to snivel again. 'And none of the servants will come with us!'

'People! I'm not bothered about what people think! I only know that I owe that man something, and this is how I can repay him, by giving him a fresh start. Goodness knows it's little enough, being a farm labourer and general packhorse when he might have risen to being mate on one of my ships.'

He sighed and took her hand again. 'Try to understand, Isobel, that it isn't ever easy for some people. They struggle all of their lives just to keep body and soul together, and then in the end they still haven't anything to show for it. It is our duty, when we have so much, to try and ease their misery.'

She looked at him coldly. 'Then do as you please, Isaac. But do not expect me to accept him. He can stay if you think that you owe him a debt, but I repeat, I will not have him near me, and that is my final word on the matter.' She slid down into the feather bed, drawing the fine linen sheets up to her chin. 'And now if you don't mind leaving me, I would like to rest.'

Isaac marched out of the house and strode purposefully down the garden and into the yard at the back of the house. Already his men were moving equipment and goods from the staith side into the yard, ready for the time when they should move into the house. His irritation cooled as he gave instructions and once more became absorbed in the day-to-day continuance of his business, and it wasn't until later in the day when John appeared with a query that he remembered the problem of Will Foster and Isobel's antipathy towards him.

'I wanted to have a word with you, John,' he said. It seemed to Isaac that he was leaning more and more on his nephew, particularly when dealing with people. He appeared to have a natural flair for talking to and understanding them and their problems, which Isaac in his impatience was lacking.

'How do you think Will Foster is managing out at Garston?' he began hesitatingly.

'It's a little early to say yet, Uncle. They will only just be settling in. We haven't had news yet from the agent.'

'No – I was thinking more of how he would manage to get about, on his crutch, you know?'

'Oh, he manages very well, he's very agile and very strong, I wouldn't think he has any trouble at all.'

Isaac nodded. 'That's what I thought. Would you come inside for a moment, I must speak to you privately.'

They moved indoors to the small back room overlooking the river which John had claimed for his own office, and sat down on the hard wooden chairs.

'I've got a slight problem, John, and although I don't like to ask you to deal with all the awkward matters, I think it would be less embarrassing in this instance if you will do so.' He got up and looked out of the window to the busy river just feet below. 'Isobel has an aversion, as you may be aware, of anything slightly less than normal.

'Damn it all!' He turned in exasperation to face his nephew. 'He's a perfectly capable fellow, but she says she won't have him near her. Isobel, I mean,' he said as he saw the perplexed look on John's face, 'and Will Foster. She doesn't like the thought of his leg!'

'You're not thinking of bringing the Fosters back!'

'No, no. I won't go back on my word. But we have

to think of something, otherwise I'll never have a minute's peace!'

'There isn't anything we can think of,' John replied in exasperation. 'And in any case he isn't going to be anywhere near Aunt Isobel. He'll be busy outside most of the time, and on the land.' He was thoughtful for a moment. 'So short of fixing him up with a wooden leg, I don't see what's to be done.'

Isaac looked up. 'That's a good idea. They can do that for him at the Infirmary.'

'But he can't possibly afford it, sir. They haven't any money at all, I know that for a fact.'

'Never mind that. Isobel has spent so much money on fancy new furniture and suchlike for Garston Hall, that I think a few guineas more won't send us out of business.' Isaac breathed a great sigh of relief. 'Go out and see him, will you, John, there's a good fellow, and arrange to get him fixed up. Wait a minute.' He pondered as John opened the door. 'Boots, long ones – up to the knee. That's what he needs. See to it, will you?

'Oh, one more thing, the new furniture will be arriving at Garston Hall any time now, so you might tell them to be prepared. Perhaps you would stay on there for a few days just to organize things?'

John was none too pleased as he left his uncle. He had organized his working days very efficiently he thought, and now because of his aunt's absurd behaviour, he had to re-arrange them. But more than anything he was extremely uneasy at having to give a man the humiliating order that when the mistress of the house appeared he was to remain invisible and out of sight like some leper.

John dismounted in the inn yard and called for ale and bread and cheese. The day was fine and he sat outside on the rough bench and felt the warmth of the sun on his face, though the breeze blew coolly.

He gazed at the tranquillity of the landscape. The

wheat had been cut and the meadows below him had been thrown open to cattle and sheep for common grazing.

How peaceful it looks, he thought. Almost as if life has passed it by. No sign of discontent or strife here, and yet just over the sea in France men of the land and in the cities were revolting against poverty and starvation, threatening both the new constitution and the old monarchy. Only last year, thousands of women had marched to the king in Versailles demanding bread for their starving families. Harvests had been disastrous and they had nothing more to lose. Since then there had been a great deal of blood shed and he understood that even the French king's life was in danger.

He stretched his legs and reflected that he could almost wish for some excitement himself. His blood had stirred when he read of the news coming from France, and yet he had been sickened by the tales of massacre. He wondered too, should he decide to go to see for himself what was happening there, where his loyalties would lie, for he had much sympathy with the starving masses.

His uncle, perhaps realizing his restlessness, had drawn him more and more into the business, in particular with the kitting out of the whaler the *Polar Star*, which after a substantial refit would sail next March, and with the promise that he would sail with her.

The landlord re-appeared holding a jug of ale. 'Will tha tek a drop more, sir? Travelling is thirsty work.'

John nodded, having just taken a mouthful of cheese.

'Going very far, sir?'

'Only as far as Monkston. Not so far now.'

'Tha'll be going to Garston Hall then?' said the landlord, his tone becoming deferential. 'Would Mrs Masterson be family by any chance, a sister or—?'

'What is it to you.' John's tone was sharp. He didn't care for the man's fawning attitude.

'Begging tha pardon, sir. I'm not meaning to be curious like, but I do have a reason for asking.'

151

John relented. 'My aunt. Mrs Masterson is my aunt. Now what is it you want, for I must be on my way?'

'Have just a drop more, it's my best.' He poured more ale into the pewter tankard, ignoring John's protests.

'Fact is, sir – dost tha mind if I sit beside thee?' He squeezed his fat frame on to the bench and John, wondering now how he could get away without seeming arrogant, moved along to make more room.

'Fact is,' the man repeated, 'I wondered if maybe Mrs Masterson was wanting any more staff. I've a daughter who—'

'I've really no notion of my aunt's requirements.'

'I've got four daughters at home,' the landlord said gloomily, 'and no wife to keep them in order. Two of them are spinsters and help me here at 'hostelry, and one is spoken for, but I want to place 'youngest if I can. Somewhere where I know she'll learn to be useful and how to behave and all that.'

He looked sideways at John, and then said confidentially, 'Fact is, she wants to go and work in Hull, says it's dull out here. All 'young folk are going, 'farmers are enclosing their land and don't need so many workers.'

John shifted uncomfortably. He knew that his uncle had struck a very favourable bargain when buying his estate. The village farmers could no longer afford to hedge and ditch their strip fields as Parliament decreed, and the richer landowners and merchants like Isaac Masterson who could afford it were buying up more and more land that had previously given a living to whole villages.

'But your daughter wouldn't have become a farmer surely!'

'No, sir, but she would likely have married somebody with a bit of land and been set up. As it is, I'm afraid of her going to Hull. She's a right bonny lass and I don't want her to go wrong.' He rose from the bench. 'If tha has just a minute to spare, sir, I'll fetch her for thee to look at.'

John opened his mouth to object; he didn't want to inspect the man's daughter like some curiosity or prize heifer, but the landlord had already reached the inn door and had raised his voice to a bellow to whoever was inside.

Promptly, as if she had been waiting for a signal, a young girl appeared, and John as he saw her, quite without thinking, rose to his feet.

The landlord smiled in satisfaction. 'This is my youngest daughter, sir. Susan's her name. If I say so myself there isn't a finer looking wench this side of 'country.'

John guessed her age to be fifteen or sixteen years, but she was well rounded, and had he been older and wiser he would have realized her charms were displayed with skill. Rounded breasts rose gently above the low neckline of her dress and she placed her small brown hands against them discreetly, drawing his attention to them and her soft plump throat. He swallowed hard and cleared his throat.

'Say how de do to 'gentleman, Susan. Show thy manners!' The innkeeper gave his daughter a playful nudge.

She ignored him and moved towards John and gave a small curtsey. 'Good morning, sir.' She looked at him coolly, no hint of subservience in her eyes as there was in her father's, and then with a catch of amusement in her voice and as if rehearsed she said, parrot fashion, 'It's a fine morning for travel, I hope tha's had a good journey.'

John felt that she was amusing herself at his expense for he caught a sparkle in her eyes and, as she spoke she turned herself around slowly, her arms outspread as if about to dance.

'Now then, Susan, behave thyself,' admonished her father.

'I'm only showing what's on offer, Fayther,' she answered, her eyes never leaving John's face until quite suddenly he found himself flushing uncontrollably. The blood thundered in his ears until he felt his head would explode and he sat down suddenly.

'I – er.' He cleared his throat again. 'I will speak to my aunt and ask if there is likely to be a position available. I can't guarantee anything, of course, as I think arrangements have been made. But I will ask,' he repeated weakly, as the girl continued to gaze at him.

She bent towards him, leaning on the table so that he was aware of the soft rise and fall of her breasts as she spoke in a husky whisper.

'I would be very grateful.' Her eyes, almost violet in colour, held his, then she lowered her lashes demurely and he saw the contours of her cheekbones and the small pink lobes of her ears.

As he rode away down the hill he twisted round in the saddle to look back. They were still there, silhouetted against the skyline, and the innkeeper raised an arm in farewell. The girl simply stood at her father's side and made no response until, as John turned away, she turned back into the inn yard and in response to her father's grin, started to spin, round and round the yard, faster and faster, her arms held wide, her skirts and petticoats flying high above her bare legs and her voice raised in laughter.

'I'm sorry, Will.'

'I can't believe what tha's saying. How can anybody say summat like that? I thought folk of thy class were supposed to be sensitive and kind!'

Will threw down the scythe angrily and turned his back.

John had found him down in the bottom field, clearing a patch of nettles and bramble where Mrs Scryven had said he would be. 'Here, Mr John,' she'd said, 'take a drop of this with thee,' and handed him a jug of sweet elderberry wine.

Will's reaction had been stronger than he'd expected as he told him that Mrs Masterson didn't want him around the house or garden when she was about.

'Why?' he asked angrily. 'Why did she have to say it? She's not likely to see me anyway. I'm hardly going to be serving her tea in her bedchamber!'

'She's – well, she's—' John searched for the right phrase to justify his aunt's behaviour. 'It's her condition!' he said in desperation.

Will grunted cynically. 'We've already heard about that. I know women do change, but they become gentler – not nasty and mean.'

'Oh, steady on!' John felt that he had to protect his aunt's honour, even though he was inclined to agree that she was being unreasonable. 'Anyway, I haven't told you everything. Sit down and let's drink this excellent brew of Mrs Scryven's, and maybe you'll be in a better frame of mind.'

'I've half a mind to pack this in and go back to Hull. Take my chance. At least I know what to expect from my own kind,' Will said bitterly.

'Your own kind as you call them couldn't help you before, why should they now?' John took a long draught from the jug. 'Anyhow, you can't go now, Maria's near her time.'

Will took the jug from him and took a swig. 'Well, seeing as tha's such an expert on these matters! Go on then, let's hear what tha has to say.'

John lay back on the grass his arms behind his head. He could understand Will's anger, he would feel the same way himself, it was rather like undermining a man's virility. He thought of his own as yet unproven manhood and gave a deep sigh as he thought again of the girl at the inn. Susan. Her name had been on his lips all afternoon, her face so constantly drifting in front of him that he felt that he only had to reach out and he would be able to touch her, to run his fingers through her golden curls and stroke the softness of her skin.

As he'd turned round after seeing her standing at the top of the hill, he'd urged his horse on to a vigorous gallop, the pounding of the hooves matching the rhythm of his pulse. He'd given a joyful yell at the top of his voice which startled both the horse and a brace of pheasants who rose from beneath a hedge in heavy, cacophonous flight, and which in turn startled him, almost unseating him.

'Well, are we going to sit here all night?'

'What! Oh, sorry. I was miles away.'

'Thinking about a lass, I bet!'

'As a matter of fact – yes, I was. Do you think it possible to fall in love at a first meeting, Will?'

'Aye, I do. But tha's better not saying owt about it till tha's sure. Lasses have a way of trying to arrange things and tha'll find thyself wed before tha knows what's happening.'

'Wed! I'm not thinking of getting wed!' He sat up with a start and thought with amusement of the reaction he would receive from his aunt should he suggest marrying the innkeeper's comely daughter. Isobel had produced a parade of suitable young ladies from amongst their élite circle of friends, and was forever suggesting that he should entertain more, but from the bevy he had met, not one had set his senses on fire in the way that Susan had.

'No, I don't want to get wed, but just enjoy the pleasure of being in love.'

Will grunted. 'Well, don't enjoy it too much or tha might find thyself wed, whether or not tha wants to. Her father might not take kindly to some young fellow squiring his daughter and not having 'right intentions. I know how it works with thy sort, so just be careful. Anyway, if tha has nowt else to tell me, I'll be getting on. Some folk have work to do.'

'No, wait, listen. This is the best part.'

Will listened whilst John outlined the arrangements he had made. 'My uncle and aunt will be arriving here in less than a week, so there isn't much time. So what I suggest is, that you go tomorrow, first thing. You'll need to stay a few days anyway to see the surgeon and get the limb fitted, and to have your boots made, and whilst you're waiting you can help in the yard.'

What John didn't tell him was that when placing the order with the bootmaker, in a fit of pique at his aunt's obstinacy, he had told the bootmaker to spare no expense in making a good pair to ensure a perfect fit.

'And thy uncle is willing to pay for all this?' asked Will slowly.

'Yes, I've already said so. We're not saying that this will answer all the problems, it might even be very painful for you, but it's worth a try, and it might just make up a little for—' He wanted to say for his aunt's behaviour, but felt there had to be family loyalty.

'I appreciate it, young John, don't think I don't,' Will replied gruffly. 'I'll go as soon as it's light.'

He didn't say why he was going, just that he had instructions to go into Hull for a few days.

'Take Tom with thee,' said Maria. 'He could go to 'Fair, and get me some stuff from 'market.'

Lizzie looked up eagerly from where she was sitting, a heap of crimson rose hips in her lap which she was preparing following Mrs Scryven's instructions for making into syrup. She had gathered them this morning and in her eagerness to please had gathered a basket of blackberries as well, thinking that she could make jam as Mrs Scryven had done. She had reached into the middle of the thicket where the biggest ones were growing, scratching her arms and face on the barbed stems.

Then to her dismay the old lady had made her take them outside to leave for the birds, telling her, 'Come October, 'Devil has spat on 'em.' Such was Lizzie's fright she had run pell mell, spilling half of them from out of the basket, back to the patch of brambles where she had found them, and flung them back amongst the tangled stems in case the Devil himself was waiting there.

Maria caught her look. 'I know tha'd like to go too, Lizzie, but I need thee here with me.' She nodded

157

her head conspiratorially, and Lizzie smiled at the confidence.

'Perhaps tha'll ask about Lizzie's brothers when tha's there, Will? She'd like to know about them – find out if they're doing well!'

Maria had heard the child at odd intervals crying softly to herself in some quiet corner where she thought she couldn't be heard. She saw too how she clung to Tom, trusting him not to leave her, and being hurt when unwittingly he did just that, being unaware in his innocence of her dependence on him. She refused to go with him when he joined the older Reedbarrow boys in their games down on the sands, believing that she would be made the butt of their boisterous antics, and yet was upset when Tom went without her.

'I'll try, if there's time,' Will answered. 'But it depends how long 'other business takes. I don't want to promise, Lizzie, and then not be able to go, tha does understand?'

'I'll go and see them, Lizzie,' Tom said determinedly. 'After I've been to 'Fair. I'll tell them that tha's all right here with us and that it's good living by 'sea.'

Maria smiled at his enthusiasm. That made three of her family happy at Monkston. Will had relaxed and was more like his old self, and Tom was full of his own importance because he was going to start work in earnest with Dick Reedbarrow. Alice was being spoilt by Ma Scryven, who was constantly plying her with syrups for her cough, and flummery made from eggs, wine and honey to build her up. There was just herself and Lizzie who were not quite happy with their new life; Lizzie because she missed her family, and Maria was saddened that she couldn't do more to help the child, but perhaps when the new baby came Lizzie would be happier.

Possibly I shall be more settled too when the child is born, she thought, for she still felt uneasy and intimidated in the vastness of the unfamiliar landscape. She missed the slow, silent, muddy waters of the River Humber whose every mood she knew, and hated and feared the constant muffled moaning of the sea outside her door, which echoed unceasingly in her ears like some ancient, lingering lament.

'I need to slip down to 'village with some stuff for that sick bairn. Will tha manage 'till I get back?' Mrs Scryven looked keenly at Maria. 'If I go now I'll be back before 'rain starts, 'sky's looking very black.'

'I think so. I don't think it's time yet.'

The dark morning sky had been streaked with scarlet as the sun rose, heralding changeable weather. She had leaned against the door, watching Will and Tom move off in the cart, Tom's face pink with excitement at the thought of going to the Fair and the promise that he could take the reins and drive once they were out of the narrow lanes of the village.

She hadn't said that today she would give birth, but when she had woken before dawn and felt a tranquil calm enveloping her, preparing her for what was to come, she knew that today was the start of a new life. A new being of flesh and blood that had been content to cling in close subliminal embrace would now with seeming insensitivity inflict pain and torment in an effort to be free of her.

She didn't tell them, because she knew that Will would want to stay. She preferred that he was out of the way so that she could concentrate only on herself and the infant she was about to bring into the world, without seeing his anxious face hovering above her and having to assure him that it didn't hurt.

Mrs Scryven knew. She had watched her throughout the day getting slower and slower as she worked at her tasks about the Hall, stopping occasionally to stretch her back or lean against a table. She didn't stop her or insist that she lie down, trusting that Maria would instinctively know when the time came.

'I'll go along home soon,' said Maria, 'I'm getting tired now so I'll rest for a bit. There's not much else I can do till 'other furniture comes anyway.'

Day by day waggons had been rolling up to the door laden with crates of pewter, silver and glass. Coffers lined with sweet-smelling herbs and filled with linen had been emptied, and the contents placed in the huge linen cupboard for airing. Fine rugs and velvet curtains made to specification in York and London were now in place waiting for the chairs, made to the design of Mr Hepplewhite, and the stuffed elegant sofas to arrive. French silk hangings and vallances which had been packed in crates had been carefully ironed and draped in sheets, ready to hang when the oak and maple four-poster beds arrived.

She sat down wearily in the kitchen after Mrs Scryven had gone and laid her head on the table. Please God, she prayed, let this babe survive, let me keep this one. Two infants she had lost within hours of birth, even though the midwife had each time successfully delivered them. They had failed to take the food which was fed to them at their first cry. The mixture of bread and milk mixed to a sloppy pap and placed into their tiny mouths by the midwife's fingers had failed to nourish them, and even the cordial which the midwife had claimed was a miracle for ailing babies and made to her own special recipe could not sustain them. Maria had watched in great distress as her babies' cries had grown weaker and they sank deeper into a sleep from which they never awoke.

When she had become pregnant with Alice her mother had taken charge of her, feeding her with her own potions and locking the door against the midwife. Alice, a tiny mite of humanity, slipped from her body with consummate ease and they thought that she was dead. Gently, her mother had wrapped her in a cloth and laid her in Maria's arms that she might hold her for comfort before they took her away, but within an hour the baby with open mouth was nuzzling to her breast and feeding contentedly on her thin milk.

There was a loud knocking on the door leading up into the hall and as Maria raised her head from the table,

John Rayner opened it and looked in. Maria rose to her feet, anxious lest he think she was slacking at her work.

'I'm looking for Mrs Scryven,' he said. 'I'm feeling hungry and thought she might have some of that delicious game pie left from last night.'

She smiled at him. What an amazing appetite he had: he had already dined on ham and eggs and slices of beef, and a large portion of apple tart.

'It must be the sea air that is making me hungry,' he said laughingly, 'or else Mrs Scryven's cooking. That apple tart—!' He rolled his eyes in ecstacy.

Maria laughed at him and moved towards the cool pantry where the pastries were kept. As she reached the door she was gripped by a sharp pain which made her gasp at its intensity. She clutched the pantry door and stood holding her breath until it had eased, and then brought out the pie and put it on the table. Again it came, the sharpness making her cry out.

John looked at her. 'Are you all right Maria – Mrs Foster?' He thought of her always as Maria, but some shyness made him hesitate over using her name.

'Maria will do, Mr John,' she gasped, 'and aye, I'm all right. It's just that I'm near my time, so begging thy pardon but I think tha'd better not stay.'

Hurriedly he picked up the plate and headed for the door. He hesitated. 'But where is Mrs Scryven? Surely you won't stay here alone?'

She shook her head. 'I'm going to my own place. Mrs Scryven will come to me there, there's plenty of time.'

Still he hesitated and as he did so she asked, 'Perhaps if tha would be kind enough to give Lizzie a shout for me, she can help me across to Field House.'

He nodded nervously and went in search of Lizzie. Maria could hear him calling her through the house and outside in the yard. He came back shortly, running his hands anxiously through his hair. 'I can't find her, do you think she's gone down to the sands?'

Maria closed her eyes in dismay. She remembered now that she had told Lizzie that she could take Alice down to the sea as long as they went down the village road and not by the cliff, and to be back home before dark. They were probably already at the house waiting for her.

'It doesn't matter,' she said breathlessly. 'I can manage, it's not that far.'

'Let me come with you,' he insisted. 'It's starting to rain and there's quite a wind blowing.'

She nodded and picked up her shawl. Perhaps she was leaving it rather late, after all. The pains were coming stronger now and she was taking deeper and deeper breaths to relieve the pressure. Suddenly she felt a trickle of warmth running down her legs and knew that her waters had broken.

'I would be obliged if tha will help me across, Mr John, and then if tha could run and get Mrs Scryven.' She stopped as another red-hot pain shot through her body, making her bend double.

He helped her out through the back door into the yard where they were buffeted by the driving rain and wind.

'Maria, I think you should stay here and I'll fetch Mrs Scryven. It's madness for you to attempt to walk across the fields in this weather!'

'I can't stay here and have my babby, how can I?' she cried. 'Oh, how stupid I am, why didn't I go back before?' She was afraid now, afraid of giving birth out here in the open, in this desolate place, alone apart from the young gentleman at her side who took her arm so solicitously, but who was more afraid than she was.

They had gone only halfway across the first field when she felt her legs weaken and she clutched him for support. 'I can't go any further,' she gasped. 'Tha'll have to fetch help, Mr John, I'm sorry to be such a trouble.'

As she sank down on to the wet grass she heard the relentless sound of the sea, as it beat and crashed against the cliffs in rhythm with the turmoil within her. In her hazy, confused state, above the noise of the wind, she thought she heard voices, one of them her mother's, and she called out tearfully, 'Ma, Ma, help me.' And then, oh blessed relief, there was Mrs Scryven bending over her, her leathery face glistening with rain and her cloak soaking wet.

'I guessed what had happened when tha wasn't back at East Field. Lizzie and Alice are there and I've told them to stay put. We'll have her back at 'Hall, if tha can manage her, Mr John.'

He half carried, half supported her back across the field, the rain lashing at them with fury, and into the welcome warmth of the kitchen, where he helped her off with her wet shawl and undid the laces of her boots as she leant against the table.

'I didn't want to have it here, what will 'mistress say when she finds out?' she cried in distress.

Mrs Scryven looked at John, an unspoken question in her eyes.

'Well, I don't think there is any reason why she should know,' he said slowly. 'Mrs Masterson isn't going to ask, she wouldn't think of it.'

'Quite right,' Mrs Scryven answered briskly. 'Now, sir, if tha wants to be useful, tha can help Maria up to my room; it's a long way up to 'top floor but it can't be helped, though I think we shall have to hurry by 'look of it.'

They climbed the back stairs from the kitchen and had reached the first landing when Maria cried out, 'It's too late – it's coming!'

John let go of her for a moment and reached across to open another door which led to the main bedrooms. 'Come in here.' He led her into a room which had been made into a temporary bedroom for him when he had arrived unexpectedly the day before. Mrs Scryven had supplied him with linen sheets and fustian blankets, and had made him a bed up on an old truckle, apologizing all the while that a better room wasn't ready.

There was a fire burning in the grate and he bent to put more coal on and give a better blaze.

'I thank thee,' said Mrs Scryven, pushing him firmly towards the door. 'If tha would build up 'fire in 'kitchen and put a pan of water on to boil, sir, I would say tha's done all tha can.'

He was halfway down the staircase when he was stopped in his tracks by a sound which sent a shiver running down his spine. He sat abruptly on the stairs. Poor Maria, he thought, poor sweet Maria! How brave she had been, and now to suffer such pain. He listened, but there was silence, and he felt now a cold dread. How could she possibly live through that? The cry reminded him of the torture that Will had gone through on board the whaler when the surgeon had sawed through his leg, and he felt sure that a woman could not possibly bear such painful torment as the cry suggested and make a recovery. What would he tell Will when he returned from Hull? How would he react to the news that his wife had gone from him?

He was sitting with his head in his hands when he heard a small cry. He lifted his head and heard it again, a thin mewling sound like a young kitten. He'd never heard a new baby cry before, but he heaved a sigh. At least Will had a son – or a daughter – to remind him of Maria. He choked and then swallowed hard as the bedroom door opened and Mrs Scryven appeared.

'Is that water hot yet, sir?'

He stared up at her. 'Water?'

'Aye, I asked thee to put on some water, Mr John.'

Uncomprehendingly, he gazed at her. 'Maria, is she—?'

'Aye, she's doing fine and she's got a bonny little lass.' Mrs Scryven beamed down at him. 'Now if I could trouble thee for hot water?'

He gave a great whoop of delight and jumped to his feet. With a bound he leapt on to the bannister which Maria had so thoroughly polished, and slid gleefully down to the bottom, his coat tails flying.

Mrs Scryven wiped the baby's face with a clean white cloth, then placing a kiss on her forehead she warmly wrapped her in a blanket and put her into the makeshift crib. She sponged Maria with warm lavender water to refresh her and gave her sips of cool water with the pale taste of rosemary in it to relax her.

'How kind thou art, Mrs Scryven.' Maria looked into the old woman's brown eyes as she gently attended to her. She had forgotten the pain and felt as if she was floating on a cushion of air.

'Tha reminds me of my mother,' she said, and tears gathered in her eyes.

'Aye, well – if things had been different!' Mrs Scryven shook her head sadly. 'But it wasn't to be. I'm reminded of it every time there's a bairn born.'

Maria lay back on the pillow and waited.

'When I was just a young wench, I got caught with a babby. I went me full time for I wanted it, even though 'fellow wouldn't marry me. Not that that mattered, there's plenty of bastards around, especially in high places. But my family were shamed, said I'd brought disgrace on 'em and wanted nowt to do with it.'

Maria put out her hand and took Mrs Scryven's in hers.

'I'll tell thee about it maybe one day,' she continued, her voice gruff. 'But not now. I lost my bairn at birth, but I've brought thee one.'

John knocked nervously on the door the next morning. Mrs Scryven had said he could go in for a few minutes. His own clothes and hairbrushes had been removed to another room and in their place were piles of clean white bed linen and strips of torn up flannel. Bowls of scented water had been placed around the room and the warmth of the fire drew out the perfume.

'How are you Maria?'

She was lying in bed, dark tendrils of hair framed her pale, smiling face. Her eyes were luminous and she smelled of warm milk and lavender.

'Look at my babby,' she said softly, turning towards the side of the bed.

He looked and saw that placed on top of a chest was

a drawer, and in the drawer was a small bundle, covered so closely that all he could see was a haze of golden down.

'Lift her out and tha can look at her properly.'

'Oh, no, I couldn't possibly. I might drop it!' he answered in alarm.

'Here, I'll get her.' Mrs Scryven bustled over and lifted the baby out of her crib and put her in Maria's arms. 'What a fright she gave us, 'little love, coming so quick.'

He bent over and touched the baby's tiny hands gently as if afraid she might break, and she stretched her fingers and curled them around one of his. His eyes opened wide and he said in amazement, 'How strong she is! What name shall you give her, Maria?'

'The choice is thine, and Mrs Scryven's – tha was both so kind.'

He was embarrassed for a moment, then looked down at the baby still holding tight to his finger. 'My mother's name was Sarah,' he said, his eyes moist.

'So was mine,' Maria smiled back at him.

' 'Tis a good name,' said Mrs Scryven, wiping her eyes with her apron, 't'was given to me at baptism.'

'Then Sarah it shall be,' said Maria happily.

'You're beautiful, Sarah,' he breathed softly and stroked her silky cheek.

'Tha'll make someone a good husband one day, Mr John. Tha must wed and have a bairn like Sarah.' Maria in her bliss was anxious to place everyone in the same state of rapture as herself.

He continued to gaze down at the infant, at the soft golden down of her hair, her tiny nails and her small pink face and fine lashes.

'Perhaps,' he said. 'Or perhaps I'll wait for Sarah.'

Mrs Scryven smiled.

10

'Pooh, what a stink!' Tom wrinkled his nose in repulsion as they clattered over the old bridge into the town.

Will laughed at his son's expression. 'It's no different from what it was,' he said. 'Tha can't have forgotten already.'

'Nay, it was never as bad as this, Fayther, never. It makes me feel sick!'

'It's no different,' his father insisted. 'Tha's just got used to 'smell of sea air, that's all. It used to hit me just 'same when I came home from 'sea.'

The smell of blubber from the processing yards hung on the air and combining with woodsmoke, as small fires were lit with damp wood in the impoverished hovels of the town, it formed a choking, nauseating fog.

They drove the waggon into the yard of the Cross Keys inn and Will walked with Tom into the Market Place. He had intended dropping the boy off and driving on to the Infirmary, but he couldn't resist coming into the town to savour the carnival atmosphere. The town was already brimming with people who had come in for the annual fair and Will felt an uplifting of spirits as he responded to the noisy, throbbing excitement of the crowd.

The Hull seafaring fraternity always tried to come home in time for Hull Fair, and if their ships were late the men would be angry and disappointed. It was the big event of the year and people saved what little money they had to buy from the foreign merchants who arrived with their packhorses laden with goods, to see the jugglers, magicians and performing bears, or to have their fortunes told by the itinerant fortune tellers.

They pushed through the crowd, passing the travelling

musicians and the hurdy-gurdy grinder, and Tom shook his father's arm as they heard the piercing voice of Doctor Black shouting out the efficacy of his potions. He was tall and thin and dressed in a long black cloak and a grey curled wig which was rather too large for him, and slipped constantly over one eye. The stall in front of him was draped with a red velvet cloth and artistically displayed on it were dozens of bottles of liquid in vivid shades of red, yellow and blue, guaranteed, he assured the crowd, to cure all ills from the pox to childbed fever.

He picked up a bottle of deep blue and held it aloft. 'This potion – made to my own receipt,' he shouted, '—on my word of honour, will cure the dreaded pox – which,' he lowered his voice to a hiss, 'is the scourge of all men.'

'Can tha guarantee it?' called a voice from the crowd.

'That I can,' he replied, turning to find the face to match the voice.

'So, tha's tried it then?' called back the heckler to the delight of the crowd.

He ignored the jeers and picked up another bottle, filled with sulphurous yellow liquid. 'This, my friends, I gave to a young man who had been bedfast all of his young life, due to a wasting disease.' Here the good doctor took out a large handkerchief and blew loudly on his long nose.

'Shame, shame!' called the crowd in mock sympathy.

'But, I am happy to say,' he continued, whisking his hanky back into his pocket with a flourish, 'that after only one week of my miraculous remedy, he had risen from his bed.' At this, wild cheering and clapping erupted from the crowd, the doctor took his bow and then held up his hand for silence. 'And – has deigned to come here today to give you proof of his well being!' He turned and with outstretched hand introduced a man who had been sitting quietly behind him and who, but for being about twenty years younger, was a mirror image of the esteemed Doctor Black.

The young man rose, his face pale because of the

amount of white chalk on it, and bowed to the crowd, his hand to his forehead, and proceeded to extol the virtues of the potions which, he said, had only recently snatched him from the jaws of death.

Tom, who was standing on tiptoe in front of Will, suddenly shouted out, 'I bet thee a shilling tha can't cure me fayther's leg!'

Doctor Black searched the crowd to find Tom, and called to him, 'A gambling man, and so young! Just one bottle, young sir, will relieve all your dear father's pain, whereas two bottles will effect a cure, and if it don't, then on my honour as a gentleman, I will return your money! Just send your poor, dear father to me.'

'He's right here,' shouted Tom cheekily and got a cuff from Will as the crowd, on seeing who it was, roared with laughter whilst the doctor, not seeing the joke, became exceedingly confused and quite put off his practised patter.

'Come on, tha young peazan,' Will laughed as they pushed their way out of the crowd, who goodnaturedly slapped them on their backs as they passed. 'Tha just might see a miracle afore long, just tha wait!'

Tom laughed. He knew his father didn't mind the joke, but he himself would be quite prepared to fight with anybody else who might make fun of his father's injury.

Will gave Tom a couple of coins which he put deep into his breeches pocket with his hand over them. He knew well enough that if he didn't the money might easily disappear into someone else's pocket.

'Watch out what tha's doing, Tom. Keep with 'crowd and don't wander off down 'alleys on thy own. It's times like this that 'press gangs and navy men are on 'lookout for young lads like thee, and tha might never see home again.'

He intended to frighten the boy, for although Tom had always been made aware of the dangers when living in the town, Will knew that these men were unscrupulous and would not hesitate to snatch boys of tender years and carry them off to the navy ships where they were worked so hard that they often died of exhaustion, or were washed overboard during violent storms and never heard of again.

'They'll not get me, never fear, Fayther, I'll punch them and shout till they let go.' Tom danced round, throwing punches at an imaginary foe and grimacing horribly.

'Aye, I reckon they'd send thee back soon enough,' said Will ironically, 'but watch out all 'same!'

Telling Tom to meet him by the Seamen's Hospital, he turned and walked slowly back to the Cross Keys. The stimulation that he'd felt as he entered the town was ebbing away. How easy it was to forget, after just a few short weeks of living at Monkston, the dangers of the town, when children were not safe alone and a man could be drawn into crime simply because of poverty. The crowd had grown larger and there seemed to be an undercurrent of tension. He saw a flash of colour and realized that there was a detachment of soldiers in the street. If the crowd grew ugly as it sometimes did, if there was resentment against the military, then street fighting began and the jail soon became full. Will hesitated, wondering whether to go back and take Tom with him. He looked back into the crowd but he'd disappeared, and he knew that he would never be able to find him.

He dismissed his fears as fanciful. Tom was still a town lad, and wary of strangers, but all the same the next time he brought him, he would make sure that he stayed by his side.

The surgeon ran his fingers expertly over the scarred stump. 'It's healed very well, Foster. Much better than I would have imagined.'

Will nodded, 'I've been sea bathing. They say salt's supposed to be good for wounds.' He had risen early every morning and immersed himself in the bitter cold sea. Maria had said he was crazy, but he'd revelled in the keen, sharp glow of his body as the water washed over him, tautening his muscles and strengthening his lungs as he took great gulps of pure air. He had also been using some of Mrs Scryven's ointment which she had made up for him, but he didn't tell the doctor that as he was sure that he would discount it, or ask him what was in it, and Will couldn't tell him as Mrs Scryven kept that secret firmly to herself.

'Now, Foster. Do you realize what it is that your employer has asked us to do on your behalf?'

'Fix me up with a wooden leg, sir. That's what I understood.'

'Not just that.' He looked down at a letter on his table. 'I have been asked by Mr Rayner, on behalf of Mr Masterson, to fit you with an artificial limb.' He gazed critically at Will. 'You are very lucky to have such generous benefactors, Foster, for such a proxy limb as they ask for would cost a pretty penny, I can tell you. However, I can't help you. I can cut you up and stitch you up, and give you treatment that will hopefully keep you in this world, but I am not in the department of providing extra limbs, wooden or otherwise. No,' he went on, 'if Mr Masterson has money to throw away, then I suggest he sends you off to London or Edinburgh, where they are skilled in such matters.'

Will stood up and leaned on his crutch. 'I'm sorry to have wasted thy time, sir. There'll be no question of me going all that way. I'll manage as I am.' He turned towards the door.

'Hold on, man, hold on. Don't be so hasty. I didn't say we couldn't do anything. I only said that *I* couldn't. I'm no good at all with an adze or chisel – not like some of you whaling fellows – I've seen some of the fine work that comes off the ships. No, what we'll do is send you downstairs and get you a peg leg, and then it's up to you to find a carpenter to make it fit comfortably. I'm quite sure that you'll manage somehow, but as I say, it's not really my province.'

Will was dismissed, acutely conscious of having taken

up the surgeon's valuable time over a matter which was of no real importance. The surgeon's priority was saving life and limb, and what happened to the patient after was of no consequence. He had agreed to see him only in deference to Isaac Masterson, whose ships he sometimes sailed on as surgeon, and but for that Will would not have expected to see him again.

The limb the Infirmary provided was crude and unmanageable, and the leather strap cut cruelly into his thigh. As he reined in outside the bootmaker's and climbed awkwardly down from the cart he felt lopsided and insecure.

'I've got some good calf leather here that I kept on one side for thee, like Mr Rayner said.' The bootmaker shook his head. 'But that limb is no good. It needs to be built up to fill 'boot. If tha can get that done, then I'll make 'boots straight away.'

'I think I can do that,' said Will. 'I just need to borrow some tools, and I know somebody who has some. I'll be back later.'

It was well after the time that Will had arranged to meet Tom and he paced up and down outside the Seamen's Hospital in some impatience. He was anxious to get to Rob Hardwick. He knew he could borrow some tools from Rob and he was sure that he would help him. Rob was a craftsman as far as woodwork and carpentry were concerned, although it wasn't his trade. Some of the scrimshaw work which he turned out during times when the whalers were becalmed was beautiful to see. He would sit for hours bent over a whale's tooth or walrus tusk, carefully etching and carving intricate designs and pictorial scenes.

Will walked through into the Hospital and asked if he could see the Swinburn boys. Tom would just have to wait for him now. He had no doubt become involved with some of his old mates and forgotten about meeting his father.

The porter looked sharply at Will. 'The eldest lad is

poorly. He's consumptive and he's fretting. There's nowt much we can do for him and 'young un won't leave his side. But tha can see them if tha has a mind to.'

Will followed him down the corridor and into a high-ceilinged dormitory. The bare floorboards were scrubbed clean and in the middle of the long room was a smoky stove which gave out a little heat as they approached it. Beds were lined down each side of the room, one or two were occupied by sick boys but most were empty with a blanket folded neatly at the bottom of the iron bed.

Jimmy sat on his brother's bed and gazed at Will defiantly. 'I'm not moving from here, not till our Ted gets better, so don't try and mek me.'

'He should be out doing his share of jobs, not wasting time in here,' the porter said chidingly. 'I'll have to report him again.'

'Do what tha likes, I'm not moving.' The child stared back at them, his thin, pinched face hostile.

The boy in the bed moved his hand limply to attract attention. 'Don't get into bother over me, Jimmy. I'll be all right, honest.'

He smiled weakly up at Will. His face was deathly white and it was obviously painful for him to speak. 'Hello, Will. I told our Jim that somebody would come soon. Has tha seen owt of our ma?'

Will swallowed hard. How could he tell this sick child that there had been no word of Annie, that she seemed to have vanished from the face of the earth?

He smiled back. 'No, but I expect she's busy trying to find work, tha'll be hearing soon enough, never fear. But we've got Lizzie staying with us out in 'country. She's got roses in her cheeks already.'

Ted nodded, as if appeasing Will in his effort to console. 'I hope she comes soon, me ma I mean, but if she doesn't—' He broke off in a fit of coughing and his brother slid down from the bed to hand him a cup of water.

Jimmy tugged on Will's jacket. 'Can we come with

173

thee? Me and Ted? We'll work, well, I will, till Ted's better.'

'It's not as easy as that, Jimmy.' How could they manage to feed and clothe another two children? He and Maria took their main meals at the Hall, but there must be a limit to how many children Isaac Masterson would be prepared to feed.

'Please,' the boy shook his arm. 'We don't eat much and we wouldn't be any bother. We don't like it here.'

'I'll have to think about it, Jimmy. I'll come back tomorrow and bring Tom. Tha'd like to see him, Ted?'

Ted nodded, 'Aye, I'd like to see Tom again.' He closed his eyes for a moment, then opening them wide he looked at Will searchingly. 'Tell our Lizzie that we thought about her, and our ma.' He closed his eyes again and dropped off into a doze.

'Has 'doctor been to see him?' Will questioned the porter as he went to the door.

'Aye, but he says it's just a matter of time. He was sick when he came here but it's just galloped away since. There's nowt anybody can do.'

'Could tha see thy way to keeping quiet about 'other little lad not working?' Will asked. 'If it's not for long?'

The man looked stonily at Will and Will put his hand into his pocket.

'Well, I suppose I could turn a blind eye, just this once.' He took the proffered coin and slipped it into his own pocket. 'It's against 'rules, but I'll not say owt this time.'

Tom still wasn't there as he came out and Will was getting angry. He left a message with the porter to tell Tom where to find him, and made his way to the Hardwick house.

The room was full of children. Mrs Hardwick had borne seventeen and twelve of them were still living at home. Rob was sitting by the fire, puffing contentedly on his pipe and oblivious to the turmoil going on around him.

'We've finished early today. 'Ship's almost fitted up, we're just waiting for 'inspectors to check her. I've been right lucky to get this job.'

He listened while Will told him what he wanted and then, tapping out his pipe on the floor, said, 'I reckon we can do better than that, but tha'll have to do most of 'carving thyself, I can't hold 'tools so well now with these fingers missing.'

They decided to scrap the wooden peg from the Infirmary and Rob searched around in the yard outside until he found what he was looking for, a strong, light piece of timber.

As they worked on the wood, carving and whittling, Will was getting anxious about Tom, who still hadn't arrived. Rob sent one of his youngsters out to look for him, but he came back in great excitement.

'There's masses of soldiers in 'town, somebody said there's been a riot in 'Market Place!'

'Doesn't surprise me one bit.' Mrs Hardwick spoke bitterly. 'Nobody can afford to buy bread and vittals at 'price they're asking. Don't they realize folks 's starving, and winter coming on as well? I'd go on a riot too if Rob wasn't in work, just see if I wouldn't!'

Rob raised scraggy eyebrows towards Will. 'She would too, believe me!'

Will got up from the chair. 'I'll have to go and look for 'young devil, and I'll flay his hide when I do find him. It's getting dark and he won't know where to find me. I can't trust that porter to be around to tell him where I am.'

'I'll come with thee, Will. We'll stand better chance of finding him if we both go.'

But they couldn't find him. Though they searched and asked and went to all the old haunts where he used to play, there was no sign of him.

'Tha'd best spend 'night with us,' said Rob at last. 'There's no sense in us looking any further. I reckon he's gone home with some of his mates and he'll turn up in 'morning.'

'Nay, I'll look a bit longer. Go on back home and I'll come back after a while. I'll not rest easy till I know where he is.'

What would he tell Maria if he didn't find the boy, if press gangs had him, or if he'd fallen in the river skylarking about? Worries beset Will and gnawed at his mind. I can't go home without him, and that's that, even if I have to stay here for a twelve month! he told himself. I'll skin him alive when I do find him! If I find him!

His search took him deeper into the alleyways by the Old Harbour and he wandered in and out calling Tom's name, his voice bouncing eerily off the walls and his crutch tapping against the cobbles.

A woman stopped him. Her clothes were the worn and shapeless cast-offs of a woman of a different kind, but she had made an effort to be fashionable, with her hair dressed high and her white cheeks rouged.

'Is tha looking for somebody special, dearie, or will I do?' Her few yellow teeth gaped into a smile and she lifted her torn skirt invitingly.

Will smiled back at her and winked. 'Not this time, love. I'm looking for my lad, he's gone missing. If tha should see one wandering about, ask him if he's Tom Foster, wilt tha? And if he is, send him round to Rob Hardwick's.'

'Aye, I will. Though I can't ask all 'young lads that pass by here. It would tek all night for one thing, and ruin my reputation for another. I don't mek a habit of accosting young 'uns!'

Will felt deep into his breeches pocket. There was just one coin left. 'Here, take this, it's all I've got but I'd be grateful if tha'd keep a look out.'

She hesitated for a moment as she looked at the coin in his hand, then waved it away. 'I don't want tha money. Not unless I've earned it.' She smiled again and drew nearer. 'Tha wouldn't be disappointed!'

Will shook his head. 'I've got a good wife at home, and besides I must look for my lad.'

She smiled wistfully. 'Then tha's both lucky, for

there's others with good women at home who still come searching for such as me.'

He blew her a kiss as consolation and turned away.

'Wait on.' She called him back. 'What does he look like, this lad of yourn?'

Will described him. 'And his hair is black and curly.'

'Well, it might be nowt, but there was a young lad this morning, making a devil of a row. Woke me up he did, and when I looked out—' she pointed to a window above her. 'There was this fella pulling a young lad along by his ear. I didn't think owt about it at 'time of course. But he was kicking and shouting at 'chap who had hold of him.' She shook her head. 'I don't suppose it was your lad. 'Chap with him was dark as well.'

'Where did they go?'

She shrugged, 'I didn't watch, I wanted to get back to bed. But they were heading down towards 'George.'

He hurried back down the High Street, even though he and Rob had already covered this ground. He looked up at the Mastersons' house as he passed and saw by the lamp in the uncurtained windows that the room was bare but for packing cases stacked against the walls ready for removal.

Mastersons are nearly ready for off, he thought. I'll have to look sharp over this business, I shall be needed out at Garston Hall.

He came to the entrance of the George inn yard and hesitated under the shadow of the pillars, wondering whether to cut through and look in the adjoining inn. Someone in there might have seen Tom. He looked across the old courtyard, at the closed stable doors ranging it with the galleried hay lofts above, and was about to move across when he heard the sound of a door opening and closing quietly above his head and footsteps coming down the wooden stairs into the yard.

There was something familiar about the shape of the man who came down the steps. He was plainly unfamiliar with the area for he felt his way cautiously and then, misjudging the last two steps, slipped, cursing. Will

177

watched him as he made his way across the courtyard to the inn. As he opened the door the beam of lamplight highlighted his shape and bearing and, though his face was turned away, Will was in no doubt about his identity.

Cautiously he climbed the stairs to the upper storey, pulling himself up by the stair rail. He listened at one door and quietly opened it. It was pitch black and smelt of damp hay. He called softly. 'Tom? Tom?' There was no sound apart from the scurryings of rats. Quietly he closed the door again and moved along the gallery to the next. As he opened it there was a sudden crash on the floor which startled him.

'Who's there? Tom is, that thee?'

A muffled shout and banging came in answer and though Will had no light, as his eyes adjusted to the darkness he saw across the straw-strewn floor a writhing bundle. He dropped down on to the floor, as the beams were low, and scrabbled his way through the bales of hay and straw. There, trussed up like a chicken, was Tom, his hands and feet tied and a filthy rag knotted around his mouth.

He started to gabble incoherently as his father released him.

'He was going to sell me to 'press gang, Fayther. He said as it was to get even. That tha owed him summat.'

'All right, all right, quietly, son. Tha's safe now. Don't worry.'

He released the ties and gently rubbed Tom's ankles and wrists where the twine had cut into him. 'Can tha manage to get down 'steps, or is tha too stiff?'

Tom rose painfully to his feet but his knees buckled beneath him.

'I've been tied up nearly all day, I can't feel my legs.' His voice was hoarse and cracked.

'Never mind, put thy hands round my neck and climb on to my back. I'll carry thee down.'

Will put both hands on the stair rail and carefully swung himself one step at a time down the stairs.

'Now sit here in this corner for a bit and keep rubbing

thy hands and feet. Stay there till I get back. I'll not be more than a few minutes.'

Reassuring the boy, he turned back towards the inn. It was hot and stuffy inside with a strong smell of whale oil burning in the lamps. The room was filled to capacity and there was a loud buzz of talk. A woman was singing boisterously as she moved in and out of the tables, filling up the ale tankards generously from a large earthenware jug, the brown liquid brimming over and slopping on to the tables.

Will raised his voice and banged with his crutch on the floor. 'Wilt tha listen.'

There was a sudden silence as the crowd turned towards him, then a woman laughed hysterically and made a ribald remark. General laughter broke out, drowning his voice. He reached out towards a table and took a glass from the nearest drinker and holding it high above his head he smashed it down on to the floor.

Its owner got up from the table, his hands clenched.

'My fight's not with thee, my friend.' Will held him off, his hand open to pacify him. He raised his voice to the now silent throng who had turned towards him, their eyes wary and their bodies tense, preparing for a fight.

'There's a man among thee, if I can call him a man, who fights with childre'. Somebody who has a grudge against me, and who instead of fighting fair and square, chooses to take my lad, who's no more than eight years old, and ties him up in a rat-infested hole, ready to sell to 'press gang!'

The crowd's voice erupted. They had no love for the pressmen or those in their pay. 'Point him out, man, we'll string him up for thee.' 'Cut his throat, that's best thing for him.'

Will held up his hand. 'I can fight my own battles.' From the corner of his eyes he saw a figure slide down into his seat, pulling his hat further over his face. 'I just want to let him know that I've marked him. That I know he's here and I'm ready, whenever he is.'

Loud cheering broke out at this and the man who had

lost his drink came over to Will. 'Just give us his name and we'll find him for thee. We want no navy agents here.'

Will refused. 'It's my fight, nobody touches my family without answering to me.'

A woman stood up and shouted across the room, 'We should do summat. 'Press men took my lad. He were just a bairn – nine year old, barely off 'breast when they took him.' Tears streamed down her worn face. 'I've nivver seen him since.' She sat down at a table, her head in her hands, her shoulders shaking as she sobbed and hiccupped drunkenly.

There were mutterings and then another woman got up. 'She's right, what are we waiting here for? My man got took and he was in good work at 'Yards, but that didn't stop 'em.' Her voice was loud and angry. 'Let's go and find 'em. Show 'em we mean business.'

There was a roar from the men in the crowd as the women and the alcohol incited them to action, and as Will made his way to the door he heard the anxious voice of the landlord imploring the crowd not to be hasty, but to stay and enjoy the fine ale.

'Come on, Tom, let's be off. I reckon we've stirred up a bit of trouble between us.'

There was no answer from Tom. He was curled up fast asleep in the corner where Will had left him. He woke him up and once more hitching him up on to his back he made his way towards Rob's house, taking a longer route to avoid the Market Place and the hostile crowds who were streaming there out of the inns and dram shops to join the fierce demonstration against the press gangs, the navy, the price of bread and countless other grievances which they felt were persecuting them.

Rob had almost finished the limb. He had shaped and smoothed and planed, tapering the timber down slimly to where the ankle should be. From a separate piece of wood he had carved a foot, rounding the ball and heel, and at the top he had taken an auger and gouged a hole for the tapered leg to fit into.

'Tha should have been a carpenter, Rob,' said Will admiringly. 'Tha might have been thine own master now.'

'Aye, I should have, instead of following me da into whaling. But money was short as it always is, and I had to go where I was sent.'

Tom was leaning against his father swaying slightly, his eyes half closed with weariness. 'Fayther, I wanted to tell thee – I wanted to tell thee about that man.'

Mrs Hardwick put her brawny arms around him and led him to the bed. 'Tell us tomorrow, chuck.' She pulled off his boots and tipped him in, dirt, straw and all, with the other children, where shivering he huddled up to the warmth of their bodies and was asleep in an instant.

'And what's 'name of this villain who steals childre'?' she demanded as Will related how he had found Tom and the subsequent events at the inn.

'Jack Crawford,' Will replied absently. 'He thinks I owe him, but it was all a misunderstanding.' He avoided telling them of the connection with Francis Morton. 'He's a villain all right, no doubt about it, he'll stop at nowt.'

Mrs Hardwick poured them both a tankard of ale, then wrapping a shawl around her shoulders said to her husband, 'I'm just stepping out for a minute. I want to see what's happening down at 'Market.'

'Just watch thy step,' Rob growled. 'Don't go poking thy nose in if there's trouble there.'

'Would I do that, Rob Hardwick? Tha knows me better than that!'

'Aye, that's just it, I do!'

The crush of the crowd was so thick in the Market Place that she could hardly get through, but had to skirt the edges, squeezing her large frame past the shop doorways and windows. Some of the shopkeepers were putting up their shutters, anxious to avoid the glass being broken if there was trouble, whilst others, keen to take advantage of the large crowd, were shouting out the excellence of their goods.

She saw two women of her acquaintance and beckoned them over. She spoke earnestly for a few minutes and then moved on to a different area, and the women did the same, going their separate ways.

Soon an angry murmur rippled through the crowd. 'Sold a bairn to 'press gang.' 'His name's Jack Crawford.' 'Call him Black Jack.' ' 'Press gang murdered 'lad.' 'To hell with 'press men.' 'Down with 'navy.'

The clamour grew louder and fighting broke out, fruit and vegetable stalls were overturned and the produce trampled underfoot. Shouts and screams and breaking glass were heard and occupants of nearby dwellings opened their windows to complain and add their raised voices to the confusion. The clatter of hooves rattled over the cobbles as the military arrived, and further reinforcements were sent for from the citadel across the Old Harbour waterway.

As the rioting reached its zenith, two figures slipped away from opposite edges of the crowd. The woman, a smile twisting her lips, put her shawl round her head to protect her from the cold night air and hurried home. The man, with his head and shoulders hunched low, slithered stealthily down the back streets, cutting through the quieter parts of the town, and headed northwards up the country roads towards Beverley. The silence of the country was broken only by the mocking call of an owl and a creaking of rope on wood. He cast a glance upwards as he scurried on and shuddered as he saw the frame of the gallows silhouetted against the night sky.

Rob had finished the limb by the next morning and Will took it straight to the bootmaker who promised to start working on the leather right away. Must feel good to have influence like Mr Masterson, Will mused. Just ask and it's done.

'Come on then, Tom,' he said on his return. 'I'll tek thee to see Annie's lads like I said.'

They picked their way through the debris which remained from last night's rioting. Broken glass from the shattered shop windows crunched beneath their feet, and scavenging dogs and drunken men searched amongst the mangled fruit and broken eggs for something wholesome.

Tom kept close to his father's side, nervously looking back over his shoulder from time to time.

'Don't worry, lad. That villain will be well clear of 'town by this time. He'll be keeping low for a bit now that his name's known.'

Mrs Hardcastle had told them of the crowd chanting Jack Crawford's name.

'What a hero tha'll be!' Will tried to keep the subject lighthearted. 'What a tale to tell to 'Reedbarrow lads, eh? Only – only try not to say too much to thy ma. Tha knows how she worries, and she'll be near her time now – might even have had 'babby. How about that, Tom? A country bairn!'

'I'm stopping in 'country,' said Tom determinedly. 'I'm not likely to get taken there!'

As they walked down the corridor of the Seamen's Hospital, two rows of children marched towards them, girls at one side and boys at the other. The girls were wearing sacking aprons over their grey dresses and their hair was tucked under crisp white bonnets. The boys were dressed in grey jackets and breeches. They all wore shiny black boots and they all carried scrubbing brushes, every other one carrying a metal pail. Bringing up the rear of the platoon was a large, formidable woman, who on drawing abreast of Will and Tom, called out in stentorian tones, 'Boys to 'left, girls to 'right,' and with not one ill-matched step they streamed off obediently.

She looked impassively at Will and then down at Tom. 'We only tek childre' of maimed or drowned seamen. And tha has to go before 'committee.'

'No, no. We've not come for us. We've come to see

'Swinburn lads. I came yesterday.' He was interrupted by the woman, who swung around, ordering them to follow her. She took them into a small office where she sat down behind a huge desk and surveyed them. She was obviously somewhat perplexed.

'Is tha a relation of 'Swinburn lads or what?'

Will shook his head. 'No, we're friends, that's all, though we're guardians of 'eldest girl till Mrs Swinburn gets back.'

'I'm matron of this institution and I need to pass on some news to Mrs Swinburn. Has tha any idea where she is?'

Will shook his head. 'No. I don't know where she is. We haven't heard.' He looked back at her earnestly. 'She won't abandon them, she'll come back one of these days.'

'That'll be too late.' She stared at them stonily. 'Eldest lad is dead. 'Died last night in his sleep. We have to make arrangements for the funeral.'

Will put his hand on Tom's shoulder for he had felt the boy shudder as the woman brusquely gave them the news.

'What about 'young 'un, Jimmy, is he all right?'

'No, he's not, he's gone mad. We've had to lock him up for his own safety. He said he wasn't stopping here on his own.' She leaned back in the chair and folded her arms. 'I know he's had a shock, but there was no need for all them 'isterics, throwing things and that. He's going to be trouble, that lad.'

'Can we see him for a few minutes?'

She looked dubious, then relented. 'Come with me then.' She preceded them down a long corridor, then down two flights of stone steps which led to store rooms. She stopped outside a heavy wooden door and took out a set of keys. 'Tha musn't think that this is for punishment,' she said. 'It's just so's we know where he is and so's he won't run away. We're responsible until somebody comes for him.'

Will looked through the barred opening at the top of

the door and saw a white-faced Jimmy sitting forlornly on the edge of a bed, his head and shoulders hanging dispiritedly. He looked up at the sound of the woman's voice, and though the matron may not have thought that he was being punished, Jimmy seemed to have different ideas, for no sooner was the door open than he propelled himself furiously towards her and attacked her stout person with small, flailing fists.

'Hey, hey, that's no way to behave.' Will grabbed the impetuous child.

'She locked me up,' he shouted. 'Said I couldn't have no dinner. Don't think I'm stopping here, 'cos I'm not.' He glared at her and made a run for the door.

Will put out his arm to stop him, forcibly picked him up as he kicked and struggled, took him over to the bed and sat down.

'Just be quiet for a minute, wilt tha, while I think on what's best to be done?'

Jimmy sat silently, his temper ebbing away, leaving a pale, tear-stained, miserable child who plucked anxiously at his lower lip. He stared at Tom, who looked away and down at the stone floor, not knowing what to say to his friend. All the things he was going to tell him about the games he'd had by the sea with his new friends, now seemed trivial and unimportant.

Will looked at the small room, the high window, the iron bed, then back at Jimmy and finally his gaze rested on Tom, who stood silently staring at the floor.

'I'd be willing to take responsibility for him, if tha can release him to me,' he said, looking at the matron. 'His ma wouldn't mind. We already have his sister staying with us.'

A gleam of hope showed in Jimmy's dull eyes and he looked towards the woman, catching his breath.

She pursed her lips. 'It's not beyond regulations – but tha'd have to sign papers, and it would only be temporary, till we get his mother's agreement.'

'Aye, aye, that's understood.'

Jimmy stole another look at Tom, not trusting himself

to speak. A small bubble appeared at the corner of his mouth and he licked his lips and swallowed nervously.

'Then I think arrangements can be made. We'll get signed up and then he can fetch his things.'

11

Isobel stood by the window watching for the carriage that would take her to her new home. She was dressed in a warm travelling dress and cloak and the weight of it made her very uncomfortable. Ellie had loosened her corset and unstitched some of the seams on her petti-coats yet she still felt very restricted and occasionally very faint.

She turned to look at the now empty drawing room. It was bare and cheerless, all semblance of elegance and charm had gone now that the furniture and ornaments had been removed. The high ceilings and cornices were grey and dusty, and Isobel was saddened. She had been happy here and she couldn't quite make up her mind whether the choice of moving house had been hers, or whether she had been skilfully manipulated.

The clerks were waiting to move in with their desks and high stools as this was to be the office where all the paper work was done. Only Isobel's own sitting-room had been left untouched, for, true to his word, Isaac had said that that could be used for an overnight stay if she required it. John was to have his own rooms also and make his home here during the week, riding over to Garston Hall only at weekends, it being considered too far to make the journey every day. Old Mrs Harris would stay on here and look after him and keep the place tidy.

Mrs Harris knocked on the door. She was breathless from climbing the stairs and yet Isobel detected a slight note of disparagement as she announced, 'There's a Mrs Moxon and a Mrs Hawk downstairs, ma-am, they say as you're expecting 'em.'

'Yes, ask them to wait, will you. I shall be down presently.'

She turned again to the window as the carriage arrived outside and Isaac stepped out.

'Isaac, I hope you were not thinking of travelling in the carriage?' she greeted him as he entered the room. 'There really will not be sufficient room. The midwife and her assistant have arrived and I would feel much safer if they travelled with me.'

'I quite agree, my dear. I shall ride alongside you. I've given Walters instructions to drive carefully.' He smiled playfully. 'Precious cargo on board, you know! I should be able to keep up, although it's quite a long time since I rode so far. I've also arranged that we stop at an inn for refreshments. John suggested it and asked that you speak to a young girl there. He seems to think that she'd be suitable for another maid.'

'Yes, I know, he told me about her, although I can't think that an innkeeper's daughter would know much about being a lady's maid. But it seems that I have to put up with these people, I don't have a choice in the matter! And what on earth is the matter with John at the moment? He's as jumpy and as irritable as can be since he came back from Garston Hall.'

'Can't say I've noticed,' Isaac replied. 'Come along, let's be off.'

Mrs Moxon fussed and fawned in the most irritating manner as Isobel was helped into the carriage. She plumped up the cushions, moving Isobel to one side as she did so and arranging blankets around her so tightly that she could hardly move, all the time muttering that madam must be kept warm.

'Warm!' Isobel threw off the blankets, 'I can't breathe with all this on top of me.'

Mrs Moxon tut-tutted, and re-arranged them again. 'I must insist, madam, or I can't be held responsible. Sir—' She turned to Isaac for support. 'Sir, I must insist – madam must be kept warm. Heat is essential for madam's wellbeing – and for 'sake of her child!'

'Best to be careful, my dear, I'm sure Mrs Moxon knows best.'

'Certainly I do, sir. Attended 'undreds of women – er – and ladies like yourself, madam, and I always insist on plenty of heat. Isn't that right, Mrs Hawk?'

Mrs Hawk had made herself a comfortable corner on the opposite side of the carriage and made no reply to Mrs Moxon's enquiry, but merely smiled drowsily and nodded her head, clutching tightly a capacious green baize bag which she held on her knee.

'For goodness sake, let's get moving, Isaac, the sooner we are there the better.'

Isobel turned her face to the window as they moved off. She didn't want to have to look at the two large, muscular women in whose hands she had placed her life and that of her child. She had had the utmost difficulty in finding a midwife to accompany her to Garston Hall, and although her doctor had assured her that the country midwives were perfectly competent, she was not to be persuaded and insisted on taking someone from town. Mrs Moxon had appeared in person on hearing that someone of her profession was required, and declared that she would be delighted to accompany such an esteemed family to the country. She would bring her own assistant and would not require the services of a doctor. Even though she was sure that the country doctor who had been so highly recommended by Doctor Stone was very efficient, she was of the opinion that it was quite improper to have gentlemen anywhere near ladies in labour.

As Isobel agreed wholeheartedly with this declaration and as Mrs Moxon appeared to be so self-confident, it was arranged that she would accompany her. It was only now that she viewed the women with distaste, as she realized that they were rough and blowsy and very inferior indeed, and although Mrs Moxon appeared to be quite clean if rather dishevelled, Mrs Hawk looked most decidedly as if she had slept all night in the clothes she was wearing now. Her dress was torn and spotted with grease and her hands were rough and dirty. But what was worse she had a most disagreeable smell, causing Isobel to put her scented handkerchief to her nose and leave it there.

The innkeeper and his daughter were waiting to greet them as the carriage drove into the yard an hour later. Isaac dismounted stiffly. He was extremely sore and had decided that next time he undertook the journey it would not be on horseback. A youth appeared to take his mount and lead it to the stable, whilst the innkeeper helped Isobel down and gave her into the charge of his daughter.

Susan gave Isobel a sweet smile and led her into a private room, closing the door firmly on the two other women who were bearing determinedly down on her.

'Please make yourself comfortable, ma-am,' she said, drawing up a chair, 'or perhaps you'd care to walk about a bit to ease 'stiffness?'

'Thank you,' said Isobel wearily. 'I am extremely shaken about.'

'I'll fetch some hot chocolate, and perhaps tha – you would care for a little bread and cheese.'

'No, just the chocolate, and would you ask my husband to join me?'

Isaac sat down with a groan a few minutes later. 'I'm going to be very stiff tomorrow!'

'*You're* going to be stiff! How do you think *I* am going to feel? I feel terribly ill already. I don't know how I'm going to withstand the rest of the journey.'

'I'm so sorry, my dear, perhaps we should have waited before moving.' He leaned towards her. 'It's just that I had this notion of our child being born in his heritage – out at Garston Hall. Do you see what I mean?'

'Hmph. It might not be a son,' she replied irritably. She had no far-fetched ideas like Isaac, and just now she didn't care where the child was born as long as she could get it over and done with.

The girl arrived with the chocolate. 'I've taken 'liberty of bringing you a small brandy, ma-am,' she said. 'I thought perhaps it might revive you a little'

'Oh, how thoughtful of you,' exclaimed Isobel. 'Isn't that thoughtful, Mr Masterson?'

'Indeed it is,' agreed Isaac, recognizing the admonishment that was implied because he hadn't thought of it first.

'So, you are the young woman who would like to come and work for me?'

Susan dropped a respectful curtsey and demurely lowered her eyes, then opened them wide and candidly. 'Yes, ma-am, I'd very much like that.'

Isobel nodded and viewed her critically. She was dressed neatly and modestly, and was extremely pretty. It would be pleasant to have someone like her around. She was certainly in marked contrast to the two harridans sitting outside now.

'Very well, you may join me in a few weeks' time. I shan't need you until then, but when you do come I shall expect you to attend me as well as help in the house.'

The girl smiled again, showing her small, even, white teeth. 'Thank you, ma-am, I'll do what I can to satisfy you.'

As Susan passed the two women who were sitting by the fire, their boots taken off and their bare toes wiggling towards the flames, Mrs Hawk whispered to her companion. 'What does tha mek of that fine young piece, Mrs Moxon?'

Mrs Moxon took a long draught of the ale which Mr Masterson had had brought for them, or rather which they had requested of the landlord when told that refreshments were available for them.

'Well, she's a fine lookin' piece, I'll say that for her. But there's summat strange that I can't put me finger on. If tha asks me – and tha did – I'd say she was moonstruck!'

'How does tha make that out then, Mrs Moxon?'

'Look at her eyes. I've brought enough babbys into 'world to know that wi' colour of eyes like that, there's summat not quite right!'

They were about five miles from Monkston when Isobel began to feel unwell. The constant jolting of the carriage and the warmth from the blankets had already made her sick, but now she had a discomfort unlike anything she had experienced before, and with dread she realized that the birth had begun.

'Mrs Moxon, I am unwell,' she said weakly.

Mrs Moxon was asleep, her mouth open slackly and emitting an occasional whinnying snort. Mrs Hawk moved across and sat beside Isobel and placed her hand on her forehead. Isobel grimaced. The woman reeked of spirits, and she had caught her several times surreptitiously placing something back into her bag, and wiping her mouth with the back of her hand as she saw Isobel watching her.

'We'll leave Mrs Moxon be, for the time being, madam.' She smiled ingratiatingly. 'She's going to need all her strength!'

Isobel paled at the words, but summoned enough vigour to reply angrily, 'Waken her immediately. She is here to attend me, not to sleep when I need her!'

Mrs Hawk took one look at the fury on Mrs Masterson's face and did as she was bid, shaking Mrs Moxon roughly by the arm.

'Now then, my lady, no need to get alarmed, nothing's going to happen for a bit.' Mrs Moxon was soothing and placatory. 'I'm afraid that you've just got to put up with 'pain 'best you can till it's over.' She laughed coarsely. 'And I can only say, madam, that it'll get a lot worse afore it gets better, so best prepare yourself.' She gave a deep complacent sigh. 'It's what I say, it's a great leveller, is childbirth, makes us all 'same – rich or poor.'

'I'm going to be sick,' gasped Isobel. 'For goodness sake do something!'

Mrs Moxon crooked a finger at her assistant, who immediately opened up the green baize bag and took out a half full bottle of brandy and handed it to her. Mrs Moxon held it up as if measuring the contents and looked quizzically at Mrs Hawk, who said nothing but merely smiled weakly.

'Have a drop o' this, madam, it'll help.' She poured

a generous glassful and held it whilst Isobel sipped. 'That's it, drink it all down.' She put more blankets on top of her patient. 'I'll just call up to 'coachie to go a bit faster.' She put her head out of the carriage window, the feathers on her hat blowing wildly, and called up to the driver, who cracked his whip and urged on the horses faster, leaving Isaac Masterson sitting uncomfortably on his horse staring after them in surprise.

'No! Stop! Stop! I can't bear it!' Isobel cried out. She was being shaken from side to side, the breath being beaten out of her as they tore along the rutted road. 'Tell him to slow down, or I shall be dead of exhaustion before we're there.'

Mrs Moxon did as she was asked. She was barely able to stand as she put her head out again, her wide behind swaying precariously, and Isobel gasped in dismay as she feared that she would fall on top of her.

'Take a little drop more brandy, madam.' The midwife held the glass to Isobel's lips again. She started to sip and then swallowed hurriedly as Mrs Moxon tipped the glass generously.

'Can't beat spirits for childbirth.' Mrs Moxon poured herself a glassful and leaned back contentedly. 'Or for a lot of other things, for that matter.' She held up the glass and gazed at the amber liquid contemplatively before taking another drink. 'Finest medicine that ever was invented.'

Isobel gazed back at her through bleary eyes. The woman was swaying and moving, even the features of her face, her nose and mouth, seemed to be shifting in a distorted fashion as if she was seeing her through water.

'Mishis Moxshon,' she began, her tongue not seeming to belong to her. 'You mushn't drink too much. I'm going to have a baby soon.'

She tried desperately to retain her dignity, but her mind was fuddled and her back ached. She wanted to get up and walk about, but in the confined space of the carriage, and even though they were now travelling at not much more than a walking pace, she lacked the ability to stand.

Mrs Hawk, at a word from Mrs Moxon, lifted Isobel's legs and stretched them out on the seat, tucking them in securely with the blankets.

'Now, madam, tha'll soon be home, and in tha own bed. Try to rest till then. Tek a drop more and tha'll happen sleep.'

Isobel opened her mouth to protest, but the glass was pressed to her lips and she was forced to swallow. Her throat burned, her body sweated from the weight of the blankets, yet she shivered uncontrollably. She slipped into a light, uneasy sleep, where she dreamed that she lay trapped in a cave with two wild horses which reared and cavorted on her swollen body.

The mist was rolling in across the fields from the sea as they arrived at the door of Garston Hall and Isobel was helped unsteadily into the house. The afternoon was dark and grey and gulls wheeled plaintively above the house, but fires had been lit in all the rooms and Isobel, in spite of herself, felt comforted.

Mrs Scryven brought in a tray. 'I've brought thee some tay, ma-am.' There was a red flush under her brown skin and her eyes were fiery, yet when she looked at Isobel they showed compassion. 'Tha'll happen be hungry, ma-am, after 'journey? There's some boiled fowl, or a little light junket to give thee thy strength back.'

Isobel realized that she was hungry. She hadn't eaten at all since early morning and, though she still felt sick and dizzy, she managed to eat a small amount and felt her strength returning.

'Where is Mrs Foster?' she demanded. 'I expected to see her.'

'She's here, ma-am, she's just showing them two persons to 'lying-in chamber. They wanted to see it – to see if it was satisfactory.' Mrs Scryven snorted as she finished speaking and she clenched her lips as if to stop herself from saying more than she should. 'There's a fire

194

lit already, though I didn't know it would be used so soon. Happen jolting of 'carriage has brought thy labour on, ma-am.'

Isobel didn't reply. She didn't want to discuss her personal affairs with servants and provide them with chit chat over their bread and ale. Bad enough having to put up with the indignities of the other two women poking and prodding roughly at her body. She put her head back against the sofa. The ache in her back had eased, and the sharp pain in her side had subsided since she had rested. She felt cooler and the effect of the brandy was diminishing.

'Can I suggest, ma-am, that when 'pains come, tha rests between 'em, to gather strength like!'

As Mrs Scryven spoke, Maria knocked quietly on the door to admit Mrs Moxon, who gasped in resentment at this advice.

'I'll not have that, madam, I'll not have anybody interfering in this business. I'm paid to do 'job and I don't want anybody else pushing their nose in. And another thing.' She paused to draw breath. 'That room up there is freezing. I'll need a lot more fuel to build up 'fire and a lot more blankets. What we want is heat!'

Mrs Scryven, with barely concealed anger, excused herself and hurried from the room, her eyebrows bristling and her lips clenched. Isobel groaned aloud, a groan that was misinterpreted by Mrs Moxon who insisted that she was helped upstairs and put to bed immediately.

'By, I can see 'flames coming out of thee!' Maria hid a smile as Mrs Scryven burst into the kitchen, her small round body propelled by her fury. She picked up a pan and clattered it on to the table, awakening Sarah who was in her crib under the table. She bent to pick her up, her anger abating as she soothed her. 'I'm sorry, my angel, did this nasty, horrid old woman, who doesn't know owt about babbies, wake thee?'

'Don't get upset, Mrs Scryven.' Maria took the crying baby from her and put her to her breast.

'But I am upset!' She sat with a thump in the chair by the fire. 'How dare they? Scum – dregs! How dare they bring in 'mistress looking like that? Half drunk, her hat hanging off – where's their respect?' Her face got pinker as she took a deep breath. 'I tell thee, Maria, I don't like what's happening. I said that I'd tell thee one day what happened to me when I was young.' She bent over, her elbows on her plump knees, her hands cradling her chin and rocked to and fro as she gazed into the fire.

'Well, it was women such as them as was sent for when I started in labour. They gave me spirits, which had never before passed my lips, and they sweated me – to get rid of 'impurities they said. But 'babby was a breech and wouldn't come, so they sent for two more women, and they gave me even more strong liquor so that I could barely stand.'

She shuddered and closed her eyes, her small brown face puckered at the memory. 'Then, while two of them held me, the other two pummelled my belly to make 'babby turn – but they killed him, and they nearly killed me. I was young and strong and I survived, but I vowed that though I couldn't have any more bairns, on account of what they did, I would deliver other mothers of their babbies, and I wouldn't use force, and I wouldn't use brutality. I studied herbs and plants and found what was best to ease 'pain, and I found that I had strength in these hands, strength to ease 'babby out without hurting its mother.'

She looked down at her small brown hands for a moment and then looked up at Maria who was silently watching her, the baby fast asleep at her breast, her small rosebud mouth creamy with milk.

'Only, mistress upstairs isn't young – and she isn't strong, not like thee and me, and I'm afeard of what they might do.'

Maria was afraid. She believed all that Mrs Scryven had told her, for she had heard similar stories, time and again. Not all the midwives were cruel, but most were ignorant, and many of them drank strong liquor and were quite incapable of helping a woman in difficulties.

'What can we do?' she asked, but before Mrs Scryven could answer the door flew open and Mrs Hawk stood there, leaning on the door frame unsteadily, her face flushed and her hair hanging greasily over her eyes.

'Where's that wood for 'fire,' she demanded. 'Mrs Moxon wants it immediately.'

Mrs Scryven rose without a word and went to the rear door where she called for Lizzie. 'Fetch some logs in, Lizzie, bring big 'uns, not 'small brittle pieces.' She turned back to Mrs Hawk who was about to return upstairs. 'Hey, just wait on and help this bairn upstairs wi' log basket.'

'With a bit of luck,' she said to Maria as she closed the door behind them, 'them logs will smoulder and keep 'fire down, they'll not give out much heat, being elm.'

All the late afternoon and early evening Isaac Masterson paced the hall floor, anxiously turning to the stairs and listening intently each time a door opened. He had been told by Mrs Moxon that his wife would be better without him, even though the baby wouldn't be born for some time yet.

'But surely I could see her just for a few moments,' he begged, 'just for reassurance?'

'Madam doesn't need reassurance,' said Mrs Moxon firmly, and closed the door on him.

'Stupid woman,' he said under his breath. 'I'm the one who needs it.'

Lizzie came through the kitchen door with yet another pan of hot water and he took it from her and carried it up the stairs. 'What are they doing with all this water, Lizzie?'

She brushed the hair out of her eyes wearily. 'It's for giving Mrs Masterson hot drinks, sir, least that's what 'midwife says.'

He looked at her sympathetically; the poor child was

worn out. She'd been up and down the stairs dozens of times, fetching wood and coal and hot water, her name constantly being called by the women upstairs.

'Is there no-one else in the kitchen to help you?' he asked.

'They won't have Mrs Scryven upstairs, sir, and Mrs Scryven won't let Maria lift owt heavy on account that she's just had her babby.' She looked at him anxiously. 'But I can do it, sir, I'm not a bit tired, I'm ever so strong.'

'I'm sure that you are.' He smiled down at her. But you're also so young and ought to be playing with your toys, he thought, not fetching and carrying like a work horse.

'Lizzie, where's that water?' The bedroom door opened with a whoosh and Mrs Moxon, almost filling the doorway, breathed in sharply as she saw Mr Masterson standing there with Lizzie.

He handed the pan to her and looked beyond her into the room. What he saw filled him with dread. He pushed the woman to one side and went in. Isobel, in just her shift but with a heavy blanket around her, was being supported by Mrs Hawk, who was walking her up and down the room, forcing her on though her legs were collapsing and she was on the point of exhaustion. There was a stench of sweat and alcohol and foul air.

'My dear.' He took a step forward but his arm was held by Mrs Moxon in a grip as strong as any man's.

'Better go, sir, this ain't any place for a gentleman. I've known men faint at a childbed, and not gentlemen like thee, sir, but great heavy brutes. Best be off.'

She turned him around and directed him towards the door, but not before he saw the mute appeal in his wife's eyes. His elegant, regal wife, her face pale and haggard and wet with perspiration, and her fair curls straggling and knotted and hanging damp with her own sweat down her back.

'Isaac.' Her voice was weak and breathless. 'For God's sake do something. I'm going to die.'

He was propelled out of the room and the door shut fast behind him. He heard Isobel wail, a terrifying, despairing cry which chilled him to the bone. Bewildered, he went down the stairs and, not knowing what he was doing, he followed a frightened Lizzie down into the kitchen.

'She's going to die,' he said, his voice flat and dull.

Maria took him by the arm and sat him down. 'It's a difficult time, sir, especially for 'first. Tha can only trust in God and providence.'

'But can I trust in those women?' He shook his head. 'It's like Hell up there, and just as hot.' He wiped his own sweat from his face. 'There's no air, the windows are blocked up with blankets, and the fire is roaring up the chimney. It doesn't seem right.' He looked at her imploringly, begging for help. 'There must be something – somebody!'

Maria looked at Mrs Scryven for a moment, then decided. 'I'm going up, I'll see what's happening. I've had enough bairns of my own to know.'

She opened the door quietly without knocking and stood unobserved. The room was as Mr Masterson had said, hot and airless. Only one rush light was burning and the flickering firelight threw out black, grotesque shadows which leapt and danced eerily over the walls and ceiling.

Her eyes were drawn to the bed where Mrs Masterson lay motionless, her pale legs and belly exposed, her eyes closed and her arms stretched wide in supplication. Only her fingers moved, clasping and unclasping in silent entreaty.

The two women had their backs to her and Maria saw Mrs Moxon sink down into a chair and reach for a bottle close by and lift it to her lips. Mrs Hawk was rummaging in the bottom of a large baize bag, then with an exclamation brought out first one object and then another. Maria drew in her breath sharply as she saw the flash and glint of metal caught by the flames of the fire.

She moved back, silently closing the door, and sped down the stairs, holding her skirts high lest she should fall, and the women upstairs hear her.

'Tha must go up, Mrs Scryven. They're going to use them new instruments!' She looked in alarm from Mrs Scryven to Mr Masterson, who had risen to his feet, his face pale and drawn.

'Forceps! Nay, only 'doctor should use them.' Mrs Scryven shook her head, then turning to Mr Masterson. 'Begging thy pardon, sir, wilt tha give me permission to attend 'mistress?'

He looked in bewilderment from one to another, speechless in his anxiety.

'Say yes, sir. She knows how. Look at my bairn, safely delivered.' Maria pointed to the sleeping baby in her crib under the table. 'Thy wife is in danger. 'Doctor must be sent for.' She shook his arm gently.

At her touch, he seemed to awaken from his vacant state and jumped nervously. 'Yes, yes. Please go up, Mrs Scryven, but first tell me where to find the doctor and I'll send Walters straight away.'

'He's in Tillington, sir, but it'll not take long to ride there. And he'll come straight away if he knows who it is.'

Mrs Scryven moved quickly, filling a bowl with hot water and washing her hands, calling to Lizzie to fetch down cotton sheets and towels from the press upstairs. Then, with a determined look set on her face, she climbed the stairs.

The women were bent over Mrs Masterson, their sleeves rolled up and their hands bloody as Maria and Mrs Scryven came into the room.

'Hey, what's going on? I said I wouldn't have thee in here!'

'Well, tha's not giving out orders any more,' said Maria softly. 'Tha's to go downstairs. Mr Masterson wants to see thee. Go on, both of thee.'

Mrs Moxon blustered. 'I can't leave my patient now,

she's having a very difficult time. 'Child might be dead. We can't move it.'

'Aye, it might well be dead if tha's been using them on it.' Mrs Scryven nodded towards the forceps, which lay on the floor where they had been dropped. 'Go on – out!'

'I'll not be responsible – if owt happens to either of 'em, it'll not be my doing!'

Maria held the door wide as an invitation for them to step through it, and hurriedly, as they saw her impassive expression, they picked up their bags and went down the stairs.

'How is she?' breathed Maria as they bent over the silent woman, her face ashen in the gloomy light.

'She's exhausted, poor lady. They've wore her out. I told her to rest between pains, but I don't suppose they let her. They've sweated her so she's no energy left.'

She ran her hands gently over Isobel's body, her small fingers moving delicately.

'Babby's still alive, I can feel it. But missus is almost gone. I can't feel her heart and her body's that still.'

She turned to Maria. 'Can tha help me get her out of bed if I take 'strain?'

'There's no need to take 'strain,' said Maria, 'I'm as strong as an ox. If we'd been back in Hull, I'd have been shifting barrels of fish by now.'

'Mebbe so, but tha's not in Hull, so I'll take 'strain,' Mrs Scryven answered sharply. 'First of all, put some blankets on 'floor. Ah, here's Lizzie. Look sharp, Lizzie, and spread out these blankets so that 'floor isn't hard.'

Lizzie did as she was told, then gently they eased Mrs Masterson down on to the floor, lying her on to her side. She moaned as they moved her and Maria felt relief. There was still some hope.

Mrs Scryven patted Mrs Masterson's face gently but firmly. 'Wake up, ma-am, don't sleep.'

Isobel opened her eyes narrowly. They were bloodshot and painwracked. 'Leave me, let me die in peace,' she whispered.

'Tha's not going to die, ma-am, we're going to help thee. But tha must try to help thaself.' Maria put her face close to hers. 'Please try, Mrs Masterson, please!'

She didn't answer but lay still; then her face wrinkled, her eyes opened wide with suffering, she opened her mouth and cried out.

'Quick, turn her on to her knees, support her arms and shoulders!' Mrs Scryven with vigorous strength turned her over into a kneeling position whilst Maria put both arms around her mistress from behind and held her in a supportive embrace.

They heard the cries as they waited downstairs, the two women shuffling their feet nervously, and Isaac with dulled eyes gazing up to the top of the stairs. Two cries, one piercing, tormented, torn out of agony, and another, fragile and imploring, as it was drawn reluctantly into its new life.

The doctor said there was no more that he could do. The next few days would determine if Isobel would live or die. He told them to keep her comfortable and quiet, and to keep the baby away from her in case she should turn against it.

'What rubbish,' said Maria to Mrs Scryven the next morning. 'I should want my babby with me, that would be one thing that would bring me back to life.'

'Happen it would with thee, Maria, but not with someone like 'mistress. She might well turn against 'poor bairn if she thought it had brought her such pain.'

'Poor little mite.' Maria bent to look at the infant, which was tightly swaddled as the doctor had directed.

Mrs Scryven came to her side. 'Aye. We'll have those bindings off soon, once she's feeding and used to 'feel of this big, bad world.'

Maria nodded. She hadn't allowed Sarah to be put into swaddling clouts, she hated to think of the delicate limbs being fettered and restrained by the tight bindings so approved by doctors and midwives.

'Will that mark disappear?' An ugly red weal showed on the baby's forehead where the brutal forceps had been used.

'Aye, I reckon so, though there might be a small scar. But her hair will cover it, never fear.

'Wilt tha be willing to nurse her, Maria? It'd save sending for a wet nurse. We'll get extra help for 'house. Master says to do what's necessary, he doesn't mind 'expense. Poor man, he's been almost out of his mind.'

'I'll nurse her gladly, I've plenty of milk for two, thanks to thee.'

Mrs Scryven was still plying her with eggs and milk beaten up to a froth with honey and caraway seeds. Junkets and jellies made from the dried wild fruits of summer slipped down her throat, giving her vitality and energy so that she felt better than she had ever felt in her life.

They heard a low moaning from the next room where their mistress was lying and hurried in. Mrs Masterson's face was pale and bloodless and she lay very still, but her eyes opened as they leant over her. She tried to speak but her mouth was dry.

Maria lifted her head and gave her a sip of spring water. She smiled down at her. 'Just rest easy, ma-am, everything's going to be all right and you've got a right bonny little babby.'

Isobel Masterson closed her eyes and turned her head away with a shudder. Then she turned back again and asked in a whisper, 'Boy?'

'No, ma-am, it's a lovely little girl.'

Mrs Masterson closed her eyes again and murmured weakly, 'Mr Masterson, please.'

Mrs Scryven rushed off to fetch Mr Masterson, who had been persuaded to lie down and take some rest. He had spent all night at his wife's bedside, watching over her, willing her to live and blaming himself for putting her life in danger.

He took hold of her limp white hand now and gently stroked it. 'Are you feeling a little better, my dear?'

She nodded and gave a deep sigh. 'I'm sorry, Isaac,' she whispered. 'I know how disappointed you must be.'

'Disappointed? Because it's a girl, you mean? Not a bit,' he said heartily. 'She's going to be a little beauty, just like her mother. Fair hair, though not much of it at the moment, and beautiful blue eyes!'

She nodded her head wearily and closed her eyes. Then with a supreme effort she opened them wide and said huskily, 'No more, Isaac. Promise me!'

Isaac, in relief and thanksgiving that his wife felt well enough to even consider the matter, promised most profoundly.

12

It seemed a bit hasty, thought Will, as they stood, cold and damp, the next morning at the graveside, the parson mumbling into his prayer book. No period of mourning to smooth the bed of death. No weeping mother to bless the short life of a child. Just himself, the two shivering boys and the matron to say farewell.

'Come on,' he said as they finally turned away. 'We'll go across to Masterson's and make ourselves useful. Then tomorrow, if my boots are ready, we'll set off home.'

They spent another night with the Hardwicks, and the next morning Will left the boys at the Masterson yard whilst he went to the bootmaker.

'Is Mr John here?' he asked one of the clerks as he left. 'I wondered if there was any message from Garston Hall?'

The man shook his head. 'He's down at 'dock side with Customs. He won't be back till late.' Masterson's have flitted already, did tha know? There's some boxes and stuff here for thee to take back with thee.'

The boots were ready. They felt soft and comfortable though the strap around his knee and thigh chafed.

He stood up and looked in the mirror that the bootmaker placed in front of him. 'What a dandy,' he said, to hide his emotion, as he saw two seemingly normal legs reflected in the glass.

'Nobody would guess,' the man said. 'But tha should take this stick, just till tha gets used to 'feel of it.'

Will thanked him and left, walking cautiously at first until he became used to the sensation of once more placing one foot in front of the other.

*   *   *

'When we've unpacked 'cart, put 'hoss into 'bottom field, Tom, and me and Jimmy will go across to 'Hall to see thy ma.'

He was disappointed that she wasn't at home at Field House. He'd wanted to surprise her, to see the look on her face as he stood in front of her without his crutch. The house was empty, though it was warm and welcoming. Clean rushes had been strewn on the floor and a fire burned in the grate. He felt a satisfying warmth enveloping him. She was a good homemaker, was Maria.

Jimmy ran on his short little legs to keep up with him as he strode steadily across the fields. This was a testing time; he wanted to see if he could keep upright on the rutted surface. The boots fitted well and he walked firmly with barely a sway save for the natural roll of a seaman.

'Wait here a minute, Jim. I'll find Lizzie and send her out to thee. Surprise her, eh?'

Jimmy nodded and sat wearily on the kitchen doorstep like a tired old man. Will tousled his hair. He knew he was worn out with the devastating events of the last few days, with the shock of finding his brother's bed empty, and of being locked up in the cold bare room, and he was quite unprepared for the long journey down the endless road to Monkston, for he'd questioned Will and Tom constantly as to how much longer they would be.

'Is it as far as 'Shetlands, Will? Or as far as Greenland?' he'd asked, for those two places were the limits of his geography.

No-one heard Will as he quietly entered the kitchen door, ducking his head at the lintel above the low entrance. Lizzie was standing at the table diligently cleaning knives and Mrs Scryven was sitrring something in a pot over the fire, whilst Maria, with her back to him, was bent low, lifting up something from a basket on the floor. Alice was sleeping soundly in a chair.

'God bless us, tha frighted 'life out of me!' Mrs Scryven was the first to see him, and Maria turned, startled, at the exclamation.

They stared in astonishment at each other. Maria's eyes opened wide at the sight of Will standing straight and upright in the doorway. Looking back at her, he was equally astounded as she stood with two babies, one in each arm.

Her eyes filled with tears as she gazed at him and coursed steadily down her cheeks. He took four long steps towards her and gathered her up in his arms. 'I didn't mean to shock thee, Maria. It's all right, it's all right.' He kissed her hair, her nose, her lips. 'I just wanted to surprise thee.'

'Tha did that, Will Foster,' she said with a husky break in her voice. 'What's happened to thee? I thought I was dreaming.'

'So did I, when I saw two babbies, but I see I'm not. What's Ma Scryven been feeding thee on?'

She laughed and wiped her eyes with the back of her hand. 'Don't get alarmed, they're not both ours.' She sat down in the chair and rocked gently back and forth. 'So which one will tha claim, Will? Which one is thine?'

He bent over to inspect the sleeping babies, so similar in size and form, one with fair translucent skin and light silky lashes edging her closed lids, the other with skin the colour of pale cream and a smile flickering on her lips. He smiled and gently stroked the soft golden down on her head. 'This one's mine,' he said. 'She's going to be a redhead, just like her da!'

Lizzie put down her polishing cloth and wiped her hands. 'I'll take Miss Lucy upstairs, Maria, if tha's finished feeding her. Perhaps 'mistress would like to have her by her for a while.'

'Tha can ask, Lizzie,' Maria answered sadly, 'but I doubt it. Perhaps when Mrs Masterson is feeling better she might take to 'poor little babby.'

'Poor!' said Will in amazement. 'Poor! How can she be? She'll want for nowt. Unless she's sick?' He peered anxiously at the tiny face.

'No, 'bairn isn't sick, but mistress is, she doesn't want to see her, let alone hold her.'

Will suddenly gasped. 'Lizzie, before I forget – I've left a parcel on 'doorstep. Go and fetch it inside, wilt tha?'

Lizzie looked curiously at Will and he nodded. 'Go on, look sharp.'

He grinned sheepishly at Maria. 'I hope I'm not going to get into bother, but I've brought summat home.'

'I think tha's got some explaining to do,' said Maria. 'Them boots for one thing, and what's inside them.' She dropped her voice to a whisper. 'Where did tha get 'money from, Will?'

He put his finger to his lips as from outside they could hear shrieks from Lizzie, and Mrs Scryven made a dash to open the door. 'I'll tell thee all about it after, just trust me.'

Maria cried again as Lizzie and Jimmy fell into the room in their excitement and hugged and skipped and squeezed, and even Mrs Scryven wiped her eyes, although, as she said, she didn't rightly know what was going on.

'So, I couldn't leave him there, not on his own, could I?' asked Will later. 'It was different when there were two of them. They would have been company for each other. But 'bairn, he looked that miserable; and then I thought what if it had been our Tom in 'same position?'

'Don't go on, Will. Of course tha did right. We'll manage somehow. And I expect Annie will come back soon, especially when she hears about 'other poor little lad.' Maria glanced at Lizzie as she sat quietly gazing into the fire with her arms around her sleepy young brother, who for once in his young life was quite happy to submit to her endearments.

13

Will reported to Isaac Masterson and gave him an account of his visit to the hospital and the fitting of his limb and boots.

'It's very good of thee, sir, to go to 'trouble and expense.'

Isaac brushed his thanks aside. 'As long as you're comfortable, Foster. That's what matters.'

They had established a good working relationship. Both men were aware of their inexperience in country matters, yet with their practicality and good judgement, and under Dick Reedbarrow's guidance, the farm had once more become established. More men were employed to prepare the land for spring sowing, and though there was no snow that settled, the wind blew cold and icy and the ground became rock hard. Cattle were bought at market, and sheep used to the rigours of the bleak landscape were bought from a local man, some for breeding and some for fattening.

'I wouldn't mind having a cow for missen, Dick,' said Will one day, 'and maybe a few hens. Maybe next year when I get my wages I'll buy some eggs for hatching. Though I'd have to save for years before I could afford a beast.'

'Oh, I'll bring thee a hen and a few eggs for hatching,' said Dick, 'soon as it's spring. And why dossn't tha get a goat for milking? It would cost thee less than a coo.'

As the weather deteriorated, they moved into the shelter of the woods to work, clearing the dead timber and making space for more planting. They spent days sawing and chopping and carting wood to the store in the yard, to be used on the fires which now were lit in almost every room.

Another girl was brought in to help in the house. Mr Masterson had seen Maria one morning when he had risen very early to leave for town. She had been clearing ashes from the grate in his study and had risen to leave, having been told by Mrs Scryven that she must not on any account continue with her work in front of her employers. Mr Masterson had frowned and she thought that he was displeased with her and resolved to get up half an hour earlier in order to avoid him, but he had instructed her that she must not under any circumstances undertake hard, rough work whilst she was nursing the babies.

'You must take care of yourself,' he said, flustered and embarrassed. 'I know my wife would tell you so if she were well enough to think about it.'

She smiled at him and thanked him for his kindness and saw to it that he had every comfort, that his tobacco and papers were always in the same place. That his brandy and glass were in easy reach of his chair, and when he was at home, baby Lucy was brought down each evening for him to look at before she was put down to sleep. He was very taken with his daughter and got into the habit of dropping into the nursery to gaze fondly at her, making kindly comparisons between the two babies and asking Lizzie's opinion on their well being. Lizzie, who slept in the same room so that she could hear their every whimper, would swell with pride and become completely tongue-tied.

But sometimes, on the nights when Isaac was away from home, Maria would wrap up both the babies and take them home to Field House and spend the night quietly with Will, leaving Lizzie and Alice with Mrs Scryven. She loved these evenings when they could talk quietly together, and share the big bed only with the babies, for Will had made another bed for Tom and Jimmy in a corner by the fire, where they whispered and joked and finally fell asleep as the shadows of the firelight dwindled.

* * *

Maria and Mrs Scryven looked up out of the kitchen window one morning as they heard the rattle of a cart. They watched as a man and a young girl climbed out and he lifted down a wooden box and deposited it on the doorstep.

'I've brought our Susan,' he said. ' 'Mistress said as she was to start now.'

They looked at him doubtfully, then at one another.

'She was taken on by Mrs Masterson herself,' he said loftily in reply to Mrs Scryven's questioning. 'She's going to be her own maid.'

'Well, we know nowt about it,' she grumbled, and muttered to Maria, 'Now there'll be trouble, mark my words. I know that lot. There'll be trouble.' She banged a pan on to the fire, spilling the water and making the hot embers spit and sizzle.

Maria ran up the stairs and knocked on Mrs Masterson's door. She was still confined to her room and had not yet been down since Lucy was born.

' 'New girl has come, ma-am – Susan. She says you've taken her on as another maid.'

A frown creased Isobel's colourless face and she gazed blankly at Maria from the depths of her bed. 'I don't remember. Did I?' She gazed into space. 'Perhaps I did. Yes, the innkeeper's daughter. Such an obnoxious man, but she was very pretty and polite.'

She sighed and leaned back against the pillows. 'I'll see her later. I am too fatigued to bother just now. I'm too weak to make decisions about maids. Do with her whatever you think.'

'If only tha – you would eat more, ma-am, you would feel much better.' Mrs Scryven's tempting trays of jellies and junkets, poached fish and coddled eggs had all been sent back barely touched.

Isobel nodded and looked at Maria through dull blue eyes. If only I looked and felt as well as she does, she thought. Though she was nursing two babies, Maria breathed vitality, her skin was smooth and clear and her black hair was thick and glossy.

'Perhaps I will see the girl after all,' she said with an effort. 'She can brush my hair, Lizzie doesn't really know how.' Young Lizzie, so afraid of hurting, was too gentle to unravel the tangled knots. 'And I will have some jelly, I think, and a little bread.'

Maria came downstairs smiling. 'I think 'mistress is feeling a bit better. We'll prepare a tray, Mrs Scryven, and Susan can take it up. Come over here, Susan, and watch what we do, then tha'll know for next time.'

So saying Maria pleasantly and firmly asserted her authority so that Susan was in no doubt as to who was in charge of the household.

Isobel slowly started to improve; the effect of having a young and vital girl about her, one with golden curls and fair skin such as she had had, goaded her into life, and Susan, so charming and obliging, painstakingly cut and combed the matted locks, smoothed the aching brow, and with Mrs Scryven's creams and lotions massaged her stiff and weary limbs which had taken no exercise since the birth of Lucy.

She was awakened one morning by the cry of a baby. She turned on her pillow to escape the sound. It persisted for perhaps five minutes without being hushed, which was unusual, for normally she wasn't disturbed as Maria or Lizzie were quick to pacify and soothe. She rose from her bed, put on her robe, and went into the next room where the crying was coming from. It was a sharp, crisp morning and the sun streamed through the window throwing a beam of light on to the crib where the babies were laid, head to toe. One of the babies cried as the sunlight caught her eyes and she moved her head from side to side to escape the brightness. Isobel hesitated, then bent over the crib and her body blocked the sunlight. The child opened her eyes and hiccupped, giving a windy smile at Isobel.

Isobel smiled back and touched her cheek, and the baby chortled and squealed and kicked her feet, disturbing the other child who lay wrapped tightly beneath her blankets. Isobel moved the covers to one side, for she thought how restricted she was, and noticed the angry scar on her forehead. She frowned and bit her lip and turned back to the wide-awake baby who watched her with alert eyes, and impulsively bent to pick her up. She felt the softness of her skin against her cheek, and the fragrant smell of milk and something like roses, as she carried her across to the window, lifted her spirits, while a protective tenderness stole over her.

'I'm sorry, ma-am, I didn't mean you to be disturbed.' Maria was apologetic as she hurried into the room. 'I had to go to 'kitchen for some warm water.' She was carrying a bowl of water with the same smell of roses.

'It's quite all right.' Isobel smiled back at her. 'It is about time I was introduced to my daughter. Mr Masterson is forever extolling her perfections.'

'She's beautiful, isn't she?' agreed Maria. 'Shall I take Sarah now, ma'am, and perhaps when I've finished washing Miss Lucy, you would like me to bring her to your room?'

Isobel stared at Maria. 'But, I thought—' She looked at Sarah and handed her back quickly.

Maria made no reply but simply put Sarah back into the crib and picked up Lucy. 'Here she is, ma-am, little beauty.' Lucy puckered up her face and let out a disgruntled wail. She was hungry, wet and uncomfortable and she punched her small fists in the air as Maria undid her sheets.

'Why is she fastened up like that?' demanded Isobel. 'the other child isn't. I am quite sure she doesn't like it.'

'No, no more do I, ma-am. But 'doctor said I had to. It's what's done to babbys, 'cept I don't agree with it for my own.'

'Then I won't have it either,' Isobel snapped. 'Take them off at once and tell the doctor that I said so.'

She turned to leave the room. 'I won't have Lucy with me just yet,' she said. 'I seem to have developed a headache. I shall go back to bed.'

* * *

213

Violent storms battered the east coast that first winter they were at Garston Hall. Tremendous seas, whipped up by north-easterly winds, ravaged the soft boulder clay, and deep cracks spread across the top of the cliffs as the base disintegrated. Before January was out six feet of land had crumbled and slithered down into the sea.

'Dost tha fancy a jar of ale at 'Raven before going 'ome, Will? I've got a right thirst on me.'

Will and Dick Reedbarrow had finished their work for the day. They had spent most of it repairing the wall of a barn which had taken the brunt of the bad weather, but now it was almost dark and they were unable to see what they were doing.

'Aye, I'll have a quick one with thee, Dick, we can do no more here.'

He called to Tom to hurry with the clearing up. 'Take 'lamp, Tom, and get off home, and straight to bed after supper.'

'All right, Da,' Tom nodded wearily. He needed no second bidding. He rose every morning at daybreak when his father called him, his eyes barely open as his feet touched the floor. He worked as hard as any man, fetching and carrying for Dick and his father. He never shirked or grumbled, for it was recognized that he was now old enough to contribute to the household funds. He fell asleep as soon as he climbed into bed, and Maria would gaze pensively at him as he lay there, his hands folded beneath his plump, winter-rosy cheeks, full of wonder at how quickly her young son was growing into manhood.

Will followed Dick into the oak-panelled room of the small smoky inn which was already full of men who were unable to work because of the weather, and as they opened the door the gusty wind whipped in behind them, causing the blazing fire in the grate to throw out clouds of smoke and soot into the room.

This was the first time that Will had come to the inn, and he nodded a greeting to some of the men. They nodded back and some held his gaze and said, ' 'ow do.'

They joined two other men sitting at a heavy, rough-hewn table, one, Ralph Graves, a man just out of his youth with dark, deepset eyes and a sullen mouth, and the other, Nathan Crabtree, who looked so old and decrepit that Will wondered how he had ever found the strength to get there.

They sat for some time without conversing, just drinking their ale and smoking their clay pipes, and Will was beginning to muse thoughtfully on the difference between the quiet atmosphere here and that of the taverns he used to frequent in Hull, where the noise, and the voice of the landlord shouting to be heard above the din, was evident from half a street away.

'I hear as thou's a whaling man.' The old man took his pipe from his mouth and interrupted his meditation.

'Aye, I was, until my accident.'

'And now tha's going to be a farmer?' Crabtree bent and tore up a long strip of paper, and lighting it from the fire held it to his pipe and sucked loudly, the flame flickering perilously close to his shaggy eyebrows.

Will hesitated. 'I reckon that would take more time than I've got,' he answered, 'I just want to earn a living. But maybe my lad will be, he's young enough.'

The old man nodded, apparently satisfied with his answer, but the younger man interrupted abruptly. 'There's plenty of us round here who want to do that, so why didn't 'maister at Garston take on one of us. We could do 'job as well as anybody – aye, and better.'

'He's tekken on local labour! Me for one,' butted in the normally taciturn Dick Reedbarrow. 'And 'ostler, and another gardener, and women for 'house.'

'I reckon if he'd known about thee, I'd still be looking for a job,' Will agreed placatingly, 'so it's my good fortune that he happened to know me. I've worked for him since I was just a lad and he's always looked after his men.'

The old man started to chuckle. 'I met a seaman when I was a lad, and he used to tell such tales as tha'd never believe. About 'Esquimaux, and unicorns and icebergs as big as an 'ouse.'

Will laughed. 'I could tell thee stories to make tha beard curl, if tha has a mind to listen.'

'About yakkeyahs?' asked Ralph, curiously.

'Aye, that's what 'whaling men call 'Esquimaux, on account of all 'yakking they do; they're grand folk for talking and most hospitable. Why, I remember once when we were frozen into 'ice and running short of food, they came with their sledges laden with caribou and duck. They brought their women with them, and though there was no impropriety, tha understands, we had a grand party, with singing and dancing and all.'

Other men had gathered round when they heard that tales were being told, and Will looked up nonplussed. He hadn't expected an audience. 'I tell thee what, I haven't wet my babby's head yet. It's 'custom in 'town to do that, and maybe tha'd join me, and I'll tell thee a tale or two before I go home for supper.'

'Aye, we have 'same custom,' said the old man. ' 'Cept tha should do it on 'day 'bairn is birthed. But we'll not refuse to drink its 'ealth for all that. Hast tha been fortunate enough to have a lad?'

He commiserated when told that it was a girl. 'I've had six lads and four lasses, and outlived 'em all. They're all in 'churchyard waiting – missus an' all – but I'm not ready yet.' He chuckled wickedly and started to cough as tobacco fumes caught his throat. His eyes watered and tears ran down his furrowed cheeks and disappeared into his stained grey beard.

'I'll tell thee summat,' he said when he got his breath back. 'That little lass o' thine might see a bit of 'istory.' He nodded his head sagely. 'We'll be part of it, even though we shan't be here, 'leastways most of us won't be.'

'I'm sorry,' said Will perplexed. 'Tha's lost me, I'm afraid.'

'That's just it.' The old man scratched his head absently. 'Lost. We'll all be lost.'

Will glanced at the other men. He thought the old fellow must be wandering in his head. But some of the others were muttering together in agreement, whilst the rest pondered silently over their tankards.

'There's nowt we can do about it. Leastways not in our lifetime.' He rumbled on as if talking to himself. 'It's gone on right through 'istory and 'istory always repeats itself.'

Dick Reedbarrow caught Will's eye. 'He's talking about destruction of 'cliffs. There's more gone over this winter.'

'Summat should be done about it,' Ralph Graves broke in angrily. 'Parli'ment should do summat. They should build a wall like we've tried to do.'

'Nay, man,' interrupted another. 'It'd cost 'undreds, and we're not that important.'

Nathan Crabtree smiled a toothless smile. 'I've tell'd thee afore and I'll tell thee again, it's part of 'istory, same as all them other towns that was lost. Monkston will go 'same way – in time.'

He wagged a finger at the assembly but spoke specifically to Will. 'What folk don't realize, is that out 'ere, time is measured in centuries. Them cliffs have bin eaten away bit by bit for as long as man can remember. Life still goes on unchanged, bairns get born and 'awd folks dee and other things go on in between, and I'm not saying that thy little lass won't grow up and have her own babbies here; but sooner or later we shall have to move back or be consumed, and our old bones'll be crushed and washed away along wi' all 'others.'

There was silence as he finished speaking and he put his head back and closed his eyes as if exhausted with the effort.

Ralph Graves surveyed Will churlishly. 'Tha'll be a bit of an expert, seeing as tha was a sea-going man. What would thee do to keep watter back?'

Will shook his head, for the man was plainly looking for a confrontation. 'Tha can't tame 'sea, never will in a million years. I've heard of 'lost towns of course, there isn't a seaman who hasn't. There's some who'll swear they've seen 'top of a steeple at low tide, or heard 'sound of a church bell through 'waves. And I wouldn't disbelieve it.'

Old Nathan nodded in agreement, his eyes still closed. 'That's reet, that's reet.'

'But as for keeping it back,' Will added earnestly, 'from Bridlington Bay right down 'coast, 'cliffs are breaking up, and some say 'land is drifting down as far as Spurn and building up 'peninsula. But it's like Mr Crabtree here says.' He was careful not to breach the bounds of etiquette by calling the old man by his first name until invited. 'Monkston probably will go 'same way, along with Old Ol'boro, Hartburn and Ravenser and all 'others, for there's no science on this earth that'll stop it.'

Nathan Crabtree started to hum under his breath and then to sing in a cracked, hoarse voice. Some of the men grinned and withdrew back to the places where they had been sitting previously. The discussion was over, but Will sat on and listened. The tune was unrecognizable and the old man had forgotten most of the words, yet here and there he caught the thread and was aware of an intangible shadow hovering within his consciousness as the old man sang.

> Where life and beauty
> Dwelt long ago,
> The oozy rushes
> And seaweed grow
> And no-one sees
> And no-one hears
> And none remembers
> The far off years.

14

'Oh what a treat! It *will* be nice to see John. He will do me so much good. I declare, I feel better already just anticipating his visit.'

Isobel smiled warmly at Isaac when he gave her news of John's arrival the next weekend. 'I have missed him terribly. Just one brief visit since we came here, I did expect that he would have been over more frequently.'

'I really can't spare him so often, Isobel. He came when you were ill, and I have been giving him regular reports of your health and that of Lucy. Also the weather hasn't been at all conducive to travelling.'

He shifted uncomfortably on the fragile chair in Isobel's sitting-room. 'Are you going to come downstairs now that you are feeling better? The doctor says that you are quite well enough.'

'Perhaps I might, I have been thinking about it.'

In truth she was getting rather bored. Her health was improving gradually, and she was entertaining thoughts of inviting her local neighbours to visit, though she did not as yet feel strong enough to go out visiting them. Invitations and cards had been left, but sadly she had had to decline for the present.

'When John comes at the weekend, I want to show him all the improvements we have made already. We've planted out hawthorn to compact the growing area, though we've left some of the old woodland for shelter, and built new pens for the spring lambs. If he has a mind and the sea isn't too rough, I thought we might go fishing.'

Isaac had bought a cobble, and he and Will had discovered a mutual interest. With rod and line they had spent several satisfying hours far out at sea. Master and servant, the expeditions reaffirmed what they already knew, that the elements rendered no distinction between men's status, and in the battle to preserve their vulnerable lives they were equal. They were not so foolhardy as to flout danger, but they both responded to the elation of landing a fish while waves towered above them, threatening to capsize their wooden ark, and they treated the sea as an awesome and terrible friend.

Isobel's mouth pouted childishly. 'Don't forget that I would like his company too, Isaac. And don't for goodness sake bore him with all your farming gossip. Why, you're worse with your talk of oats and the price of wheat and sheep than you ever were with your ships!'

'Isobel!' He rose from the chair impatiently. 'Our ships keep us in comfort, you seem to forget that. We have property, servants, and the farming isn't a whim, I'm not just playing at it! I intend to succeed. I intend to make this land efficient and profitable. I intend to co-operate with the local community so that they might have a share in the success of this venture.' Indignantly he paced the floor and Isobel grew alarmed.

'Very well, Isaac, do please calm yourself. You are making me feel quite faint.' She reached for the smelling salts on her table and immediately he was contrite.

'I'm sorry, my dear. Do please forgive me. I know how irritating you find business talk. But don't you see, I'm sure that the people around here think that I am just amusing myself and don't take me seriously, and I should hate to think that you felt the same.'

'Why, Isaac, as if I should do that. I am perfectly aware how important it is to you, and you must not take any notice of these other people, whoever they are, their opinion is of no account whatsoever. Now, shall I ring for tea?'

Isaac had once explained to John that in order to have the respect of one's work force, it was necessary, in his opinion, to show capability oneself, and with farming there are no instant results to show success or failure. He knew that there was antagonism towards unscrupulous rich merchants coming from town into the country. They bought up the scattered strips of land from the peasant farmers who could not afford to enclose them as the government decreed, and evicted them from their homes, leaving them destitute and without any means of gaining a livelihood.

Isaac intended to use local labour, though he knew that the larger land holdings would be easier to work with fewer men employed, and should in theory be far more efficient. Only time would tell whether this was correct but, being a considerate man, he was uncomfortable as he passed through the small village and felt the animosity of some of the men who lounged outside the doors of their cottages and who turned morosely to watch his carriage drive down the muddy road.

'When you are feeling well, my dear, do you think that it might be a good idea if you paid a visit to the villagers? Get to know them, and let them get to know you? Let them see that you are interested in their welfare?'

She stared at him stupefied.

'I think it would show that we mean well,' he said, pacing the floor and trying to engender some enthusiasm. 'That we do wish to belong.'

She gave a deep sigh. 'I don't think you realize, Isaac, that I am still in a weakened state and am quite likely to catch some dreadful disease that might be harboured in those houses.'

He raised his hands in protest. 'Heaven forbid that I should suggest that you take tea with them! But to take them some comforts and pass the time of day would be charitable.'

She smiled sweetly at him. Yes, of course she would like to be considered charitable, to do good deeds. Just as long as it wasn't too taxing on her energies. And, she mused thoughtfully, her circle of contemporaries would be more than impressed when they discovered that her new life as a gracious benefactor was filled with compassionate and bountiful acts of goodwill.

'When I am up and about again, Isaac, I will do what I can.'

He sat silently as Susan brought in the tea and carefully poured it from the silver teapot. 'Mrs Scryven's just made them honey cakes, ma-am. She says she hopes that you'll try them.'

Isobel nodded. 'Will you ask Mrs Foster to come up. I need to speak to her about the arrangements for the weekend when Mr John will be here.'

Susan bobbed, a smile hovering about her lips, and left the room.

'Pretty girl, that one. What eyes she has!' Isaac sipped his tea. 'I can't see you keeping her for very long. Some young fellow will snap her up, mark my words.'

'Isaac, really,' she tutted. 'Pray don't mention it. I should hate to lose her, she's such a comfort.'

Isaac bit into the soft, sticky texture of a honey cake and spoke with his mouth half full. 'We'd find another maid soon enough, but we'd never find another cook like Mrs Scryven. What an angel, what delights she produces! She's the one we must look after!'

'Has Mr John arrived yet?' Isobel stretched and yawned and inspected the breakfast tray which Susan had brought in response to the bell. Fresh bread, kidneys and newly laid eggs were there to tempt her jaded appetite, and a small vase of spring flowers, snowdrops and the slender stems and starlike yellow flowers of winter jasmine, were set upon the crisp white cloth.

'Yes, ma-am. He got here about ten-o-clock.' The girl drew back the curtains, letting in the sunlight. 'It's a grand morning, ma-am.'

'Mm, so it is. I have decided to come downstairs today, so would you prepare my yellow morning dress, and we'll use the front drawing-room so be quite sure that it is warm.'

'Yes, ma-am. 'Fire is lit already. Mr Masterson said to tell you that they'd be back about eleven and will take breakfast then.'

Isobel ate sparingly, and then rose from her bed. She had slept well and felt refreshed. Some of her old sparkle seemed to be returning and she was looking forward to greeting John and hearing the news and gossip of Hull, for Isaac gave her none.

She stood in her night robe and surveyed the view. Snowdrops were appearing in scattered drifts across the lawn, and here and there in sheltered corners were splashes of gold from winter aconites. She leaned forward to look towards the round tower at the east end of the Hall as her gaze was caught by another shower of gold, which tumbled and cascaded over the grey stone. Winter jasmine delighted her eyes. It must be nearly spring, she thought, unaware that its beauty had been there to enchant all the winter had she only cared to look.

As she gazed she saw figures approaching from across the fields towards the pasture land, three people, one of which she knew to be Isaac, his stocky figure in his greatcoat and tall beaver hat instantly recognizable. The two others walking on either side of him she was unsure of. John, it must be John. Her face softened into a smile. He looked taller, broader, since she had last seen him.

She watched as Isaac and John turned to the other man, who swung his stick jauntily on to his shoulder, and John threw back his head and laughed as if at a joke. As they came nearer she narrowed her eyes in order to see if it was anyone she knew, but the face was unfamiliar, and she would surely have remembered the thick beard and mass of curly red hair, like a beacon atop his broad shoulders, made wider by the thick padded jacket he was wearing. A new friend of John's perhaps, although somewhat older. How annoying of Isaac not to tell her; she did prefer to be prepared to receive extra guests.

She turned towards the door as Susan knocked and waited with hot water. 'Has Mr John brought a guest, Susan? I have this moment seen him with someone.'

The girl joined her at the window, but the men had

disappeared from sight behind the high hedge which sheltered the lawns from the open paddock.

'Nobody told me, ma-am, but then they wouldn't.'

Isobel raised her eyebrows at the veiled hint of sarcasm in her voice, though if Susan was expecting a response from her mistress, then she didn't yet know her well enough.

'I won't wear my yellow after all,' she said thoughtfully. 'I think I am still too pale. Get out my rose figured silk, it will give me a little colour. And then you can dress my hair. Do hurry up, girl, don't just stand there, the morning is practically over.'

She came down the staircase slowly, her legs trembling a little at the unaccustomed exercise. Isaac heard her through the open door of the drawing-room and came hurrying out to her.

'How delightful to see you downstairs at last, my dear. John, come here and greet your aunt.'

John, smiling, bent to kiss her hand, then gave her a warm embrace. He held her out at arms' length in order to see her better. 'How well you look, Aunt Isobel. Motherhood suits you very well. A turn or two around the garden once the weather is warmer, and you will soon have roses in your cheeks.'

She laughed merrily. 'Come, John, you surely know me better than that. It is not yet the height of fashion to acquire the country girl look.' She turned to Susan who was hovering behind her. 'Tell Mrs Foster to bring us fresh tea and chocolate.'

'Yes, ma-am.' Susan slipped away, but not before looking into John's eyes which had caught hers, and giving him a demure smile, the tip of her pink tongue showing between her white teeth.

'So, John,' said Isobel as she sat graciously in the chair which they had placed for her by the fire. 'Where is your mysterious friend? Where are you hiding him?' She moved the firescreen nearer. She had taken the trouble to wear a touch of powder to hide the dark shadows beneath her eyes, and brushed a little colour on her cheeks, and didn't want the heat of the fire to redden and scorch her delicate skin.

'Mysterious friend? I don't understand.' John gazed at her quizzically.

'Come now,' she laughed teasingly. 'I saw you. Both of you. You didn't think to tell me of an extra guest, Isaac?' she added reprovingly, but with a smile in her voice.

The two men looked at each other and Isaac shrugged his shoulders. 'I don't know who you mean, Isobel. There is no-one here but us.'

'Well, I must have been dreaming,' she said gaily. 'I dreamed that I saw you and John with a giant of a man.' She smiled girlishly. 'With a mop of flaming red hair.'

Maria, who had knocked and quietly entered with a tray, hesitated, her breath held.

'With red hair!' John exclaimed impetuously. 'The only red hair around here is that old sea dog Will Foster.'

Isaac threw him a warning glance, but it was too late. John had forgotten the circumstances in which Will's presence was deemed to be undesirable.

Maria put down the tray and whispered, 'Shall I pour, ma-am?'

Isobel, pale beneath her false colour, closed her eyes momentarily and gestured negatively with her hand to dismiss her.

John glanced at Maria as she withdrew, her face as impassive with a slight flush to her cheeks as his aunt's was pallid and confused.

'You must have seen us with Foster, that was it, I expect?' said Isaac dubiously. 'We were just inspecting the land.' He nodded several times as if replying to his own question. 'That would be it. Just showing John what we've been doing,' he finished feebly.

Isobel made no reply but deliberately attended to pouring the tea and chocolate as if that was the most important matter in hand and which required her full attention. That she was embarrassed and ashamed was known only to her, for to any observer the discussion was concluded and the mistress of the house was already turning the conversation with considerable dexterity on to other, safer subjects.

Her reason for being embarrassed was not so important to her, although she felt an angry stab of hurt pride that she hadn't seen that Foster was only a common labouring man, that by his bearing she had mistaken him for a gentleman, although of course, she excused herself, as she smiled and attended agreeably to the conversation between Isaac and John, I did only see him from a distance.

Her shame, which she could admit to no-one and which she didn't wish to acknowledge even to herself, stemmed from the morning as she had risen from her bed and looked out of the window and seen the freshness of the day. She had suddenly been aware that she was alive and recovered from childbirth, that her body though frail was whole, and the sight of a handsome man, virile and strong, reminded her in a way that no lady of her station would ever confess that she was, after all, a woman.

'Mistress has gone to rest before supper, Maria.' Susan had come into the nursery where she found Maria nursing Sarah, whilst a contented Lucy, fed and free of her bindings, kicked and cooed as Alice tickled her toes.

'Take an hour's rest, while tha can, Susan,' said Maria. 'We'll happen be up late tonight as Mr John is here.'

'I'll tek a short walk first,' the girl replied, looking out of the window. 'I could do with some air.'

Maria smiled, telling her to be back before dark, and changed Sarah to her other breast. She felt a little tired and closed her eyes. She wondered what had been the talk this morning when she had heard Will's name mentioned. It couldn't have been much, as she'd heard John laughing later, though the mistress looked drawn. Sleep stole softly over her, and Sarah too, satiated with milk, let slip the nipple from her tongue and slept, her small satisfied mouth nestled against her mother's warm breast.

The sky was gathering dark across the horizon and grey clouds chased swiftly before the wind as John strode briskly along the cliff top. Below him the restless ocean crashed and beat against the shore, reminding him that soon he would be leaving the safety of dry land and riding the backs of the great white waves towards the wastes of the polar regions.

He cut back across the cliff, keeping leeward of the dense hawthorn hedge, and made towards a thick shelter belt, where elm, hazel and ash grew in profusion, with the tangled stems of blackthorn, bramble and ivy at their feet. A pile of logs from autumn felling lay neatly stacked, a flush of pale and fleshy fungi clinging to them.

He whistled softly between his teeth and narrowed his eyes as he caught sight of a sudden movement and a glimpse of something white. Someone was in the wood and it wasn't Will or Reedbarrow or one of the labourers, for they would have shown themselves. Poachers perhaps, after a rabbit or hare, though it would have been more usual to wait until after dark.

'Hey. You in there. Come on out. Show yourself.'

A figure emerged from behind the woodpile, a girl wearing a grey shawl over a woollen dress and starched white apron.

'Susan? What are you doing out here, all alone?'

'I came out for a walk, Mr John. It's my time off.' She pulled her shawl around her. 'But it was too cold on 'cliff, so I came in here for shelter.'

He smiled down at her. More likely a tryst with a local farmer's boy, he thought, yet he hoped not for he had a strange sense of envy at the notion.

'Shall I escort you back? It's getting dark and it's most unwise for you to be wandering about alone so near to the cliffs.'

She thanked him and walked in silence beside him, her small feet taking two steps to his one.

John cleared his throat. He was very conscious of her presence so close to him. 'Are you settling in at Garston Hall?'

'Aye, I thank thee, sir.' Her voice, though broad with the dialect of the district, was soft and caressing as if she was stroking him with her words. 'I'm very grateful to thee for getting me 'position.' She looked up at him, her violet eyes dark in the evening shadows.

He felt a shiver run down his spine and it wasn't the effect of the cold east wind, for he was warm within, the blood flowing fast in his veins, though his hands trembled. How gentle she was, how sweet and delightful. So different from the exotic creature she had seemed when she had taunted him at her father's inn. He strode out faster, his mind agitated.

She picked up her skirts and in her haste to keep up with him, she stumbled in the rough grass and fell heavily to the ground.

'I do beg your pardon, I was rushing you. Please, let me help you.' He bent over her as she made no attempt to rise.

'I've twisted my foot, Mr John. I don't think I can stand.'

He helped her up and felt the softness of her dimpled elbows and the sweet warmth of her breath against his face as he lifted her.

'If tha could help me across to 'old barn yonder, sir, happen I could sit down for a minute.'

He hesitated. Was it possible to compromise a servant girl by being alone with her in an empty barn? He dismissed the thought: she would never have suggested it had it been so. The rules were quite different with females of her class, he felt sure, and yet, he wavered again. He knew instinctively that someone like Maria would never jeopardize her character by being alone with a strange man. He recalled the night of Sarah's birth and how anxious she was to be rid of him.

But there was nothing for it, the girl couldn't walk and it would be quite improper for him to carry her. The thought brought him out in a cold sweat. Not that she would be heavy, for she was small and not too plump, just nicely rounded, and with her arms around his neck, it would be no effort at all.

'Come, then,' he said, his voice hoarse. 'Lean on me and I'll assist you.'

The barn was but half a meadow away, and he wished it twice as far. With his arm around her waist for support, he could smell the soft warm scent of her flesh and feel the rounded contours beneath his fingers. The sensation aroused an aching, burning need.

The loose straw rustled beneath their feet as they entered and there was a sudden scurrying of mice into the dark corners. He unfastened his greatcoat, his fingers fumbling with the metal buttons. It was large and loose, of warm cloth and he spread it out on the floor.

'Thank you,' she murmured softly as she sat down and took off her shoe.

He knelt beside her to examine her injury. There was no sign of swelling or bruising, but her bare foot was cold, and gently he warmed it within his hands, stroking her toes with his fingers to avoid hurting her.

'I don't think you have sprained it. Just a painful wrench. It will no doubt be better by the morning if you rest it.'

Her eyes watched him as he spoke, dark, deep unfathomable pools within the contours of her face. She shivered. 'I'm so cold, Mr John. I can't go on until I'm warmer.'

'We must get back, they'll be worrying about you,' he croaked, his eyes held fast by hers. He unfastened her other shoe and spontaneously began to warm her other foot.

She shook her head. 'I'll not be missed just yet,' she said softly. She gave him her hands, small and chubby. 'I'm cold all over, Mr John.'

He started to rub them into life, slowly at first and then faster. He moved his trembling hands to her arms, her shoulders, still briskly rubbing, until she cried out. 'No. No, not like that.'

He drew away with a gasp, what was he thinking of? His breath was coming fast, his mouth was dry and he licked his lips nervously.

'Not like that, Mr John.' Her eyes gazed into his and he was drowning. 'Slowly, slowly – to get 'blood warm.'

She reached out her hand and gently stroked his face, tracing patterns down his forehead and nose and out-lining his lips. He opened his mouth to take a breath and she slipped her fingers between, touching the smooth wetness inside his lips and probing the tip of his tongue with a sensuous touch until he groaned out loud.

He drew in a sharp breath as with her other hand, she slowly unfastened the row of buttons down the front of her dress, revealing the swelling curve of her breasts, and placed his hand upon them, arching her body towards him.

The pounding in his head and the fire in his loins threatened to engulf him as bewitchingly she incited him. He was unaware that she had loosened his shirt and breeches until he felt the scratching of her small sharp nails upon his buttocks and with a strangled cry he pulled away from her and started to tear off his shirt. She half sat up on his coat, her curving breasts pointed and nipples aroused. She gazed at him for a second as he struggled with his buttons and then started to fasten up her dress.

'We'd best be getting back,' she murmured, her eyes cast down. 'They'll be missing me.'

'What?' He looked at her unbelievingly. 'But you said—'

She looked up at him and smiled, then lowered her lashes demurely. 'We don't want to do summat we'd be sorry for, Mr John.'

'Oh, but please.' He was desperate, there was an ache inside him that must be assuaged. 'Please – just stay a little longer, you must.' He was begging now.

She shook her head as if shy, but there was a gleam

in her eyes that told him that perhaps she could be persuaded. He stroked her cheek and neck and fondled her tousled hair. 'You are so lovely.' The fire within him raged as he rained passionate kisses upon her. She resisted for a moment, then reaching up she drew him down towards her and the warmth of her body.

'If tha's sure, Mr John, that it's all right. That tha won't regret it after.'

'No, no, how could I?'

She lifted her skirts, inviting him to explore the delights of her velvety skin, the curves and valleys of her yielding body and the soft glade in which to lose himself.

He started to pant, his breath catching in his throat. He opened his mouth to shout but no sound came. Skilfully, she led him down the road to joy and willingly he followed in an exquisite, consuming frenzy. A tumultuous exultation overcame him as the climax came, and from far away he could hear her laughing softly.

Dazed, he lay on the crumpled coat and watched as she dressed, her face calm and unperturbed. The experience had been beyond all expectations, more magnificent than he had ever imagined. And yet now he began to feel uneasy. He was taking such a chance, what if they should be discovered? He thought guiltily of his uncle's reaction should he find out. He would consider that he had taken advantage of his position to romp with a servant girl, even though she had been a more than willing participant.

She caught him looking at her and gazed back at him. No decorous, blushing damsel, she leant forward and put her tongue between his lips, slipping it in and out like a small pink snake. 'There,' she said. 'Now, that'll have to last thee.'

He moved away and began to dress, his desire appeased. He felt a shameful need to get away before it was too late. 'I'm sorry, Susan,' he began.

She looked at him sharply, her fingers poised in the

act of untangling her dishevelled curls. 'Sorry? What for?'

'I – I hope I didn't hurt you.' His cheeks coloured and he was glad of the shadows. 'You know!'

She put her head down now and lowered her lashes. 'Not much. Just a little bit.'

'Are you – I mean, were you – a virgin?'

She turned her head away, and covered her face with her hands. 'How could tha say such a thing, Mr John? Tha knows very well that I was.' She took a deep breath like a sob and laid her hand on his arm imploringly and gazed into his face. 'I just hope my fayther never finds out!'

Leaving the barn, they walked in silence. He was full of remorse and cursing himself for a fool, and though she leant heavily on his arm she didn't attempt to speak to him. He watched her as she went round to the back of the house, through the yard to the kitchen door, and smiled ironically as he turned away and took the winding drive round to the front. Her wrenched foot seemingly had mended: there had been no sign of a limp, in fact she had almost skipped before turning to wave goodbye.

He handed his dusty greatcoat to Janey Reedbarrow who opened the door to him. 'Would you see that it is cleaned before I leave tomorrow, Janey? I must have brushed up against something.'

The girl bobbed and took it from him. ' 'Master was asking where tha was, sir. Supper will be ready in half an hour.'

He hurried upstairs to wash and change. He could hear his aunt's bell ringing furiously and he wondered what excuse Susan would make for being late. He eased off his boots and lay down on his bed, and a sudden smile creased his face. How marvellous – and yet how terribly wicked. His mortification began to dissipate now that he was safely back and undiscovered. All regret was vanishing as he felt renewed vigour and satisfaction flowing through his body. So this is what it is like, he observed to himself, savouring again the remembered delight. This is manhood.

'Where hast tha been?' Mrs Scryven's face was lit up with fury. 'Mistress has been ringing and ringing for thee. Tha'll catch it good and proper, and tha'll deserve it.'

Susan gazed unmoved into Mrs Scryven's face and then turned away to hang up her shawl. 'If tha must know, I went for a walk and I fell and twisted my foot, and it's taken me a long time to walk back.' She limped across to a chair and sat down and stretched out the offending limb.

Mrs Scryven viewed her suspiciously. 'Who was tha with? Tha's been wi' some village lad, I'll be bound. Just look at 'state of thee and thy clothes.' She pointed at her crumpled dress and disarranged hair.

Susan's upper lip curled. 'I've been with no village lad, nor will I.' She laughed. 'I've got more sense than that. There's bigger and better fish for catching than them round here.'

The round face of Mrs Scryven flushed with anger at the brazenness of the girl, but she was stopped in her brusque reply as the kitchen door opened and Janey came in carrying Mr John's coat, followed closely by Maria, who on seeing Susan gasped.

'Tidy thyself up and get upstairs this minute or I'll not answer for 'consequences.' She pushed her off the chair and out of the kitchen.

On reaching her mistress's door, Susan knocked hesitatingly and with a tear glistening in each eye told how she had caught her foot in a deep crack at the edge of the cliff and had lain in pain for a long time, hoping that someone would come, and finally as it got darker she had had to drag herself back, knowing that the mistress would need her. She gave a little sob as she finished her explanation and her lip trembled.

Isobel sighed impatiently. 'Well, don't let it happen again. If you must go walking make sure that it is somewhere safe and not so far from the house. I will not have my staff wandering all over the countryside when they should be indoors attending to their duties. But I will say no more this time. Be quick now and help me dress, Mr Masterson does not like to be kept waiting for his supper.' No sympathy was extended for the foot but neither was any expected, and Susan smiled her grateful thanks through the oval mirror as she carefully arranged her mistress's satin gown, and pinned on her ringlets.

'Don't go on about 'poor lass,' Maria gently chastised Mrs Scryven. 'She's not as bad as tha says.'

They were alone together in the kitchen early the next morning and Mrs Scryven's temper was not improved by the contrariness of the kitchen fire, which was emitting choking black smoke and no flame, making it difficult for her to cook or boil water for the Mastersons' washing.

Mrs Scryven shrugged and muttered, and then turned sharply to Maria. 'And I'm telling thee to lock up thy man. She's from a bad lot.'

'She might well be, but tha can't blame her for that,' Maria answered crossly as she laid the trays to take upstairs. 'It isn't right, especially when she's no mother to guide her.'

Mrs Scryven put her face near to Maria's and breathed softly, 'And does tha know why not? They make out that her ma's dead, but she's not. She's doing a good trade in some big town. Didn't like 'quiet life out here so she left. Took one daughter with her and left three others with him.'

'Poor man,' Maria murmured sympathetically.

'Poor man nowt,' was the hissed reply. 'What else should he expect? Where dost tha think he met her? Wasn't in church, I can tell thee. And don't feel too sorry for him, for them other two lasses keep him in little luxuries that tha can't afford from a village inn.'

'Even so,' Maria was lost for words. 'It doesn't make Susan—'

Mrs Scryven smiled slyly and nodded, she'd won her battle. 'Then tell me why half of 'village lads are always hanging round here? And not just lads. Martin Reed-barrow, who should know better, is always here with some excuse or other.' She put up her hand as she saw the look of protest on Maria's face. 'I know he's a free man now his wife's laid to rest, God bless her, but it doesn't make it right, not when he's got childre' as old as her.'

They discussed it no further, for Susan and Janey came into the kitchen and Lizzie followed, with a baby in each arm and Alice hanging on to her skirt, her thumb in her mouth.

'I'll take Mr John's tray,' Susan said. 'Janey, tha can take 'master's.' She picked up a tray laid with tea and thin slices of bread.

'It's all right Susan, I'll take it,' said Maria. 'Help Mrs Scryven with 'fire and hot water, and Janey, when tha's taken master's up, set 'sideboard for breakfast. Mr John 'll want a good meal afore he sets off back to Hull.' She smiled at Mrs Scryven. She didn't really believe all she had said, but it wouldn't do to take any chances.

When she knocked on John's door and entered to his reply, she found to her surprise that he was up and dressed. He had thrown the curtains wide to let in the daylight, and was seated on a chair pulling on his boots.

'Good morning, Maria, what a lovely morning.'

She glanced towards the window. It was cloudy and overcast and not very warm. 'Chance of rain, I think, sir. Were you thinking of leaving early?'

He shook his head and smiled at her, seemingly in very good spirits. 'No, Mr Masterson wants to go fishing first for an hour or two. We arranged it with Will yesterday. So tell Mrs Scryven to get her kettle ready, we shall have a shoal of fish for her to cook for dinner.'

'I'll do that, Mr John, and I'd best pack thee some vittals to take if tha's going to miss breakfast.' She laughed shyly, her cheeks flushing prettily and he laughed with her. She still sometimes forgot and spoke in the flat Hull dialect. She was not often careless when speaking with Mrs Masterson, for she knew how inflexible she was, and she hated to see those cold blue eyes fixed disdainfully on some forgetful wrongdoer, but not needing to be heedful with Mr John, she sometimes slipped back into her own unaffected manner.

As she returned downstairs she called to Janey who was about to enter the dining room with a tray of dishes with cold fowl, game and rolled herring, 'Take those dishes back to 'kitchen. They'll not be needed.' She also told Mrs Scryven, who had already started to cook kidneys and bacon, that breakfast wouldn't be needed yet after all.

'Can anybody else eat this afore I throw it out?' Mrs Scryven paused in the act of scraping the contents of the pan into a bucket. She would have to start again with fresh food when the gentlemen returned, she couldn't give them food that had been re-heated.

'Aye, I can!' Will poked his head around the door, and with a grin took the pan from her.

'Will Foster,' exclaimed Maria, 'tha's already eaten gruel.'

'Aye, but I'm a growing lad,' he said, chewing a crisp rasher of bacon. 'Besides, we're off fishing and it'll be a bit nippy out on 'ocean, tha needs plenty of fodder inside to keep out 'cold.'

Maria laughed at the thought of Will ever feeling the cold. He was so accustomed to freezing conditions whilst whaling that the biting east winds that blew along the coast affected him not at all.

'So get prepared, Ma,' he added to Mrs Scryven. 'There'll be a bucketful of fish for thee to cook.'

'I've already been told,' she replied sharply. 'So tha'd better clear off out of my kitchen and go and catch it, or we shan't be eating it till tomorrow.'

Will stowed away the basket of food that Maria had insisted they brought with them into the bow of the cobble and then sorted out the bait which he had gathered the day before. Sandworm and lugworm and boiled shrimps were best for hook and line fishing which was what they would do today. If they were lucky they might catch cod or flat fish, and there would be plenty of herring and mackerel.

He looked up from what he was doing as he heard a soft whinnying snuffle, and saw Martin Reedbarrow leading his mare down the slipway to help them launch. The sandy beach was quite shallow and not very suitable for launching a boat as heavy as a cobble, and a good deal of effort was needed to get it into deep water. Already it was chocked up on greased timber which, as the horse pulled, would roll the boat into the sea.

Up on the cliff top behind Martin he could see the small figure of Jimmy, who waved and shouted something to him. Will shook his head, he couldn't hear what he was saying.

'Can I come with thee?' Jimmy plunged down the slope and ran eagerly up to him, jumping up and down in his enthusiasm, his eyes bright with excitement. 'Tha said I could one day.'

'Aye, but not today. Not when 'master's here.'

'But—!'

'But nowt. I've told thee, not this time. I will take thee, and that's a promise. I'll take thee and our Tom and show thee both how to fish and sail.'

Jimmy turned sulkily away. 'I wouldn't be any bother.'

Will didn't answer him. Jimmy could be very persistent sometimes, so obstinately determined to get his own way that often it was easier to give in to him. He looked up again towards the cliffs where the soft red clay gushed a steady stream of water which ran down and round the interlaid layers of gravel, sand and boulders. If only Mr Masterson and John would hurry up. It was already late and they ought to have moved off an hour ago. The weather didn't look very promising, the wind was blowing hard and there was a heavy sea running. Then he saw the two men rounding the cliff top and making their way down the crumbling face by the broken steps.

'Beggin' tha pardon, sir.' Martin touched his forelock as they reached the sands. 'Them steps isn't safe. Tha'd be better off comin' down 'village road another time.'

'Yes, I think you're probably right.' Isaac was breathless with the effort of climbing down the uneven steps. 'It's a long way round, that's all.'

'If tha's ready, sir,' Will interrupted, 'we'd best be pushing off and getting under way.'

The two men were dressed in their warmest coats and woollen hats, though they weren't wearing their padded arctic jackets as Will was. He had discarded his fine leather boots today and brought out his old waterproof sea boots and was wearing just one, this and the stump of his wooden limb making an odd pattern in the damp sand.

'There she goes!' As the boat rumbled off the logs and the bow hit the water, Will and John hoisted themselves on board to join Mr Masterson who was already seated on the wooden planking. As they picked themselves up, John gave a gasp and then a laugh. 'Young varmint!'

A pair of small hands were clutching tightly to the side of the cobble and two thin legs dangled in the sea as Jimmy clung on desperately. As Will and John had pushed the boat, he, under the guise of helping, had flung himself on board in a frantic leap as the boat had hit the waves.

Furiously, Will yanked him on board. 'I'll give thee a taste of summat when I get thee home,' he hissed. 'I told thee tha couldn't come!'

Turning towards Mr Masterson, he apologized. 'I'm sorry, sir, I'll have to row back, 'water's too deep to put him over. Though I must say I've half a mind to drop him in it.'

'Leave him, leave him,' said Isaac. 'It'll maybe do him good and he won't be in such a hurry to stow away another time.' He stared good-humouredly at Jimmy

238

who was wringing the water from his breeches. 'A dose of seasickness should cure you.'

Jimmy grinned up at him. 'I'll not be sick.'

'Sir,' reminded Will sharply as he prepared to hoist the sail. 'Don't forget thy manners.'

'I'll not be sick, sir,' Jimmy repeated. 'I'm going to be a seaman like me fayther.'

Isaac looked puzzled for a moment and looked at Will. 'Is he one of your sons? I thought he was working on the land?'

'No, sir. This is Jimmy Swinburn, he lives with us until his ma comes to fetch him.' Will reckoned he could do without a parley on Jimmy just now. The wind was freshening from the north-east, inducing a long deep roll of the sea which broke high over the bow.

'Me fayther worked thy ships, sir. Alan Swinburn, he died on 'Polar Star.' Jimmy blinked his eyes as tears gathered and drew in a deep gasping breath. 'I'm going to be a harpooner and work on Masterson ships.'

Isaac Masterson nodded thoughtfully. He remembered Swinburn, not the most reliable of men, yet the company had a policy of looking after the families. 'Are you now? Well, you must come and see me when you're older and we'll see what can be done. What age are you?'

Jimmy drew himself up as straight as he possibly could from his position at the bottom of the boat. 'I'm ten, sir.'

'He's nearly seven, sir,' shouted Will over the noise of the wind. 'And he has an ower long tongue.'

John laughed cheerfully. 'I doubt he'll reach ten if he keeps throwing himself into the sea.' He reached for the sack of bait. 'Now, come on, young fellow, if you're staying on board then you must pull your weight, there are no passengers on this trip. You're in charge of the bait and you must make sure that the hooks are baited and ready for use as soon as we need them.'

The cobble was a robust boat, built to withstand the rigours of the rough and uneasy German Ocean. It had previously been used as a pilot boat, and was reliable and seaworthy, but it was not easy to handle and needed an experienced crew to manage the capacious four-cornered lug sail. Will soon found that he was skipper, for although Isaac Masterson had had many years of experience in sailing ships, he was quite willing to follow Will's instructions as the current took them out to the open sea.

They covered about four miles before they dropped anchor to fish. Mackerel and herring were in profusion, and for two hours they hauled in one fish after another until the baskets were stacked high with the glistening silver bodies. The white fish were not so plentiful, though they caught four small cod, and, to Jimmy's ultimate delight, he pulled in a flounder unaided.

'If tha's ready, sir, it would be prudent for us to get back.' Will had been watching the weather closely for the last half hour. The sky was rapidly darkening, a storm was gathering in the east, and the sea birds, foretellers of bad weather, were flying before it as they made for the shelter of land. Shrieking kittiwakes and noisy herring gulls flew above them as they headed for the safety of their nests on the lofty white chalk cliffs of Flamborough Head.

'Ready when you are, Foster. We've enough fish here to feed the village, so we'd better leave some for next time.' Isaac's face was red and blotchy with the wind and salt air and his eyes watered, but he had a look of satisfaction as he spoke.

'I can't imagine that this sea will ever run out of fish,' said John as he shifted a sack of sand ballast. 'What a harvest!'

As they weighed anchor the wind freshened and shifted, the sail filled and they clung on tightly to the straining ropes as the waves buffeted them, drenching them with salt spray.

They could barely see a smudge of land as they dipped and rose between the watery ridges, but they knew they were being carried further from their home base and northwards towards the sweep of the Bridlington headland.

'All right, Jim?' Will glanced down at the boy who sat below him. Jimmy nodded, not trusting himself to speak. His face was deathly white though his mouth was red as he clenched his lips together in a tight line. 'Here, tie this rope round tha waist,' Will shouted. 'Make a good knot and lash 'other end to thole pins. Then if tha wants to lean over 'side, tha'll be safe.'

'I'll not be sick,' the boy protested, but nevertheless he fastened the rope around him, and within a few minutes as the boat was flung high into the air and then sank low into the following trough, to his immense fury he succumbed to his first wave of seasickness.

'We'll have to seek shelter in Bridlington Quay, sir,' Will yelled, his voice hoarse as he battled to keep an even course. 'We won't make it back against 'wind. There's going to be a real blow.'

As he spoke the wind rose again, whipping up the frothy white spume as a huge wall of water hovered then broke above them, making them gasp for breath as it washed over them.

'Get hold of 'pigging and start bailing, Jimmy.'

Jimmy took hold of the wooden pail and, a true seaman's son, forgot his sickness as he bailed frantically, glad of the line which held him fast, while the three men fought to keep the cobble steady.

There was a fleet of vessels sheltering already in the safety of the bay as they approached the choppy, broken sea at the mouth of the harbour. The long, exposed coastline was renowned for the sudden shifting of currents, the vagaries of gusting winds and vaporous sea frets which came down in an instant to hide land from view. There were few sheltered harbours and the ships' masters and fishermen were glad to be within reach of a haven to protect them from the icy wind which blew across the northern waters.

A small boat rowed out to take them to shore as they dropped anchor in the deep water of the harbour. They loaded two baskets with fish and their gear and tipped two other baskets of fish back into the water.

'I'll try for a carriage, sir.' They had gone into the nearest inn and asked for a room where they could dry their clothes and get warm. 'You go inside, whilst I am making enquiries.' John hurried out into the street and Will drew Jimmy near to the fire, politely elbowing some of the blue-jerseyed seamen out of the way. 'Can he come by? 'Lad's wet through.'

Isaac hesitated in the doorway of the private room that the landlord had directed him to, then turned into it. There was a good fire burning and a pair of comfortable chairs. The landlord brought him a glass of ale and a hot rum and set it down on the table.

'My man and a boy are through in the other room. See that they get what they want, will you?'

John returned after ten minutes looking harassed. 'I've managed to get a carriage, but we have to pay double the price. The driver was very reluctant to take us. He says that he was along that way last week and the roads are waterlogged.'

'I don't mind what it costs,' Isaac replied testily. He was beginning to feel cold and shivery and he was very wet. 'I just want to get home and out of these wet clothes, and Isobel will be getting worried.'

The rain came down in torrents as they climbed into the carriage, and John realized that he would have to stay at Garston Hall another night. By the time they arrived there it would be too late to start the journey back to Hull. The roads were not good to travel on in the dark and besides he was too tired and wet, though not as tired and wet as he would be once he was away whaling, nor as cold. As he settled back on to the hard, unsprung, leather seat he was suddenly struck by a thought. 'Sir?' he said to Isaac. 'Would it be permissible to bring young Jim inside?'

'Why not? The boy looks frozen stiff, he wasn't really dressed for a fishing trip. Tell Foster to pass him down.'

So Will handed him down and Jimmy took his first

and only ride on the inside of a carriage, whilst Will turned up his collar and pulled down his hat over his ears and sat hunched next to the coachman, sharing with him the vista of the grey landscape seen through a curtain of pouring rain.

'Oh, I've been that worried about thee. I thought 'worst.' Maria flung her arms around Will and then Jimmy. She stripped the boy of all his clothes and stood him naked in front of the range. Mrs Scryven put a poker into the fire, went into the cold pantry and brought out a jug of ale and one of milk to make a hot posset.

'Try not to worry about me, Maria. What will be, will be. And besides,' Will gathered her up in his arms as he saw her anxious expression, 'don't ever forget that I'm a seaman, always will be. And if 'sea should take me when my time comes, then that's 'way I should want to go. No earthen grave for me with worms eating my flesh.' He smiled down at her and joked. 'I'd rather be floating with fishes, with seaweed in my beard. Now, come on, lass, dry thy tears and let's get started on that fish. We're starving, aren't we, Jim?'

The door opened and Tom came in. His hands were dirty and his face smeared with mud. He left his mudcaked boots by the door and sat wearily down in the nearest chair. 'By, I'm that tired, Ma. We've been trying to plough but it's that wet and clarty, 'oxen got stuck fast.'

Maria laughed as she heard Dick Reedbarrow's expressions coming from her son's mouth.

'Tha should have been wi' us, Tom.' Jimmy sipped his posset and grinned at Tom, his eyes alight. 'We've had a right grand time.' He proceeded to tell of the day's events, with several supplementary embellishments, and culminating with the ride inside the carriage.

'I'll take thee next time, Tom. Only we'll pick a better day.' Will smiled at his ploughboy son as he sat half asleep in the warmth of the kitchen.

'What?' Tom stirred himself and sat up blinking. 'I'm

not that bothered, Da. Dick said I can help with 'sowing as soon as 'weather changes and I thought I might make a patch at home. Plant some 'taties and cauliflowers and some corn. Tha'd like that, Ma?'

Maria nodded and smiled at his enthusiasm but glanced at her husband.

'But tha'd like to come fishing some time, wouldn't tha, son?' said Will slowly.

'Oh, aye. I'll come with thee, Da. If I have 'time. But I'm going to be a farmer, so I can only come when 'weather won't let me work 'land.'

His young face was earnest as he tried to make them understand, and Will felt a vague ripple of regret as he nodded in silent agreement, and wondered why, when the sea, which he believed coursed through his veins alongside his blood, hadn't run also into his only son.

'Do you realize that I have been alone all day, whilst you have been sitting out there in that silly boat. If you had wanted fish for dinner, I'm quite sure that Mrs Scryven could have ordered some.' Isobel walked up and down the drawing room in anger. 'It has been raining all afternoon and I couldn't even step outside to relieve the boredom.'

'I'm sorry, my dear. It was most unfortunate, but a terrible storm blew up and we were lucky to get back at all.' Isaac looked hurt. 'I thought at least you might be a little worried.' He blew his nose loudly. He was sure he'd caught a chill.

Loftily she gazed at him. 'Why should I be worried? You've been in shipping all your life. You're hardly likely to fall out of a little fishing boat.'

Sighing, he poured himself another brandy. 'No,' he said, 'you're perfectly right, of course.'

John took a stroll around the grounds after supper. His aunt had forgiven them and was genial enough at table. They had had an excellent meal of stuffed mackerel and baked cod and he felt relaxed and pleasantly tired and would soon go to bed, ready for an early start tomorrow. The rain had stopped and there was a fresh clean smell of wet earth and seaweed. He walked down to the edge of the garden where the pasture began and stood in the semi-darkness, his arms folded, listening to the murmuring of the waters and looking out at the dark streaked sky towards the horizon.

His senses alert to the sounds of the night, he was suddenly aware of a girl's laughter, and, with a sudden quickening of his pulse, he recognized it as Susan's. He drew back within the shelter of the hedge, for he didn't want to spy, nor did he want to startle her. She laughed again, a teasing, playful laugh which made his stomach tighten. She wasn't alone. He heard the answering deep voice of a man, one he had heard only today. They came into view, dark shadows against the skyline, their arms around one another, and then he with a laugh picked her up and swung her round as if she was as light as a feather, her legs and skirts swinging shamelessly.

He watched them as they returned to the house, skirting the forbidden garden, knowing their place, and returning via the stables and yard, unaware that they were being observed either by John or Will, in the shadows with a small sleepy child on his back and another one trudging wearily by his side as they made their way back home.

John didn't of course expect Susan to share in any aspect of his life, but the fact that she had led him from the greenness of youth to the delights of manhood gave him a sense of possession. He was hurt that she should turn from him to another so easily. He didn't remember now that he might have found himself in an undesirable predicament, and, as he walked back to the house, for the second time in his life he had a sensation of loss and felt very much alone.

15

John didn't return to Monkston for another six weeks
and then it was to say goodbye, for he was due to sail
on the *Polar Star* the following week. There was a first
sweet breath of spring in the air, a newness which seeped
into the house as they opened wide the windows
and doors, and into the bones of those who were
aware of it. Narcissi and crocuses were showing tips of
colour from within their shafts of green, and birds were
nesting, flying busily across the lush green lawns with
trailing straw and strands of sheep's wool in their
beaks, up into the gaps and crevices beneath the red-
brown pantiles and deep into the safety of the prickly
hedgerows.

'It'll be like stepping back in time, going back to winter
snow and ice,' said Maria.

John had slipped, unseen by his aunt, into the kitchen
to say goodbye to Maria. 'Yes, it is. It's like another
world out there, majestic, magnificent and terrifying.'

'God go with thee, Mr John, and tha'll be in our
thoughts, and Will especially will be thinking of thee out
on 'ice. He'll miss it, more than he'll ever say. We're
very lucky being here, and we've thee to thank for that,
but Will will be restless, I know, for a week or two after
'ship has sailed.'

'I was hoping to see him before I go,' he said. 'Do
you know where I can find him?'

'Aye, I do, but first come and say goodbye to my
babbies.' She led him to a warm corner of the kitchen
where the crib was hidden from any draughts.

'Here's thy cousin, Miss Lucy.' Lucy stared at him
from her pale blue eyes, her fine, fair hair almost
covering the faint scar on her forehead. Her bottom lip

246

trembled as he leaned smiling over her, and he pulled back in alarm.

'It's all right,' laughed Maria, 'she's a bit careful who she smiles at. She smiles at 'master and she smiles at me who feeds her, and she loves Sarah and Lizzie, but for 'rest she only tolerates them.'

'So, a real lady,' he said, 'and what of Sarah, will she give me a smile?' He reached into the other end of the crib, and Sarah with an excited squeal grabbed hold of the short fair beard which he had been trying to grow for weeks as protection against the cold winds of the arctic. He picked her up and she made no objection save to hold on tighter to his whiskers. Removing her fingers from his hair, he held them to his lips and blew noisy raspberries through them. She chuckled in glee and patted his face with her other plump hand.

'Oh, Sarah, will you be faithful until I return home, I wonder, or will you give your heart to someone else whilst I'm gone?'

Maria smiled as she took her from him. 'We'll keep reminding her that she owes a lot to thee, Mr John.'

'No, never do that, Maria,' he protested. 'I only want her to know that I was here at the beginning of her life, and that she'll always be someone very important.'

He left them then and used the back door to go and look for Will. As he rounded the stable block he almost bumped into Susan. He nodded politely and walked on, but she turned to him. 'I hear as you're going away – sir,' she added, almost as an afterthought.

'Indeed, yes.' He gave her no more information, and with a slight smile moved on.

'Mr John?' She held him back with her mild words and reluctantly he turned.

'Are you going to be away for long?' Her eyes held his.

He shrugged his shoulders, confused by her presence and lost for words. 'Possibly.'

'Would you like to say goodbye properly?' Her smile would have melted an icecap. 'I could slip away.'

He was amazed at her boldness, though her voice and manners were modest and unassuming. Yet as he watched her, his colour mounting in embarrassment, he thought he caught a challenge in her eyes, defying him to refuse her offer and mocking his caution.

'I think not. We were perhaps a little foolish.' He was defensive, yet didn't want to offend her. 'You are very beautiful, Susan, and I – we – let our emotions carry us away in the heat of the moment. I would not want to upset your chances of a worthwhile relationship with someone else.' He cleared his throat. 'Someone who could perhaps offer you more than I can.'

Her nostrils quivered and she smiled a twisted, derisive smile. 'Tha's talking of marriage? Somebody of my own class, tha means?'

'Yes, of course,' he said. 'For you must know that I can offer you nothing.'

She turned away, contempt souring her lovely face. 'We'll see about that, sir.'

He stood staring after her. There was a definite threat in her tone. She surely wouldn't tell his uncle? If she did, it would mean instant dismissal for her and acute embarrassment for him. He could never look another woman in the face again if word got out, though his male friends would think it fine sport, not to have tumbled a serving maid, but having been found out.

'What am I to do, Will?' he asked when he eventually tracked him down in the wood where he was splitting logs. 'I've upset a young woman. My own stupid fault, I just got carried away and I'm very much afraid that she feels I've let her down.'

'Did tha promise her owt? Marriage or such?'

'Good heavens, no. Nothing like that, that would be quite out of the question.' His brow creased into lines. 'But I got the impression she thinks I owe her something.'

'Mmm. Is this 'same young woman that tha'd fallen in love with 'last back end when tha was here?' Will bent to pick up a log and hid a wry smile.

248

'Yes, the same. But I know better now, she's not what she seems.' He gave a deep sigh. 'I even have my doubts as to whether she was a virgin.'

Will put on an expression of grave shock. 'Tha never bedded a maiden, sir?'

John had the grace to blush and stammeringly answered, 'Well, she said she was.'

'Oh, aye. Well, and of course tha would know.' Will nodded thoughtfully. 'Of course tha would. Well, now tha knows what happens when tha plays with fire – tha gets tha fingers burned.'

'Yes, I realize now, but what am I to do?' He paced up and down the patch of woodland in his agitation.

'Well, what I would advise thee to do,' said Will, sitting down on a tree stump and wearily stretching his aching leg, 'I would recommend a sea voyage. Preferably somewhere far away, like Greenland, and stay there until she gets tired of waiting for thee.'

'Do you think that she will forget about it? That it will have blown over by the time I get back?' John's face lightened with relief, then darkened again at Will's reply.

' 'Course, she might be so besotted with thee, that tha'll never be able to set foot on land again.' Will saw no reason to let his young friend off lightly, and considered that a few weeks ruminating on the folly of his ways was the best remedy for the rashness of his indiscretion.

John sat down on the log beside him and moodily stared down at the ground. 'Why aren't you wearing your new boots?' he asked suddenly.

Will was silent for a moment. 'It's a sort of protest,' he said bluntly.

'I don't understand.'

'No, I don't expect tha would.' He got up from the log and walked up and down, swinging his leg exaggeratedly. 'Out here, on my own, I can be myself – Will Foster, 'man with one and a half legs. I don't have to pretend, like I do with my boots on, that nowt has happened and I'm just 'same as I ever was.'

249

John rubbed his fingers through his beard. 'It's me, isn't it? It's because I'm sailing on the *Polar Star* and you're not?'

Will turned his back and looked out towards the sea, unseen because of the dip of the land but its presence known by the persistent, rhythmic thrashing of the waves across the sands.

'Aye, that's it, I suppose. It's just a year since my last voyage.' He turned to face him, his face bitter. 'I know I'm lucky. This is a job that hundreds would give their other leg for. But it doesn't help me when I know that men are going off to do a man's work, and I'm here – a servant at 'Big House – out of sight and hearing, unable to hold my head up as a man should.'

'I had no idea that you felt this way, Will. I thought you'd settled here.'

'Oh, aye. I've settled all right, even Maria's settled when she thought she wouldn't.' He put his hand on John's shoulder. 'It's difficult to explain. It's not that I don't like it here, I do. I like to be here by 'sea. 'Air's good and we've got a grand house. It's just that I've never been behodden to anybody before, apart from ship's master, and I was always treated as a man by him, as part of a team.' His face soured. 'Not hidden away like something too ugly for ladies to look at.'

He stopped as he saw the expression of pain on John's face. 'I'm sorry, Mr John. I don't mean to chide. I've just got an attack of gripes. I'll be all right when 'ship has sailed.'

'Mr John?' John frowned. 'You've never called me that before.'

'No, sir. But thou art 'master's nephew and it's time I learned my place.' He put out his hand to shake John's. 'Now be on thy way, young mariner, and God speed thee home again.'

John turned and looked towards the wood as he reached the crest of the undulating meadow, but Will had turned his back. He was holding an axe, his arms high, and, as John watched, he brought it down on to the timber with a resounding crash.

The whaling ships plying the northern seas sent messages home with the crews of other ships who were sailing back into port, and Isaac reported that he had heard from the *Polar Star*. 'They've reached the Orkneys. The sea is calm and they should be sailing in a few days as soon as they've finished taking on supplies and extra crew.'

Isobel dismissed Susan from the room as Isaac came in with the news. He looked tired: he had spent most of the last two weeks in Hull since John had sailed, and was discovering just how indispensable his nephew was.

'I miss that boy, but he has to go.' Wearily he sank into a chair and reached for the brandy decanter on the table beside him. 'It's so important that he learns every aspect of the business if he's to take over from me eventually.'

Susan moved silently away from outside the door where she had stayed listening and smiled archly to herself. She slipped into the kitchen and gaily greeted Will, who was bringing in baskets of logs for the fires.

'How do, Will.' She glanced around the kitchen. Mrs Scryven's back was turned and Maria and Janey were out of the room. She reached up and gently tugged his beard, drawing herself up close so that her lips were close to his, and said softly, 'Is tha well, this fine day?'

He removed her hand from his beard and playfully smacked her rump as he would a child. But it was no child who boldly caught his hand and held it for a moment as she waited for his reply.

'I'm well enough,' he said, withdrawing his hand. She smiled, amusement showing in her eyes, and raising her eyebrows moved away as Mrs Scryven turned around.

He scratched his head thoughtfully as Mrs Scryven gazed stonily at him and at Susan's retreating back as she went out of the door.

251

'She's trouble, that lass. Just mark what I say, Will. She's out to cause trouble.' She pointed a wet, urgent finger.

Will shrugged. 'Not for me, Ma, I won't be tempted. But I can see she might lead some poor fellow a dance.' He smiled a wide, disarming smile. 'Somebody not used to 'wiles and tricks of women like I am.'

'Hmph, there's no man yet who can best a woman if she's set her mind to it.' She came up close to him, the top of her head reaching only halfway up his chest so that he had to bend his head down to hear her whispered words. 'If tha has a friend who needs a word of warning, then give it, before it's too late.'

Maria came into the kitchen with a basket of clean linen on her hip and stood watching them with an amused expression. 'And thee my best friend, Ma Scryven, I would never have thought it of thee.'

'Aye, well, we're never too old, or too young,' she answered darkly. 'So don't say tha wasn't warned.'

Will remembered her words a few days later when Martin Reedbarrow sought him out. 'I hope tha doesn't mind, Will. But seeing as we're of an age, I thought I'd ask thee first, for I don't want to mek a fool of missen.'

'Ask me what?' Will looked up at the broad-shouldered countryman who topped him by a couple of inches, but who wouldn't look him in the eye and kept his gaze firmly on his boots as they walked along the cliff top.

'I'm thinking on getting wed,' he said, a slow blush crimsoning his face.

'There's nowt wrong with that as far as I can see, Martin. Tha's a free man.'

'Oh, aye,' said Martin. 'That's not a worry. My poor lass has been buried this last twelvemonth, and it's hard, I can tell thee, trying to bring up a family without a woman. Youngest babby's gone to Tillington to be nursed, and our Nellie does well to look after other childre', 'though she's only a bairn herself.'

'Well, tha'd best be getting wed then, if tha can find

somebody willing to take thee and thy brood on board.'

'That's just it. Lass I'm tekken with is only 'same age as our Janey and I don't know if it's right.'

'If tha's both willing, then it's right enough. But I can't see a young maid tying herself down with a readymade family 'size of yours.'

Martin shuffled his feet. 'Well, she's almost said as she will. 'Says as I'm 'sort of man she cares for.' He shook his big head from side to side. 'I'll tell thee, Will, I can't believe as how somebody like her would look at 'likes of me. I'm fair bowled over. I'm on fire wi' thought of it.'

Will's brows furrowed anxiously. 'Well, that's as may be, but it doesn't mean she'd make thee a good wife and mother for thy bairns. Fancying looks of some lass isn't same as sharing thy life with her.'

Martin looked defiantly at him. 'Well, she's shared my bed already, said she trusted me to look after her and make it right.' A look of pure beatification lit up his open, honest face, then, as he saw Will watching him, he looked away in confusion. 'Anyway, I've made my mind up. I shall ask her next time I see her.'

They stopped as they came to the boundary of Garston land and Martin cut through a gap in the hedge. 'I shan't care what folk say. If it's what we want, it's nowt to do wi' anybody else.'

'Nobody's saying it's not right, Martin. Just be sure, that's all, don't let her string thee along.' Will smiled to lighten the mood. 'I'm not saying tha's a fine catch, but tha's got a good piece of land and tha needs some strong lass to help thee with it, not some flibbertigibbet who doesn't know how.'

Martin's face flushed with anger. 'Susan's no flibbertigibbet. She's a good worker. She ran her father's inn practically singlehanded before she came here. He was nowt but a tyrant, that's why she left.'

Will rubbed his beard in bemusement: the situation was beyond him. He could see that if he said anything more, Martin's temper would explode, and he was obviously so blinded by the girl's charms that his judgement was impaired.

He looked out at the grey sea, barely a ripple disturbing its flat surface, unable to look Martin in the eye. 'I didn't realize it was Susan that tha was talking about. Well, if tha's made up thy mind, I'll wish thee well. She's a fine looking lass.'

Martin frowned at him from over the top of the newly budding hedge. 'Aye, I meant Susan. Who else is there round here? And I'll thank thee to treat her wi' respect. I've told thee all of this in confidence, remember?'

Will swallowed hard. He had no wish to fall out with Martin. He raised a hand as he turned to walk back. 'I'll remember, Martin, I wish thee luck with thy plans.'

Susan waited another two weeks before confronting Mrs Masterson. She drew a faint smudge of soot beneath her eyes to darken them, and on her rosy cheeks she brushed some flour.

'I am visiting the Smallwoods for dinner, Susan. Tell Walters to have the carriage at the door in an hour, and I think I shall wear my grey—' She stopped as Susan leant on a chair and put a hand to her head. 'What is the matter with you? If you are feeling ill, leave the room at once and send Mrs Foster to attend to me.'

'No, no, ma-am, I'm not ill. Leastways – not exactly.' She clasped her hands together imploringly and took a deep, sighing breath. 'Oh, ma-am, I don't know how to tell you.' She hung her head and gave a shuddering moan. 'But I must.'

Isobel surveyed her in horror. She was going to tell her something perfectly appalling, she could tell. She sat down and reached for her smelling salts. 'Do I really need to know?' she said faintly, 'If you've been falling out with the other servants, then you must settle it between you.'

'No, ma-am, it's not as simple as that. Oh, how I wish that it was.' A tear slipped down Susan's cheek and she carefully wiped it away with a piece of clean white linen.

Isobel leant back in her chair, closed her eyes and waited. She might have known that things were going too smoothly. The household was running well, her social life improving now that she was getting to know people. There was bound to be something to spoil it.

'Well, come along then, if I have to know, then you'd better tell me.'

'You're not going to like it, ma-am, and I would hate for you to turn against me.' The girl gave a little sob and turned a tear-stained innocent face to her mistress.

Isobel sighed and silently waited.

' 'Fact is, ma-am, I'm in trouble. In 'family way.' She put her hands to her face and her shoulders shook with silent, shuddering sobs.

Isobel rose to her feet, a look of disgust on her face. 'You wicked, wicked girl. How dare you – and in my employ.' She turned away so that she didn't have to look at her. 'You will have to leave immediately. I can't possibly keep you here now.'

'Yes, ma-am, I realize how wicked it was – but, but, it wasn't all my fault, ma-am.'

Isobel turned towards her and regarded her contemptuously. 'Don't pretend to me, young woman,' she said icily. 'No woman should put herself in a situation where a man can take advantage of her.'

'But I trusted him, ma-am. On account of who he was. I never thought that he would force me.' She broke into loud sobbing.

'For goodness sake control yourself, Susan.' She glared at the girl. 'Are you telling me that someone forced his attentions on you?'

'Yes, ma-am.'

'And you were not a willing, er, participant?'

She shook her head, her hands covering her face in shame.

'Then he should be horsewhipped. Is it a local man? Someone you were seeing regularly?'

Susan raised her head and stared at her mistress with

open eyes. 'No, ma-am. I said as how you wasn't going to like it, ma-am.'

Isobel felt a cold fear clutch at her heart. Not Isaac. He wouldn't, would he? No, not even though he no longer shared her bed. Not with a child such as this, not under his own roof.

Coldly she stared back at the girl. 'What is it you are trying to say? Is it one of the men here?'

That was it, of course. It had to be one of the staff. A sudden wave of anger swept over her. Will Foster, it was probably him. Well, it would serve Isaac right for employing him, giving him too much authority, now he'd have to get rid of him as well as the girl. But then Maria would go as well and she couldn't do without her. Oh, what a mess.

She was sure that Isaac would be sympathetic, probably even want to keep the girl on in their employ. He would say it was their duty and dismiss her own views on servants' morals as being petty and narrow-minded.

'Not one of 'servants, ma-am.' Susan paused to let her words sink in, then with her head hung down, she wrung her hands together and whispered. 'A gentleman, ma-am.'

Isobel lowered herself carefully into a chair. 'A gentleman? No gentleman would do such a thing.' As she spoke she knew it wasn't true. It would be considered no more than sport for some young buck to take advantage of a servant girl, willing or not. She racked her mind to think of who had visited the house who would be capable of such unprincipled behaviour.

Susan lifted her head and looked her mistress straight in the eyes. 'Mr John, ma-am.'

She sat dumbfounded, her tongue and brain frozen, unable to speak. Susan reached for the smelling salts and silently handed them to her, but she waved them away.

'How dare you say such a thing,' she croaked as her voice returned. 'My nephew is the last man to—' Words failed her.

Susan nodded her head. 'Mr John it was, ma-am. That

day when I was late back. When I said that I'd hurt my foot. I was afraid to tell you, ma-am. I thought as you wouldn't believe me – and I didn't want you to dismiss me. It was in 'barn, ma-am, he made me go in with him.'

'Stop. Stop this minute,' Isobel screeched. 'Spare me the sordid details. Get out of here. I will speak to you later, and do not discuss this with the other servants.'

'No, ma-am,' said Susan meekly, dropping a curtsey as she went, 'of course I won't.'

Isobel calmed herself and then rang the bell loud and long. Maria, hurrying up the stairs, passed Susan coming down.

'What's wrong?' Maria was anxious. Susan usually answered the mistress's bell.

Susan shrugged her shoulders. 'Got a fit of 'vapours if tha asks me. I can't do owt right for her.'

Maria waited for her mistress to speak. She was obviously upset about something, her cheeks were flushed and she had run her fingers through her immaculate curls, disarranging strands of hair which hung around her forehead.

'Maria, help me dress, that girl Susan is useless. I'm going to be late for my dinner, and I don't suppose she has told Walters to bring the carriage.'

'I'm sorry, ma-am, I'll do it, I can't think what's got into her. I'll give her a good talking to.' She helped her mistress into a padded, whaleboned frame and slipped her grey silk gown over the top.

'I may decide to get someone else to dress me, she really is most unsatisfactory.'

Maria couldn't hide her astonishment. She had thought that Susan could do no wrong. Mrs Masterson always sent for her rather than anyone else. 'Has she misbehaved, ma-am, for if so?' Maria knew that instant dismissal was normal in that case.

'In a manner of speaking, but I don't wish to discuss it. Not until I have spoken to Mr Masterson.' She had already said more than she intended.

'Would you like Janey to attend you, ma-am? She's very well behaved and quiet.'

'Very well, she can attend me when I return. She's a village girl, isn't she? At least that should please the locals,' she added waspishly.

As the carriage trundled along the potholed road towards her neighbours in the next village, she pondered on the dilemma. If the story was true then they would have to pay the girl to keep her quiet, for although it was not unusual for sons of gentry to father bastards, to Isobel the thought was repugnant. She felt that the family would be the laughing stock of the area if word got out, and that she could never again face society. John shall answer for this, she thought angrily. It seems he sailed just in time, but I shall be waiting for him on his return.

The following evening when Isaac returned from his business she told him, and let him know in no uncertain terms of her feelings on the matter.

'Wild oats, my dear, wild oats. I agree that it is most unfortunate that it should happen right here on our doorstep, hmm, so to speak, but it is a fact of life that these things happen.' He chuckled, then changed it to a cough as Isobel glared at him. 'She's a beauty all right, he probably just got carried away. And she might well have been willing, no matter what she says to the contrary.'

'I dare say that you think it is of no consequence,' his wife said coldly, 'but I have now to find another maid, for I can't possibly keep her under the circumstances.'

'Plenty of young girls in the village who will be more than willing to come, my love, don't you worry about that. I should imagine that once they hear that Susan is going they will be lining up at the door.' He stopped as his wife gazed icily at him. 'Not that we will want to shout it from the roof tops, of course. Give the girl another shilling if you think it will keep her quiet, and then when John comes home and admits that the child is his, he must contribute towards it. That'll teach him to be more careful in future.'

Isobel sent for Susan the next day. The girl looked well and the roses were back in her cheeks, and though she hung her head, suitably chagrined, as Isobel lectured her, she wasn't as subdued as she might have been.

'So we have decided that you are to be given your wages and a sum of money to help you, although of course that does not imply that we accept that our nephew is responsible. That will be decided when he returns, for as you know he is at present at sea and will not be back for some considerable time.'

'Could I speak, ma-am?' Susan raised her head and looked at Isobel, her violet eyes deep and fathomless. 'It's just that I wanted to tell you that I'm courting a young man, and that I had to tell him what happened.'

Isobel drew herself up straight and was about to speak.

'I had to tell him, ma-am,' Susan hurried on. 'I was that upset, and he wanted to know why I kept on crying, and even though I know you said I hadn't to tell a soul, well, I had to in the end, and he said that even though I was spoiled – well, he would wed me and bring 'bairn up like it was his own.'

She watched unblinking as Isobel heaved a silent sigh of relief. Then she smiled and for some reason Isobel was reminded of a little cat she had once had which used to chase the mice in the garden, patting and pawing, chasing and releasing.

' 'Only thing is, ma-am, he doesn't have any money to get wed. He was hoping to set up on his own, but if he weds me and a babby coming along, well, it won't be easy.' A tear glistened, 'I don't know what other chance I've got, ma-am. Me fayther won't have me for sure, he's that narrow. I should have to go on charity.'

Isobel tried hard not to appear too relieved. 'Very well, I'll see what can be done. How much money would this young man require?'

'Ten pounds, ma-am.' The reply was sharp and decisive.

Isobel's eyes opened wide at the sum.

'He's got 'offer of a bit of land, ma-am,' the girl went on quickly before she could raise any objection. 'It's not very good, as all 'best has been sold to 'big landowners,' she smiled sweetly, 'but it's over near Beverley, so I should be out of 'district.'

Isobel made up her mind instantly. She was sure that there would be money in the house, though it was a pity Isaac wasn't here. She really didn't have a head for figures and it did seem an uncommonly large amount just for a miserable piece of land. But she would tell him on his return. 'Very well, that does seem to be the best solution, although it is a very large sum of money. I hope he uses it well.'

Susan smiled, her face lit with pleasure. 'Oh, he will, ma-am, he will. I'll make sure of that.'

The next day with the money handed over and safely tucked under her skirt, Susan made her departure. She packed her box and left it in the room which she shared with Janey and slipped out of the kitchen door. Mrs Scryven, busy stuffing a fowl for the evening meal, looked up as the door banged and lifted her head towards the window.

'Where's that young hussy gone to?' she demanded later as Maria came in. 'She's been out some time and I need her to take in 'tray to 'mistress.'

'She's out of favour with 'mistress, Ma,' said Maria. 'I'll go in with it.'

Isobel was sitting gazing down into the garden, her sewing lying idly on her lap. The scent of newly cut grass mingled with the perfume of spring flowers and drifted in through the open window. Narcissi were nodding their heads in the soft breeze, their pale yellow heads reflecting the afternoon sun. Bluebells and violets unfolded beneath the flowering almond trees, and blue and white periwinkle trailed and twisted into tangled wreaths beneath the blossoming blackthorn hedge.

'Are you glad you came here, Maria?' was the surprising question as Maria put down the tray.

Maria hesitated. 'Yes, I think so, ma-am. Though I miss Hull and all my old friends. But I'm very happy here, ma-am,' she added quickly lest she sounded ungrateful. She glanced out of the window to the smooth green grass and neat edges and clipped laurel bushes. 'And I love 'smell of flowers and grass.' She laughed and turned towards her mistress. 'It's better than 'smell of blubber, ma-am.'

Isobel nodded in agreement, her thoughts elsewhere.

'But it's 'sea that I can't get used to.' Maria stared out of the window, forgetting where she was and who she was with. 'Tha can always hear it. 'Sound never goes away. Constantly calling, telling me summat and I don't know what.'

Isobel, drawn from her reverie, turned sharply. 'I hope you are not fey, Maria. I cannot tolerate that sort of nonsense.'

'Oh, no, ma-am, I'm not, though I believe my mother was.' She refrained from telling Mrs Masterson of the strange sensations that sometimes came over her, which she was sure had some hidden meaning that she couldn't comprehend. She had attempted to explain them to Mrs Scryven, who she hoped would understand, but who only nodded her head, smiled a gentle smile and said quietly, 'We'll face what comes.'

'I wanted to ask you about Susan, ma-am. She went out this afternoon and hasn't come back yet.'

'I've dismissed her, so she won't be coming back.' Isobel's tone was curt. 'She has misbehaved. You can look for another girl for the house and I will have Janey to attend me. She is very obedient and will suit me, I think, once I've polished her rough, country ways.'

'Yes, ma-am.' Maria hid her astonishment. 'Where shall I send Susan's things?'

Isobel shrugged. 'I've really no idea. Perhaps her father will collect them. I expect she will stay with him until she marries her young man.'

Maria smiled and raised her eyebrows. 'Will said that Martin was going to ask for her, but I didn't realize he already had. We didn't think she'd have him.'

'Martin?' said Isobel as she sipped her tea.

'Martin Reedbarrow, ma-am, Janey's father. He's not a young man though. About 'same as my Will, I'd say.'

Isobel frowned. 'Where does he live, this man.'

'In 'village, ma-am. He's got a nice piece of land.' She shook her head sorrowfully. 'But he badly needs a wife for all his poor motherless bairns.'

'No,' said Isobel slowly. 'That isn't him. Someone else, I understand. Thank you, Maria, that will be all.'

Will was riding back from the mill at Aldbrough when he saw Susan on the carrier's cart travelling in the opposite direction. She waved cheerfully and blew him a kiss and then put her finger to her lips and winked impudently. He gazed after the cart in surprise, and then grinned. She was up to something, no doubt about it, for she shouldn't have been out in the middle of the day. She'd be in trouble if she was found out, which she certainly would be, though he wouldn't give her away.

Martin ranted and raved when he found out Susan had gone. 'I've been made a fool of, Will, by a slip of a lass. Why, if I knew where she was, I'd give her a right tanning and bring her back, just like I would our Janey.' His confusion was increased by the ale he had drunk as he wallowed in his cups at the village inn.

'No, tha wouldn't,' said Will as he watched his friend unsteadily pour himself another tankard. 'Tha's not first to fall for a young lass, and she isn't thine to bring back. She'd made thee no promises.'

'But what I can't understand.' Martin leaned drunkenly across the table to peer at Will. 'Where's she gone? I've searched and asked for three days and nobody's seen sight nor sound of her since she left Garston Hall. Not even her fayther. Her poor old fayther who says he's worried out of his mind. Poor old gaffer.' His eyes filled with tears.

'I shouldn't worry about her, Martin. I'm sure she'll

come to no harm,' said Will, with the vision of the carrier's cart heading for town and the smiling figure of Susan on it still fresh in his mind. 'She's got a good head on her shoulders.'

'Aye, she has, and a lot more than that, I can tell thee.' He put his head down on the ale-puddled table. 'But I was right smitten, Will,' he moaned, 'I was right smitten.'

'I suspect the young minx might have fooled us, my dear,' mused Isaac as Isobel told him what she had learned from Maria.

'But why should she want to do that? She was so lucky to be here.' Isobel was nonplussed.

'It isn't everyone's idea of bliss, being cut off in the countryside, you know. Especially a young, attractive female.' He glanced sideways at his wife. 'She's probably heading for Hull and all its amusements. She might not even be, er, in trouble at all.'

Isobel was shocked. 'Surely she would not make up such a dreadful story?'

'It is quite possible, I'd say.' He put his thumbs in his waistcoat pocket and smiled cynically. 'It's just as well we only decided to give her an extra shilling or so, she might have asked for more.'

Isobel turned pale. She would have to tell him, he would be sure to find out. 'She did,' she said. 'I gave her ten pounds.'

'You gave her what?' Isaac's mouth dropped open.

She didn't feel the necessity to repeat the amount. There was nothing wrong with his hearing.

'Then she might well have fooled us,' he said gravely, 'but there's not a thing we can do about it. We have no proof that what she said about John was, or was not true. Not until he comes home, and then it will be too late to take any action.' He laughed suddenly, throwing his head back. 'Imagine that,' he spluttered. 'Imagine being taken in by a slip of a country girl.'

* * *

Eleven months passed before the *Polar Star* returned to her home port, her decks and timbers torn and battered where she had been frozen into the ice. She had been heaved clean out of the water by the crushing, cracking pressure of an advancing floe, and held in a vice-like grip by the relentless ice which piled above her, there to remain until the thaw set in.

There had been little food left and the crew were put on short rations, with the result that scurvy manifested itself. Four men died of the disease and two more from cold and exhaustion. Some of the sick men were carried across the field of ice on the backs of their healthier shipmates and transferred to ships which were still afloat, but many other ships were trapped themselves in that ferocious landscape and were in danger of being torn apart.

'He's lost, isn't he, Isaac?' Isobel had said sadly. 'Our poor dear John is gone from us?'

Isaac had put his arm around his wife's shoulders comfortingly and shook his head. 'We won't give up hope, not yet awhile.'

Maria and Will too were uneasy that long winter. Maria wished that she could go down to the jetty at the mouth of the River Hull and keep watch down the broad expanse of the Humber, as she knew that wives and mothers and sweethearts would be doing as they waited anxiously for the ship's return and that of the other missing vessels. Will stared out across the sea from the safety of land, his senses in turmoil as he prayed for the protection of the men and boys who defied the seething water, and remembered the cold which froze their beards, their food and fingers, and the fear of the closing, advancing ice.

It was decided not to mention the matter of Susan, for John was thin and ill when he finally came home, and Isobel was so relieved to see him safely back that she carefully obliterated the incident from her mind. Besides, the girl had not been seen in the district since the day she left.

He spent a month at Garston Hall, sitting in the garden when it was fine with a blanket wrapped around him, and being nourished by Mrs Scryven's cooking. He was an older, soberer man, his youthful vigour had temporarily deserted him, and the dreadful voyage had had a profound effect on his view of the world.

Whereas his first voyage on the *Polar Star* had been challenging and dangerous, and the sight of the towering icebergs had filled him with awe and excitement, with the youthful certainty of his immortality he hadn't felt at any time that his life was in danger. On this passage there had been many times as he had chipped away at chunks of glacier ice to supplement their fresh water supply, or made hazardous journeys across the ice on foot to shoot birds and seals to add to their dwindling amount of salt meat and biscuit, when he had thought that he would never see his home or family and friends again.

He watched with quiet amusement as his cousin Lucy and Sarah tottered unsteadily by Lizzie's side. One silky fair head and one tangled mop of red curls played happily together in the room at the top of the house which had been designated a nursery.

As he recovered, fed on quantities of Mrs Scryven's Yorkshire Pie, the topping of thick crust hiding deep layers of tender pigeon flavoured with sweet bay and lovage, a cure, she assured him, for a weary traveller, he began to have qualms of conscience. He thought of his companions from the ship who had no such comfort as this, and of the widows who had been left to fend for themselves, and one fine morning he rose and packed his bag and returned to Hull. His aim was to improve conditions for the seamen who sailed in Masterson ships, that their life on board, though perilous, might have some little comfort, and in this he had his uncle's full support.

Will saw little of his former shipmate, and John's visits to Monkston were less frequent as he became more and more involved in the whaling industry. Isaac made him a partner, and their company prospered with the

265

addition of his youthful enthusiasm and as the need for blubber and whalebone continued to rise. More industries sprang up to produce oil for lighting and heating, lubricants for machinery, household goods like brushes and blinds, as well as the accessories of fashion, stays and corsets and parasols.

Increasingly, decisions were left to Will with regard to the running of the farm. Though Dick Reedbarrow decided when to plough and when to sow, Will found that he could strike a good bargain in the buying of stock and grain, and his reputation increased with the local farmers. He had regular fortnightly discussions with Isaac Masterson when he would report on problems and policies, and yet he never met his master's wife face to face until Lucy and Sarah were four years old.

He walked one day alongside the coppiced woodland, where the hazel was sending up a dense mass of thin straight shoots which soon they would split and use for sheep fencing and securing thatch to the cottage roofs, or making supports for hay ricks. He could smell the sweet aroma of hay as he turned towards the meadow. The weather had been fine and dry and the men had turned the hay, exposing it to the sunlight and ensuring a good crop of dry winter feed for the livestock.

He smiled as he heard the sound of childish laughter and looked over the hedge into the garden where Lucy and Sarah were playing. Lizzie was nearby and she waved to him cheerfully.

'Chase me, Sarah,' Lucy called. 'Chase me, and then I'll chase thee.'

He stopped to watch them as they ran around the garden, laughing as Lucy took a tumble head over heels into the shrubbery. She started to laugh and then her laughter turned to tears and she started to scream shrilly in pain.

'It bit me, it bit me,' she screamed as an angry cloud of wasps flew up from the ground where she had fallen and buzzed menacingly around her head.

Will ran round the side of the hedge and into the

garden and scooped up the hysterical child, then came to a sharp stop in front of Mrs Masterson.

Isobel had been strolling idly on the terrace, her cream parasol held above her head to keep away the sun and the insects which were such an annoyance to her. She heard the children calling and descended the stone steps into the garden, calling to Lizzie in admonishment at the clamour they were making as they chased around the lawn, when Lucy fell and she found herself face to face with Will Foster.

'She's all right, ma-am. Just a wasp sting. She must have fallen on to a nest. I'll get 'gardener to smoke them out.'

Isobel gazed at him in confusion, her cheeks flushing slightly. She had avoided him for so long, not daring to face his disability, and now he was standing in front of her, tall and straight and her own child clinging to him with her arms around his neck. For the need of something to do she put her hand up to comfort the fretful child, although the crying exasperated her.

'Don't want Mama. Want Maria,' Lucy cried and petulantly pushed her mother's hand away. 'Maria make it better, Will?'

'I'll take her in, ma-am, and they'll put some vinegar on it.' Will didn't smile at the woman who employed him and from whose sight he had been barred, but merely displayed a politeness which was natural to him but which he didn't at this moment feel.

He carried Lucy across the wide lawn towards the back of the house, tickling her face with his rough beard to make her laugh, and leaving Isobel staring after them. Lizzie took Sarah by the hand and dropping a curtsey turned to go. Sarah too gave a little bend of her knee and then waved her hand at Isobel. 'Mama make Lucy better,' she smiled sweetly.

'I met 'mistress today.' Will remarked to Maria later when they were alone. 'I think she was surprised to find that I hadn't got two heads.'

'Don't be bitter, Will. She can't help being 'way she is.'

'Happen not,' he replied. 'She's a fine looking woman. Could be handsome if only she smiled more!'

It was later that evening, after Lucy was brought down to say good night to her father, that Isobel broached the subject which had occupied her thoughts for most of the day.

'We must get a governess for Lucy, Isaac,' she said firmly. 'It is time she was taught to read and write, and how to behave.'

'She behaves beautifully,' answered the indulgent father. 'Though I agree she could learn to read. She is a very intelligent child and it wouldn't go amiss.'

'Her behaviour is not all it might be,' Isobel replied. 'If you could have heard her this afternoon!'

'She might well make a fuss. Very painful are wasp stings, especially for such a little mite.'

'I'm not talking about the wasp sting,' she answered sharply. 'I'm talking about her language. She does not speak as a lady should, she has picked up a lot of rough expressions from the servants.'

'She spends most of her time with them.' Isaac answered back in the same tone of voice, for he was quite aware of how little time his wife devoted to their daughter, like most other ladies of their society. This pained him for he was devoted to Lucy and showered her with gifts; a hobby horse was made for her, a windmill on a stick, and colourful puppets and dolls were brought from foreign lands.

'Exactly,' she said. 'And now it is time for her to leave them, and her education to begin. We will employ a well-spoken young woman, not a country girl, who will teach her good English and then later perhaps French.'

Isobel began to plan out loud, and Isaac with a quiet sigh surreptitiously picked up his newspaper. 'Lizzie can stay on to help in the nursery: she's very patient with Lucy and usually makes her behave. Yes, that's what we will do. Will you advertise in the newspapers, Isaac? The sooner we start the better.'

But it took longer than she had anticipated. Several young women came that winter, took one look at the bleak, harsh landscape and felt the brunt of the east wind and declined the offer. Others who came Isobel didn't care for, and one forbidding, dictatorial widow induced in Lucy a screaming fit after which she wouldn't go near her.

Finally, there came to Garston Hall an amiable woman of thirty, whose husband had died leaving her in straightened circumstances when they had been married less than a year. That she was fond of children was obvious from her gentle manner, though she was firm and expected obedience, and though her accent was northern, her home formerly being in a village near York, there was no trace of the wide vowels customarily used by the inhabitants of that pleasant city.

Isobel was delighted to employ Mrs Love and she could start immediately, the only hindrance being that Lucy flatly refused to stay for lessons in the nursery unless Sarah was there as well.

'It would not be a bad thing, Mrs Masterson,' explained Mrs Love to a harassed Isobel. 'In my experience, children often work better with other children, it gives them stimulation and competitiveness.'

Isobel reluctantly agreed for the sake of harmony. 'As long as you are sure that Sarah won't hold Lucy back,' she said. 'She is after all a servant's child and cannot be expected to have the same degree of intelligence.'

Mrs Love smiled tolerantly at her employer's reasoning and said she would see that she didn't.

Lizzie brushed their hair, tied Lucy's long straight strands with a silky ribbon and put Sarah's unruly curls beneath a bonnet. They both wore aprons over their dresses, Lucy's of soft blue silk and Sarah's of crisp white linen, and were presented to Mrs Love to start their formal education.

Lucy could no longer follow Sarah into the kitchen to

be petted and spoiled by Mrs Scryven, she was confined to the nursery or the garden when fine, and brought to the drawing room in the evening to say good night to her beloved Papa, and recite to him the lessons she had learned.

Maria missed her a great deal and shed a tear or two, though she was rewarded with a hug whenever Lucy saw her. 'She's been almost like my own,' she explained to Mrs Scryven, 'and now I've lost her.'

'She'll grow apart, though she'll not forget thee who nursed her, no matter how great a lady she becomes.'

'And our Sarah taking lessons, whatever next?'

'Next is Sarah taking lessons from me. It's time she started.'

'Whatever does tha mean, Ma, taking lessons from thee?' Maria laughed. 'Tha's never going to teach her to cook, she's far too young.'

'Not to cook,' exclaimed the old lady impatiently, 'anybody can see she's not big enough to reach 'range nor strong enough to lift a pan, but she's old enough to come with me, come summer, to gather herbs and flowers and get to know their uses. To tell by 'smell and colour and shape what they are and what they're used for, and she can help me to gather them for drying and for making simples.'

'But why not teach Alice, she'd be more use to thee than young Sarah?' Maria looked searchingly at her friend.

She shook her head. 'It's got to be Sarah,' she answered. 'I made me mind up 'day she was born that she would carry on 'craft after me.' She looked sideways at Maria through narrowed eyelids. 'It isn't everyone who has 'gift,' she said softly, 'but Sarah has it and she'll have all 'knowledge by 'time I'm gone.'

'What nonsense tha talks sometimes.' Maria laughed uneasily. Her own mother had walked for miles along the river bank gathering nettles and cowslips, primroses and meadowsweet to concoct into soothing cough syrups, sedatives or salve for weeping sores, but she

270

never passed on the lore to Maria apart from teaching her the use of pot herbs to enhance their simple cooking.

'And teach Alice how to sew,' added Mrs Scryven firmly. 'She's too frail for rough work, but there'll always be a place for her if she turns a neat hem.'

Maria agreed. Her eldest daughter was always a source of worry to her, for although her health had improved since coming to Monkston, she had a fragile look and too many feverish colds. When the rest of the household gathered in the fields to help bring home the harvest, Alice stayed indoors fighting for her breath, or helping Mrs Scryven to bake large quantities of food for the hungry harvesters who sat to eat at the huge table, and who brought into the kitchen with them the choking dust which filled her lungs and reddened her eyes.

She proved to be a nimble and tidy worker, and as she sat painstakingly over her needlework her sister Sarah was taken by the hand when she wasn't at her lessons and shown where to find wild herbs and grasses, and splashed her chubby hands and tiny feet in the Holderness drains and streams where marsh marigolds and yellow iris and water lilies grew.

Mrs Scryven led Sarah and Maria one afternoon to her own thatched cottage. The thick walls were built of mud, brick and pebble and the windows were closely shuttered against the elements. She opened up the door with a heavy iron key, unfolded the wooden shutters and led them inside. The two small rooms smelt dank and fusty, and one was empty but for a metal trough and feathers strewn about the floor.

'I kept a pig in here last winter,' said Mrs Scryven, 'but, by, he did stink, so I shifted him out and just kept 'hens inside.'

The other room was barely furnished with a plain wooden table and two chairs, but the walls were lined with cupboards, and as she opened the doors, a sweet scent of aromatic herbs drifted round the room. Boxes of rose petals, blue borage and purple lavender were stacked on the shelves, and Sarah clapped her hands in delight and ran her fingers through their delicate, perfumed contents.

The small garden had a profusion of lavender bushes and roses, foxgloves and crab apple, larkspur and the creamy, heavily scented flowers of the elder, and the air was filled with their perfume and the hum of bees. They crossed the perfumed grass of chamomile, to bend and breathe in the scent of purple thyme and marjoram, mint and sage, and Sarah measured herself against the giant smiling sunflowers, grown for their edible seed and the glorious yellow dye from the petals.

'This is all mine,' said Ma Scryven. 'My very own, not tenanted like Reedbarrows' yon.' She pointed to the adjoining land where Martin and his father rented the farmhouse and land from a local landowner.

'And one day it will be thine,' said the old lady to Sarah, 'for I've nobody else, so mark well what I tell thee.'

And Sarah looked at the garden and at her mother and at Mrs Scryven; she gazed abstractedly out at the sea, shimmering and glinting beyond them, and with a sob hid her head in her mother's skirts and wept.

Lucy made a fuss when Sarah went off without her, and in order to humour her, her father came home with a pony and little trap which she learnt to drive around the meadow. Isobel had made for her a green velvet riding coat and a hat with feathers, and she stood proudly in the trap showing her skill and flicking her whip, whilst her admiring father applauded.

She fussed too when she saw Sarah with a cloth, polishing the furniture. Sarah generously went to fetch one for her and both were found by Mrs Love on their hands and knees under the dining room table, their hands and faces sticky with beeswax. Lucy screamed furiously when told by Maria that she wasn't allowed to join in these pleasures, that only the servants could do so, whilst Sarah looked on in confused bewilderment and wondered why grown people should spoil their games.

16

'This is 'last time that I'll fetch thee back, Jimmy.' Will was furious with the boy. 'I haven't 'time to be chasing all over 'countryside looking for thee. I've got work to do.'

Four times in the last year Jimmy had collected his few belongings and left home, and each time Will brought him back.

Jimmy looked down sullenly at his feet and made no reply.

'This is 'last time,' Will repeated. 'Next time tha can take thy chance and go, but remember there'll be no apprenticeship for thee with Masterson's, they'll not take anybody who's unreliable.'

Jimmy kicked a tuft of grass. He never got very far before being discovered: the first time he went in the wrong direction and headed towards Hornsea up the coast instead of down to the port of Hull where, he told Tom, he had been hoping to find a ship which would take him on. This time he had reached the village of Aldbrough, but as he sat on a stone at the side of the road pondering whether to continue on his journey or give in to the pangs of hunger and return, Will had overtaken him.

He had started work on the land under Tom's command, but he hated every minute of it and argued with Tom about the work to be done until Tom finally complained to Dick Reedbarrow, and he was given the menial tasks of collecting and bundling brushwood for kindling, and raking and weeding the circular drive around the house.

'I don't want to work on 'farm,' he muttered sullenly as he climbed up into the cart and they turned back for Monkston.

'What tha wants has nowt to do with it,' Will replied sharply. 'Tha has to help out, everybody does, even young Sarah has started with little jobs.'

Jimmy made no answer but sat peevishly silent behind Will, his lips curled and his tongue stuck out at Will's broad back.

'Another year, and then Masterson's will take thee,' Will said, looking over his shoulder. ' 'Mister said he would, when tha reaches twelve, but only if tha behaves. If tha's going to be a seaman tha has to obey 'rules, other lives might depend on it.'

Will's patience was sorely tried by Jimmy's behaviour. He expected pranks and scrapes from a lad, Tom had done his share as he had himself, he remembered, but Tom had settled down now that he was working, whilst Jimmy seemed to be getting worse. His behaviour was aggressive and he could be cruel. In a fit of temper he'd trampled down Tom's vegetables of which he was so proud, but he refused to admit to it, complaining that he always got the blame, and it was widely suspected that he and Paul Reedbarrow were the culprits when a hayrick on Martin's land caught fire. Paul had been given a leathering by his father and told to keep away from Jimmy, but Jimmy swore that it wasn't him and Maria insisted that they must believe him.

'He misses his ma, I expect,' she said in mitigation as Will had let him off with a warning.

Will exploded. 'What makes thee think that Annie would do better than we do by him?' he roared, his face flushed with anger. 'There's hundreds of lads far worse off than him, and they don't go round setting fire to other folk's property. I tell thee, Maria, one more prank like that and he'll get such a tanning he won't sit down for 'rest of week.'

Maria sighed. They had made allowances for Jimmy because he wasn't their own. He wasn't like Lizzie, who had never been a trouble to them. She was affectionate and kind, and was like a little mother to Sarah. Will was right, something would have to be done about Jimmy.

Lizzie swept the floor at Field House and strewed fresh rushes. She loved to do these jobs for Maria and today, because Mrs Love had taken Miss Lucy and Sarah out walking down by the sea to collect shells and pebbles, she had an hour free.

She laid a fire ready for lighting when Will came home, for though it was the height of summer the thick stone walls kept the room cool and the fire was needed for cooking. She filled a bucket with water from the well and sang softly to herself.

Her thoughts very rarely strayed to her home in Hull, though she thought sometimes with sadness of her mother. Yet even the memory of her was fading. She was secure and safe here with Maria and Will and Tom, and if only Jimmy would settle down she would want for nothing more.

She heard a whistling outside and went to the door. 'Hello, Tom, what does tha want?'

'I'm that parched, Lizzie. I was just passing and thought I'd stop for a drink of water.' He smiled at her, his teeth white in his brown face. He was growing strong and muscular and though they were both thirteen, he was a good head taller than she was.

She drew him a cup of water and he drank thirstily. 'Thanks, Lizzie,' he said, wiping his brow, 'I'll just go in and get my cap and then be off.' He took a deep breath of humid air. 'It'll rain afore long, I can smell it.' As he spoke a growl of thunder rolled across the sky from far out at sea. 'See,' he laughed. 'What did I say?'

Lizzie stood at the door waiting for him to come out again, thinking that she'd better hurry up and get back to the Hall before the rain came, when she saw Jimmy and Paul Reedbarrow coming towards the cottage. They didn't see her at first as they were skylarking about, pushing and chasing each other. Jimmy stopped when he did see her and then swaggered towards her, with a sheepish Paul coming up behind him.

'Where does tha think tha's off to, Jimmy Swinburn?' she asked tartly.

'Where does tha think tha's off to, Jimmy Swinburn?' he mimicked in a high falsetto voice, his hands on his hips.

Paul laughed loudly, but Lizzie didn't smile.

'Tha shouldn't be here, Jim. Tha should be working.'

'And who says so, eh?' Jimmy put his face close to hers and she backed away.

'Come on, who says, Mrs Clever Clogs?' He poked her in the chest with his finger.

This brought more encouraging laughter from Paul and he did it again but harder.

'Don't do that, Jimmy, it hurts,' said Lizzie, pushing away his hand.

'Pull her dugs, Jim,' Paul's eyes gleamed lewdly, and he leaned forward to poke at her.

'Don't touch me, or I'll tell.' Lizzie, frightened, crossed her arms on her thin, budding chest.

'I'll touch thee if I want.' Jimmy thrust his face towards hers and she backed, trapped, against the wall. 'And I'll bray thee if I want. Tha's only a stupid lass.' He lifted his hand towards her, his face menacing.

She raised her arm to defend herself. 'No, don't, Jimmy, don't, please.' Her voice rose shrilly and tearfully. 'Tha's not to hit me.'

'Get off her.' Tom appeared from the doorway and roughly grabbed Jimmy by his shirt and dragged him away.

'What's up with thee? Hitting a lass, and thy sister at that.' Tom's dark eyes glowered down at Jimmy.

'It's nowt to do with thee, what I do.' Jimmy glared back furiously. 'If I want to hit her, I shan't ask thy permission.'

Paul cheered. 'No, he won't.'

As Tom turned to tell Paul to be quiet, Jimmy lashed out with his fist, catching him unawares on the side of his face. Jimmy started to run but he collided with Paul and Tom caught him, tripping him up so that he sprawled on the floor. Furiously Jimmy grabbed Tom by the leg and they fell in a heap, hitting and punching and rolling in the dust, with Paul shouting and cheering them on, and Lizzie crying and pleading with them to stop.

'Stop. Stop,' cried Jimmy breathlessly as Tom finally sat on his chest. Tom gave him one more thump for good measure and then let him go.

'If I catch thee tormenting her again,' he said warningly, 'tha'll get worse next time.'

Jimmy made a coarse gesture and ran off to join Paul, catcalling once they were safely out of range. 'And get back to work.' Tom shouted after him. 'They'll be looking for thee.'

Lizzie was sitting on the doorstep, her head resting on her knees, gently rocking, tears rolling down her cheeks.

'Did he hurt thee, Lizzie?' Tom bent towards her. She shook her head but turned away.

'Don't cry then,' he said, embarrassed. 'He didn't mean it. He was only showing off in front of Paul.'

She looked up at him, her face ashy and streaked with tears. She wiped her eyes on her apron, and pushed back a strand of straying hair beneath her bonnet. 'He did mean it,' she gulped. Her voice broke and she drew in a deep shuddering breath as long-forgotten memories came flooding back. 'They always mean it.'

'Tell me if he bothers thee again.' Tom awkwardly touched her arm, mindful of some agitation in her that was not wholly to do with the incident that had just taken place. 'Come on, Lizzie, I'll walk back with thee.'

He put his arm round her shoulder protectively, and she shyly put hers round his waist as they walked back across the fields.

'I'll look after thee, Lizzie,' he pledged. 'I'll not let anybody hurt thee again.'

It was hard unremitting rain which lashed down and a galeforce wind which buffeted him as Will turned into the kitchen yard at the latter end of the day. He

277

hammered loudly on the door with his stick, for it had been bolted inside to stop it from being blown open.

Maria opened it cautiously as the wind threatened to tear the heavy wooden door from her grasp, and laughed to see him in such a sorry state. His hair hung in a mass of wet curls and his coat and breeches were soaking wet.

'Tha'd better get dried off in front of 'fire,' she said, moving away some wet washing which was draped in front of it, filling the kitchen with steam. They had started their wash day early in the morning, but the sudden downpour of rain had soaked the dry sheets and they had to be dried all over again.

He shook his head and then sneezed violently. 'I'm not stopping, I only came to ask if tha's seen 'lad? I can't find him any place. Jimmy, I mean.'

'I thought he was with thee,' Maria neatly folded a pile of fresh linen. 'He said he was coming to thee this morning.' Exasperated, she stopped what she was doing. 'I hope he hasn't run off again.'

Lizzie looked up from the table where she was carefully pressing the tucks and pleats in one of Lucy's dresses, her eyes wide and nervous. 'He hasn't run off, Will.' She rubbed her hand across her mouth diffidently. 'I saw him this afternoon.'

'Where? Where did tha see him?' Will's voice was harsh and she jumped.

'He was at Field House.' Her voice shook, and she spoke in barely a whisper. 'He was with Paul Reedbarrow.'

'Lizzie?' said Will puzzled. 'What's up, love? I'm not blaming thee.' He came towards her to console but she put down the heavy iron and fled from the room.

'Well, what does tha make of that?' said Will, bewildered. 'What did I do?'

'Take no notice,' exclaimed Maria. 'She's growing up is our Lizzie. Full of laughter one minute and tears in 'next.' She folded her arms and faced him. 'But what about Jimmy?'

'Young peazan. He's not been at work all day. He's

got to pull his weight, Maria, it's not fair to 'other lads. I'll have to give him 'strap, it'll be 'only thing to cure him. Paul's been told to keep away from him. They're nowt but trouble when they're together.'

Maria was anxious: she knew Will didn't like to resort to the strap. Tom had felt it no more than twice in his life and Jimmy not at all.

There was another loud banging on the door and Mrs Scryven, her face red from the heat of the range, complained loudly that she wished everyone would get out from under her feet.

Martin Reedbarrow stood at the door, as wet as Will had been. 'I'm glad I've caught thee, Will. I'm right bothered.' His large round face was worried. 'Our Paul's missing and somebody said he'd been seen with Jim.'

'Aye, that's right. Young varmints won't listen. But Jimmy'll get a tanning when he gets home and that'll keep them apart.'

'I'm not bothered about that.' Martin shuffled in the doorway until Maria made him come in as they were losing the heat in the kitchen.

He looked uneasily at her and then back at Will and lowered his voice to a murmur. 'I wouldn't have missed him, but I saw that 'boat's gone from where I keep it, and I'm afeard that they might have taken it out.'

Will stared in disbelief, but it was just the sort of crazy prank that Jimmy would get up to. He loved fishing and went out regularly with Will and Mr Masterson or any other man who would take him. He'd been out with Martin in his small boat and was inclined to boast to Tom and the other lads of his prowess with the oars, and of the fact that he was never sick.

Lizzie had crept back into the room and heard the quiet words. She whispered, her face white, 'They ran off towards 'cliffs.'

Garston Hall was half a mile from the cliff edge and they went as fast as they could, Will lagging behind Martin and cursing his disability, though he soon caught up, as Martin, his large lumbering frame unused to

279

moving quickly, became out of breath and had to slow down.

'See, this is where I keep it, 'rope's been cut,' he said breathlessly.

Will peered over the edge. He could see the protruding stake sticking out halfway down the cliff and the dangling rope blowing rhythmically from side to side.

'I keep it hanging here so's it doesn't get knocked about by 'sea,' explained Martin. 'Our Paul knows that he hasn't to go out on his own!'

Will stood up straight and with his hands framing his narrowed eyes looked out at the raging ocean, the crashing waves flecked with white. 'That's a wicked sea,' he said soberly. 'If they have gone and are not just larking about somewhere, then they don't stand a chance. Not just 'two of them.'

Above the wind they heard a voice calling them and expectantly they both looked back. Nathan Crabtree was standing in the doorway of his cottage beckoning to them. His was the last house in the village and nearest to the sea, the rickety garden fence only yards from the cliff edge.

'Them two lads of yourn were here this after',' he shouted in a quavering voice. 'They were messing about down 'cliff and I shouted at 'em to watch out. It's not safe just here, but they didn't tek any notice. Didn't think they would,' he grumbled.

'Did tha see 'em take 'boat, Nathan?' Martin asked.

The old man shook his head and ducked back inside the doorway out of the lashing rain. 'Didn't see owt after they went down 'cliff. I could see 'rain driving in over 'sea, so I came in and shut 'door.' He clamped an empty clay pipe between his gums and stared out at the sodden grey sky. 'They're going to get wet,' he said gloomily. 'We all are.'

Maria had been to fetch Tom, and he had raced around the village calling at houses where he knew Paul and Jimmy had friends. Most of them were indoors now, sent scuttling inside as the storm broke. None had seen the two boys.

A loud crack of thunder broke, swiftly followed by a flash of lightning which lit up the sky and illuminated a small crowd of villagers who had gathered as the news travelled. Varying suggestions were made, but heads were shaken and lips were pursed as they considered the futility of ever finding them.

Tom felt a small hand tugging at his as he stood by his father's side.

'Don't tell on him, wilt tha, Tom?'

The words were whispered and he looked down questioningly at Lizzie. Rain was streaming down her face and mingling with her tears.

'Don't tell about what he did today. It's like tha said, he was only showing off.' She snuffled and looked at him pleadingly. 'He didn't mean it.'

He squeezed her hand and shook his head. 'Nay, I won't tell. But get off home, there's nowt to be done here.'

'We'll take thy hoss and cart, Martin,' Will decided, 'and drive down 'coast. If they haven't turned over there's a chance they'll be carried by 'current down towards Kilnsea.'

Martin agreed, glad to be doing something rather than gazing out at the empty grey landscape, and went off to harness up the horse.

'I'll come with thee, Da,' said Tom.

'Nay, stay with thy ma and Lizzie. They'll be upset and need thee.' Will shook his head despondently. 'I don't hold out much hope, son, that's an angry sea out there.'

Martin had brought a heavy canvas tarpaulin to cover them as they crouched over the reins and drove down the narrow winding coast road. Occasionally they lost sight of the sea as the road skirted around the backs of villages, and sometimes they had to get out of the cart and lead the horse, as the track wound perilously close to the cliff edge. The mare snorted and shied as the rain

281

continued to fall and the harsh peals of thunder startled her, but presently the rain eased and then stopped, leaving the air fresh and salty.

It was getting late into the evening, but they stopped in two villages and knocked on bolted and shuttered cottage doors where they could see a gleam of light showing, and asked the men within if they would be sure to search the sands as soon as it was light. One or two of them put on their coats straight away and said they would go down immediately to look for the boat, but Will felt sure that it would be driven on past this straight stretch of coastline and down to the nearest inlet between Owthorne and Tunstall.

As they approached the small hamlet of Owthorne, where the dozen houses clustered around an old steepled church, they came across a group of villagers who, with oil lamps held high to give them their only light, were hurriedly carrying their few pieces of furniture, bedding and straw mattresses from out of their homes, and moving chickens and livestock from buildings which were on the very edge of the cliffs.

They were compassionate about their problem, as Will and Martin explained about the missing boys, but harassed and anxious as they battled to move back from their own inevitable slide down the muddy cliff face. Some of the women were crying and several of the men, they could see, were too upset to speak.

The two men got down from the cart to help as they saw an old man struggling to move a heavy plough from where it was stuck in a muddy rut. 'God bless thee,' he croaked, his sea blue eyes swimming with tears. 'I'll remember thy lads in my prayers, for they're surely gone from thee.'

The road was gone, broken completely away, and they were redirected, skirting behind the village and down a track not much more than a footpath, until they came across the coast road again.

'We'll go down as far as Dimlington Heights,' said Martin wearily.

They had searched visually in the small bays, but there was nothing to be seen or heard, only the squally, white-flecked waves rushing in, and the howl of the blustering wind. 'We'll get 'best lookout from there, up on top by 'beacon.'

The moon came out from behind the scudding clouds as they reached the high point of the cliffs. Over one hundred feet of glacial clay towered above the sea, and on top of this there stood a beacon, set there along with others all around the country at the time of Queen Elizabeth, the torch ready to be lit in warning should an invasion come from the sea.

From this vantage point they could see down the coast towards the tip of the low-lying Spurn Point, where the glimmering yellow glow of the lighthouse flame flickered steadily, and a fleet of vessels anchored in the deep water were riding the waves, waiting for the pilot boat to guide them through the mudflats of the Humber into the sanctuary of harbour. But the sands below them, gleaming white in the moonlight, were empty, and despondently they turned their backs and headed for home.

The sky was beginning to lighten, showing long streaks of the white, red and gold of dawn as they retraced their journey back as far as Owthorne, periodically stopping to look and listen. They saw as they approached the dark straggle of houses stretched along the cliff top and the villagers still busy moving belongings from the houses most in danger. Slowly, they drove towards them when a sudden shout made them sit up sharply. Heads were lifted and backs straightened and the small knot of people abruptly dropped what they were doing and rushed towards the cliffs. Someone waved urgently to Will and Martin and shouted something incomprehensible. They cracked the whip, urged the horse on and saw that it was the old man they had helped with the plough.

'It's a fisher boat,' he called. 'Come in to land.'

They gave him the reins and threw themselves down

to the ground to peer over the crumbling cliffs.

'Tek care,' shouted the man. 'It's ready to fall any time.'

The cliffs here were not so high, and twenty feet below they saw a fishing boat being dragged ashore. 'That's not my boat,' said Martin, his voice fatigued and despairing.

There were five or six village men up to their waists in water helping to pull the boat on to the narrow strip of sand. One of them looked up and called, 'They've found 'em, they've found 'poor bairns.' Gently and carefully they were lifting out of the boat two still forms.

'Are they drowned?' A woman's troubled voice asked the question, and Will shuddered as the seaman's old superstition of never saying the dreaded word came back to him.

Cautiously, taking each step with care, the boys were carried up the slippery slope and laid gently down on the ground.

'Nay, they're not, though they should be by rights,' a fisherman, his face red and raw from the stinging spray, answered. 'We saw 'boat two miles out as we were heading for home. They'd lost their oars and shipped a deal of water. They were lying that low beneath 'troughs, it's a miracle we saw 'em at all; and a bigger miracle they didn't turn over. They were lying in 'bottom of boat, I doubt they'd have lasted much longer. They were just about finished.'

Will and Martin bent over the boys. The fishermen had put their own coats over them, but they lay exhausted and shivering on the wet ground, unable to speak, their lips blue with cold.

'I'm sorry about thy boat,' the fisherman added. 'But we couldn't risk towing it, we had difficulty getting 'lads out of it and into ours without tekkin' a dip. She'll be washed up further down 'coast I expect, but she'll not be much more than firewood.'

'It doesn't matter about 'boat,' Martin said gruffly. 'As long as 'lads are safe.'

Will shook the fishermen by the hand. 'God bless thee and watch o'er thee.'

They nodded quietly, recognizing a fellow mariner. 'And thee, my friend.'

Exhausted, cold and wet, they travelled back, the two boys huddled silently in the back of the cart, weak and tired and frightened. Presently, as they came towards the familiar lanes of Monkston, Paul leant on his elbows and pushed back the tarpaulin that covered them. 'Fayther?' he said, in a small voice. 'Fayther? Will I get a leathering when I get home?'

Martin glanced sideways at Will and a flicker of a smile touched both their lips. 'Nay, lad, tha's suffered enough already,' he said leniently.

Something like a sigh came from behind them.

'I'll wait a day or two 'til tha's recovered, it'll give thee summat to look forward to,' he added.

'It's not fair,' Jimmy protested vehemently. He didn't object to the leathering, although his behind stung where he had received the strap. But to be told he had to pay towards the boat, he felt, was too much.

'Tha's on 'books as a casual labourer,' Will rebuked him harshly, 'and when tha wages are due I shall hand them over to Martin.'

'But he said he didn't care about 'boat. I heard him.'

'But *I* care about it.' Will's voice rose. 'And tha'll pay towards it, so instead of 'money being saved for thee, like Lizzie's is, it'll go towards another boat.'

He had another surprise due for Jimmy, but first he must see Mr Masterson, who nodded gravely when he was told the story and directed Will and Jimmy to seek an interview with John.

'So you want to be a whaling man?' said John sternly. He sat behind the desk in the timber-clad office in the High Street looking every inch a sober business man in his dark grey tail coat, the white frill of his shirt sleeve showing at the cuff. He was tall and athletic looking and sported a short curly beard. His blue eyes glinted as he looked at Jimmy, standing alongside Will, his hair neatly brushed and his cap in his hand.

'Yes, please, sir,' Jimmy replied solemnly, having been well rehearsed by Will and Maria.

'Well, I can offer you an apprenticeship,' said John, 'but of course there are certain conditions to be met.'

Jimmy's eyes sparkled and he took in a deep expectant breath.

'First of all, you can't start until you are twelve, which I understand is in nine months time?'

'Yes, sir,' he replied, less exuberantly; he had thought that he would be able to start right away.

'And next, we only take boys of good character, who are responsible and reliable. So after the next nine months I will expect to receive an honest statement of your behaviour from your guardian here, and if it is satisfactory then you can join the Masterson fleet.'

Jimmy stared back at John, turning his cap round and round in his hands until he finally dropped it on the floor and, blushing, bent to retrieve it.

John continued. 'The work is hard and the hours are long, it isn't a job for a weakling or a shirker.'

Jimmy stood up straight, his chin held high.

'However, you have been recommended by Mr Foster, and his word is good enough for me, so make sure that you don't let him down.'

'I won't, sir.' The voice was quiet and submissive, and Will glanced curiously at this new Jimmy.

John rose to shake hands with Will and then with Jimmy. 'If you will wait outside, Swinburn, I wish to speak privately to Mr Foster.'

Jimmy, not a little surprised at the esteem shown to Will by this fine looking gentleman, left the room, touching his forelock as he went.

'So, Will,' laughed John, stretching back in his chair and putting his hands behind his head. 'Was that all right? Did I play my part well?'

'Aye, tha did well,' he replied, pulling up a chair as John indicated. 'It's 'only threat that's going to work with him. 'Only thing that will keep him out of trouble for 'next nine months.'

He accepted a tot of rum which John offered and raised his glass. 'God bless all seamen.'

'Amen to that,' replied John, raising his own glass. 'And now tell me the latest news of the countryside, and how is your lovely Maria and the adorable Sarah?'

17

Maria made regular visits to the village, first of all to accompany Mrs Masterson, who had finally decided that she couldn't put off her husband's request to visit the tenants any longer, and then alone because she became anxious about some of the villagers, particularly the families with young children and the very old, like Nathan Crabtree.

Isobel, too, was anxious. She was quite sure that disease was lurking in every corner of what she regarded as their dark and verminous hovels, and that she would be infected. She mentioned her anxiety to Maria who in turn confided in Ma Scryven, who sniffed and humphed and then made up a sweet-smelling ball of eucalyptus, pennyroyal, tansy and mint for her to carry to deter flies and smells. She wore her thick woollen cloak to ensure that no infection would get through to her, and her face could barely be seen beneath her hood.

The visits were not successful. Isobel in her anxiety seemed haughty, and the villagers were distrustful of her. They took the gifts she offered, which were handed to them by Maria, and nodded their thanks and stared at her through the window of her carriage, for she didn't descend from it.

'Tell them I have a bad headache, Maria, and cannot get out. Indeed I can feel one coming on quite severely.'

Maria handed over flour and some offal to a pale, scrawny young woman who stood at her cottage door, a baby at her shrunken breast and three small children sitting listlessly in the dust.

'I'm grateful to thee, Mrs Foster.' Her voice was hoarse and low and Maria had to bend to hear what she was saying.

'They're Mrs Masterson's vittals, she's brought them,' Maria explained. 'She's a little unwell today or she would get down to speak to thee.'

'Best not to, I reckon,' the woman replied. 'I'm not well missen and 'bairn is ailing. Me milk doesn't seem to satisfy him.'

Maria looked anxiously back at Mrs Masterson, who was impatiently tapping her fingers on the carriage door, and then took a quick look at the silent child, its pale mouth slack against his mother's nipple. 'Does tha get enough to eat?' She was perturbed by the child's stillness.

The woman shook her head. 'Me man's gone off to Hull to find work, but I've not seen owt of him for nearly a month. We're living off what other folk can spare us.'

'Come along, Mrs Foster,' called Mrs Masterson sharply. 'We must be getting back.'

'I'll come again as soon as I can,' Maria whispered as she turned to enter the carriage. 'I'll bring thee summat for 'babby.'

'I'm sorry, ma-am,' she said apologetically as she sat uneasily on the edge of the seat. 'Might I have permission to visit that young woman again? She hasn't any food and her baby is sick.'

'You have your time off if you wish to make further visits,' said Isobel irritably. 'Just be careful that you don't catch some nasty fever and bring it back. I wouldn't want Lucy to become ill.'

'No, ma-am,' said Maria, chastened but wondering if it was possible to catch the disease of starvation, which she was sure was what the woman and her children were suffering from.

'Could we make one more call, ma-am?' she said hurriedly as she saw her mistress about to tap on the carriage window to tell Walters to turn for home.

Mrs Masterson sighed, then grudgingly agreed. 'Providing that it won't take all afternoon, Maria. I am ready for a rest now. These visits quite exhaust me.'

'I promise it won't, ma-am, and there will be no need

for you to get down, unless of course you want to.'

'Which I don't. Whom do you intend to visit?'

'Old Mr Crabtree, ma-am, he lives alone down near 'cliff edge. Will told me about him, said he ought to move out of his house and further into 'village, but he won't be persuaded.'

'He sounds like an obstinate old man to me,' said Isobel disinterestedly. 'But if you feel we should go then let us hurry up about it.'

Maria called up to Walters to go as far down the lane as he safely could and whilst the carriage waited she picked her way quickly down the uneven and broken surface towards the dilapidated cottage.

Nathan Crabtree saw her coming and stood waiting at the door, an old blanket wrapped around his shoulders. ' 'Didn't expect fine company today,' he said. 'I'd have trimmed me beard had I known.'

Maria smiled. 'Mrs Masterson has sent thee a few vittals.'

He peered into the bag which she handed to him. 'Mrs Masterson didn't send these,' he said. 'I know 'smell of oatcakes. These is Ma Scryven's bakin'.' He cackled wickedly. 'She doesn't forget that these is me favourites.'

She laughed with him. 'No, she doesn't forget. She said to tell thee that she'll come when she can. Her rheumatism is bad just now and she can't walk so well.'

'Aye, well, we're all getting old and it's time some of us was moving on.' He wiped a watery eye. 'But 'good Lord teks his time. He doesn't seem to be in any hurry to see me, anyroad.'

'Perhaps He thinks tha's still some use here, Mr Crabtree.' Maria felt sad for the lonely old man.

'No use to man nor beast,' he said bluntly. 'I've done me share o' labour, it's just a matter o' waiting.'

'Would tha come and live with us, Mr Crabtree?' Maria said impulsively. 'Over at Field House, I mean. We've plenty of room and it would be company for thee, and tha'd get plenty to eat.'

The old man's eyes creased with humour and he

smiled toothlessly. 'I haven't had an offer like that from a young wench in a long, long time.'

Maria smiled, took his wrinkled, blue veined hand in both of hers and patted it gently. 'I have to go now, mistress is waiting, but think on what I say. Tha shouldn't be here all alone, it's not safe any more.'

He watched her as she hurried back to the waiting carriage, and as it moved off he looked down at the hand she had held; he stroked it gently with his forefinger and then held it close to his face. He closed his eyes and breathed in the long-forgotten scent of womanhood.

'Maria, where's Will?' Lizzie ran swiftly up the stairs to the linen room where Maria was putting away clean sheets and inserting sprigs of lavender and rosemary in the folds to sweeten them.

'Somewhere out in 'fields I expect. Why, who wants him?'

' 'Mistress has arranged to travel to Hull, only Walters didn't come as he should. I've just been round to 'stable to fetch him and he's laid out on his bed, not fit to move.'

She came further into the small room and dropped her voice to a whisper. 'I think he's had a drop too much, 'place stinks of liquor.'

Lizzie wasn't given to exaggeration and she had seen enough inebriated men in her young life to know that the loud snores which Walters was emitting were drunken ones.

'I'll go and tell 'mistress that Walters is poorly. Run and find Will and tell him he's needed back at 'house. Quick as tha can, Lizzie.'

With a nervous grin, Lizzie ran off as she was told and Maria went in search of Mrs Masterson. She found her, dressed in her travelling clothes, restlessly walking the floor of the drawing room.

'What is happening, Maria? I sent Lizzie to see where Walters is and now *she* has disappeared. I'm not at all pleased, I particularly wanted to be off early today.'

'I'm very sorry, Mrs Masterson, ma-am. But Walters

is sick and not fit to travel. I've taken 'liberty of sending for Will if you need to go specially today. I didn't want to risk Walters being taken poorly while you were on the road.'

'No, of course,' said Mrs Masterson, exasperated, and sat down whilst she pondered on whether or not to cancel her visit to the milliner's to buy a new hat or risk being driven into town by Foster.

'Is your husband capable of driving the carriage, Maria?'

'I don't know, ma-am, that's why I've sent for him. He's driven a cart into Hull often enough these last six years, and knows 'road well.' She stopped as Lizzie came into the room.

'Beggin' your pardon, ma-am,' Lizzie bobbed, 'but Will Foster is here if you want to see him.' She was hot and flushed after chasing all over the estate looking for him, finally finding him as he answered her shout, down on the shore with some of the village men as they inspected the state of the cliff.

On his way back to the house Will had examined the drunken Walters as he lay insensible on the straw in the loft above the stable, and knew without a shadow of doubt that he wouldn't be conscious for several hours, if at all that day. He'd swiftly swilled his hands and face under the pump in the yard to make himself presentable and run his wet fingers through his hair, and now waited in the hall for his instructions from Mrs Masterson.

She surveyed him critically from piercing blue eyes, tapping the floor with the tip of her parasol. 'I can cancel my visit to town if there is any doubt that you can handle the horses, Foster, though I particularly wished to go today.'

He inclined his head. 'No need to worry, ma-am, I've handled 'pair before, Walters showed me how.' He didn't add that he had driven the carriage on two other occasions when Walters had been too drunk to stay on the seat. 'I'll just have to harness up, and change my

292

clothes,' he indicated his muddy coat. 'I'll be as quick as I can.'

Walters was several inches shorter than Will, though considerably wider around his middle, and although the dark red coachman's coat with its shiny black butons, which he found hanging on a peg, was too short in the sleeve, the fit was fairly comfortable. Will caught sight of himself in a window and rakishly adjusted the cocked hat on his thick hair, winking at Lizzie as she watched him through the window.

'I wish I could've gone, too, instead of Janey.' Lizzie gazed forlornly after the disappearing carriage. 'I'd like to have a look at 'shops some time, and 'ships in 'river.'

Maria put her arm around her in consolation. She knew that the girl was thinking of Jimmy, who with a supreme effort had conformed to the rules laid down to him, and had left them when he'd reached the age of twelve to join the whaling fleet. Maria was not a little relieved to see him go. He was a vexatious, restless child who made her feel uneasy, and there were times when she could see shades of his father in him. Although Lizzie had cried when he went, she too seemed less anxious and calmer since he had left.

They never had any message from him, and although they knew when his ship sailed, and had reports from John Rayner that he was shaping up well, he never once came to see them when he was in port, but stayed in lodging houses in the town. It was as if they had never been a part of his life and Maria knew that Lizzie once more had been hurt.

Will had been in the middle of a heated debate down on the shore when he'd heard Lizzie calling for him. The men had gathered there during working time, as the issue under discussion was considered to be of paramount importance requiring an immediate decision.

'We're talking about our homes and livelihood. God knows we don't have much, but we're going to finish up with nowt,' said one irate villager.

'Aye, look at Owthorne, there's not much left, 'church is teetering on 'edge and can't be used for worship. It's a disgrace, summat should be done.'

Will had agreed with them; he'd seen the extent of the damage to Owthorne church. The churchyard was gone and the sea washed around the base of the cliff only yards below its cracked and broken walls. But without wanting to appear discouraging, he didn't see what could be done about the cliffs at Monkston.

'We can build a wall down on the beach along 'worst parts,' Ralph Graves butted in. 'There's enough of us if we put our backs into it.'

'What of?' Dick Reedbarrow had been sceptical. 'We can't build it of clay, and that's 'only thing we've plenty of round here!'

Graves was scathing. 'Don't give us any encouragement, wilt tha?'

'Tha's got to be practical, lad. No use putting effort into summat without thinking about it first.' Dick stood his ground stoically. 'I'll do all I can, but it's got to be talked about. Discussed, like.'

Martin had a suggestion. He scraped his boot in the soft sand as he searched for the right words.

'It'd take a long time maybe, but if all them that has a cart or waggon could go down 'coast to collect 'rubble and waste from houses that's already gone ower cliffs, then we could fetch it back here to build a wall.'

Some of the men nodded hopefully. It was the best suggestion they'd heard so far.

Will had shaken his head despondently. 'Tha doesn't stand a chance of building a wall strong enough. Other villages have built them and it didn't work. Tha can't keep 'sea back.' The men stared at him sullenly. 'It's just impossible. Tha doesn't seem to realize 'power of 'ocean.' He pointed far out to sea where the grey waves flicked lazy white crests. 'That's where 'power is, not just here by 'cliffs, but out there, pounding away on 'ocean bed. Power that's never seen, nor imagined, not unless tha's seen a ship battered and torn by 'waves as I have.'

'Tha doesn't have to come in on this,' said Graves sarcastically. 'We'd best have a show of hands for them that's willing.'

'I'm willing to help,' Will interrupted protestingly. 'I just don't think it's going to work.'

He pondered on the problem now as he waited in the Market Place whilst Mrs Masterson made her purchases. Old Nathan Crabtree was the biggest worry, he mused, and though he'd agreed to help to strengthen the cliff just below his cottage, he thought it a better idea that they try again to persuade him to leave his home and come to live with them as Maria had suggested.

He shuffled impatiently as he waited and took off his hat, letting the breeze ruffle his hair; he was going to be behind with his work now, what with the village meeting and now the drive into Hull. He was provoked by Walters shirking his responsibilities; it wasn't the first time that he'd found him drunk in the stables and he was fearful that he might one day go out under the influence of drink and turn the carriage over. On the rutted roads around Monkston care was needed, as he'd realized today. But the most annoying trait about the man was his arrogant and surly manner, and Will would not expect, or receive, any thanks for covering for him today.

He gazed around the Market Place. Things looked very much the same as they used to. There were still swarms of people gathered around the stalls outside the church, or watching the performing bands of showmen; but as he had driven into the town he had seen that old slum buildings and a disreputable house of correction had been demolished, and fine new red brick houses were rising in their place. He wondered where the slum dwellers had gone, for the new buildings were far too grand for them. Gone too was the old gaol and where it had been was a new, broad road lit up with street lamps. Even King Billy had been cleaned up, he mused, as

295

he looked down the long street and saw the gilded statue glinting. Maria would like to see that, he thought, it was always a favourite of hers, yet never once had she asked to come back to visit the town where she had been born.

A young boy took hold of a rein and stroked one of the horses. He looked up at Will. 'Spare me a copper, mister,' he said cheekily, though his pale eyes were anxious. 'I've had nowt to eat since yesterday.'

Will felt in his breeches pocket but there wasn't any money there. He put his hand into the inside pocket of Walters' coat, found a coin and threw it down to the boy. He'd consider that a return for a favour from Walters. He watched the boy as jubilantly he ran off, shouting back his thanks. It could well have been Tom a few years back, he thought. Who knew what depths they might have sunk to had they stayed in the town, hawking or thieving, pilloried or gaoled? And here he was, dressed in fancy clothes, driving a carriage and pair and handing out money to beggars.

He climbed down from his seat as Mrs Masterson and Janey came out of the shop. Janey was carrying several parcels tied up with ribbon, and as he reached out to relieve her of them, he was suddenly jostled from behind by a man who seemed to appear out of nowhere, and who bumped into Janey, sending the parcels scattering on to the road.

'Look out,' Will ordered. 'Watch where tha's going.'

Mrs Masterson drew back hastily into the shop doorway as the fellow tore past. He didn't speak or apologize, but ran on, leaving them staring at his disappearing back.

'I don't think anything's damaged, ma-am,' said Janey as she picked up the scattered parcels.

Will handed Mrs Masterson into the carriage and for a moment gazed thoughtfully down the street. A strange feeling of disquiet had come over him, a vague sensation of familiarity with the stranger who'd glowered at him from under his hat. He tried to dismiss the thought. Probably it was someone with a grudge against the richness of Mrs Masterson's appearance, the fine carriage and obvious wealth, but the thought worried away at him as he drove down the High Street on his mistress's instructions to call at the Masterson office.

'Will?' Janey put her head out of the window as they waited. 'Tha knows that fellow that nearly knocked us over?'

'Aye, what of him?' Will leaned down from the box.

'Well, I've just seen him again, round 'corner. He's been watching us. He seems a bit shifty to me.'

'What does he look like, Janey?' Will had caught only a glimpse of him as he ran past them.

'Can't hardly see his face for his great black beard,' she answered, 'and he's got thick bushy eyebrows. Looks a proper villain to me.'

'Tha can't go by appearances, Janey.' Will smiled down at her; he could see she was apprehensive by the worried frown on her forehead. 'Why, look what a handsome fellow I am, tha'd never tell from my face what a scoundrel I am.'

She laughed back at him, her round face, so like her father's, creased into dimples. 'I don't believe that of thee, Will.' As they were talking Mrs Masterson came out into the street on John's arm. He handed her in to the carriage and came to speak to Will.

'Why are you here, Will?' he asked. 'Enjoying the sights of the town?'

'No, sir, Walters is sick, and Mrs Masterson needed to come to Hull.'

John raised his eyebrows. 'Sick?' he queried. 'Again? What's the matter with the man? He was ill not long ago. Is it serious?'

Will hesitated. 'Not exactly.' He cupped his hand and made the motion of drinking. 'Just a temporary condition, I would say.' He didn't want to get the man into trouble, but felt nevertheless that a warning might be in order.

John nodded. 'I understand. Perhaps a second coachman might be a good idea? I might suggest it to Mr Masterson, but forget I ever mentioned it.'

*   *   *

The village men worked unceasingly every night for two weeks. They worked by lantern or moonlight until the early hours of daybreak. Most of them were working men and couldn't take time off during the day, and they were anxious to build the wall before the onset of winter. Every available means of transport was taken along the sands and every piece of brick or masonry, boulder or cobblestone that they could lift was loaded up, carried back and deposited at the foot of the cliffs.

Will and Martin, who were working as a team, brought back their last load of the night and viewed the heap despondently.

'It'll make a wall no higher than a man,' said Will wearily. 'And first storm of 'winter will wash it away.'

'That's what me Da says,' Martin answered gloomily. 'He said it was hopeless, that's why he wouldn't come to help. Said we'd have been better building some cottages further back.' He eased his aching back. 'But it was surely worth a try, wasn't it?' he asked, anxious that his idea was sound. 'We can't move a whole village, church 'n all, now can we?'

'No, 'course we can't,' Will replied, privately agreeing with Martin's father. 'Course it was worth a try. At least we've tried to do summat.'

There was a west wind, which blew off the land and dispersed out at sea, during the latter part of October, and so the wall held, much to Martin's delight. But as November approached, the weather suddenly became much colder, the wind changed to easterly and there were a few snow showers.

'I'm right bothered about that young woman and her bairns,' Maria said one bitterly cold morning. 'If tha'll cover for me, Lizzie, I think I'll slip over. 'Babby was poorly again 'other day and I said I'd take some syrup for him.'

Sarah slipped off her chair and put down the sketch which she was drawing of a spindle shell that she had

298

found on the sands, and went to the cupboard where the syrups were kept. She pulled a stool over and climbed on to it, reaching in for one of the bottles which were kept there.

'This will do him good.' Solemnly she handed the bottle to her mother. 'It's thyme and honey, it'll give him strength.'

Mrs Scryven smiled to herself and then, answering Maria's unspoken query, said, 'Aye, 'child's right, that's 'best thing for him.'

Sarah jumped down from the stool, her red curls bouncing. 'I made it myself, so I know it's good,' she said earnestly.

Maria hid a smile as she surveyed her small daughter. 'Well, in that case, miss, tha'd better come with me and administer it and we'll see if it works.' Her smile faded. 'Though I think 'poor bairn might be past our help.'

Mrs Scryven packed a basket of food and Maria held Sarah's hand as they took the shorter way across the fields to the village. Sarah skipped at her mother's side, there were no lessons today as Mrs Love was confined to her bed with a cold and Lucy had gone visiting with her mother.

They knocked on the closed door of the cottage, but on receiving no reply Maria opened it and called out, 'Mrs Vickers, is tha there? It's Mrs Foster, I've brought thee some medicine for 'babby.'

The room was dark and Maria stepped inside. 'Mrs Vickers?' There was a snuffling and whispering coming from the opposite corner and as Maria peered towards it, she could make out the shapes of the woman and three of her·children lying huddled together on a straw mattress on the floor.

'Can I open 'shutters?' she asked, but did so without waiting for a reply. The dim light filtered into the room showing empty desolation.

The children sat up pale and wide-eyed and looked listlessly at Maria and Sarah and the basket of food which she held.

'We've brought some syrup for 'babby,' Maria said softly to the woman who was lying silently with the baby in her arms. 'Can tha sit up?'

Mrs Vickers smiled and wearily pulled herself up. The baby was wrapped in a thin, dirty grey blanket and she gently pulled it away from his face. 'Come on then, lovey,' she crooned. 'See if tha likes what this kind lady's brought thee, for tha doesn't want owt that I've got to offer.'

She smiled patiently at Maria. 'He doesn't seem to be hungry, but he's stopped his crying at last, so we can all get some sleep.'

Maria poured the syrup into a spoon and held it to the baby's mouth, then with a soft cry she drew back, her hand trembling.

'Let me give it, Ma.' Sarah took the spoon from her but Maria snatched it back, spilling the sticky syrup.

'Mrs Vickers,' she cried compassionately. 'Doesn't tha realize thy babby's gone? Poor little mite's passed on.'

The woman hugged the dead baby against her, rocking it steadily. 'Don't tha dare say such a wicked thing.' Her voice was harsh and fretful. 'He's asleep, that's all.'

She laid him down tenderly and covered him with a blanket. 'Just as well he's sleeping, for his fayther will be in in a minute and there's no dinner ready for him.' She got up from the mattress and ignoring them both walked over to the empty hearth and put a kettle on it.

'Sarah?' Maria whispered. 'Can tha find thy way back and ask Ma Scryven to come straight away? Tell her that Mrs Vickers is sick and 'babby has died. I'll stay here until she comes.'

Sarah walked quietly across to the bed and gazed at the still little body, then she tenderly stroked the pale cold cheek with the tips of her fingers. She smiled at her mother and at Mrs Vickers who was suspiciously watching her. 'Don't worry,' she said quietly, 'the babby is better now, he's not hurting any more.'

Mrs Vickers put her hands across her eyes and sank slowly on to the floor. She rocked backwards and forwards until finally her body shook with convulsive sobs.

'What really surprised me was that Sarah wasn't at all afraid,' Maria explained to Will later that evening as they sat together in the firelight at Field House. 'She even stroked 'poor bairn's cheek. It was as if she understood about death without being told.'

'No need to be afraid.' Will looked up from his supper. Maria seemed tired and strained, the baby's death had upset her, and he noticed for the first time the fine lines which had appeared around her eyes and the scattering of silver threads amongst her dark hair. 'Think of it as snuffing out a flame, just before a final sleep.'

She nodded and pushed away her bowl of soup, her appetite having deserted her. 'I can't help thinking of those other bairns going off to 'charity. Poor Mrs Vickers is going to be a long time before she'll be well enough to look after them. They looked so dowly and miserable as they went off in 'cart.'

Will went on eating. 'Don't think of asking, Maria,' he said, without even looking up. 'We can't take on any more bairns. We can't be responsible for all 'waifs and strays in 'kingdom, no matter how sorry we feel for them.'

She opened her mouth to speak.

'I'm not saying any more on 'matter,' he said. 'I'll put word about in Hull next time I'm there, and maybe their father will turn up and rescue them.' He got up from the table. 'Who knows, he might have made his fortune. On 'other hand,' he added bitterly, affected just as much as Maria was by the injustice of poverty and the peck of troubles that befell those like Mrs Vickers who couldn't help themselves, 'If he has, he might well be drowning his sorrows with it.'

'I was only going to ask if tha could go and see Mr Crabtree,' she complained. 'He went right out of my mind, what with 'worry over Mrs Vickers's childre'. Weather's getting bad, he ought to be moving out. I saw some huge cracks in his wall last time I was there. His place will hardly last over 'winter.'

He bent and kissed her on her forehead. 'Aye. I intended going anyway. I'll go first thing in 'morning. There's going to be a bit of a blow tonight, by 'sound of it.'

She rose and put her arms around him, burying her head in his chest. 'Hold me tight, Will. I feel so strange and uneasy.' She shivered. 'It's been a miserable day and I'm that tired. I'll go to bed now, though whether I'll sleep with that wind howling is another matter.'

He kissed her again, tenderly on the lips. 'Aye, go to bed. Tha'll feel brighter in 'morning.' He stretched. 'I'll just take a last look round, then have a jar down at 'Raven with Martin.'

'Does tha have to go out tonight, Will? It's so wild out there.' She was unduly anxious. 'Stay in, please.'

'Tha calls that wild?' He smiled at her consolingly. 'It's nowt but a capful of wind.' He reached for his thick jacket. 'I feel a bit fidgety, like thee. A walk and a drop of rum'll mend matters. Go to bed now, I'll try not to wake thee when I come in.'

He picked up his crutch which was leaning in a corner by the door. He wouldn't bother to strap on his limb or wear his boots tonight, for he didn't intend to be long – just one drink and then home again.

Maria sat staring into the fire after he had gone, trying to understand her uneasiness, her thoughts still lingering on the Vickers baby, when she felt a small warm hand in hers. Sarah stood solemnly in front of her, her red curls tousled, her brown eyes clouded with sleep, and her bare toes curling against the cold floor.

She put her arms around her mother's neck and climbed on to her knee. Maria hugged the child, pressing her warm body to her, and it seemed as if she drew strength from her as Sarah patted her hand and whispered soft endearing words, so soft and low that she could neither hear nor understand, but which lessened her melancholy and brought her comfort.

Will turned up his collar as he walked across from Field
House towards the cliff. The wind was rising steadily
and he could hear quite clearly the resounding thunder
of the sea swell. He recalled his surprise when they had
first arrived in Monkston at the nearness of the village
to the sea. Since then the cliff had steadily eroded bit by
bit, slipping away into the waters until the village which
stretched haphazardly along its length now faced the sea
like the ragged front line of an army about to do battle
against the might of an invincible foe.

'Perhaps I'd best walk up towards old Crabtree's
tonight,' he muttered to himself. 'Make sure that he's
all right.'

He turned towards the village, cutting through a small
copse which afforded a little shelter from the blast of the
wind. Most of the leaves had fallen and were lying dry
and crisp on the ground, whilst the bare branches
silhouetted against the sky shifted and creaked against
each other, buffeted by the increasing gusts. He stopped.
His senses, attuned to the night cries, questioned a
different sound, but the bark of a fox distracted him, and
with a shrug he walked on.

Nathan Crabtree's cottage was in darkness, the
shutters at the window blocking out any lamplight that
might have been seen, and he pondered for a moment
on whether or not to knock and risk disturbing the old
man.

He made his way to the bottom of the garden, looked
over the brink at the sea, and was disturbed to see that
a large chunk of cliff had fallen since he had last been
there. He bent down and in the darkness scrabbled his
hands around on the ground near the battered old fence,
finding to his consternation wide cracks which ran from
the cliff edge and under the fence, snaking their way
towards the walls of the cottage.

It's not going to last much longer, he thought, I'll have
to warn 'old fellow, or it'll be too late.

He hurried back through the small garden, crushing

decaying leeks and sorrel in his haste, and raising his crutch banged loudly on the door, calling out the old man's name. 'Nathan. Nathan, wake up. Can'st hear me, Nathan?'

He put his ear to the door and listened intently but there was no sound from within. He walked to the window and banged again, this time on the heavy wooden shutters, but still there was no response.

Hesitating for only a moment he spun round and pushed out of the gate. I'll fetch an axe from 'Reedbarrows, he thought quickly. I'll have to break down 'door, he can't stay there any longer, and turned towards the direction of the Reedbarrows' farm further along the cliff.

He almost fell over the man who was standing by the fence, so quickly did he come across him. 'Is that thee, Martin?' He peered in the gloom at the bulky figure in front of him.

'Tha doesn't remember me, then, Foster?' The voice that sneered was rough and antagonistic.

'I can't see thy face, do I know thee?'

'Tha should – we're what tha might call old comrades. Partners – that might be a better name. Aye, that's it. Partners. We had a bargain once, thee and me, and somebody else who'd better remain nameless – only 'partnership split up 'cos of thy double crossing.'

'Crawford!' Will drew in a hasty breath. 'What's tha doing out here? Tha's never seeking me out – not after all these years?'

Jack Crawford turned so that he was facing the sea and Will recognized by the reflected light the seamed face of his enemy.

'Seek thee out! Course I'm seekin' thee out. It's 'cos of thee that I had to leave 'town. Four years I stayed away, and all because tha gave my name to 'Hull mob.'

Will felt his anger rising. What sort of man was this, that could abduct a child and then feel aggrieved at being found out? 'Tha's mad,' he raged. 'Tha brought it on thissen. Tha was bound to be found out. Hull has no love for navy agents, or babby snatchers.'

Crawford reached out and grabbed Will by his coat. 'Four years,' he hissed, his spittle flying as the squally gusts buffeted against them. 'I had to go as far as York before I could find any jobs to do, half starved I was, and all because of thee.' He pushed his face towards Will, still holding his coat in a tight grasp. 'And I haven't forgot that old score. Tha still owes me for that.'

Will thrust him from him. 'Tha's nowt but a fool, Crawford. I explained all that to thee; all that stuff was taken back, back to where it belonged.'

Crawford's laugh was devoid of any humour. 'Tha's still keepin' up that old tale, is tha?' He leaned forward. 'So how does tha account for 'tidy little house yonder?' He jerked his thumb back in the direction of Field House.

'It's not mine, how could I afford owt like that? It belongs to 'man I work for. I pay him rent for it out of my wages.' It was Will's turn now to glare at Crawford. 'Anyroad, how does tha know where I live? How did tha find me out here?'

Crawford smiled, the tips of his broken teeth protruding against his heavy beard. 'I've been lookin' for thee ever since I came back, only I couldn't find thee, and I couldn't ask for fear of questions. I only knew tha'd left town. And then as luck would have it, I saw thee.' He sneered. ' 'Didn't know thee at first, dressed up in tha dandy clothes and driving a fine carriage, not until tha took off thy fancy hat and I saw thy red hair, though I couldn't work out how tha managed to have two legs.' He folded his arms in front of him and smiled in satisfaction at his own cleverness. 'Didn't tek me long then to find out where tha was hiding.'

He threw back his head and roared with laughter and the rain, which had started to come down steadily, ran glistening down his face. 'I've been right under thy nose these last few days, sleeping in 'stable with thy friend Walters.' He looked slyly at Will. 'He was right glad to tell me about thy special boots and how tha's old Masterson's right-hand man. Tell anybody owt, he would, for 'price of a glass or two.'

Will listened to the man, inwardly seething. He could guess what was coming next.

'Aye.' Crawford nodded, smiling maliciously. 'Masterson'll be right glad to know what sort of man he's employing.'

'What is it tha wants from me, Crawford?' Will restrained himself from grabbing the man and hitting him. 'I've no money. I work for less out here than I did at sea.' He laughed mirthlessly. 'How about a few cabbages or a couple of rabbits? That's what we call luxury. Or I'll catch thee some fish. We eat well out here, providing we grow it or catch it, otherwise we starve, just 'same as town folk.'

Crawford caught hold of him again. 'Tha knows what I want. I want 'way in to 'big house. Tha knows thy way round in there, and where 'stuff of value is kept. I know they don't keep a dog inside, Walters told me that already. So I need to know when Masterson is away and for thee to let me in after dark when his lady's in bed.'

'Tha's crazy. When will tha get it into that thick skull that I want no part in owt of that sort? I'll work for what I need, and I don't need much, so tha's wasting thy time.'

'Then in that case I'll be in touch with Masterson first thing in 'morning, and tell him about 'part tha played in 'robbery over near Beverley.' He dropped his voice to a malicious whisper. 'Even drop a hint or two about Francis Morton. They never did find out who stuck him.'

Enraged, Will shook him off. 'Take thy hands off me, scum, and get back to 'kennel tha came from. There's no place for 'likes of thee around here.'

He fell heavily to the ground, retching, as Crawford's fist, hard as iron, made contact low in his stomach, and whilst he was trying to regain his balance, he felt the thud of pain as Crawford's boot struck his ribs. He was vaguely thankful that he was wearing his padded jacket, but wished that he had put on both of his boots, as he tried to make purchase on the soggy, broken ground.

'Fight fair,' he gasped. 'Man to man, if tha knows what that means.'

In answer Crawford kicked out again, and Will grabbed his boot and brought him down. They grappled violently, first one then the other trying to gain mastery as they rolled over and over.

Crawford was the heavier of the two men and though Will was muscular, he was disadvantaged and eventually Crawford held him down, the weight of his body taking his breath away as he knelt on his chest, with one hand held in a tight grip against his throat.

He saw the gleam of the blade as Crawford drew the knife from the top of his boot, and saw too the smile hovering on his lips as he drew back his arm to strike.

Will's arms were free and he hit out with all his strength, catching the other a blow against his chin with his fist, jerking it upwards and striking again with his other hand. Crawford was thrown off balance and Will heaved him away. As Crawford struggled to rise, Will rolled over and managed to stand, leaning on the fence for support. The two men eyed each other, their hands taut and fingers clenched, panting in short, rapid breaths.

'Watch out.' Will suddenly shouted. 'Tha's near to 'edge.'

Crawford laughed wildly. 'Does tha think tha's fighting wi' bairns?' He threw himself on to Will, who ducked and landed a punch into his ribs. Winded, Crawford had stepped back and was gathering himself for another assault, when without warning the cliff started to slip, the deep cracks opening up wider, and Crawford with a short startled cry disappeared backwards over the brink.

Will crawled forward slowly on his stomach and, grasping a clump of grass, eased himself out as far as he could to look over the rim. He narrowed his eyes and searched below, but it was too dark to see anything but the foamy tops of the waves lashing below against the darker shadow of the newly built sea wall.

'Crawford!' His voice was tossed away by the screech of the wind. He swore vehemently under his breath. He would have to go down and look for him, blast his eyes.

He started to rise, but as he did so he felt the ground give way beneath him; the grass which he clutched so tightly came away in his hands and he was suddenly falling and slithering, tumbling and rolling down the cliff, to land face first in the sand.

Dazed, he picked himself up after a moment. His hands were scratched and bleeding from trying to stop the momentum of his fall, and there was a cut on his forehead where he had been hit by flying debris, but he was thankful that he had no bones broken.

He dragged himself over the pile of muddy clay and boulders and made his way back through the shallow water to where he thought Crawford had gone over. It had been a heavy fall, the clay was piled up in immense heaps across the narrow strip of sand and he found it difficult to walk or see in the darkness. He had no crutch, having dropped it during the struggle with Crawford, and he fell constantly over boulders lying half hidden in the sand.

Crawford was lying spreadeagled across the makeshift sea defence, his legs half buried by the soft clay that had fallen with him. His skull, split wide open by the impact with the boulders on the top of the wall, oozed blood and brains which clung to his hair and beard. His eyes gazed sightlessly towards the night sky and his mouth opened wide in a frozen grin.

Will turned away, sickened by the sight, and sank down on a pile of stones, his head in his trembling hands. Why did this have to happen? He thought he had safely left the past behind him when he had come out here to Monkston. I should have known, he thought bitterly, that sooner or later it would catch up with me again.

But what to do now about Crawford's body? Should he go for help and try to explain away the man's presence out here at Monkston? It would mean bringing in the law and the law might well choose not to believe that Crawford fell accidentally, especially if Walters was questioned and told that Crawford had come seeking Will out.

Uppermost in his mind was the fact that conceivably Crawford's name was known to the magistrates, and that by being linked to a thief and ruffian, by even a tenuous thread, he might well be dismissed by Isaac Masterson.

Numb with apprehension, he sat shivering, watching the water as it lapped around him, and it wasn't until he realized that the tide was on the turn that he thought of Martin Reedbarrow's boat. Martin had bought another small boat from a Bridlington fisherman, which Will had insisted that Jimmy should help pay for before he left to start his apprenticeship, and he kept it tied up on a timber groyne on the sands just below his land.

Will started up, an idea hovering at the back of his mind by an association of thought – of death, and of burial at sea.

'Not that he deserves a decent burial,' he muttered grimly. 'I'd just as soon see him swinging from 'gibbet 'till he rotted.'

He scrabbled to move the wet clay away from Crawford's legs and with a great heave thrust him off the wall and down on to the sands where he lay in a crumpled heap. Breathlessly, for Crawford was a big, wellset man, he dragged him down to the water's edge and dumped him there, his body leaving a trail in the wet sand.

Stumbling, he made his way along the sands towards the groyne which was partially submerged in the sea, the boat rocking wildly in the boisterous waves. He half walked, half swam up to his waist in water until he reached it, and hauling himself over the bow he slipped the painter from the groyne. Steadily he pulled on the oars, feeling the drag of the tide as it turned, and rowed back to where he had left Jack Crawford's body.

It was difficult getting him into the boat, for he had

309

to drag him through the water, keeping tight hold of the rope to stop it drifting away and knowing that if he beached the boat too high on the sands, he would never be able to push it off again with the weight of the body in it. He finally heaved himself on board, and lay panting and exhausted at the side of Crawford, letting the tide carry them away from the shore.

The tide was running fast and strong but the wind was against him, great squally gusts which threatened to turn the boat over and drive it back to the shore. His arms and shoulders burned as if on fire as he pulled on the oars, and the skin of his palms rose into blisters as he battled desperately to keep the boat from being submerged as it dipped and dived through peaks and troughs, huge waves lashing over him until he was soon soaked through.

He rowed on until he judged he was about half a mile out, where the depth dropped beneath the sandbanks and the currents began to eddy and change. He shipped his oars and struggled to lift Crawford's body over the side. For a moment the dead man hung suspended half in, half out of the boat so that he was dangling face down into the turbulent water. Then, with a final surge of strength, Will lifted him by the legs and pushed him over the side. Panting with exertion, he watched as a gigantic wave like a cavernous mouth hovered momentarily above them before crashing down, consuming Crawford within it.

He battled now to turn and row against the tide and head for the shore. The wind was with him but the currents were strong and he felt himself being carried along, his own puny efforts having no effect against the aggressive sea.

So exhausted was he that he was tempted to lay down his oars and let the boat drift with the tide until it turned, but he knew that by then he would be miles out at sea, with no hope at all of getting back, that in the deepest water the small boat would be swamped, unless by some miracle he was picked up by another vessel, as young

Jimmy and Paul had been. He hardly felt that Providence would smile twice.

'Dear God, I'm not ready to meet thee yet,' he cried angrily. 'Just one more chance. Just this once!'

With another effort he swung round again, pulling on the oars. The wind had increased and as he felt the combat between tide and wind a strange exhilaration filled him. He filled his lungs with great gulps of air and started to chant, 'Pull. Pull. Pull!' He hurled the words into the air and with each shout strove to best the opposing waves.

The German Ocean had an infamous reputation among those who sailed it. Cunning, tricky and devious, with its powerful tides, hidden sandbanks and changeable currents, it could smash a boat to pieces and carry it to unfathomable depths within minutes, or rock it as gently as a child in a crib on its serene and placid surface. As Will struggled, he felt the boat being driven into a deepwater channel, where the opposing currents whirled above the uneven sea bed. With the flow of water driving him back along the sea furrow and the raging wind at his back, he pulled ever harder towards land. There was a following sea now and he knew that he had a chance.

Next time I'll be ready, I promise, he vowed as the boat beached, and silently he said a prayer of thanks for deliverance. He dragged the boat the last few yards across the sand towards the groyne which now stood clear of the water, and slipped the painter back over the wooden stake, hoping that Martin wouldn't notice the score marks in the sand.

Wearily he stumbled back along the sands towards the slipway which joined the lane, but stopped abruptly as he found his way barred by another huge fall of cliff. Scattered about the sand were heaps of stone and boulders, and as he peered into the gloom, he saw timber joists and broken furniture and clumps of what looked like straw piled amongst the heap of debris.

Puzzled, he picked up some of the straw and rubbed it between his fingers. It was thatch. With a growing sense of unease he looked up to the top of the cliff and saw on the skyline the torn and jagged edges of a building teetering on the cliff top.

He heard the sound of voices as he stood gazing bewildered, his mind confused and his body weary. He let himself fall and half sat, half lay on the wet sand, the piece of crumpled thatch still held fast in his hand.

As he waited, a line of flares and oil lamps swung unsteadily down the cliff face; like will-o'-the-wisps they dipped and danced in the darkness as the village men who held them climbed precariously down over the broken surface.

Ralph Graves held his flare high, the shadows it threw making his face grotesque and his eyes hollow. 'Here – look here. It's Foster. What's tha doing out here? Hast tha tummelled ower 'cliff?'

Will didn't answer, but just sat, the men gathering in a ring and staring down at him.

'Fayther?' Tom pushed his way through the crowd. 'Da! Ist tha hurt?'

Will shook his head, too spent to speak, but unwilling in any case to give explanations.

'I saw Mr Crabtree's house go over, Fayther. I came to look for thee at 'Raven, only tha wasn't there. We can't find old Crabtree, he must have gone over 'cliff.'

Will nodded. 'I tried to wake him,' he said hoarsely. 'I knew 'cliff wouldn't last 'night out.' He shook his head. 'I tried, but I couldn't make him hear.'

'So tha went ower with it?' Martin Reedbarrow, crouched at the side of Will, peered at him curiously.

Will put his swollen, bleeding hands to his head. 'I don't know. I can't remember.' As he spoke it seemed that he couldn't recall the sequence of events. His mind was a confusion of thoughts; of locked doors which he couldn't enter, and fights on raging seas, of the devil grinning at him, and of broken ground which opened into huge crevices and swallowed him up.

'Let's get on.' Ralph Graves spoke up. 'We've got to find Crabtree.'

'Aye.' Martin rose to his feet. 'He might be lying hurt somewhere. Let's spread out a bit, only mind where tha's putting thy feet. Don't go treading on him.'

They found him curled up on the sands beneath the cliff, his blanket still wrapped around him and his nightcap askew on his head. Not a cut or a bruise was on his body, and he lay with a still, contented countenance. His house had fallen about him and the earth given way beneath him, but he had slept on in the deep sleep which had come at last to claim him.

Will leaned heavily on Tom as they made their way back home. Without his support he knew he would have had to crawl, his body so ached with fatigue and his spirits were so low.

'Don't make a fuss, Maria,' he complained, as she put on the pan to heat water to bathe his swollen hands. 'I'm not hurt, just a bit shaken up, that's all.'

'But tha's drenched through,' she said anxiously as she helped him off with his sodden coat. 'I hadn't realized that it was raining so hard.'

'I fell into 'sea,' he said abruptly. 'I lost my crutch and it's not easy walking on 'sands with only one leg. Alice, pour me a tot of grog, there's a good lass.'

She poured him a good measure, handed it to him and waited as he tossed it down and held out the mug for another.

Sarah came and stood at the side of his chair. She took hold of his other hand with both of her small chubby ones and gently turned it over. The skin was broken on the tips of his fingers and thumb and the flesh of his palm was puffy and swollen. She gazed at it without speaking, a disturbed, troubled look on her face.

He wrinkled his nose and winked at her to allay her childish fears, but she gazed back at him absently, without seeing. A profound stillness gathered around his small daughter as she looked deep into his eyes, down into the essence of his being.

Then she smiled gently at him, her face lighting up

313

from within. As he smiled back, he sensed the stillness flow from her towards him, drawing him in and wrapping around him protectingly, and his troubled conscience responded and became calm. With a discernment which mystified him, he realized that this child knew without words of his anxieties and fears, and she was telling him to be still; that the devils which tormented him had gone and that the storm within him was over.

18

Mrs Masterson had graciously given a recommendation on Alice's character, even though she hardly knew the girl, and was therefore instrumental in obtaining for her a position as a seamstress in a high-class dress-making establishment in the fashionable coastal resort of Scarborough.

She was thirteen years old when she took a tearful farewell of her family. Scarborough was too far away for frequent visits, the hours were long, the work was demanding, and for the first few weeks Alice went home to her shabby lodgings, ate her supper and went to bed, crying herself to sleep.

As time passed, though, she emerged from her cloud of misery and looked around her with fresh eyes. She became less unhappy, and began to enjoy her new surroundings and the merry company of the other girls at work. She was persuaded, with some trepidation at first, to visit the theatre, and taken to watch the horse racing on the sands and the Morris dancers who entertained the ladies and gentlemen who came to the spa town for the mineral waters and the sea bathing.

The air was considered to be highly beneficial in Scarborough, and with the restraints of home and the dependency on parents gone, a sparkle came to her grey eyes, her cough diminished, and a few heads were turned at the young, dark-haired girl with a spring in her step and the promise of beauty just unfolding.

It was natural, therefore, that when Sarah reached the same age, Maria should ask her mistress to do the same favour for her second daughter. This time, however, Maria was in something of a quandary as to what type of work Sarah would be suited for.

Will was of the opinion that she could do better than just going into service, for wasn't she able to read and write as well as Miss Lucy? It was a pity she wasn't a lad, he said, for she could get a job in Isaac Masterson's office as a clerk. But as Maria tartly reminded him, had she been a lad then she wouldn't be able to read and write as well as she did.

They were impressed when she brought home Mr Masterson's discarded newspapers and read to them, giving them news of the war which, after an uneasy peace, had broken out once again between Britain and France. Items of national importance, as well as shipping and industrial reports, all were read with understanding and without hesitation or stumbling. She also read them news of the rapidly expanding whaling fleet in Hull, which was now a major port, and of the ships which were pushing ever further north to track down the whales.

But the very fact that Sarah was so clever bothered Maria more than a little, for who would want a housemaid who could read and write probably better than her mistress?

'I wondered, ma-am, if she would be suitable for someone with a large family, to assist with the childre', until she's a bit older, then perhaps she could be a companion or a lady's maid?'

'Hmm, I will give it some thought, Maria,' Isobel said, which Maria knew meant that she would ask Mr Masterson when he came home.

'It perhaps wasn't a good idea for her to take lessons, after all, Isaac. I would not like to think that we have spoiled her chance of employment.'

Isobel was consulting her husband as they sat over supper the next evening, and neither of them was prepared for the emotional outburst from Lucy when she heard that Sarah might be taken away from her.

'But, Lucy, she has a living to earn. Had she been living anywhere else but here she would already be in service,' Isobel explained irritably. 'She has been very, very fortunate.'

Isaac sat quietly and finished his wine, saying nothing, waiting for the heated debate to subside.

'She can't go,' cried Lucy passionately. 'Who would I talk to, walk with? Papa, she's my friend, she's been with me all of my life, you can't let her go.' She burst into tears and rushed from the room.

'It seems to me that Mrs Love has been rather lax in teaching Lucy decorum,' said Isobel coldly. 'I must speak to her. There are other kinds of instruction to be considered as well as education.'

Isaac pondered no more than a day. If Lucy was going to be unhappy without her childhood companion, then there was only one solution. He asked Maria to send Sarah to him that he might talk to her.

She stood smiling before him, a tall girl for her years with the rounded plumpness of budding womanhood. Her long red hair was thick and curly, and she had tied it with a brown ribbon in the nape of her neck, though several corkscrew tendrils had escaped and danced around her cheeks.

Sarah was not intimidated in Mr Masterson's presence, unlike Lizzie who still scuttled out of sight whenever he appeared, or Janey who giggled behind his back at his heavily jowled chin and his crooked, old-fashioned wig. Sarah considered him to be an eminent friend, one who was kind and generous, for he had often brought her presents too when bringing them for Lucy, one to be treated with respect.

'You wanted to see me, sir?' She dropped him a slight graceful curtsey.

Her voice was soft and her brown eyes met his in an open gaze.

'Your mother tells us that it is time you went away to seek employment, in service or such capacity.' He sat back in his leather armchair and linked his hands, looking at his fingertips. 'Is this what you want?'

The smile disappeared from her face and a shadow

317

crossed it, a fleeting look of unhappiness which she was unable to hide.

'It's what I must do, sir,' she replied. 'I can't always be dependent on my parents.' She hesitated. 'Or on you and Mrs Masterson, you have already given me many advantages, and I'm very grateful.'

He liked her self-possessed manner, her gentle way of speaking, but above all her repose, which was very soothing. Lucy would do well to emulate some of her qualities.

'So, if you didn't go away, what would you like to do?'

'I haven't really thought about it, sir,' she answered reflectively. 'I have always known that one day I would have to go away.' Her eyes became luminous for a moment and she bit her lip, saying with a tremulous smile, 'I suppose that what I really want is to stay here for always, and for nothing to change.'

'What, no fancy to work in other places, or find yourself a husband?'

She smiled shyly. 'I would like to see other places perhaps, but I would still like to come back here. I feel as if I might be needed.'

'Be needed?' he queried. 'In what way?'

'I don't know, sir.' She blushed. 'It's just a feeling that I have.'

He didn't really understand her but he smiled kindly and nodded his head. 'Well, what if I said that we needed you. That Miss Lucy needs you and wants you to stay. What would you say to that, eh?'

There wasn't very much that she could say, so she waited patiently for him to continue, her hands clasped in front of her.

'Suppose I offered you a position, such as you might obtain elsewhere, with a similar salary and conditions, but here in this house as companion to Miss Lucy. A position where you would be independent of your parents, but able to see them, not only on your days off, but at other times during the course of your duties. Now how does that sound?'

'It sounds wonderful, sir. Thank you, oh, thank you! May I go and tell Lucy – Miss Lucy, I mean, sir?'

'Er, no, I will tell her myself, and Mrs Masterson. But go and tell your mother and your father, by all means. They will be delighted, I'm sure, that they are to keep you for a little longer.'

He hadn't of course mentioned what salary she would receive, but he would give her the going rate, or perhaps a little more. He felt sure that whatever he gave her would be more than repaid if it meant that Lucy would be happy.

'I'm not sure that it is a good idea, Isaac,' Isobel complained. 'They already spend far too much time together. I very much fear that we shall take Sarah out of her own class. Still, as long as she realizes her position, and you too, Lucy. Never forget that you are the daughter of the house, and that Sarah is a paid companion.'

Lucy tossed her head sulkily. 'Sarah never forgets, she never has.'

Indeed, Sarah had always known instinctively, or been taught at her mother's knee, she didn't know which, that there was an invisible barrier between herself and Lucy, that, although they had played together and slept in the same crib like sisters, there were times when she had to draw back, to become less than she was in order that Lucy could become more.

The realization had come to her when she was still a small child, when she and Lucy had been taken in the carriage to visit the Smallwood children. They had played and taken tea in the nursery, but when the time had come to depart, Lucy had been taken to the drawing-room to say her goodbyes to her hosts, whilst Sarah was bidden to wait in the hall.

Now she knew what to do. Whilst Lucy took tea in the drawing-room with her elders, Sarah was escorted to the kitchen, there to be observed with some curiosity by the Smallwood servants. In response to their curious questioning she adopted the local dialect, for she knew already the ridicule her normal accent could bring, having suffered from the jeers of the Monkston village children.

'Mrs Love, isn't it splendid?' said Lucy. 'Sarah is to stay with us. She's not going away after all.'

Lucy was so delighted that she flung her arms around Sarah and whirled her around the room. The old nursery had been transformed into a schoolroom with a work table for them and a desk for Mrs Love. There was a large cupboard for their books and paintings, and the walls were adorned with maps and quotations.

'Miss Lucy, please behave,' said Sarah primly. 'I cannot tolerate such unseemly behaviour.' Her voice matched that of Mrs Masterson so well that Mrs Love turned away to hide a smile.

'Am I still to instruct you in your lessons, Sarah?' she enquired. 'Or is this to be your free time?'

Sarah and Lucy both gasped, Sarah with dismay because she so enjoyed the lessons with Mrs Love, who knew the answers to practically everything and was so patient and kind.

Lucy rushed to Mrs Love and put her hand across the teacher's mouth. 'Oh, hush, please, Mrs Love. Don't let's ask. Let's pretend that we hadn't thought about it and continue as we are doing.'

Mrs Love agreed. She felt it a pity that Sarah should lose the opportunity of prolonging her education when she had the intelligence and understanding to absorb knowledge. And so, almost by mutual agreement, on the rare occasions when Mrs Masterson entered the schoolroom, Sarah would fold her arms across her knees and assume a slightly bored expression, or pick up a piece of sewing as if for all the world she was patiently waiting for Miss Lucy to conclude her lessons.

They put on their cloaks and stout boots one bright day during the following autumn and walked down the long winding drive to the village. The horse chestnut trees were shedding their leaves and a thick crisp carpet of brown and gold covered the ground and crackled beneath their feet.

Sarah waved to some of the women who looked out of the cottage windows as she and Lucy and Mrs Love passed by. She knew them all and they knew her. They had given her apples or plums or some other treat when she was small and had visited them with her mother or Ma Scryven.

'Is tha well, Mrs Alsop?' she called to an old woman, and beamed when she received a toothless, nodding reply.

Lucy turned up her nose and rebuked her for her coarse language, but Sarah shrugged and said nothing, though she caught an understanding glance from Mrs Love.

'I want you to look for fossils and shells, Miss Lucy, and, Sarah, will you look at the cliffs and see what you can find?'

With a pocket full of shells, Lucy soon tired of searching and picked up instead the shiny, coloured pebbles that lay so prettily in the sand. Sarah thought that she had been given the less interesting project for there appeared to be nothing of interest in the wet clay. Thin rivulets of water ran down from the top of the cliff and formed shallow red pools on the sand. She climbed higher up the cliff, searching for a foothold in the muddy clay.

'Don't climb too high, Sarah,' called Mrs Love and Sarah shook her head. She knew how far to climb and where to put her feet. Neither Mrs Love nor Lucy realized how familiar she was with this stretch of coastline.

This was her territory, where she came to be alone, to listen to and watch the sea. Where on warm summer evenings when the tide was coming in she would take off her dress and petticoat and clad only in her shift would wade out into the sea until the waves gently lifted her off her feet and she could no longer feel the sandy sea bed, and she would float as her father had taught her, and let the sea carry her on its back and deposit her on the shallow, sandy shore.

Sometimes she sank deep and let the waters wash over her, holding her breath until she felt lightheaded and dizzy, when her mind filled with illusions of insubstantial strangers who were vaguely familiar, who called to her, begging her to follow. She tried to reach them, but always on the point of contact, when her hand reached for theirs, they would slip away from her leaving her with an obscure sadness. Then she would rise out of the water, reaching for the surface with her arms held high and her lungs bursting.

One day this summer as she'd emerged from the water, her wet shift clinging to her body, she found Paul Reedbarrow standing by the water's edge watching her, a sly grin on his face. She didn't like him, though she knew he had once been a friend of Lizzie's brother Jimmy. He seemed shifty and had made no attempt to move away, but stood staring at her, his mouth wet and slack in a foolish smile. She had put her dress on top of her wet shift, instead of drying herself in the sun, and climbed the cliff, her clothes and hair streaming. She hadn't been down to the sands alone since, for she knew that he might be there, watching and spying.

'There doesn't seem to be much worth finding, Mrs Love,' she called down. 'Just a lot of soggy clay.'

'There's more than that if you look carefully,' was the answer.

She continued to scrabble with her fingers, poking in the crevices, dislodging small pebbles and showering a sandy deluge down on to Mrs Love's head.

'I've found a piece of wood, but I can't get it out. It looks like old driftwood, from a ship or something,' she shouted. 'Yes, and a piece of bone.' She scraped around the edge of the object with a pebble. 'Oh, no, I think – yes, it is, it's a piece of claw, quite large, a gull perhaps, I can't really tell.'

Enthusiastically she put her finds in her pocket and moved along the cliff, holding on to the tough sedge grass and sea lavender that sprouted out of pockets of wet clay.

'Come on, Sarah! Haven't we finished yet, Mrs Love?' Lucy was bored. 'I want my tea.'

'I won't be long.' Sarah prodded and poked again, pulling out clumps of grass. 'There's something here. Oh, I wish that I had Tom's knife with me, it would be so much easier.' Then she remembered the pins in her hair. She took off her bonnet and removed one of the whalebone pins that were holding her hair in place. Her curls cascaded down her back and she threw the bonnet down on to the sands below.

'I won't be long now,' she called, and with the sharp point of the pin she continued to scrape.

'There,' she said triumphantly as she slid down the cliff to where Lucy and their teacher were waiting. 'Look at that!' She held out her stained hands to show them her find.

'Ugh, what is it?' Lucy peered at her hand with a distasteful expression on her face. 'It doesn't look very nice.'

Mrs Love took it from her and examined it carefully. 'It looks like a large tooth,' she said, 'but I don't know what kind or from what.'

The colour was light and the edges were smooth and round. 'Whatever it's from,' she said, 'it has been there a long, long, time. Like the piece of driftwood it's been washed there by the ocean at some distant time in history, and pounded into the clay. Or perhaps this part of the land was below the water during the great flood the Bible tells us of.' She shook her head regretfully, 'I fear that I am not sufficiently knowledgeable to tell.'

Sarah stared at the tooth, stroking and smoothing it with her fingers, her thoughts drifting away, her breath shallow. She heard the pounding of the waves and thought of the unknown creature immersed in the sea. Perhaps it had fought a losing battle here with some other stronger creature and its body had been left to batter against the coast; or maybe it had come to the end of its natural life miles out at sea, hundreds of years ago, and the tide eventually had carried it here, its bones mingling and becoming one with the grains of sand and particles of rock, but for the one tooth embedded in the cliffs for posterity.

The sound of the sea grew louder so that it filled her ears, banging against her eardrums; her vision became blurred and she swayed dizzily, she felt as though she was being carried along on a rushing, dipping bed of turbulent water and her legs trembled and crumpled beneath her.

'Sarah! Oh, Sarah – Mrs Love, do something quickly. Sarah is ill.' Lucy was frantic with alarm as she knelt over Sarah's prostrate form.

'It's all right, she's fainted, that's all.' Mrs Love gently patted Sarah's face. 'The climb up the cliff must have overtaxed her.'

Sarah stirred and her pale lips parted. 'I'm all right,' she said weakly. 'Just let me rest a moment.'

Mrs Love looked around her at the long empty stretch of sand. 'How to get her home is going to be a difficulty.'

'I'll go for help,' Lucy said determinedly.

'No!' cried Mrs Love and Sarah simultaneously, both aware of the consequences should Mrs Masterson discover that Lucy was wandering the countryside alone, no matter what the purpose.

Sarah sat up and feebly brushed the sand from herself. 'I shall be able to manage, really.' She didn't want a fuss, though she did feel a little weak. How silly of me, she thought, what a thing to do, fainting like that.

'Look. Look. There's Cousin John,' Lucy jumped up and waved frantically to the figure above the cliff. 'And your father, Sarah. Now all will be well. They will help us home.'

The old steps were long gone, though subsequent village children had attempted to make footholds for easier descent, and John slid and clambered down the slippery surface to assist them, the wet clay staining his clothes.

Sarah protested that she was quite able to stand and walk alone, but she was overruled by Lucy who demanded that John must carry her. With great solicitude he picked her up, insisting that he should at least help her as far as the slipway where her father would be waiting.

'I'm so sorry, Mr John,' she said softly. 'I could have managed.' She smiled at him, her brown eyes level with his blue ones. 'I'm quite heavy, I think?'

He wrinkled his nose. The wind was blowing her hair into his face, and he laughed. It was a pleasurable sensation, like being stroked and caressed by gossamer, and her body was soft and warm within his arms.

She lifted her hand to move her hair away from his face, and as he turned towards her she inadvertently touched his cheek. He drew in his breath involuntarily and looked at her, wondering if it was a deliberate gesture, but she smiled back at him, her lips parted and her eyes innocent. 'I've lost the pin.'

'What?' His mind was confused and he felt his heart begin to race.

'The pin! From my hair.'

He put her down as they reached the slipway and waited for the others to come.

She held out her open hand, stained with sand and clay. 'I was using it to prise this out of the cliff.'

He hardly heard what she was saying, heard only the sound of her voice as he watched her lips move. He saw the line of pale golden freckles which ran across the bridge of her small straight nose and the way her cheeks dimpled as she smiled.

'It was a lesson, you see!' Her face wore a puzzled expression as she realized that his attention was focused elsewhere.

'A lesson?' He shook his head as if to waken himself. A lesson! Great Heavens, what was he thinking of? She was just a child, not yet grown into womanhood, even though she was in his cousin's employ; and here he was, with thoughts that he should feel ashamed of.

He took hold of her hand, deliberately and firmly so as not to be misconstrued, to look at the object she held there, but felt instead a force running through her fingers into his, an electric charge which tingled and sparked, kindling and melting her flesh with his.

'What's that in thy hand, Sarah?'

John started and dropped her hand as Will came up behind them.

'It's part of a tooth, I think, Fayther.' Sarah answered her father, but her eyes held John's, a look of bewilderment on her young face.

'Aye, it's a tooth all right. It's a whale tooth. Where did tha find it?'

'It was buried in the clay, about halfway up the cliff.' She indicated vaguely back down the sands.

Will looked out to sea thoughtfully. 'It's been there a long time, I reckon, but everything gets washed to shore sooner or later.'

'But not always in the same form.' Mrs Love joined the conversation as she and Lucy came up the steep slope towards them. 'I was just explaining to Miss Lucy and Sarah about the remains of animal and plant life deposited here, when Sarah became unwell.'

Sarah held out the tooth to John. 'Would you like to keep it? It will perhaps bring you luck next time you sail.'

He took it from her. 'I don't often get the opportunity to sail these days, but yes, thank you, Sarah, I shall keep it always.' His voice was unsteady as he gazed down at her. 'Now, perhaps we had better return home,' he said, glancing at the others, 'so that Sarah can rest. I was just about to return from my walk, as I expect visitors this afternoon, when I saw Will – er, Foster. So it will be my pleasure to escort you.'

'I can't think what got into thee, child.' Will walked at his daughter's side, chiding her gently, whilst the others came behind. 'A strong lass like thee, fainting like that.'

She smiled and took his arm. 'It was nowt, Fayther,

but this child is also a woman, and it's the time of my monthly flux.'

He gazed down at her, young and fresh-faced, with a look of awakening beauty, and shook his head in wonder. It seemed but yesterday when she was born and now here she was with a woman's mind and body.

He sighed. 'Time is measured by 'seasons out here, Sarah. As summer follows spring and reaping follows sowing, so 'years have slipped by without us even noticing.'

'That's what is so wonderful, Fayther.' She turned an animated face towards him, her eyes glowing. 'It's like the flowers and herbs pushing their way up through the earth every spring, nothing can stop them; not the frost or the snow, and we know that when they die in the winter, it's not for ever, that next year it will start all over again.'

Her face had a radiance which began deep in her eyes and spread to her lips so that her whole face was glowing. 'And that is what is happening to us, we are constantly growing and renewing and creating, one following another. Do you know what I mean?'

He put an arm around her and laughed at his ardent daughter who had discovered the meaning of life and was attempting to explain it to her father, who knew nothing.

John watched them from behind and tried to shut out the sound of Lucy's chatter as she hung on to his arm. He wanted to concentrate on the fullness of feeling, the profound stirring which he felt within him as he watched the two figures in front. The tall frame of Will, his red hair fading to the colour of dark sand, bending down to listen to Sarah, whose hair reminded him of the spiralling autumn leaves which were falling from the trees, leaving a splash of red and gold.

He felt a sense of envy as he watched her take her father's arm, and tried to put his thoughts into perspective. He had watched her grow, as he had watched Lucy, but Sarah had always been special because he had been there at her beginning. He had heard her first cry, and seen her first stumbling steps. 'Genesis,' he murmured, and Mrs Love glanced at him curiously.

It wasn't a purely physical sensation which held him in its grasp, for he was now a man of some experience and he acknowledged her for the child that she still was. This was something more. He recognized an awareness growing within himself, that his other brief love affairs had been but the first sip of wine, a mere apprenticeship to prepare him for what was to come.

'Tell me about your visitors, John.' Lucy's eyes lit up at the prospect of company.

'Stephen Pardoe, you have met him already, and his sister Matilda.' John answered his cousin vaguely as they awaited tea in the drawing room and he gazed out of the window at the dusk gathering over the garden.

Mr Pardoe and his sister had arrived at the house shortly before their return, and were now in their rooms changing from their travelling clothes after the long journey from their home in London.

'Is she very pretty?' Lucy gazed at herself in the gilt mirror.

'Who?'

'Why, Miss Pardoe, of course. Who else, silly?' Lucy laughed, arranging her curls as she preened at her reflection.

'Oh, yes – yes, she is. Very pretty.'

'And are you going to marry her? Is that why she's here?'

'What are you talking about, Lucy?' He turned irritably away from the window. 'What nonsense is this?'

'Nonsense? I don't call it nonsense. Why should anyone come all the way from London if it wasn't for some purpose?'

He sat down on a sofa and spread himself, tapping his fingers on the upholstered arm. There had been a purpose, he had to admit. Miss Pardoe was attractive, and talented, and intelligent, which was why he had invited her along with her brother to meet his relatives.

'Stephen Pardoe is one of my best friends,' he answered sharply, 'and as his sister is not familiar with this part of the country, I felt it would be hospitable to invite her.' He got up again and paced the room. 'They will be travelling on again in a few days to visit friends in Harrogate.'

'Well!' said Lucy with a gleam in her eyes. 'If you're not in love with her and going to propose marriage, I can't imagine why you are being such a cross patch!'

Her face suddenly creased in alarm as a thought struck her. 'Oh, don't tell me she's refused you already?' She flung her arms around him. 'Oh, my poor John! How can you bear it?'

He disentangled himself from her sympathetic embrace. 'Lucy, do behave. There is nothing to tell. I assure you, you would be the first to know. Now be a good girl and please ring again for tea.'

Isobel too thought that there was a purpose to the visit, for although John had brought parties of house guests before, this was the first time that he had specifically invited an eligible young lady, even though ostensibly she was merely accompanying her brother.

And eligible she certainly was, as Isobel had ascertained during her discreet enquiries. That Stephen Pardoe's father was a banker she already knew, and subsequently discovered that his only daughter Matilda was the apple of his eye. No expense had been spared on her education in the arts and in music. She had a delightful singing voice, it appeared, and was an accomplished painter and needlewoman. Moreover, everyone who had met her testified to her charm and beauty.

She surveyed her from across the dining table. Delicate garlands of fragrant dried lavender and thyme decorated the table, the candle light flickered and the flames in the hearth glowed, reflecting the lustre of the silver and glassware on the table and giving a deep burnished gleam to Miss Pardoe's dark hair.

Isobel felt complacent. The dinner had been excellent. She had to admit that there was no-one they knew who had a cook as fine as Mrs Scryven. She had excelled herself today, and they had dined on watercress soup, sole stuffed with thyme, lambs' kidneys sautéed with juniper, and wild duck with piquant crabapple jelly. Miss Pardoe must surely be impressed, and they had yet to sample the dessert, lemon balm soufflé and mulled pears with cream. She gave a small belch; she was getting fat, she knew, and she looked with some envy at Miss Pardoe's tiny waist; at the silk-embroidered bodice above her looped skirt, which showed a glimpse of matching petticoat.

'Miss Pardoe says I may visit her in London.' Lucy's eyes sparkled with excitement. 'Oh, Papa, may I, please? Do say I can.'

Isaac looked anxiously across at Isobel. 'Well, I'm not sure, you are a trifle young.'

'But of course I intended to include Mrs Masterson in the invitation.' Miss Pardoe inclined her head towards Isobel and graciously smiled her request.

'That is most generous of you, Miss Pardoe, but as Mr Masterson says, Lucy is a little young to savour the delights of the city just yet.'

Lucy's face puckered and she looked as if she was going to cry, but her mother's eyebrows rose appeasingly as she spoke again. 'But if the offer could be kindly extended to next autumn when Lucy will be almost sixteen, then we should be delighted to accept.'

Mrs Masterson and Miss Pardoe both smiled. They understood each other perfectly. Lucy nearing sixteen could attend balls and parties and be seen as an eligible contender for the marriage stakes, and her mother had a year in which to prepare her.

'Sarah, what fun it will be! Dances to go to, and grand parties, and lots of young men who will all fall in love with me!' Lucy picked up her skirts and whirled around the schoolroom the next morning. 'Oh, how I wish that I could go now.' She sat down on the floor and put her arms around her knees, closing her eyes dreamily. 'Don't you think that Matilda Pardoe is absolutely beautiful, and that her brother is the most handsome man you have ever seen?'

'Yes,' said Sarah, 'and no.'

'What do you mean, yes and no?' Lucy frowned.

'I mean, yes, Miss Pardoe is very beautiful, and no, Mr Pardoe is not the most handsome man I have ever seen.' Sarah concentrated hard on threading sweet-scented myrtle and sprigs of rosemary together to make a posy.

Lucy got up and stood over her watching as she entwined small pink late rosebuds and pale green ivy with a length of vine, interweaving it with leaves of lady's mantle. 'You are clever, Sarah. Will you show me how to do that?'

Sarah shook her head. 'No, you are going to be far too busy learning how to be a lady, and besides you haven't the patience for it.'

Lucy shrugged. 'No, I expect you're right. I would get bored.' Idly she picked up some sprigs of dried lavender and pressed them to her nose. 'I'm bored now. There's nothing to do out here. I wish I could have gone out visiting with Cousin John and the Pardoes. I consider that it was very unkind of them not to have asked me.'

She sat down at the table opposite Sarah. 'Who do you think is the most handsome man you have ever seen, if it isn't Stephen Pardoe?'

Sarah looked down at her flowers. 'Well, my brother Tom is very fine looking, don't you think?'

Lucy pouted her lips. 'Oh, yes, I agree, he is, in a robust sort of way. But I favour Grecian features myself. You know, a noble brow, a classical nose.' She gazed pensively into space. 'Like Mr Pardoe in fact. But anyway,' she added emphatically, 'you can't include brothers. You have to choose someone else. For instance, who was that village boy who was staring at you the other day when we were out walking?'

'Joe Reedbarrow? Is that who you mean?'

'I don't know. I don't remember seeing him before.'

Sarah smiled. It was hardly likely that Lucy would notice the local village boys who hung around when they had no work to do, for she never looked at them but kept her eyes averted. But Joe Reedbarrow had doffed his cap as they went by that day and had moved aside to let them pass.

'He's just come back to Monkston to live with his father. His mother died giving birth to him and he's lived in Tillington with the woman who nursed him. But now his father needs him back to help on the farm.' She frowned. 'His brother Paul is a ne'er do well and does nothing to help his father, and his grandfather, old Dick Reedbarrow, is failing badly.'

Lucy shuddered. 'How dreadful. How perfectly horrid to die like that. Mama almost died, you know, giving birth to me. But your mother helped her.' Her face was a picture of frightened innocence. 'Oh, Sarah, I hope it doesn't happen to me. I declare I shan't have any babies if I can help it.'

Sarah stared into the distance, her thoughts vague and undefined, and her eyes clouded. 'I'd help you if I could,' she whispered vacantly. 'Only, I'll be too far away.'

'What do you mean, Sarah? Where will you be?'

'I don't know,' she said remotely, 'I don't know.'

Lucy jumped up, 'Oh, come on, do. Don't let us get melancholy and think on sad things. Choose who is the most handsome man in your opinion and let's pretend.'

'I can't think of anyone just at the moment.' Sarah's face was inscrutable though her lips trembled, 'and in any case, I'm too busy making a love posy for someone else to think about myself.'

Lucy's attention was caught instantly. 'Oh, who is it for? Sarah, do say.'

'Only if you promise not to say a word to a soul.' Sarah looked up at Lucy. 'I mean it. It's to be a secret.'

Lucy promised, hand on heart, but was none the less disappointed when she was told that it was for Lizzie, who she considered was very plain and shy, although she thought her kind and accommodating. 'I never thought of Lizzie being in love. I didn't think of servants in that way.'

'There is no reason why not, Miss Lucy,' said Sarah reprovingly. 'We do have feelings just the same as everyone else.'

Lucy was contrite. 'I didn't mean *you*, Sarah. I'm sorry. I didn't think what I was saying. Please say you forgive me.' Her eyes brimmed with tears. 'What a beast I am; of course Lizzie should be in love, she's a dear, sweet creature and deserves the best.' She patted Sarah's arm earnestly. 'Tell me who it is, do.'

Sarah sighed. She couldn't be cross with Lucy for long. She always made the most outrageous remarks without thinking of the effect they might have on other people's feelings, and then was devastated when she realized they were hurt.

'Why, Tom, of course. Couldn't you guess? And he doesn't even notice.' She sat back to admire the effect of her arrangement. 'But he will when I have finished with him.' She threw back her head and laughed, her humour restored and the unaccountable thoughts which flitted through her mind melting away. 'I shall give him a magic drink, Lucy, spiced with love potions, and hide fragrant herbs beneath his mattress to enchant him.'

Lucy stared wide-eyed at Sarah. For once she was tongue-tied. After a pause she gulped and whispered, 'Can you really do that?'

Sarah drew close to her and grasped her by the shoulders, staring deep into her blue eyes. 'Of course,' she whispered. 'Shall I make one for Mr Pardoe, so that he falls madly in love with you?' Her eyes gleamed mischievously, 'And shall I turn you into a mouse, and set the cat on you?'

'Oh – oh, Sarah, what a clown you are! I really

333

believed you for a moment. You are too bad, teasing like that.' Lucy gave a deep sigh of relief. 'I really did believe you.'

She looked thoughtful for a moment. 'But just in case the love posies *do* work, could you make one for Miss Pardoe, so that she will think of John, and one for him so that he will think of her?'

Sarah flushed and started to clear the debris of flower stalks from the table. 'Not now, Lucy, I haven't got the right herbs or flowers. Perhaps later.'

'Oh, but we must, Sarah. I insist, and I will help you.'

Whether the posies which they placed at the bedsides worked their spell, they could only guess. Lucy declared it to be an old wives' tale, for Miss Pardoe announced that she had never slept so well, a sound dreamless sleep as soon as she had drawn her bedcurtains, though John came down to breakfast looking tired and drawn and said he hadn't had a wink of sleep all night, and was touchy and irritable and barely ate a morsel of food. He apologized to the Pardoes for his ill-humour and Matilda had looked at him rather coldly.

They departed on the fourth day, renewing their promise of a meeting soon, and as soon as their carriage had left John announced that he would go back to town the next day, instead of staying on as planned.

'Miss Pardoe is very charming, John!' Isobel threw in the remark in as casual a manner as her directness would allow.

'Indeed. Most agreeable.' He had a dull headache that wouldn't go away. Too much brandy after supper had obviously not agreed with his digestion.

'Will you meet them again when you next visit London?' she probed anxiously.

'I shall see Stephen in the course of business, I expect, but it's doubtful if I will meet Miss Pardoe. She has a very busy social calendar, I believe.'

Isobel jumped in with both feet. 'You could do worse than look in that direction for many advantages,

John. She has great charm, perfect breeding and, as I understand it, a considerable fortune.'

'In that order, Aunt?' John allowed himself a smile.

'You may laugh, but the matter requires consideration. You will soon be thirty, just the right age for a man to wed, and Miss Pardoe is just past twenty-one. She surely won't wish to wait much longer to be married.'

'I understand that she has had several offers already, Aunt,' he said stiffly, 'but has turned them all down. Miss Pardoe seemingly isn't willing to tie herself to some scheming young buck, or a gouty rich old man, just for the sake of conforming to society's whims.' He bowed, excused himself and headed for the door.

'In that case, she should view you very favourably,' was her parting rejoinder, 'as you are in neither of those categories.'

He wished that he hadn't invited the Pardoes. Although he had been charmed by Matilda and had entertained vague, romantic ideas concerning her, he was adamant that his aunt would not be allowed to matchmake. He had seen the light in her eye the moment he had introduced his guests and knew instantly that she would start to scheme.

'Well, I won't allow it,' he muttered testily as he hurried briskly across the hall. 'I'll make my own decisions.' His head still ached, he had had the most abominable night's sleep again. The flowers by his bed had pervaded the room with their sweet, heavy perfume, and instead of soothing, it induced in him wild, restless dreams which caused him to cry out, waking him up, so that sleep evaded him and he had lain awake gazing into the grey of the morning, hearing the breathing of the sea and seeing a gentle smiling face beneath a cloud of hair, not black as night, but shining bright as the sun.

He knocked on the door leading to the kitchen and heard the scurry of those inside. Mrs Scryven opened the door and beamed at him, her round face more wrinkled and brown than he remembered.

'Mr John! How pleased I am to see thee.' She bobbed

a crooked curtsey and invited him in to the warm kitchen, the mouthwatering smells there whetting his taste buds.

He smiled at Lizzie, who he thought looked brighter and prettier and not so pale and wan as formerly.

'Mrs Scryven, I have the devil of a headache. Have you something hidden away in those cupboards that would clear it?'

She peered up at him, her eyes narrowing to slits. 'I have something to take away an ordinary pain in thy head,' she said, her voice low, 'but I can't take away 'cause. Only tha can do that, sir.'

He stared back at her. What on earth was she talking about? 'It's just a headache, Mrs Scryven, nothing more.'

She nodded her head. 'Well, we can soon fix it if that's 'case, sir. Just one moment, please.'

She pulled out a drawer in a large oak dresser and took out a pale, faded green leaf, its texture crisp and crumbling. 'Try this, Mr John, 'flavour is bitter, but tha'll find it works.'

He chewed it as she directed and pulled a face. 'It's vile! I shall forget the headache now that I have that revolting taste in my mouth!'

She nodded, her mouth twitching, and bade him sit down whilst she poured him a small glass of her own ale. He drank thirstily, it was cool and aromatic and he hoped that she would offer another, but she didn't; she stood politely waiting for him to finish and then took the glass from him, waiting for him to leave.

'Good day, sir.'

He heard the crisp rustle of Sarah's gown as she crossed the hall towards the stairs and he swung round to return the greeting. She smelt of summer, an essence of roses and sweet woodbine, and for a moment he was filled with a longing to bury his face in her hair and breathe in the fragrance.

He realized that he was staring as she gazed hesitatingly down at him from the foot of the stairs, a look of puzzlement on her face.

'Is there something wrong, Mr John?'

'Sorry, er, no, not at all. Good day, Sarah.'

He was confused. This young woman standing before him was his cousin's companion, a child almost, a servant. No – no, not a servant! He couldn't think of her as a servant, no more than he could think of Maria and Will as servants. Mrs Scryven and the others, yes, they were there to serve, that was their function. They expected their master's patronage as their right, just as they expected to be fed and clothed as their right. But Will and Maria were his friends, and this was their daughter, who in her innocence was setting his thoughts in turmoil and turning his world and his plans upside down.

She smiled and turned to leave, one hand holding a book, the other clasping the bannister rail.

'Sarah?'

She turned back, her eyebrows raised in query.

He couldn't remember what he was going to say, though he felt that it was important; his wits had wandered away like his elusive dreams, leaving him abstracted.

'Oh, hmm, I was just going to tell you – that I once slid down that bannister rail!'

She laughed suddenly, her face childlike, expectant and surprised. 'Did you? What fun!'

'Yes. On the day you were born, in fact.' He smiled back at her. His headache had lifted and he felt a sudden elation and an alarming desire to do it again. 'You won't tell my aunt, will you?'

He watched the pleasure on her face at the anticipation of a shared secret, and saw streaks of gold gleaming in her brown eyes as she laughed.

'I won't tell,' she answered and impulsively put out her hand. 'I promise.'

He took it and held it for a moment, abstractedly stroking the soft young skin with his thumb.

Gently she withdrew her hand from his. 'Was there something more, sir?'

337

'What?'

'Was there something more you wanted to say?' Her eyes held his.

'Oh. No. I beg your pardon, Sarah. Nothing more.'

19

Tom strode briskly through the yard at Garston Hall and across the lush meadow. It was a good idea of Sarah's that he should take Lizzie with him on the journey to Aldbrough. A trip out together would mean they could have a good talk like they used to when they were young.

Nowadays it seemed that there was never time, everyone was always busy. Only at mealtimes when they were all seated at the big table in the kitchen at Garston Hall did they talk, and then it wasn't proper conversation for there was always a bell ringing somewhere and somebody would have to jump up and attend to the demands of the gentry.

If there was a big party on with a lot of guests, and his mother and Ma Scryven were too busy to stop and eat, then Tom and his father would collect a basket of food that had been prepared for them and take it home to Field House where they ate in silence, neither of them bothering to speak without the women there to prompt them.

But he wanted to talk to Lizzie. She bothered him, made him feel nervous somehow. She had changed recently, become distant, and it seemed that at times when he came across her she would deliberately avoid him. She'd got something on her mind, he was sure of that. He frowned, his dark eyes bewildered. Perhaps he had upset her without meaning to. Something he had said. He sighed at the whims and fancies of women with all the profundity of a young male.

'Hello, Lizzie.' He put his head around the door. 'Sarah said I would find thee here.'

Lizzie looked up from her mending. It was her day off and she chose to spend it here at the place she thought of as home, away from the bustle of the kitchen at Garston Hall. 'Did tha want me for summat, Tom? I'm not specially busy, just doing a bit of stitching.'

He came in, sat down opposite her and stretched out his long legs. 'Mustn't it be grand to sit down just when tha feels like it, like 'gentry do?'

'Then I'm just like 'gentry today,' she said as she stitched a tear in an apron pocket. 'It's my day off, to do what I like with. I can sit, or walk or do my sewing. Today I can pretend to be Mrs Masterson.'

Tom looked at her. Her cheeks were pink from the fire and she had let her long fair hair fall from its customary knot and had tied it loosely at the nape of her neck with a blue ribbon, which, he noticed now, matched her eyes.

He rubbed his dark bristly chin with its three days' growth of beard. He'd grown tired of scraping his whiskers and had decided that the time had come to put away his youth and grow a beard.

He cleared his throat nervously. 'There's just one difference though, Lizzie. Tha's much prettier than Mrs Masterson.'

She blushed and looked away. 'Well, she is quite old,' she answered awkwardly. 'She used to be pretty.'

'Aye,' he said. 'But our ma is still bonny, and she's only about 'same age as 'mistress.'

'That's because 'mistress is never really happy, and Maria is good and gentle inside, and it always shows through. Besides,' she said, smiling wistfully, 'she has your da, and he tells her that she's lovely and that makes her so.'

There was no privacy in the kitchen at Garston Hall and Lizzie had seen the bond of affection between Will and Maria, the impulsive touching of hand on hair, the spontaneous warmth. She noticed these things and basked in the reflected comfort which she knew had been absent in her own parents' lives.

Tom stood and looked down at her. 'Lizzie?'

She raised her eyes in query and he saw the silky

340

lashes, only slightly darker than her hair, which encircled them. 'Yes?' she answered softly.

'Er.' He ran his fingers through his thick black hair and scratched his head. 'I have to go to 'mill at Aldbro' to tek 'grain. Would tha like to come for a ride?'

She felt inconsistent emotions of disappointment and elation. It wasn't what she wanted him to say, but the thought of sitting next to him in the waggon filled her with a disturbing pleasure.

'Mrs Masterson would have to have a chaperone. She wouldn't travel alone with a man. It wouldn't be seemly for a lady.' She tried to be arch, but she knew it didn't suit her, so she giggled instead.

He looked at her in astonishment. 'But we're practically brother and sister, Lizzie. Why would we want a chaperone?'

She winced and stared at him. How could such a bright, shrewd, handsome lad be such a dullard? 'It was a joke, Tom,' she said briefly. 'I'll just get my shawl.'

There was a constrained silence between them as they sat side by side on the jolting waggon. Tom clicked his tongue and cracked the whip over the horses' haunches as they pulled out of the village and on to the long road.

'Ist tha cold, Lizzie?' He saw her shiver and reached for a clean sack to put over her knees. 'Perhaps tha'd rather have stayed by 'fire, than come out on such a day?'

The morning was grey and cloudy, though it wasn't raining, and the road stretched on in front of them, the bare fields shorn of their crops and supporting a scattering of cattle and sheep.

'No, I'm enjoying it.' She looked around her. 'It's not often I get out of 'village.'

'Wouldn't tha like to work somewhere a bit more lively, like Hull, or Scarboro', like our Alice?' he asked, looking sideways at her.

She clasped her shawl closer to her. 'Oh, no, Tom, I couldn't. I'd be that scared of being on my own. Besides, I need to be near to folks that I care about.'

He opened his mouth to say something, but then closed it again when he couldn't find the words.

'It's a pity there isn't a mill a bit nearer,' she observed after a time. 'It's a long way to come to grind corn.'

'That's what I've been saying for long enough,' he replied eagerly. 'There's enough folk traipsing up and down this road to warrant building another one a bit nearer to Monkston.'

He mused over this line of thought for some time. 'Tillington. That would be 'best place. Not Monkston, it hasn't got a hill, and anyway at 'rate it's falling into 'sea, there's not going to be owt left to harvest.' He nodded thoughtfully. 'But Tillington – there's that rise behind 'church. That would be a good place to put a mill. It would catch all 'wind blowing on or off 'sea. Nowt to stop it – straight off 'Wolds or straight off 'sea. By, if only I had some money, Lizzie,' he protested earnestly, 'that's what I would do. Buy some land and build a mill.'

'That's a grand idea, Tom.' She turned to him and joined in his enthusiasm. 'Then all 'farmers would come to thee, even big ones like Mr Masterson.'

'Aye,' he said, carried away with the idea. 'They'd be doffing their caps at me to keep in favour. Then when I was rich enough, for millers do get rich, I'd buy another bit of land and build a house, and keep a carriage for my wife to drive in, just like Mr Masterson does.' He turned laughing towards her. 'How does that sound, Lizzie?'

She bent her head and answered quietly, 'It sounds right grand, Tom. I hope as tha'll still talk to them as used to know thee, when tha was poor.'

He drew in the reins, and the horses bent their shaggy heads to eat the grass at the side of the road. 'Lizzie?'

She turned her head away to hide the tears that were glistening on her cheeks.

'Lizzie, what's up? Why ist tha crying?' He gently wiped away the tears with his fingers and she didn't notice the roughness of his ploughman's hands.

'I don't know, Tom,' she whispered so that he could hardly hear her, 'I suppose it's because I can't bear to think of thee doing summat without me.'

He put both hands around her face and turned her so that she had to lower her eyes or look at him. 'How could I ever do owt without thee, Lizzie? Tha's part of my life, always have been. I said a long time back that I would tek care of thee, and I meant it.'

Bashfully he kissed her wet cheek, tasting the salt of her tears and sensing a deep emotion within her and a great happiness unrolling inside himself. 'I shan't ever be rich – tha knows I'm only boasting about that. But if tha'll have me, just as I am—?'

Her tears started to flow even faster now, and she could hardly speak she was so overwhelmed. 'Oh Tom,' she sobbed, 'I'm so happy. If only tha knew how long I've been waiting for thee!'

He put his arms around her and held her close and she lifted her trembling lips to his. The inward conflict of loving affection he had felt as a brother towards her, which had been rocking unsteadily for so long, vanished, leaving in its place a glorious, passionate elation which left him bewildered and totally bemused.

'Tha'll wed Lizzie in church then, Tom?' Mrs Scryven viewed the young couple critically as they stood blushing in the kitchen after announcing their intentions.

'Aye, nowt less.' Tom was determined on that score.

Will shook his head and lit his pipe. 'Tha's ower young, Tom. I reckon tha should wait a bit.'

'What difference does it make, Da,' Tom stood straight and tall facing his father, 'whether we wed now or later?'

'Babbies is 'difference,' said Will, looking at his son. 'Once they start coming, thy youth is over and tha's got responsibilities of other mouths to feed. It's not easy, lad, thy ma and me know only too well.'

Lizzie blushed and looked down, slipping her hand out of Tom's, embarrassed at the scrutiny of the family and the knowing grins of the other servants. They shouldn't have blurted it out like that in front of everybody, but they were so excited they wanted everyone to share their happiness.

Maria caught her gaze and smiled. 'No, it's not easy, but I wouldn't have had it any other way, Will, and nor would thou, if tha's honest.'

Briskly she dismissed the other servants about their tasks, and sat down to talk to Tom and Lizzie. 'Tha'll have to give up thy room here, Lizzie, once tha's wed, and live with Tom and us at Field House. It'll be like old times when we first came here, except that we've more room now that Sarah is living here at Garston, and Alice hardly ever comes home.'

She gave a small inward sigh. Alice didn't visit them as often as she might and Maria missed her.

'We were having a laugh, Lizzie and me,' said Tom, feeling a sense of pleasurable possessiveness as he linked Lizzie's name with his. 'About what we would do if we were rich.'

'And how would tha manage to get rich, son? Can we all share in 'secret?'

'It's like this, Da. I'll buy a piece of land and build a mill and become a miller, and 'money will start pouring in like 'grain that I'm grinding.'

Will laughed. 'I always knew tha'd make a good tradesman. It's a good dream, Tom. But first dream of finding 'money to buy land, and tha won't do that with a wife and bairns to feed.'

He looked across at Lizzie and said soberly, 'I'm only saying it for thy own good, Lizzie. Tha knows I only want best for thee and Tom, and that's why I'm saying wait a bit.'

She shook her head. 'Tha's been better than a fayther to me, Will, and I hope that I've been as good as a daughter should be.' She swallowed nervously. 'Only I have to go against thy wishes this time. I love Tom and I want to marry him, and to have his bairns. And if we have to struggle, well, I shan't mind that either.

Everybody I know has lived in poverty – me ma and da, and Maria and thee until we came out here to live. This has been like heaven to me – to have clean clothes and good food, and now that I know that they exist, well, I shan't give them up, and Tom and me'll work to have them always.'

She stopped, too overcome to go on. Tom gazed at her in amazement. It was the longest speech he had ever heard her make and he swelled with pride. What couldn't he achieve with such a woman behind him?

Will too looked open-mouthed in astonishment at the formerly quiet and timid Lizzie. Then he limped across the kitchen and planted a huge kiss on her cheek. 'Well done, Lizzie. Tha's quite right, and I give thee both my blessing.'

Sarah had come into the kitchen unnoticed and stood quietly by the door listening to the conversation. She smiled at Lizzie and then came over and gave her a hug. 'I'm so glad,' she said happily. 'Now I shan't lose a sister.'

She reached up and gave Tom a kiss. 'You're very lucky, Tom, Lizzie will be good for you – you'll be good for each other.' She looked at him seriously. 'I overheard what you were saying about a mill. Why don't you ask Mr Masterson about it? He would probably be interested in building one if it meant less travelling with the corn.'

Will looked thoughtful. 'Tha could well be right, Sarah. I can't think why we haven't thought of it before. 'Miller at Aldboro' is getting past it and can't cope with all 'work.'

He turned to Tom, a commanding tone to his voice. 'It's hard work being a miller. I've watched them, they work all 'hours that 'wind blows; but we could do with one a bit nearer and it would bring 'price of flour down for 'locals.'

Tom stared. It had been a joke, just a bit of make-believe, and now suddenly the idea was assuming reality. He glanced at Lizzie, whose eyes were wide in wonder, and then back to his father who he realized was perfectly serious.

'He'd never pay out, would he?' he asked incredulously. 'Would he buy some more land, does tha think?'

'I think he might.' Sarah answered him. 'He's a business man, after all, and if he thought it would bring him a profit! Anyway, it would be worth asking him.'

Maria and Mrs Scryven had been quietly listening to the discussion without making any comment. Maria shook her head in disbelief. 'Surely he would have done it already,' she said cautiously, 'if there was a profit to be made?'

'Happen he hasn't thought of it,' Mrs Scryven said slowly. 'And if he had, he would know that it wouldn't be any good here at Monkston. Now, if he had land at Tillington, that would be a different kettle of fish to be boiled.'

'That's just what I said,' said Tom, his voice rising in excitement, 'Tillington is just 'spot for a mill – on that piece of high ground near 'church.'

'Ah, well, now that does give thee a problem.' Mrs Scryven sat back in her chair and folded her arms and rocked gently backwards and forwards. 'That bit o' land isn't for sale!'

The others looked at her curiously. She would know if anyone did what was available.

'Does it belong to 'lord of manor then, Ma?' asked Will eventually, when it became obvious that she wasn't going to say anything more without some persuasion.

'No,' she said with some satisfaction.

'To one of 'big landowners then; or – I know,' Tom butted in. 'It must belong to 'church.'

'If it belongs to 'church, then tha'll never get tha hands on it,' Will said sardonically. 'Come on then, Ma, whose is it? And will they sell it, always supposing that master will put money up for it?'

She shook her head positively. 'I said, didn't I, that it wasn't for sale?' She gazed round at them and a beaming smile of complacency lit up her face. 'That land belongs to me.'

'Of course! I remember tha told me that a long time back.' Maria declared. 'It belonged to thy fayther.'

'Aye, it did,' she answered. 'We lived there when we were bairns, me brother Ben and me. 'Cottage is still there, though it's not much more than a hovel now. 'Thatch has fallen in and it was full of blackbirds and sparrows last time I was up there.'

'But tha won't sell it to 'master?' Tom's expression had changed from animation to disillusionment.

'What would I do with 'money?' she said, looking at him keenly. 'What else do I want at my time of life, save a good meal once a day and a warm bed?' She shook her head and went on steadily rocking. 'No, I've got them already, so I've no need for owt more.'

Just the hiss of the fire and the shifting of coals in the grate broke the silence as she finished speaking. Maria got up to light a lamp as the daylight diminished and she patted Tom's arm as she moved past him and smiled gently. She could see the disappointment as his dream faded.

'Never mind, Tom, perhaps Mr Masterson knows of another bit of land somewhere,' said Lizzie consolingly. 'It's worth asking him, if tha dares.'

'Just wait on a bit,' interrupted Mrs Scryven sharply. 'I only said I wouldn't sell it. I said nowt about me giving it away.' Her face creased into a smile and she started to chuckle, holding her arms around her plump body as she rocked to and fro and laughed at her own ingenuity.

'Give it away?' Tom gasped. 'Tha can't go giving land away!'

'It's mine to do as I like with,' she answered. 'Ben left it to me when he died, and I've no family of me own to pass it on to.' Her glance took them all in as they quietly watched her. 'Tha's all been like family to me and I'd intended to leave it to thee, all properly drawn up, before I passed on.'

She smiled up at Sarah who was leaning over the back

of her father's chair. 'Sarah knows she's to have 'cottage here at Monkston, and seeing as tha's going to wed Lizzie, Tom, then there's no sense in waiting till I'm in my grave. If tha's intent on being a man o' business, then tha'd better speak to 'master straight away about a loan to build a mill on thy land.'

To the family's amazement, Mr Masterson was in favour of the idea, and agreed to a loan on condition that he should retain shares in the mill once the loan and interest were paid off.

Tom had approached him in some trepidation. He knew what he wanted to say and do, but was very much afraid that he would become tongue-tied in front of Mr Masterson and put his case badly, and that the master would think him an idiot.

'Collect all your facts, Tom, and speak plainly,' Sarah advised. 'He won't bark at or bite you, but he doesn't like folks who wander from the point. Ask Fayther to make you a proper appointment to see him, then he'll know that it's important.'

Will went with him and stood quietly by whilst Tom explained what he had in mind. He was nervous at first, but when he realized that his employer was listening in all seriousness, his confidence grew, and Will was proud of his son's perceptiveness in recognizing a need in the area that could be turned to his own advantage.

'You know nothing about milling, Tom, how will you go about learning?' commented Isaac Masterson as he viewed the determined young man standing before him. 'You need to know about the quality of grain as well as the grinding and dressing of it.'

'I've already had words with 'miller at Aldbro', sir.' Tom replied. 'He's giving up soon, he can't climb steps so well, and he said he'll take me on for six months if tha'll release me. And there's a man in Tillington who used to work at a mill until he fell off 'sails and broke both his legs. He said he'd be glad to help; he can load

348

sacks and do general work, though he can't climb to 'top any more.'

He took a deep breath. 'I don't mean to boast, sir, but I reckon I can do it anyway.' He held his hands in front of him and rubbed his fingers together. 'I've got a feeling for 'grain and owt that grows. I've no doubts on that score.'

Isaac Masterson released him at the end of the month, and until that time Tom went about his work in a daze, unable to comprehend that soon he would be his own master.

Lizzie brought him down to earth with her sound common sense. 'We'll put off getting wed for twelve months, Tom. I'll keep on working here at Garston and that way we shan't need to spend any money, for tha'll not be earning owt over at Aldbro'. Tha can't expect 'miller to give thee a wage as well as learn thee 'trade.'

She sighed and put her arms around his broad shoulders. 'I'll miss thee, Tom. It'll be 'first time we've been apart since we were bairns.'

He kissed her soft warm lips. 'I'll be home for a day at Christmas, and I'll have to keep coming over to Tillington to see how 'millwrights are getting on, then we'll plan 'wedding as soon as 'mill is built.'

Lizzie asked Sarah if she would teach her to read and write. 'Somebody will have to write out 'bills and keep accounts,' she said, 'and Tom won't have 'time or 'liking for it, so I'd better learn.' So Sarah set her simple exercises and she spent dark winter evenings laboriously bent over her writing, or reading aloud to anyone who would listen.

Mrs Love told Mrs Masterson of her intention to leave her employment in the coming summer. 'There is nothing more than I can teach Miss Lucy, ma-am. Her French is adequate for what she requires, as is her art and literature. But I am willing to stay on until you depart for London if you wish.'

'I would be pleased if you would,' said Isobel. 'Perhaps if you could spend part of each day in conversation, so that Lucy is able to converse on diverse subjects, should the need arise during her stay in the capital.'

Mrs Love tried various topics. They discussed Bonaparte, who had crowned himself Emperor of France, a subject which caused Lucy to put her head on the table and fall asleep. The Third Coalition between Britain and its allies against France brought on such a severe headache that she had to be excused and go to lie down in her room; and she declared quite firmly that the new invention of the mobile steam locomotive would be undoubtedly dirty and noisy and merely a whim, and couldn't possibly operate as efficiently as men or horses.

The journals which her mother had ordered, however, were filled with the latest fashion ideas, with hats and hairstyles, and with the doings of illustrious players who graced the stages of London's famous theatres. On these topics Lucy became animated and very well informed, and Mrs Love was able to look Mrs Masterson in the eye and tell her in all honesty that she was quite sure that Lucy would be perfectly at ease in drawing room conversation.

'What will you do, Sarah?' Mrs Love asked, as winter blew out in a fury and heralded a cold, wild spring. 'Will you go with Miss Lucy to London as she wants you to?'

'I suppose I must, if that's what she wants. She is my employer as well as my friend, so I must do what she says – though I don't want to go.'

Mrs Love took her arm as they walked. The wind buffeted them and they put their heads down against it. Both had felt the need for air and exercise after being confined to the house for days because of constant rain and howling gales.

'You don't have to go. You can become independent if you wish.' She gave Sarah's arm a shake. 'You are a highly intelligent young woman, you're wasted playing nursemaid to a spoilt child.'

Sarah gasped at the outspokenness of the woman by

her side. She had never thought of Lucy as being spoilt. It was perfectly natural that Lucy would expect her own way over most things, although she, Sarah, had her own methods of ensuring that she didn't always get it.

'You could be a teacher or a governess. Come and stay with me at my home when I leave here. I will teach you all I know. We will read and discuss books to further your knowledge.' Mrs Love, who was normally so calm and serious, was eager and enthusiastic with her proposal, and Sarah was flattered that she should think so highly of her.

'You're very kind, Mrs Love, and I do thank you for the offer. I don't know what to say.' She looked across the fields towards the village; they were on higher ground here with a shelter belt of trees at their backs. The wind blowing off the sea shrieked through the trees, bending the young saplings until their branches almost touched the ground, and scattering the last few remaining leaves of oak and beech which had clung so tenaciously all the winter.

'I don't know how I can ever leave here, that's the problem.' Her eyes gazed past the straggle of houses towards the heaving, swelling sea, beyond the foamy crests which surged and broke outside the irregular sandbanks, and towards Flamborough Head, whose white cliffs she could just see if she narrowed her eyes. The lighthouse beam blinked its cold white light in the blank greyness which was the merging of boundless sea and sky.

Mrs Love shivered. 'How I have managed to stay so long in such a desolate place, I can't understand.' She smiled at Sarah. 'It can only be the company which has kept me so long, but I shall not be sorry to go inland again, away from this constant wind and wicked grey sea.'

'It isn't wicked,' Sarah cried impetuously, her emotions aroused. 'You have to understand it.' She opened her arms wide as if to embrace the breadth of the ocean. 'You have to know its moods and contradictions, and when to leave it alone or when to welcome it. And you can't do that unless you have known it all of your life as I have.'

'Your life is only just beginning, Sarah.' Mrs Love turned to her earnestly. 'Don't waste it, or let it erode away like those cliffs down there.'

Sarah closed her eyes to shut in the quick hot tears which were gathering. How could she explain to this enlightened, rational woman, when she didn't have the words but only an unaccountable feeling deep within her, that she was bound here; that she was rooted as firmly as the young trees in the wood behind them which bent compliantly with the wind? That her whole being, her body and spirit, was embodied here, in the same way that the horizon united the sea and sky.

The summer passed in a bustle of activity to prepare Lucy for her sojourn in London, and hours were spent poring over patterns and fabrics, and being measured and fitted for new gowns to be worn at the parties and social gatherings to which, Miss Pardoe had written, she would most certainly be invited.

Mrs Masterson too took the opportunity to order new outfits, for she also had been invited to stay in the city for a month, and her normally severe features took on more animation as Lucy's enthusiasm affected her.

Mrs Love took her leave of them, and Sarah sadly said goodbye. She would miss her kind and understanding friend and teacher, and she promised that she would write to her as soon as she had made a decision about her future. She travelled with her into Hull, where Mrs Love was to catch the afternoon diligence to York, and then directed the coachman, Harris, who had taken the place of Walters, to drive on into the Market Place where she had to call at the milliners to collect a selection of bonnets on order for Mrs Masterson.

Sarah had a natural grace and bearing and wore her simple clothes well, and the elegantly dressed woman who greeted her with affected deference as she entered the wallpapered and draped salon, looked at her inquisitively when she learned of her errand to collect millinery for her mistress.

'I know Mrs Masterson well, of course,' she said, dropping her pretentious accent, 'and I do believe I met your mother once, before you were born.'

Sarah raised her eyebrows in curiosity. Her mother had never mentioned that she knew anyone from such resplendent surroundings as these.

The woman threw back her coiffured head and laughed. 'I don't suppose she would remember me. I was just a maid in the Masterson household then. Ellie's my name and I've often wondered about those two unborn babbys. I recognized your red hair,' she added. 'You're a Foster all right.'

Sarah smiled and looked around the shop. Hats swathed with satin and roses decked the stands, and displays of fur pom-poms and feathers were artistically arranged on draped silk in alcoves. 'It's lovely,' she said. 'You must prefer it to being a maid.'

'It's mine,' Ellie answered proudly. 'All mine. Miss Brown made me a partner five years ago, and when she died last year she left it to me. She never married, you see, and she knew I wouldn't. We're both business women, and you can't be doing with families when you've a living to make.'

She looked contentedly around her and re-arranged a satin hanging. 'Here,' she said, and picked up a rose, cream with a flush of pink on its delicate petals. 'Have this with my compliments.'

Sarah stroked the soft silkiness and put it to her nose.

Ellie laughed. 'There's no scent, my dear. That's real silk. That would cost a lot of money if you were to buy it in London.'

'Oh,' said Sarah in surprise. She couldn't imagine why anyone would want to spend money on imitation flowers when it was so easy to grow real ones.

'But you can have it as a gift,' Ellie continued. 'Just for old times' sake.'

She showed her out of the door, insisting that Sarah passed on her regards to Mrs Masterson. 'Tell her that Miss Ellie was asking about her,' she said, and pointed to the sign above the window where in shiny gold lettering was the name, 'Miss Ellie. Milliner.'

Sarah was confused by the noise of the crowd and the clatter of carriers' carts on the cobblestones as she left the shop, and held tight to the boxes containing the precious hats and bonnets. Instead of turning right to make her way to the Masterson yard where Harris had said he would wait for her, she turned left and found herself in the thick of a crowd of women all hustling down the Market Place towards the butchery.

She was fearful that her parcels and their contents would be crushed, so she dodged out of the crowd and turned down an alleyway, hoping to be able to take a short cut back to the High Street. She knew that the old town streets crisscrossed each other but, being unfamiliar with them as she very rarely came to Hull, she soon found that she was quite lost in the maze of lanes and squares.

Her eyes opened wide in dismay as she passed some of the slum dwellings and saw groups of ragged children playing barefoot amongst the seeping open sewers, or sitting in the dirt sharing their crusts of grey bread with the swarms of flies which were hovering about them.

She started to walk quickly as she saw that they had noticed her and were starting to follow her. She was beginning to feel sick. There was a strange, fetid smell hanging over the town – she had noticed it earlier but now it seemed to be stronger – a heavy, oily stench combined with a strong acrid burning which hung in the oppressive warmth, like the singeing remains of burnt feathers left on a fowl which Mrs Scryven might have plucked.

'Hey, miss. Spare us a penny.' The shouts of the children came nearer and she started to run. She had no money with her or she would have given them some, but they probably wouldn't believe that. She thought that she must look very rich in their eyes, and she was afraid, not for herself but for the safety of the contents of her boxes.

She turned a corner and heaved a sigh of relief. She had reached the river, and she knew that she couldn't be far from the Masterson warehouse which ran down from the High Street to the riverside.

The narrow waterway was crowded with ships and barges, and ropes and crates littered the staith side making it difficult for her to walk, hampered as she was by her burden.

'Excuse me, miss, but tha shouldn't be here. It's private property, and besides it's not safe. Tha might tummel in 'water.'

She glanced over her shoulder to see if the children were still following her, but they had given up the chase and gone back, and she turned to explain to the porter who had shouted to her that she was lost and to ask for directions. Taking her eyes from the wooden planking for a moment, she stumbled over a rope and dropped one of her boxes. By the time she had retrieved it the man had disappeared, and with a gesture of impatience she sat down on a crate to wait for someone else to appear.

It was mid-afternoon and the sun was still high in the sky. The stench increased with the heat and she held her handkerchief to her nose as she sat and watched the silver ripples of water trapped between the mass of craft which lay packed tight in the river, and wondered how the seamen managed to manoeuvre the ships into the dock, or out into the broader reaches of the Humber, without crashing into each other.

Gradually she became aware, first of all of a pair of shiny leather boots, and then two long legs clad in tight grey breeches. A white frilled shirt with arms folded in front completed the picture as she raised her eyes, and there stood John Rayner watching her.

'Sarah? What *are* you doing here?' His voice was severe but a smile hovered around his eyes.

She got down from the crate and brushed her skirt. 'I got lost, sir. I tried to take a short cut to avoid the crowd and lost my way. I was looking for the yard, I'm to meet Harris there, but I had to sit down for a moment, I felt so sick with the dreadful smell.'

He relieved her of some of her hat boxes. 'The smell is part and parcel of my livelihood, Sarah – and of your father's at one time. We get used to the odour of blubber boiling, but I have to admit that I never can get used to the stench of burning from the charnel houses.' He stopped. Perhaps he shouldn't have said so much. He certainly wouldn't have mentioned it to Lucy, who would probably have swooned here on to the wooden stage, but Sarah just nodded and accepted the statement as a fact of life.

'Harris is already here and getting anxious about you. Would you take my arm, Sarah? It's difficult walking along here, the staith is narrow and not meant for leisurely walks by ladies in long dresses.'

He knew that with care she was perfectly able to skirt the barrels and crates without any assistance from him, but he had an overwhelming desire to have her hand on his arm and feel the touch of her fingers through his shirt sleeve.

'Please excuse me for being without my coat.' He glanced down at her and saw the warm flush on her cheeks. 'The weather is so hot that it's more comfortable working without it. When my clerk told me that he could see a lady wandering alone by the river, I ran out without stopping to put it on.' His voice became serious. 'It isn't safe for you to be alone around here, Sarah. Sometimes violence breaks out without any warning at all and you could be caught up in it. You could be robbed, or fall into the river.'

It was true that he had hurried out of his office as his clerk had called to him, but he had already seen her from his window and had responded to an unwarranted yearning to waylay her before she found her way round to the stable yard.

'I beg your pardon, Mr John. I didn't mean to cause a nuisance.' She took her hand from his arm as they approached the building. 'If you'd be kind enough to direct me to where I can find Harris, I won't keep you any longer.'

Harris wasn't in the yard, and they found him sitting on a bale of straw in an empty stall drinking thirstily from a jug of beer. He got up, a guilty expression on his face as they entered looking for him, and apologized profusely. 'I don't usually drink when I'm working, sir, but it's that 'ot.' He stammered nervously as he explained, the memory of Walters's dismissal after a final bout of drunkenness fresh in his mind. 'I'm waiting on 'farrier to fix a shoe on one of 'greys. I daren't risk driving home with it loose.'

'That's all right, Harris. But go inside and ask for some bread and cheese. That'll soak up the beer.' John nodded to Harris affably and the young coachman looked visibly relieved at being let off so lightly.

Sarah hesitated as they came back into the yard, not knowing where to go.

'Come inside, Sarah, out of the heat and I'll get my housekeeper to bring you some refreshment.' John led her inside and up the stairs into a small sitting-room next to his office and invited her to sit down and make herself comfortable whilst he rang for tea.

Whilst he was out of the room she looked curiously around. It was undoubtedly a man's room with no feminine touches, save the vase of flowers set on a small polished table by the window. Leather armchairs and plain rugs were set upon the dark wooden floors, and paintings of whalers and sailing ships adorned the walls, but the room was redeemed from complete masculine severity by the cream blinds and billowing white muslin curtains at the long windows. It felt cool after the sweltering heat outside but she wished that the windows could be closed to keep out the awful, pervading smell. She walked across to look out and, as she bent to smell the flowers in the vase, her eye was caught

357

by an object on the table which she picked up, cradling it in her hand.

She started as he silently came and stood beside her. 'It's the whale tooth I gave you,' she said softly. 'You kept it!'

The pale ivory gleamed as if it had been polished and had been placed in a glass dish on a small cloth of rich brown velvet.

He shook his head when she asked him how it had acquired its sheen. 'No polish or oils, but every morning and every night after supper, I hold it in my hands and smooth it with my fingers.'

He took it from her to demonstrate. He wanted to tell her how he imagined that it was her own smooth skin that he was stroking, and that the velvet was chosen to remind him of the colour of her eyes. Not that he needed such a reminder, for he was constantly aware of Sarah and her dark eyes as he looked out from his window at the deep brown of the river when the evening sun splashed it with gold, when he saw the burnished gleam of his chestnut mare, and most of all when he had ridden the long country road to Monkston this past winter and observed the richness of the brown earth.

As he looked at her now, she was gazing back at him, a tremulous, hesitant smile hovering on her lips. He put down the ivory and, without thinking what he was doing, he took her hand and gently raised it to his lips. Tenderly he brushed her forehand and then turned it over to kiss her warm palm.

Instantly she snatched her hand away. Her face became confused and fearful and her eyes filled with tears.

He was aghast at his unintended effrontery, and stammered out his apologies. What must she think of him, a man in his position apparently taking advantage of her alone in his room?

'Please forgive me, Sarah. I didn't mean to offend you.'

She hung her head, her cheeks burning. 'I'm sure you didn't mean any offence, Mr John.' Her voice trembled.

'I know that there are gentlemen who take advantage of servant girls – Janey has told me about them – but I know that you are not like them.'

Horrorstruck that the notion should have even crossed her mind, he put his hand under her chin and lifted her head. 'Sarah! I would never hurt you. Never in a million years. Please believe me!'

She nodded her head silently, and desperately he wanted to kiss away the tears that were lying moist on her cheeks.

'It's just – it's just that you look so beautiful, I didn't think what I was doing.'

She became embarrassed and moved away, toying with the strings on her bonnet which she had loosened.

He wanted to say, I love you, Sarah! To open wider the window and shout it to the crowds outside. But as he looked at her he saw the innocence of her face and knew that she wasn't ready, that such a proclamation would dismay her, that she would take fright and run away, and he would lose her trust for ever.

The housekeeper knocked and brought in tea, pouring it for them before leaving the room, and silently they sat drinking it, Sarah staring down at the thin china cup and John trying to think of something to say to ease the situation.

'Have you forgiven me?' he said eventually, trying to make light of the subject. 'It won't be the last time that someone will steal a kiss from you. I guarantee that a few London gentlemen will be swayed by your charms.' He hadn't meant to be flippant but, with a sinking feeling in the pit of his stomach, realized now that that was how it sounded.

She drew herself up and met his gaze. 'Excuse me, Mr John, but I think you forget that I am Miss Lucy's companion. It's hardly likely that I will be meeting any gentlemen. Menservants perhaps, but I will not tolerate any familiarity.'

He had been rebuked, as severely and politely as it was possible for her to do so in the circumstances, and it brought home to him the fact that she was about to endure an intolerable situation. As Lucy's childhood friend and companion she was neither servant nor gentlewoman, and though while living in a country district like Monkston there was no difficulty, as servants and gentry worked together in harmony for their mutual good, she would find things very different in the London society she was shortly to enter.

He sat on at his desk after her departure, ignoring the mass of paper work waiting for his attention, his hands clasped under his chin and a wave of depression washing over him as he thought of his own predicament. He had come to love someone who in the eyes of society was beneath him. No matter that she was sweet and gentle and more of a lady than many that he knew, to declare his love for her he would be ostracized by his own class and laughed at as a fool by hers.

20

Maria and Mrs Scryven rose at four o'clock and Sarah at five, in order to be sure that the trunks and boxes were properly packed and ready to be loaded on to the carriage when it arrived at nine for their departure to London.

Mrs Scryven had prepared a hamper of food and drink for their journey, and Maria had brought warm blankets and pillows down into the main hall in case the weather was cold, or the inns where they would break their journey were not warm or comfortable enough.

There had been some discussion between Lucy and her mother as to whether either Janey or Lizzie should accompany them also, and indeed Isobel had voiced the opinion that either of them would in fact be of more use than Sarah. Then John had announced his intention of escorting them, and there wasn't room for anyone else in the carriage, and Lucy had stated quite firmly that Sarah should come with them.

'You'll love it, Sarah, once you're there, I know you will, and you can still come to the parties and watch the fun even if you can't join in.'

Lucy was a little unsure of what Sarah's position would be in someone else's household, but declared that they needn't worry about it and that it would be resolved to everyone's satisfaction. She didn't want Sarah to miss the experience, no matter how she insisted that she would be quite happy to stay behind.

The decision was made final when they received a letter from Miss Pardoe to say that she would supply a maid for Mrs Masterson, and one for Lucy and her own two cousins, who would also be staying with her.

'Then you don't need me, Lucy, if you are to have the

company of other young ladies.' Sarah had clutched at straws as the day of departure drew nearer and her despair grew at leaving the remote sea coast, the green undulating meadows and slow meandering streams where she so firmly belonged.

'But I might not like them,' said Lucy petulantly. 'They might be very dull.' She tossed her fair curls and, glancing in the mirror for reassurance, touched the pale scar that lay hidden beneath the wisps of hair on her forehead. 'They might look down on me for being provincial and countrified, and I must have someone to confide in. Now I won't hear another word. I insist that you come, and that is all that I shall say on the matter.'

The whole household gathered outside to see them off. Maria's eyes glistened proudly as she saw her daughter, dressed in a new moss green gown and cloak, travelling away to places that she only knew by name, and, with a gathering sense of her own esteem, turned to look at the house of which she would be complete mistress for a short while, answerable only to Mr Masterson. Mrs Scryven, now that she had grown into old age and was less able, was content to potter in the kitchen, leaving arduous tasks to the young maids and decisions and responsibilities to Maria.

Will watched them drive away, a sad smile hovering about his mouth. He alone had seen the despairing look, hidden beneath a bright smile, as Sarah waved goodbye. 'It's not for long, lass,' he'd whispered as he bent to kiss her cheek. ' 'Place'll still be here when tha gets back.'

Lucy and Mrs Masterson sat side by side facing John and Sarah. Sarah tucked herself into the corner, lest her feet should brush his or the jolting of the carriage should cause her to fall against him, causing them both embarrassment, for he had spoken very little to her on his subsequent visits to Garston Hall since their encounter in Hull, and she felt awkward and confused.

But on the third day of their journey, Mrs Masterson complained that Lucy was fidgety and that she could get no rest because of her constant shuffling, and insisted that Lucy changed places with John.

Sarah then was unsure which was the worse predicament; to have him sitting so close that she felt he could hear even the imperceptible movement of her breath, and when he nodded off to sleep to feel his head touching her shoulder; or to have him sitting opposite her and to know that whenever she lifted her gaze, his eyes would be fixed upon her, only to look away when he saw that he was observed.

Rain started to fall heavily as they approached the town of Sleaford where they were to spend the next evening, and by the time they reached the inn there was such a deluge that it was impossible for them to step down from the carriage.

John reached for his cape. 'I'll go inside,' he said, 'and make sure that the rooms are ready. Stay there, Aunt, until the rain eases.'

'Sarah, go with Mr John,' Mrs Masterson commanded. 'Make sure that the fires are lit and the beds are aired.'

Sarah rose obediently, but John protested. 'She will catch her death.'

'Nonsense,' replied Mrs Masterson. 'Of course she won't, Sarah is not at all frail. A drop of rain won't hurt her.'

'No, ma-am, I'm quite use to getting wet, and this rain isn't any wetter than Monkston rain.' Sarah smiled as she spoke. She was so relieved to be getting out of the close confines of the fusty carriage that she would have braved any storm, and the rain on her face was cool and refreshing as she stepped down. Never the less, the turbulent movement of the carriage had unsettled her and, momentarily, she put out her hand to clutch John's arm.

He gathered his cape around her. 'Take hold of me and we'll run for the door.'

She put her arm around his waist, and he slipped one around her shoulder to support her as they hurried across the wet slippery cobbles of the coachyard towards the porch where the landlord was waiting.

'I'm sorry, sir, but I'm fully booked up. I'm waiting on a party now. If you an' your wife could drive but 'alf a mile down the road to the next 'ostelry, you'll get fixed up there right enough.'

Sarah thought she would die with shame at the landlord's error, yet realized how the misapprehension had occurred, when their two figures had been so close beneath the cape and they laughed so familiarly at each other's drenched appearance. She wondered how John could be so calm and dignified as he explained that they were in fact the expected party, that their rooms had been booked in advance, that they would require hot water for washing and that the ladies would require tea immediately and hot food as soon as possible.

She followed the landlord's wife up the narrow staircase and was shown into the rooms they were to occupy. They were small and crowded with dark and heavy furnishings, but there was a bright fire blazing in each small hearth and a copper hod filled with coal at the side of them.

She tested the beds. They were comfortable and well aired, with the warming bricks still in them, and she longed to lie down herself and rest her aching body, to lie alone in the darkness and gather to herself her confused and bewildered thoughts, and turn them into some kind of order and reasoning.

'I shall take a walk before I sleep.' John finished his supper and stretched. They had taken their meal in the privacy of the small sitting-room downstairs which the landlord had allocated for their use. 'Will anyone come with me now that the rain has stopped?'

Mrs Masterson declined most firmly and Lucy peered out of the window. 'There's not much to see, merely a street. I don't think I will, thank you, John. You must go though, Sarah, to keep John company.'

Sarah couldn't protest: Lucy's bid was couched in

such terms that she felt she would be considered churlish to refuse.

John smiled sympathetically. 'Just a short walk, Sarah. I'm sure you must be tired?'

'Just a little,' she answered, feeling at that moment very tired indeed and, for some inexplicable reason, extremely tearful. 'Though a breath of air would be very pleasant.' She turned to Mrs Masterson. 'If you will excuse me, ma-am, and if you are not too tired to wait, I'll attend you and Miss Lucy on my return.'

'No, I will retire now, and you must do the same, Lucy. We have another long day ahead of us tomorrow.' Mrs Masterson rose and went to the door. 'Good night, John, don't overtire yourself.'

Sarah attended to their wants, helping first of all Mrs Masterson, then Lucy out of their dresses and stays and into their bedgowns. She unpinned Mrs Masterson's hairpiece which she thought must have been very hot and itchy to wear all day, and took down Lucy's long hair and brushed it, then helped them both into bed. Finally she lit a candle at their bedsides and turned down the lamps and went along the corridor to her own small room.

Mr John can't surely be waiting, she thought, I've been such a long time, but she unhooked her cloak from behind the door and went downstairs. The inn was noisy; she could hear the raucous sound of men's laughter and she hesitated about going through the main room to the front door, and instead slipped into the sitting-room where they had taken their meal.

John was lying sprawled in his chair sound asleep. He had taken off his boots, and his stocking-clad feet were turned towards the cooling embers in the grate. His shirt was unbuttoned at the neck and she could see the curly hair of his chest beneath his collar bone.

As she stood quietly looking at him, determining whether or not to wake him, he stirred in his sleep, a smile hovering about his mouth. Involuntarily she smiled back, a warmth stealing over her, and she thought how much younger he seemed when his defences were down, his air of self-assured confidence slipped away.

Gently she touched his arm to waken him, but he merely sighed deeply and turned his head away. She bent over him and stroked his neck, the way she knew people did with babies, to waken them gently without fright, and he put up his hand to hers to stop the tickling. He opened his eyes wide and looked at her and she looked wonderingly back at him, her pulse throbbing in her throat, for he groaned softly and closed his eyes again.

'Mr John!' She squeezed his hand which still held hers. 'Mr John, wake up. You must go to bed.'

He opened his eyes again and gazed back at her. 'Sarah?' His voice was deep and throaty. 'I thought I was dreaming.' He looked down at the small hand held in his palm. 'But I see that I wasn't.' He dropped her hand abruptly and turned away, putting his hands to his forehead. 'Oh, God,' he groaned softly. 'What am I going to do?'

Alarmed, she stood back from him. She started to tremble, a hammering began in her ears and spread through her body, her pulses raced, and she felt faint. She could hear the strange, yet familiar sound of powerful, rushing water, and it seemed as if the ground was going to give way beneath her.

The room was becoming darker and she took hold of the back of his chair. Some force was dragging her down into unconsciousness but she fought back, gasping for breath and trying to keep possession of her senses.

John abruptly jumped up as he became aware of her paleness and distress and caught her by her arms. 'My dear, you are ill. Come, sit down.' He sat her in his chair and poured a glass of wine from the bottle still on the table. He held the glass to her mouth whilst with trembling lips she sipped the sweet red wine.

'You should be in bed. It's been a long tiring day.'

'Your walk?' she questioned weakly.

He knelt beside her. The colour was returning to her cheeks. 'Could you manage a turn around the square? The air might be beneficial.'

She nodded. 'Yes, I think so. I do usually take a short walk before bedtime.'

The air was fresher after the rain, and mist was rising from the road, hovering in drifts about their knees. They laughed together as they looked down and saw that their feet had disappeared.

'That's better.' John smiled at her. 'You have been very solemn these last few days. Not as happy as I am used to seeing you. I was afraid that you were unwell or displeased over something?'

She dared not admit that it was he who was making her ill at ease, that his presence made her nervous, but that his absence made her more so. She could not confess that she was irritable and unsettled when he was not there, and filled with a confused, incomplete happiness when he was.

Instead she answered softly, 'I feel as if I am adventuring into the unknown. As if all my own familiar people and places have abandoned me and set me adrift.'

'But, Sarah!' He took her arm. 'We are here, Lucy, and my aunt. And you know that I—' He stopped short, not knowing how or what else to say, and finished lamely, 'I won't let anyone be unkind to you.'

'I know.' She sighed and they walked back towards the inn. 'I'm just being silly.' She laughed to cover her insecurity. 'Don't tek any notice, maister. Tha knaws I'm just a daft country lass.'

He threw back his head and laughed with her. The landlord was in the hall as they went upstairs, and John turned to him as he saw the knowing look on his face and put him firmly in his place. 'Will you be sure to send early tea to my cousins and my aunt in the morning, and bring me hot water at six. We shall be away straight after breakfast.'

Sarah smiled at him gratefully as he left her at her door. He bent to kiss her hand and then impulsively he

367

kissed her cheek. 'Good night, cousin,' he called, and noisily made his way to his own room.

Mrs Masterson was snoring gently and Lucy was idly playing with the ribbons on her dress as they approached London. Sarah leaned towards the carriage window, looking out at the tidy new streets and parades of shops and houses which were being built on the edge of the city. As they clattered on the volume of traffic increased, and Lucy then sat up and took notice as grand carriages, barouches and chaises sped by and she tried to see the occupants.

Presently they drove along wide thoroughfares with fine handsome houses, and John pointed out places of importance, and for Sarah's sake singled out the green parks and gardens which he said were in the heart of the city.

'We're almost there,' he said. 'Perhaps you should waken your mother, Lucy.' As he spoke they drew alongside a wrought-iron fence which bordered a residential square and came to a halt at a high, guarded gate. At a word from Harris, the coachman, the man at the gate unfastened the lock and the carriage rolled slowly along the wide street.

There was a green area set in the middle of the square and on the left as they approached were small neat dwellings of two and three storeys, with painted panelled doors leading straight on to the street. On the opposite side were much grander houses of five floors; and although in essence they were all similar, with their classical façades and tall windows, and four or five stone steps leading to the wide front doors, some were superior to others. It was at one of these that the carriage drew to a halt, and from whose door, as if by signal, a uniformed footman appeared to open the carriage door and help them descend.

As they approached the steps to the elegant, columned portico, a smiling Miss Pardoe was there to greet them, a second footman and two housemaids in attendance.

Mrs Masterson was enchanted with the house, which was fronted by fine, black, wrought-iron railings and was spacious and elegant within, with an outer hall and then an inner hall with central pillars, tall windows and sculptured busts and paintings adorning the white walls.

Sarah was given a small room adjoining Lucy's and to this she retired, after helping the maid to unpack Lucy's and Mrs Masterson's gowns, unfolding them carefully from their wrappings and shaking them free of creases. A perfume of lavender and mint had risen from them as she did so, and the young girl, who said her name was Rose, had wrinkled her nose in pleasure.

' 'Course, you come from the country, don't ya?' She had a nasal whine to her voice and Sarah smiled. It would be no use to adopt her native Yorkshire dialect here for the benefit of the servants, for she knew that they would not understand a word she uttered.

'Yes, we do. We grow our own lavender and mint, and we place it around our clothes and bedding to keep away the moth.'

'So do we,' said Rose. 'Only we buy ours down at the market. We don't 'ave the bother of growing it ourselves. Can't anyhow, 'cos we don't 'ave a garden of our own.'

Sarah's room, which was behind Lucy's, had a window overlooking the back of the house, and she peered out into the dusk. The house had adjoining walls with its neighbours and these abutted around a small courtyard. From the dim light coming from the basement, which she assumed housed the kitchens, she thought she could see the shadow of ferns and plants growing down there.

Perhaps that is a garden, she mused. There has to be a garden or some grass somewhere, or where do the ladies walk? Even Mrs Masterson, who was not over fond of fresh air, took a walk two or sometimes three times a week, if the weather was kind, around the lawns of Garston Hall.

She had seen the green area in the middle of the square as the carriage had rolled up to the house, but in the

369

bustle of their arrival, she had not had the chance to take proper notice of her surroundings, but saw only that the grass had an iron railing around it with a closed gate.

'Excuse me, ma-am.' Sarah dropped a curtsey as she knocked and entered Mrs Masterson's room. Mrs Masterson was dressed and waiting for the supper bell. She looked very grand in her dark blue draped silk gown and transparent muslin sleeves. The maid had dressed her hair as she had requested, with feathers and small pearls attached to fine net to adorn it.

'I wondered, ma-am, if it would be permissible to sup in my own room this evening?' She felt desperately tired and in no mood to answer questions from curious servants in the kitchen. She also knew that she would be in the way, that the last thing the cook needed would be a stranger in her kitchen when they were busy preparing and serving food to the household and guests.

'I'm sure that will be perfectly in order, Sarah. Unless of course you can make yourself useful.' She gazed thoughtfully at her and then nodded her head carefully so as not to disturb her coiffure. 'And then you may go to bed. Lucy and I won't be needing you any more tonight, the maids seem to be very capable and will help us to bed. Just lay out my new green morning gown, for I understand we are to be at home to visitors tomorrow, and then you may retire.'

Sarah closed the door quietly behind her. She felt superfluous. Lucy was dressed, and already giggling and laughing in Miss Pardoe's cousins' room as they waited to go down to the dining room. Her nervousness at being thought provincial was forgotten, for on being introduced to them she had seen at once that she was much prettier than they. She had conceded to Sarah confidentially that whilst the elder, Cassandra, had a certain dignified elegance, Blanche was really quite dumpy and plain, and she didn't think at all that she would ever grow out of it.

Sarah's private opinion was that though Miss Blanche was no beauty, she seemed kind and had a nice smile, whilst Miss Cassandra had no warmth whatsoever, and no amount of elegance could compensate for her total lack of civility.

She made her way down the winding back staircase towards the sounds and smells of the kitchen. Rising heat, the clattering of pans and loud voices alerted her as she reached the lower floor and she hesitated outside the door for a moment before taking a deep breath and firmly rapping with her knuckles. There was no cessation of sound, only the shriek of someone chastising an inferior for letting a pudding boil dry.

She opened the door and looked in. The room was crowded with people. Maids in black with trim white aprons and caps, scurried hurriedly with trays of dishes which they handed to waiting footmen, whilst red-faced girls dressed in grey stirred pans over the huge smoking range, and ducked to avoid the slaps which the cook was handing out to all and sundry as she wrestled to get the food served to the ladies and gentlemen waiting upstairs.

Sarah slipped unnoticed into the room and put on an apron which was hanging behind a door. She went towards the range and looked into a pan. The sauce in it was bubbling furiously, so she drew it away from the heat and took up a wooden spoon to stir it gently. The young girl at the side of her looked at her open-mouthed and then dipped an awkward hesitant curtsey.

'You don't need to dip to me.' Sarah smiled at her. 'I'm Sarah Foster, companion to Miss Masterson.'

'We 'eard abaht you,' said the girl, wiping a sweating brow with the back of her hand, 'from Rose. She said you wasn't at all stuffy, but neither was you common.'

The cook came up and pushed the girl away, telling her to look sharp and drain the vegetables. She looked at Sarah curiously, then took the spoon away from her and examined the sauce. 'Thank you, miss, I reckon you've saved it from burning. Them girls 'ave no idea in their 'eads. Full of sawdust, they are.'

'I'm glad I could help,' said Sarah. 'I didn't want to get in the way and only came down to ask if I might take my supper in my room? I'm very tired after our journey.'

'Bless you, miss, 'course you can. I wouldn't expect that you'd want to eat down 'ere in the kitchen.'

'Oh, but I would!' Sarah was abashed. 'I do at home. I mean – unless I eat with Miss Lucy.' She blushed in confusion. 'Things are different there – not quite so formal as in the city.'

'I understand, miss.' Cook nodded sympathetically as she viewed Sarah's quandary. 'I'll get Rose to bring you a tray up, just as soon as the gentry 'ave been served.'

It hadn't been her intention to be waited on, she could have carried her own tray, but rather than complicate matters when she could see that Cook was anxious now for her to go, she thanked her and slipped out of the kitchen, only to hear her say to no-one in particular, 'Poor young woman, doesn't know where she belongs.'

Sarah slept well in the narrow feather bed and rose as usual at first light. She washed and dressed and then looked in at Lucy who was sleeping soundly. Quietly she crept downstairs and into the kitchen, where she found the same young girl that she had spoken to last night kneeling on the floor feeding sticks and small pieces of coal into the range in an effort to relight it.

'Cook'll kill me for letting it out,' she said when she saw Sarah. 'I was supposed to mend it before I went to bed, only I forgot.'

Sarah helped herself to a slice of bread and some cheese which she found in the cool pantry and poured a cup of milk. It was thin stuff compared with the thick creamy liquid from their own cows at home. Then she asked the girl if she could tell her how to get into the garden.

'Do you mean the garden in the square?' she answered in surprise. ' 'Cos that's kept locked, and anyway we can't go in it.' Confusion showed on her sooty face. 'Leastways, *we* can't, but I don't know about you, miss.'

Sarah felt exasperated. 'Well, what about the garden at the back, surely we can get out there?'

The girl looked at her blankly. 'If you mean the yard – yes, you can go out there. Through that door there.'

Sarah opened the door which led her into a small dark hallway, and, fumbling, found another door which was locked and bolted. She turned the large iron key and slid the bolt and found herself in a small, confined courtyard which had indeed a few poor plants and wilting ferns. An ivy struggled up one of the walls to reach the light and in the middle was a palm tree. It seemed incongruous to Sarah for it to have a home in such surroundings, for although it looked as if the courtyard had once been a pleasant area in which to sit, judging by the wrought iron seat, stone urns and statuary which were there, it now had a neglected air, made worse by the old cooking pans, brushes and rubbish which had been thrown there.

She opened a gate in the wall and looked down a long narrow passage leading out into the street. She decided to take the risk of getting lost and walked down it for a considerable way before taking a left turn which brought her round to the front of the street and opposite the enclosed garden.

Cheerfully she ran across the road and looked through the railings at the grassy area. Small beds of roses were set at the side of a gravelled path which ran all the way round, and slender ash and London plane trees with their smoothly mottled trunks and black branches marched alternately between them. She was delighted to see that the trees were still in full leaf and had not yet started to fall, their cascading branches casting small pools of shade over the grass, and for the first time since she had left home she felt herself relax. The birds were singing and plump pigeons were pecking at the gravel on the path making their comforting, croaking cry.

She walked on until she came to the gate but saw to her dismay that not only was it closed but chained and padlocked, so that there was no hope at all of her getting in to walk there as she had intended. What kind of place is this, she thought angrily, when they lock up grass and trees, and she shook the gate until it rattled. She walked round to the other side of the garden, hoping to find another entrance, but there was only the one. As she continued around the perimeter, she looked across the square towards the Pardoes' residence where she saw that a groom was standing, holding a glossy bay mare which John was preparing to mount.

She ran across the road towards him, calling his name. 'Mr John, Mr John, are you leaving already?'

'Sarah, what are you doing out here so early?' He ignored her question and looked down at her, a furrow wrinkling his brow. 'How did you get out, the doors have only just been unlocked?'

'I came out through the back, through the courtyard. I wanted to walk in the garden, only it's locked, I can't get in – Mr John, are you going home?' Her voice broke as she tried to cover her dismay that he might be returning north.

He dismissed the groom who was listening with interest to the young woman who had dashed across the road in a most unladylike manner, her red hair and skirts flying, to accost the gentleman visitor in such a familiar way.

'I'm not leaving, Sarah. Not yet. Merely going out for a ride into the park.' He saw the relief on her face and explained gently. 'But I shall be leaving in about a week. I can't stay as long as I would wish, I must get back to Hull. Mr Masterson can't manage alone for any longer.'

She nodded. 'I understand. If you should go to Monkston, will you please tell them—' She looked away.

'Yes, what shall I tell them, Sarah?' He wanted to sweep her up behind him and carry her off, away from this city of brick and stone, of statues and monuments. She looked so defenceless and vulnerable standing there in a fine London street, like a wild flower grown from a seed which had been dropped by a careless bird, and left to struggle for survival or wilt and die.

'I'll tell them, shall I, that you have seen the great parks and gardens, and the rich carriages and beautiful ladies, and that you still think that Monkston is the only place on God's earth that you would want to be?' He smiled quizzically at her and settled his restless mount as, puzzled, Sarah nodded her head.

'Yes, please. Though I haven't yet seen any of those places.'

'You shall. It will be my pleasure to escort you and the young ladies this afternoon if nothing else has been decided. You shall see that London is beautiful, and though I can't offer you the lashing of the waves of the German Ocean, I can show you the ancient Thames as a substitute.' He bent down and touched the top of her bare head and wound a curl around his finger. 'Now off you go inside, it will be considered unseemly for you to be wandering about the streets alone. This is not Monkston, Sarah, and you cannot expect to do the things here that you would do at home.'

21

There was a promenade of high fashion as ladies, colourful as summer flowers in dresses of soft draped silks cut shorter to show their ankles, paraded amongst others who favoured the classical Grecian style of transparent muslin with high necks and trailing skirts, who strolled with their friends in the afternoon sunshine.

Sarah longed to get out of the carriage and walk through the vast grassy areas of Hyde Park and enjoy the autumn sunshine, or sit beneath the trees as so many other people were doing. But Lucy and her new friends were content to drive around slowly, watching the crowd; to see, and to be seen from the open carriage and to acknowledge gracefully, but with some covert giggling behind their fans, the young men riding by who tipped their hats towards them.

'Look, look. Cassandra! There's Mr Anderson. See him – on the stallion!' Blanche pointed excitedly across the park to where a thin-faced man seated on a black stallion was talking to a group of people.

Cassandra raised her eyebrows and closed her eyes in a supercilious gesture. 'What care I?' she said, but her cheeks turned pink and she fanned herself vigorously.

Lucy questioned eagerly. 'Do tell! Who is the gentleman?'

Cassandra shrugged, but Blanche, her eyes alight with excitement, leant confidentially towards Lucy. 'He's been calling quite regularly since we arrived at Cousin Matilda's. We rather think that he's taken with Cassy!'

'Don't be ridiculous, Blanche! He is simply a friend of Stephen's!' But a cool smile stole over Cassandra's haughty face and she lowered her eyelids, whilst Lucy and Blanche giggled into their handkerchiefs.

Sarah glanced at John, who raised his eyebrows at the girlish laughter and conversation and smiled, rather cynically, she thought, which was unusual for him, before calling to the driver to move on to the next part of their tour. As he did so, the rider on the stallion cantered across to them.

'Hold on, Rayner! Where are you off to with a carriage full of pretty ladies? Don't keep them all to yourself, there's a good fellow.' He looked down on them from the height of his glossy black mount, his gloved hands holding the reins firmly as it cavorted impatiently.

' 'Afternoon, Anderson.' John's voice was polite but impersonal. 'I believe you have met Miss Cassandra and Miss Blanche Hamilton. May I present my cousin, Miss Lucy Masterson, and her companion, Miss Sarah Foster – Mr Bertram Anderson.'

Bertram Anderson touched the brim of his bicorned hat at each introduction and his dark eyes lingered over each of them in turn. It seemed to Sarah that they rested longer on her, taking in her hair, lips and bosom, and she felt vaguely uneasy under his scrutiny.

'Shall we have the pleasure of your company to-morrow evening, Mr Anderson?' Cassandra, wishing to attract his attention, grew bold. 'Miss Pardoe is giving a concert. It promises to be quite splendid.'

'Indeed, yes, I shall be there.' Anderson smiled, showing gleaming white teeth beneath a thin black moustache. 'In fact, nothing would keep me away now that I know there will be such delightful company, as well as excellent music and the Pardoes' famous hospitality!'

He raised his whip. 'Until tomorrow, ladies.' He nodded to John, dug his heels into the horse's flanks and cantered off down the park, sending up a cloud of dry dust and scattering flocks of pigeons.

Lucy squealed and bit her handkerchief. 'Oh, what a rake he is, did you see the way his eyes flashed? Cassy – what a catch he must be!'

'Lucy!' John's voice was sharp. 'That's enough. You

know nothing about him. Contain your comments until you do!'

'I can assure you that Mr Anderson is from a very good family, Mr Rayner.' Cassandra's voice was cutting. 'One of the best, *and* he is due a considerable fortune!'

'I am sure that your information is quite correct, Miss Hamilton.' John smiled to offset his former tone. 'But Lucy should not jump to conclusions at a first meeting.'

Cassandra sat back in her seat and refused to take part in any further conversation, and Lucy, chagrined, sat sulkily silent. It was left to Sarah and Blanche to make desultory conversation to ease the situation as the carriage turned for home.

'What I fail to understand,' said Cassandra as she stepped into her blue muslin gown, 'is why Mr Rayner can be so stern over some proprieties and yet at the same time allow Sarah to be so familiar and call him Mr John?' She watched as Sarah fastened a necklace around Lucy's neck. '*And*, Sarah, you were seen very early yesterday morning, chatting to Mr Rayner in a most intimate manner, out in the street of all places!'

Rose blushed as she buttoned up Cassandra's dress, it was she who had passed on the information, given to her by the groom.

Sarah said nothing but concentrated on fastening the necklace.

'Oh, I can explain that,' said Lucy airily. 'John, and Sarah's father knew each other years ago and became friends – of a sort! In fact, it was all very exciting and very brave and romantic!'

'Oh, do tell us, Lucy. What happened?' Blanche sat down incautiously in her eagerness to hear and tipped over the chair, showing her stockings and pantaloons. Cassandra frowned at her severely but Lucy only giggled.

'Well, when John was just a boy, he went to sea in one of Papa's ships – and somehow or other, I don't know exactly how, he fell into the water, and had it not been for Will's bravery he would have drowned.'

'Will?' Blanche smoothed down her dress.

'Sarah's father, silly! He rescued him and had a terrible accident because of it.'

'Of course he would expect a good reward for rescuing the owner's nephew, wouldn't he?' asked Cassandra, careless of Sarah's presence. 'That is the usual thing, I believe.'

She, like Lucy, read romantic novels, usually with a happy ending or a reward for good behaviour. Lucy, with a sudden spurt of loyalty, in defence of her friend's father, who had many times in her childhood carried her on his shoulders, or had placed her small hand trustingly into his large one, became his vindicator, and hotly denied the fact that any of the seamen, least of all Will, knew that John was anything more than an ordinary seaman.

'And that is why he is called Mr John, it's what everyone calls him; Will and Maria – and everybody!'

She stopped awkwardly as Cassandra assumed a bored expression and picked up a hand mirror to examine her face.

'Fetch my pearls from my room, will you, Sarah? I think they will look better than the silver pendant.' Cassandra made the request without looking at Sarah, but kept her face turned towards the mirror and made a petulant *moue*, and Sarah, glad to get away, slipped quietly out of the door.

'You will have trouble with that girl, mark my words.' Cassandra took it upon herself as the eldest to deliver a lecture to Lucy. 'You cannot expect to behave in the same way here as you do in the country. Sarah must know her place.'

'Did you see the way Mr Anderson looked at her this afternoon?' Blanche was elated and quite unaware of the seething jealousy she was arousing in her sister. 'She is, of course, very lovely – such skin, and that beautiful hair!' She gave a deep sigh and clasped her hands together. 'Do you think that perhaps Mr Rayner is secretly in love with her?'

'Don't be ridiculous!' cried Lucy and Cassandra in scornful unison.

'Hurry, Sarah, and do up your hair, we are ready to go down. The bell will be going any minute.' Lucy, in her pale blue gown, tapped her fan impatiently as Sarah cleared up the discarded clothes and ribbons which had been left lying on the floor and chairs. Rose had disappeared, anxious to see the guests who had started to arrive.

'You go, Lucy. I'll be along in a minute.' Sarah started to brush her hair, her mouth full of pins.

'Sarah?' Lucy hesitated by the door and patted at a curl nervously. 'I think that perhaps you should call me Miss Lucy whilst we're here.' She waved her hand in an exaggerated fashion. 'You know what these people are like – such sticklers for protocol!'

Sarah stared at her. 'But – I always do,' she whispered. 'Whenever there is anyone else present.'

'Yes, I know,' answered Lucy defensively, 'but I mean, when they are not. Just in case anyone should overhear, you know, and think it strange.'

Dismay washed over Sarah and she hung her head. She had been expecting something of the sort since Lucy had so obviously come under the influence of Cassandra, and miserably she realized that their friendship as it had once been was over. Mrs Love's words that she was playing nursemaid to a spoilt child came back to her, and with a sudden perception she saw Lucy as she really was, a frivolous young woman, her breadth of view as circumscribed as the novels she read or the mirror she looked into.

'Very well, Miss Lucy.' She lifted her head. She was as composed as it was possible to be under the circumstances. 'If that is what you wish,' and she bobbed her knee. Lucy, looking slightly embarrassed, gave a small shrug of her shoulders and left to join Cassandra and Blanche who were making their way downstairs into the concert room.

Sarah bit her lip and pinched her pale cheeks to put back some colour and continued to brush up her hair, but her heavy curls kept falling out of their pins and she was in no mood to bother with it. In exasperation she pulled it back from her face, tying it in place with a piece of cream lace which matched her dress.

As she looked into the mirror she realized that the neckline of her dress was far too low. The dress had been made for Lucy, who had taken a dislike to the pale cream colour when it was finished, saying it made her look pale and washed out, and she had given it to Sarah. It would never do to be indiscreet, Sarah told herself now. She fished around hurriedly in her box, for the bell was ringing downstairs, brought out the cream silk rose which Miss Ellie had given her and placed it in the centre of the heartshaped neckline to hide the rise of her breasts.

John stood by the door watching the seats fill up with invited guests. The inner hall was being used for the concert and already the musicians were seated and tuning their instruments.

Amused, he saw that Lucy and her companions were seated together on a long sofa at the side of the room, a perfect vantage point from where they could watch people coming and going, and make comments to each other from behind their fans, and yet they were not too close to the music for it to be an intrusion. He looked for Sarah, but she had not yet come down.

He bowed as Miss Pardoe arrived and murmured his approval of her appearance. She was dressed in a gown of soft draped silk the colour of old rose which admirably suited her fair skin and dark hair. She was a beautiful woman, and he knew her also to be not only intelligent but kind and considerate and an excellent hostess.

The guests were hushed, the quartet about to begin and John had taken his seat when the door leading to the corridor at the other side of the hall opened and

Sarah slipped quietly in and took a seat at the back of the room.

He caught his breath as he saw her. The flame in the sconce on the wall above her head threw out shafts of light which flickered on her hair, making it glimmer and shine as if it too was on fire. Though she wore no powder or paint, her cheeks had a soft warm flush and her eyes were bright and luminous. He watched her in profile, and though outwardly her countenance was calm and serene, he thought he detected an undercurrent of tension or emotion beneath her tranquil beauty.

Her beauty! How blind he had been not to have seen it before. The child with her dancing curls who had charmed him with her chatter and laughter over so many years had unknowingly transfixed him with her loveliness. He felt an unendurable desire to kiss her wide mouth, which was usually so quick to smile, but seemed now to have a wistful sadness. He wanted to run his fingers through her mane of glorious hair; but most of all he wanted to protect her vulnerability which she hid so well beneath a veil of self possession.

The music had begun, but he could not have recognized the melody or the composer if his life had depended upon it, for his thoughts and eyes were mesmerized by the sight of Sarah. She could so easily be considered a lady, he thought as he watched her. But would a lady's life spoil her? If artifice and manners were expected of society's ladies, then would she lose her natural spontaneity and gaiety?

He gave a deep audible sigh, and, conscious that he might have been overheard, he glanced furtively around at his neighbours. They were not aware of him. Most were listening intently, or in some cases politely, to the music, but some, he noticed, men and women, but mostly men, were looking at Sarah.

Anderson was one of them, a crooked smile on his lips. John felt a cold anger that Sarah should be sullied by even a fleeting glance from such a philanderer. An unprincipled seducer, Anderson's character was known in all the gentlemen's clubs, though his reputation had not yet reached the ears of the ladies. He was careful to pursue only those who would not, or dare not, complain, and his standing in society was secure.

John's gaze returned to Sarah and he saw with a start that she was gazing at him, an appeal in her eyes as if willing him to look her way. Their eyes met and were held. He felt a current reaching out and linking them, conducted it seemed by the strains of soft music played hauntingly somewhere in the background of another world. He let it lift him, transport him, towards her welcoming arms.

When Sarah had slipped through the side door into the hall, she looked for an unobtrusive seat, but most of the chairs and sofas were taken. She looked for Miss Lucy, but she was chatting animatedly to her companions, and although there was an empty seat nearby, Sarah hesitated about taking it without being invited, and sat instead alone on a chair by the door.

Had she been in a happier frame of mind she would have looked forward to this evening with great anticipation, for this was the first time she had attended a concert, or listened to music played on any instrument except the drums of the military, or the reed whistles and fiddles played by the boys and men in the village to celebrate harvest time, when the labourers and the village women would drink cider and ale and dance the night away.

But tonight she felt a sadness drawn around her, a loneliness, made worse by Lucy's desertion. I should have known, I should have anticipated it, she thought. My mother must have felt the same when Lucy was banned from the kitchen and her charge. It has to be, we are from different worlds, and when we get home— She realized that Lucy would not want to stay in Monkston, that the provincial theatres and society of Hull and the north, which had formerly attracted her, would now pall after savouring the delights of London.

Sarah looked across at her. Lucy's face had a brightness about it in spite of the white powder which she had carefully brushed on it. Sarah thought that she looked like one of the pretty, fragile fashion dolls with her curls and frills and flounces.

I can't stay here, she thought, hemmed in by these London streets and great buildings, no matter how magnificent – not even if Lucy commands it. *Miss* Lucy – mentally she corrected herself. I can still go to Mrs Love if I wish. She sighed, but I don't want that either. Oh, how I miss the vast lonely plains of Holderness, the enormous sky that has no end – and the sea – the wildness and grandeur of the sea – that everyone who doesn't understand it says is grey and threatening. If only I could feel the wet spray on my face and stand and stare at its measureless, boundless horizon.

She stifled a sob and looked round to see if anyone had noticed. One or two gentlemen who were looking her way smiled and raised an eyebrow at her, and that odious Mr Anderson inclined his head towards her. She looked away. There was no-one she could confide in, no-one who would understand. Lucy was too wrapped up in her own affairs and Mrs Masterson was unapproachable. Miss Pardoe came into her view. How lovely she was and how kind, she would understand her feelings, she was sure, she had spoken kindly to her several times, but she wouldn't of course dream of approaching her.

John! Mr John. She saw him on the other side of the room, where he seemed to be engrossed, not listening to the music but staring towards Mr Anderson, who in turn was looking at something or someone near her. We would never let anyone be unkind to you, he had said. Well, no-one was being unkind, but she needed to talk to someone and she knew instinctively that she could depend on him, that he was her friend, in spite of their social differences. There was even something more than just friendship, a special bond which she had yet to find the meaning of.

She willed him to look towards her. She could do this,

she knew how, although she didn't know why she knew. Sarah had thought, when she was a child, that everyone could communicate with each other by thought. But it was a gift, Ma Scryven had explained, a gift which you must control until you needed it.

At last he looked her way and she held his gaze, willing his thoughts to lock into hers, but she was taken unaware by the power which erupted between them, a force stronger than she had ever known, stronger than the energy of life. She felt his mind and hers uniting, and it was as if her whole being was melting and dissolving into his and becoming one. Slowly she smiled, her body and mind filled with an inner, unbelievable happiness; yet somewhere within the poignant strains of music she could hear an echo of incomprehensible sadness.

She closed her eyes to unfasten the cord which bound them and concentrated fully on the music. Music of Mozart of which she knew nothing, and yet which seemed so familiar that it opened up her emotions. The notes of a flute soared and she could hear within it the sound of the sea, and the haunting cry of a gull as it swooped and dived above the headland, giving out a shrill warning of imminent danger as it flew before the wind in a storm.

Startled, she opened her eyes. Something was wrong. She was needed, but by whom? Involuntarily she stood up and gazed wildly around the room, her eyes wide but unseeing, and with a silent cry in the back of her throat she picked up her skirts and ran out of the room.

She stood hesitating in the corridor, not knowing where or which way to go, her senses returning, leaving her drained and bewildered. She heard another door open from the hall and turning towards it saw Mr Anderson coming towards her.

'My dear young lady, I fear you are unwell. I saw your pallor and your swift departure from the music, and came at once to enquire if I could be of assistance?' He bent over her solicitously, a concerned frown upon his face.

'You are very thoughtful, Mr Anderson, but it is nothing really. A slight headache, it will be gone shortly.'

'But I insist!' He took her arm.

She allowed herself to be led into a small anteroom where attentively he helped her into a chair and poured her a generous measure of brandy.

He pulled up a footstool to sit at her feet and in fright she drew back into the chair.

'Please, do not be alarmed. I intend no hurt. I simply wish to feast my poor eyes on your beauty.'

'Mr Anderson. Give me room, please, sir.' She felt suffocated by his presence. 'If someone should come in!'

His eyebrows rose quizzically. 'You are afraid for your reputation?' He smiled and took hold of her free hand and raised it to his lips; she looked around for somewhere to place the glass of brandy that she might at least have one hand free, but laughingly he took hold of her wrist, holding her fast. 'Now I have you. No, don't struggle, I shan't harm you.'

'Sir, I beg you to leave me. You are not behaving as a gentleman should.' She was afraid and near to tears.

'So, you are familiar with the habits of gentlemen?' He fingered the rose at her breast, still keeping tight hold of her so that she felt the warmth of her own hand as well as his against her skin.

'A rose for a rose!' His mocking expression faded and he studied her face. 'You must know, Miss Foster – Sarah, that I am besotted by you.'

He leaned forward and touched her lips with his, and she crouched further back into the chair to escape him. 'Please, sir. I beg you. I am nothing to you; a servant merely, but worthy of respect.'

'A servant!' he whispered softly. 'Of course you are. Why else would we be here? And you could serve me very well. I would treat you well, buy you pretty clothes and trinkets. You could be the toast of the town and the envy of all your friends.' He let go of her hand and took hold of her foot, and gently ran his fingers around her ankle, 'What say you?'

She flung the contents of the brandy glass with one quick, sharp movement across his face and jumped to her feet. 'I say you are no gentleman, sir. Now please let me pass.'

He rose from the footstool to face her, the brandy streaming down his face staining his frilled cravat. He lifted his hand to strike her, but then with a smile he took hold of her roughly and pulled her towards him. 'That's what I like, Sarah. A woman of fire and passion. What a pair we would make.' He crushed her to him, bending her body to his and searching for her lips with his own, until she felt the pressure of them on hers, and the taste of blood in her mouth.

John had seen Sarah's obvious distress and flight from the room. She had made little disturbance, but one or two people had turned round as the door whooshed to a close. He was trapped by occupied seats between him and the door, and he waited impatiently on the edge of his seat for the finale before he could politely withdraw.

The outer hall was empty, as was the corridor. He opened the front door and looked out to see if she had gone out for air, and then ran across the road to the garden, but that was locked and empty save for a few squirrels chasing up and down the tree trunks in the gathering darkness. A footman appeared on the steps and enquired if he could be of assistance, but John waved him aside and came back into the house.

Perturbed, he walked back down the corridor. There was a hum of conversation and laughter coming from the concert room, as guests rose to take refreshment, but as he hesitated in the dimness his ears became attuned to another sound, of voices coming from a room on his left. Slowly, not wanting to cause embarrassment to whoever might be inside, he opened the door a crack, then with an exclamation as he saw Sarah's dishevelled appearance and plight, he let it fly open with a crash, startling both Sarah, who fell back into a chair, and Bertram Anderson.

'My dear fellow,' began Anderson, adjusting his stained and crumpled cravat. 'You might have knocked.'

Furiously John clenched his fists. 'How dare you have the audacity to take advantage of this young woman. You are a scoundrel, sir!'

Anderson smiled mockingly. 'What nonsense. We were merely having a *tête-à-tête*, were we not, Sarah? Not jealous, are you, Rayner? Got an arrangement with her, have you? Lucky devil! She's a beauty all right, but you'd better watch out, she's going to be in demand.'

John took two swift steps forward and Anderson stepped back in alarm as he saw his raised fist.

'Steady on, Rayner. Nothing to get too upset about. You know how the ladies tease. It's more than a man can stand once the blood is up!'

John pinned him against the wall and Sarah in distress ran towards them. They none of them heard the door open, but they all turned swiftly as Matilda Pardoe's quiet voice requested the meaning of the disturbance.

She stood with her back to the closed door, and without taking her eyes from them felt for the key and turned it. 'Gentlemen. I trust that you will settle your differences elsewhere and not in my father's house. He would be much alarmed!'

John, contrite, came swiftly to her side and bowed apologetically. 'I beg your pardon, Miss Pardoe. It was unforgivable, I had no intention of causing you embarrassment.'

'Oh, come on, Matty. Rayner and I were only fooling about, and this little thing got in the way.' Anderson waved in Sarah's direction, but didn't look at her, and a slow flush suffused her cheeks.

Matilda Pardoe raised her head and looked coldly at Bertram Anderson. 'When I give you permission to use my name, it is Matilda, not Matty, Mr Anderson, and until such time I would prefer my courtesy title. However, if it is the case that you and Mr Rayner were simply indulging in horseplay, then nothing more need be said.' She looked across at John for confirmation.

He drew in his breath. She surely knew him better than that? As he hesitated he thought he saw a request in her eyes, an appeal for moderation, and suddenly he understood the implications if he should tell her what had really happened.

There would be a scandal; his word against Anderson's that he had burst into a private room in her home and found him entangled with a young woman. Anderson would deny it, of course, or else assert that it was a romp with a willing maidservant, which all his cronies would believe, but which would leave Miss Pardoe embarrassed and Sarah compromised and without a shred of character. The consequences could not possibly be tolerated.

'A misunderstanding, Miss Pardoe. I apologize most profusely.'

'Then the matter is closed.' She turned and unlocked the door, holding it open, inviting them to leave. Anderson went first, bowing to her and ignoring John and Sarah completely, and John, glancing at Sarah who was still standing as if frozen to the spot, followed him.

Miss Pardoe closed the door after him, her face serious as she indicated that Sarah should take a seat. Her hands shook as she did so and she clasped them together so that Miss Pardoe, who had started to pace up and down, wouldn't notice.

'Sarah.' She glanced at the gilt clock on a side table. 'I haven't much time as my guests will be looking for me, so I will be brief.'

Sarah trembled. She was to be sent home in disgrace, she knew it. Whatever would Mrs Masterson say?

Miss Pardoe stopped her pacing and sank on to the footstool where Mr Anderson had sat, the folds of her skirts falling around her like a shower of rose petals. 'You may think that you have been betrayed. That I wouldn't believe what probably happened in here this evening, that Mr Anderson tried to take advantage of you, and that Mr Rayner,' here she hid a slight smile, 'that Mr Rayner came to your rescue.'

She got up from the stool and started to pace again. 'Well, I can tell you that I do believe it. I do believe that Mr Anderson is a seducer and that Mr Rayner, from what little I know of him, is a gentleman.'

She turned towards Sarah, who was alarmed by the anger in her face. 'But there is nothing I can do about it. Nothing, nothing, nothing! My hands are tied. I am a mere female like yourself, and bound by men's rules!'

'Please, don't upset yourself, ma-am.' Sarah was horrified at the thought of the trouble she had caused. 'He didn't hurt me, Miss Pardoe, just frightened me.' She fingered her swollen lip and Miss Pardoe, noticing the gesture, shook her head.

'Don't you realize, Sarah? It's not just you! It's all women. They're all at the mercy of men like Anderson, especially young women like you. However, you may be sure that this matter won't rest here. We cannot get Mr Anderson refused admission at his clubs, but he will not be dining here again, and people will wonder why and speculate. And sooner or later he will go too far.'

She walked to the door. 'Go to bed now and rest. I will send supper up to you and say you are unwell if Miss Lucy should ask. You wouldn't, I'm sure, wish to face Mr Anderson again this evening, and I cannot give him marching orders in front of my guests, much as I might wish to. Besides, you deserve a little comfort, I think, after your ordeal.'

She turned to leave, then with a slight hesitation turned back. 'It was fortunate that Mr Rayner was passing by the door. He seems to take an interest in you; to be considerate of you?'

Sarah swallowed nervously. 'Yes, ma-am, he is always very kind towards me. He's known me all of my life, ma-am. Since the day I was bor , in fact. He was there when my mother needed help.'

'Indeed?' A fleeting look of ease came into Miss Pardoe's face and she suddenly smiled. 'Then Mr Rayner is indeed a champion of women. We must nurture him, for they are very rare.'

22

Sarah's sleep was disturbed and broken by strange, disjointed dreams. She could hear voices calling to her but she knew not who the voices belonged to. Images of her mother and father came into her mind, and unclear distorted pictures of Ma Scryven, who was whispering something into her ear, but no matter how she strained she couldn't hear what the old woman was saying, her voice coming and going like the sound of surf on the shore. She sat up in bed and put her head in her hands, trying to clear it of tangled thoughts of home and family, of Mr John and Mr Anderson fighting over a silk rose, and her own distress when she tried to pick it up and found that it had crumbled away in her hand.

She was weary as she dragged herself out of bed the next morning, wakened by Rose who brought up water for washing and who noisily opened the shutters, then whispered in a low voice her apologies for the day before when she had revealed that Sarah had been seen out in the street talking to Mr Rayner.

'It's that Miss Hamilton,' she hissed resentfully, 'she worms information out of folks. I didn't mean to tell, honest.'

'It doesn't matter, Rose. It isn't important,' Sarah replied as she sat on the edge of the bed, trying to rouse herself.

'No? Well what I say is, what folks do ain't nuffing to do with anybody else, and besides a bit of 'anky panky never did anybody any 'arm.' She winked wickedly as she went out, a broad smile on her face.

They spent the day sightseeing, gazing at monuments and strolling through parks and gardens, and though

Sarah would normally have taken delight in such an excursion, the ancient trees, ornamental shrubs and exotic flowers laid out in brilliant display failed to lift her spirits. She had a deep-seated foreboding of some forthcoming event which cast its shadow across her path.

They were escorted by Miss Pardoe and her brother. There was no sign of John that day or the next, but the following morning she met him as they crossed the hall. 'Mr John, I would like to speak to you, if you can spare the time.' She had no clear idea what she wished to say, only that she must tell him of her anxieties.

'Then it must be today, Sarah.' He spoke softly, mindful of listening ears. 'Tomorrow I leave early for home.'

'I see.' She spoke calmly, not showing the dismay that gripped her.

'Sarah?' He spoke urgently, but before he could continue Mrs Masterson came hurrying down the stairs, greatly agitated and waving a letter in her hand.

'John, John! Thank goodness you are here, and you too, Sarah – no, stay, I wish to speak to both of you.'

Sarah's heart sank. So Miss Pardoe had spoken to Mrs Masterson after all. She glanced at John but his manner was collected.

'Is there something amiss, Aunt? You appear upset.'

'I am upset, John! Something quite dreadful has happened!' She put her hand to her brow. 'You must do something about it.'

He opened a door to the morning room. The sun was streaming through the windows into the elegant room and he suggested that they sat down.

'Have you had bad news?' He indicated the letter in her hand.

'Read it!' she said. 'It is from Mr Masterson. I cannot leave for five minutes but that the household falls apart!'

Sarah closed her eyes. So there *was* something wrong at home, she had known it all along.

'What is so strange, however, is that there is a letter

for you, Sarah. From Lizzie of all people! Now when did she learn to write?'

She waved the opened scrap of paper towards her. 'She says that your mother is ill, as is Mrs Scryven. What are we to do? How will Mr Masterson manage without a cook or housekeeper?' She glared at Sarah as if it were her fault that such calamities had befallen the household and handed her the crumpled note which Lizzie had laboriously penned.

'I wish you was at ome.' The letters, large and spaced out, indicated Lizzie's determination to convey an urgent message. 'Maria is sik and Ma S is so porly she won't last long. She keeps axing for you and mayster as gowt and can't get owt of bed Me and janey is at our witsend love Lizzie.'

Sarah looked at Mrs Masterson, who in turn looked at John who was reading Mr Masterson's letter.

'Mr Masterson says that your mother is ill with a fever, Sarah, and Mrs Scryven is confined to her bed. He fears that she won't get out of it again. I'm sorry,' he said as he saw the pain cross her face. 'My uncle is also bedfast with a bad attack of gout.'

He turned to Mrs Masterson. 'What would you like me to do, ma-am? I am at your disposal. I intended returning tomorrow, but I can quite easily go tonight if you wish to return home earlier.'

'I?' She looked at him in astonishment. 'I cannot possibly return. I cannot leave Lucy alone here, and there are so many things planned. I would not insult Miss Pardoe by even thinking about it!' She had become quite pink and flustered at the thought of it. 'Besides, if Mr Masterson has the doctor visiting him as he says he does, there is nothing I can do to help him.'

She drew herself up in her chair. 'You must return, Sarah. Lucy will have to manage without you. You will be of more use at Garston Hall than you are here, which is what I said before we came away, and no-one would listen to me.' She looked pious for a moment then added condescendingly, 'I know you will be disappointed, but you have been very lucky. Lucy has been very good to you, more than was merited, I'm sure you would agree.'

She stared at her and Sarah could feel her hostility though she didn't understand the reason for it. 'So off you go, get your things together. If Mr John wants to leave today, don't keep him waiting.'

Isobel, in fact, was pleased to have an excuse to send her home. She had seen Lucy's fair skin and hair turn colourless at the side of Sarah's vibrant glow, and knew that others had seen it too. The contrast was too marked and, though she couldn't fault Sarah on her manners or behaviour, there had been much comment on Miss Lucy's lovely companion which she had found very hard to tolerate.

'Is it in order, Aunt, that Sarah travels alone with me?' John put the question after Sarah had left the room.

'Good heavens, why ever not? She is a servant after all, and she won't be worried about such proprieties.' Isobel adapted the rules to suit her own inconsistent whims. 'And besides, I know, and I'm sure she knows, that she will be perfectly safe with you.'

It was not yet dusk as the carriage pulled away from the house and out of the iron gates on to the main carriage-way. Sarah heaved a sigh of relief and turned to look back. The street was deserted and the gateman was pulling the two gates together and locking them. Only Rose and a footman had been there to see them off. John had suggested that Sarah should pay her respects to Miss Pardoe early in the day so that they could slip away as soon as they were ready. She had done so, and also said goodbye to Lucy, who was deciding which dress to wear for that evening's entertainment.

'What do you think, Sarah, shall I wear the pink or the yellow?' She had held first one, then the other in front of her.

'The pink, Miss Lucy, it enhances your colour.'

She had turned and given Sarah a bright smile as she

left, but no hug as she might once have done, and no message for the sick at home.

Sarah settled back against the soft leather upholstery and prepared herself for the long journey.

'I'm sorry that your visit has been cut short, Sarah, but I'm sure there will be other opportunities to come to London.' John gave a thin smile, 'I don't think we shall be able to keep Lucy away.'

'I don't think so, Mr John. I'm no longer necessary to Miss Lucy. She can manage quite well with a personal maid. She no longer has any need for a companion, except perhaps when she returns home to Garston Hall.'

She saw the frown on his face. 'It's perfectly all right, sir. I'm not sorry to be returning. In fact I'm so happy I'm almost bursting.' She smiled, her face radiant, then it clouded as she thought of her sick mother and Ma Scryven.

'But if you are not to be Lucy's companion, then what will you do? You cannot become merely a housemaid, you have more to offer than that.' His tone was anxious and he rubbed his chin thoughtfully as he looked at her. 'What must we do with you, Sarah?'

'I haven't yet decided, sir. I only know that I'll not leave Monkston. The time spent here in London has determined me on that. I belong there, nowhere else.'

John had told Harris to go as fast as possible, changing teams when necessary, and they would travel through the night stopping only briefly for food and rest. But on the second evening he decided that they would stay overnight at an inn. Harris was tired and he could see that Sarah was quite exhausted, though she was anxious that they didn't stop on her account.

'I'll see to 'osses and then go to bed, sir,' said Harris wearily. 'We'd best have an early start again in 'morning if we're to reach Hull before nightfall as tha wants.'

Sarah's body trembled with tiredness from the jolting of the carriage, but she ate a little supper and then asked John to excuse her, saying she would go to bed.

'I shall go to my room also,' John rose from the table.

'I'll read for a short while. I'm not yet ready for sleep, even though I'm tired.' He looked drawn and troubled, and she longed to smooth his forehead, to soothe away his weariness.

She paused at her door, her hand on the doorknob. 'I have some herbs with me which would help you sleep,' she urged. 'They only require hot water.'

He laughed at her and refused. 'You're turning into another Mrs Scryven. God bless her,' he added soberly, 'I hope we are in time, Sarah.'

She smiled sadly. 'I pray we are. Good night, sir.'

She undressed slowly, folding her gown and petticoat neatly so that she could dress quickly in the morning, and slipped her nightshift over her head. She lay on top of the bed and drew just a sheet over her. Although the weather was cooler as they came further north, the room was stuffy. There had been a big fire burning when they arrived which she had damped down with water from the jug on the washstand, making it spit and hiss and send out columns of sooty smoke into the room.

She must have dropped asleep instantly, for she hadn't blown out the candle which was still burning, its flame flickering steadily, when she awoke with a start some time later. She sat up shivering and drew the blanket around her. The room was cold and the fire was almost out, the red embers burnt away to fine grey ash.

A cup of camomile is what I need to warm me and make me sleep, she thought. But I have no hot water. Could I, I wonder, find a maid to ask for some? I'll see if there is someone about.

She put her shawl around her shoulders and taking the candle she padded barefoot to the door and looked out. A lamp was burning low on a table in the corridor, and she saw the shadow of someone coming quietly up the stairs. She drew back into the doorway in case it was another guest at the inn, then spoke a whispered greeting to John as he passed her door.

'What's wrong, Sarah? Are you not well?' He was

396

alarmed at seeing her there in only her nightclothes and shawl, her hair loose and hanging down her back.

'I was going to find someone, to get some hot water for an infusion.'

He looked down the silent corridor. The inn was quiet and all he could hear was the regular sound of the pendulum clock in the hall below, which seemed to keep time with the thump of his own heartbeat.

'Wait there, Sarah. My fire is still in, I'll bring you some.'

As she stepped back inside her room she realized that he must have been out, for though he was bareheaded, his greatcoat was draped around his shoulders. Perhaps he, too, had been unable to sleep.

He knocked quietly on the door a few minutes later, a dish of hot water in his hand.

'May I make you a cup of camomile tea?' She opened the door and indicated the table where she had placed two cups and the bag of dried flowers. 'I have enough for two and it will help you sleep.'

'Sarah!' He put the dish down on the table. He tried not to look at her as he spoke, but his eyes were drawn to hers, to her white throat and the narrow ribbons round the neck of her thin shift below the shawl which she held discreetly about her.

He glanced away to the floor so that he might not embarrass her, but she appeared to be unabashed as she poured water into the cups, and unaware of his discomfiture as he gazed at her small brown bare feet.

'I shouldn't be here, Sarah. Don't you know that it isn't wise to invite a man to your room?'

His voice cracked hoarsely as he spoke. He wanted to stay. He wanted to stay all night. There was within him a wildness which desired to capture her innocence, but also a tenderness which wanted to protect; and he knew he was bound on his honour as a gentleman to leave her here, and go back down the corridor, frustrated and wanting, alone to his room.

'But you wouldn't harm me, John? I wouldn't have

invited you otherwise.' His name slipped so easily and familiarly from her tongue. There was a softness flowing from her, a glow which lit her upturned face.

'I wouldn't harm you.' Impulsively he traced with a finger the wispy curls on her forehead, her freckled nose, her lips, where he tenderly drew their outline. 'I would not harm you, Sarah, because I love you.' He spoke softly, his blue eyes lingering on her face. 'I love you, Sarah. But you know that already, don't you?'

She nodded, her eyes following the strong curve of his cheeks, the straightness of his nose, and she raised her hand to stroke his beard.

He caught hold of her hand and gently kissed it. His fingers stroked her bare arm, and with a soft groan he gathered her into his arms. 'It seems as if I have waited a lifetime for you, Sarah.'

She smiled, her lips apart, as she felt their love reaching out, entwining and enfolding their receptive minds and bodies, and reached to touch his mouth with hers. 'You have,' she whispered tenderly, 'only it is mine, not yours.'

It was growing dusk as they clattered through the familiar streets of Hull on the third day and swiftly changed the sweating horses at the yard so that they might continue the last part of the journey with more speed.

They sat smiling at each other, sitting close that they might touch or whisper, but as they drew nearer to Monkston and saw the patchwork of brown earth and green and yellow fields, and the streaked evening sky above them, they drew apart and grew silent, each lost in their own thoughts.

Presently John spoke quietly, taking her hand in his, 'I love you, Sarah, and I want to marry you. I want you to be with me always.'

She leant towards him and kissed him. 'And I love you. I always have, ever since I can remember. Not like this, not the same, but I have always loved you.' She turned sadly away from him. 'But we can't marry. You know as well as I do that it is impossible.'

He started to protest, but she put her hand over his mouth. 'They wouldn't allow it, not your family or mine. Not Mrs Masterson, nor my father.' Her dark eyes were wet. 'We would be shunned. We would have no friends, nor family, we would be quite alone; and it's family which gives meaning to our existence, without it we couldn't endure life!'

'You would be my family, and I yours,' he said passionately. 'Without you, Sarah, my life has no meaning – has never had, when I think about it. I have not had the advantage of a long, loving relationship with my parents as you have.'

'Are you not content,' she wept softly, 'that we have this love? Is it not enough to know? Do we have to make it commonplace, to talk of marriage, when we have a union in our love for each other?'

'No,' he cried angrily, and she was shocked by the violence of his manner. 'It isn't enough. I need more. I need to have you near me, to show you off on my arm, to introduce you as my wife, not hide you away as if we were ashamed!'

She said nothing, but gazed out into the darkness so that he couldn't see her distress.

As they pulled to the top of the Aldbrough hill, her voice broke as she said, 'I can see the sea. We're almost home.'

He put his arm around her and kissed her wet cheek. 'There have been times when I wished never to see the sea again,' he said. 'But it gladdens me now to know that it welcomes you back.' He turned her face towards him so that she had to look at him. 'We must resolve this matter, Sarah. We can't just leave it like this. When shall I see you again?'

'In time, John, all in good time.' It was as if she were the older, wiser person, consoling him. 'I must first see to my mother and Mrs Scryven, and to Mr Masterson. We have plenty of time in which to decide.'

They were passing the churchyard at Tillington. The grey stones of the new spire built on to the old church the year before pointed skywards like a cautionary finger and she gave an involuntary shudder.

John too looked out at the white gravestones leaning sombrely in the darkness. 'I haven't the time, Sarah. I'm already over thirty. I've waited long enough, I want you now.' He put his arms around her and kissed her passionately. 'I want you now, not next week, next year, but now.'

'I knew tha would come home, if tha could.' Will greeted them as they drew up at the door, relief showing on his lined face. 'Thy ma's a bit better, Sarah, 'fever has passed, but Ma Scryven's only just hanging on, it's as if she's waiting for thee.'

He touched his forelock to John. 'I thank thee for bringing her safely home, sir. I would've been worried about her travelling all that way, it's not safe for a young woman alone.' He lifted their bags down and carried them inside. 'Mr Masterson is still abed, he said to go up as soon as tha got here. He's been in a lot of pain and we did what we could for him, but it's not easy with Maria and Ma being so poorly.'

He shook his head wearily and put his hand to his eyes. 'You wouldn't believe how fast 'fever took hold, Sarah, half 'village has been sick. I thought we were going to lose thy ma.'

'Don't worry now, Fayther.' Gently she took his arm. 'I'm here to help you. Together we'll pull her through.'

John stood and watched them as father and daughter turned and went through the kitchen door. She looked back before she entered and gave him a small, still smile, then with a stony face he climbed the stairs.

Sarah was quite unprepared for the marked difference in her mother. It was just over two weeks since she had left for London but it seemed like a lifetime as she sat by her bed and gently stroked her pallid cheek. Her once thick dark hair hung thin and straggly, and wisps of white framed her gaunt features.

'I'm much better, Sarah,' she whispered. 'Just a little weak, that's all. I'll soon be up and about. But look to 'maister, poor man, wilt tha? And to Ma Scryven. I haven't seen her, they wouldn't let me get up, but I think she hasn't long.' Maria's voice trembled as she spoke of the old woman who had been like a mother to her for the past sixteen years.

Sarah climbed the stairs to the top of the house where Ma Scryven had her room and quietly opened the door. Lizzie had kept the curtains closed during the day to keep the brightness of the small square window from hurting the sick woman's eyes. There was a dim lamp burning on the table by the bed and Sarah turned it up to be able to see the small bundle of humanity curled up in the bed.

The old woman looked like some small animal who in its pain had crawled for comfort into its final resting place. Her hand was under her cheek and her knees drawn up to her chest. Her eyes were closed as Sarah bent over and listened for her breathing. Softly she touched her cheek and instantly she opened them. She gazed as if unseeing and then closed them again with a small, quiet sigh.

'It's Sarah, Ma. Can you hear me?' She sat on the side of the narrow bed and stroked her hand. There was a faint but perceptible movement of the head and Mrs Scryven opened her eyes again.

'Sarah!' Her name was uttered softly and with effort. 'I've been waitin' for thee.' Again she closed her eyes as if the effort of speech was too much.

Sarah waited again, not wanting to disturb her, and presently got up from the bed and moved across to the window and drew back the curtains. There was no cloud and the deep vault of night-blue sky was scattered with stars. In the silence she could hear the steady rhythmic thrash of the waves as they beat on the shore. There was a sudden quiet movement behind her and she turned to see Ma Scryven looking at her, her small eyes bright.

'Sarah?'

'Yes, I'm here. Can I get something for you?' Sarah knelt down so that her face was level with the small wrinkled one in the bed.

'I've everything I need,' said the old woman. 'I don't need much for my journey.'

Sarah felt a great emotion rising up in her as she faced the sight of death before her.

Mrs Scryven must have sensed her fear for she gave her a small twisted smile. 'Don't be afraid, Sarah. When 'time is right, death is welcome. It's only in youth that we spurn it.'

She put out her hand. It was still and cold in Sarah's. 'Tha must tek my place here after I'm gone. Tha knows about herbs and potions and there's many folks who'll need thee, poor folk who don't know how to fend for the'selves.'

She must have seen the hesitation on Sarah's face, for she added softly, 'Tha must put on one side thine own desires.' She looked as if she wanted to say more, but the effort was too great and Sarah bade her not to tire herself.

'I am going to rest,' she said wearily. 'I'm ready for it.' She closed her eyes again and then suddenly said in a clear voice, 'Open 'window, Sarah. I've a great want for a breath of sea air.'

Sarah rose from the floor and slid open the window. The thin curtains billowed as the air blew in with a rush and she leant out and took a deep breath. How good it was to be home again. There was a sharp coldness, as if autumn was meeting winter for the first time and she could taste the salt on the air. She smiled as she inhaled. Yes, this was where she belonged. She felt happy and full of vibrant life. She was home, and she was loved and loved in return. She turned back into the room to tell her old friend her secret but her smile slowly faded. Ma Scryven had slipped silently away.

* * *

'You'd better get back to the office, John. There will be decisions to be made that the clerks can't deal with. I'm much easier now.' Isaac sat in an armchair, his swollen legs on a footstool. 'Sarah's made me comfortable.'

She had made him a potion of herbs, and wrapped his sore joints in comfrey leaves, and to please her he had submitted to her administrations. However, he found that his discomfort had eased. Whether it was her medicine or the fact that he was being cared for he couldn't decide for, although Lizzie and Janey had done their best, he knew they were nervous of him and scuttled out of his presence as soon as their duties were done, whilst Sarah made sure that everything was within his reach, that his cushions were plumped up and his books were by his side. The only thing that she had moved away so that he couldn't get at it was his brandy decanter, and she laughingly refused to give it to him.

'That'll be a treat to look forward to, sir,' she'd teased. 'Just as soon as you are moving about again.'

John stood with his back to his uncle, gazing out of the window. Yesterday they had buried Mrs Scryven. Will and Tom, Martin Reedbarrow and his son Joe had carried the small coffin in front of this window so that Mr Masterson might pay his respects, and then taken it round to Maria's window where she leant, pale and unsteady, on the sill and said a silent goodbye to her old friend. He and Sarah, Lizzie and Janey had walked behind, to be joined by the villagers, who followed them to the small church which sat precariously on the headland only yards from the sea.

He had not had a chance to speak to Sarah alone until that same evening, when, as he went out for a stroll, he'd chanced to see her walking towards the churchyard with a bunch of flowers.

'Be careful here, Sarah.' The graveyard stretched to the cliff edge. 'I can't think why they still use it, why they don't use the graveyard at Tillington.'

'Ma Scryven asked that she should be buried here. She said she was within sight of home and all of us. We were the only family she had.' She'd smiled sadly then, and he'd known that it wasn't the right time to talk about their future.

'I wanted to talk to you, Uncle, before I leave.' He sat down beside Isaac. 'I wanted to ask you what would be expected of me should I decide to marry?'

'Oho,' Isaac's face brightened. 'So, there's something in the wind, hey? My word, your aunt will be pleased to hear that.'

'No!' John got up in some agitation and his uncle looked at him in surprise. 'I'd rather you didn't discuss it with my aunt, not yet. Nothing has been decided. I merely wanted to hear your views.'

'If that is what you wish, John. I know, women do tend to get carried away over these issues. Well, you must make a good contract, of course, that goes without saying. Heaven knows we don't need the money, but a suitable dowry enhances the alliance.' He smiled. 'I imagine there won't be any difficulty there?'

John ignored the question and looked so solemn that Isaac too grew serious. 'And if I do not make a good contract? If the woman I wish to marry has nothing, no dowry to bring, what then?'

A flush came to Isaac's face. 'Why, then I must think again about your inheritance if you are foolhardy enough to make an inappropriate match.' He stopped as a memory long gone raised its head. What was it? Some girl and John in his youth, some fifteen, sixteen years ago when they first came here? He sighed, he couldn't remember, his memory was failing.

'I have Lucy to consider, you realize,' he said rather sharply. 'You must be mindful that she will be in your charge when I am gone, until she marries that is; and I cannot risk her losing her dowry should your wife not have money of her own to fritter away.'

He saw the expression of hurt on John's face. 'I'm sorry, John, it isn't a matter of trust, but you know that that is how things are done.' He leant forward and spoke quietly. 'You and I both know that there are ways around this situation.' He waved a finger con- spira- torially. 'Marry well, and take your pleasure elsewhere if you are so inclined.'

John bowed stiffly to his uncle, his face cold and pale. 'As I said, sir, I wished only to know your views and you have explained them perfectly. There will be no question of my having an illicit relationship. None whatsoever. When I make the decision, I intend to make only one contract and no other.'

Mrs Masterson and Lucy didn't return until November, and then with some reluctance, Lucy complaining bitter- ly that she was missing dozens of parties and balls, and enthusing about the quality of the players who graced the stages of the London theatres. She clasped her hands in ecstasy as she told Sarah of the night when she had seen the Prince Regent, and that she was sure that he had noticed her for he gave a slight bow in her direction.

'But Cassandra Hamilton seemed to think, quite wrongly of course, that he was looking towards her.' She laughed playfully and shook her curls in an affected manner. 'We all know that he prefers ladies of a fair complexion.'

Sarah waited patiently for Lucy to finish so that she might ask to be excused. It hadn't been easy re- organizing the household whilst her mother had been ill, but she had found a woman from Tillington who was a good plain cook, and with Mr Masterson's approval had taken on two more housemaids to clean the house, which had assumed a neglected look in spite of Lizzie's and Janey's efforts.

'And, speaking of Cassandra Hamilton, what do you think?' Lucy once more had claimed Sarah for her confidante.

Sarah shook her head. She had no wish to know.

'She's promised to Mr Anderson! He's spoken to her father already.' Lucy's face was animated and she waited expectantly for Sarah's response.

'I'm delighted for them,' she replied evenly. 'I can't think of a couple more suited.' She suppressed a shudder as she recalled the unwanted embrace of the odious Bertram Anderson, and even felt a little sympathy for the disdainful Miss Hamilton who was seemingly willing to join her life to his.

Lucy dropped her voice. 'Of course there is a whisper that he's quite a philanderer, but from what I understand of it, one needs a man of experience when contemplating marriage – you know what I mean, Sarah?' She nodded her head significantly and pursed her lips.

'No, Miss Lucy, I'm afraid I don't know, and I must ask you to excuse me, I have duties to attend to before supper.' She gave a small curtsey and left the room before Lucy could bid her stay. She was dismayed by Lucy's attitude, and saddened that she had acquired this thin veil of worldly sophistication since her stay in the capital.

Mrs Masterson too had come home demanding change. The house had to be redecorated in the brighter colours she had seen in London houses. The withdrawing room was to be papered with red, embossed wallpaper, new carpets ordered and sparkling chandeliers chosen from Italian catalogues. The staff were given new uniforms and their old ones given to the poor.

She hesitated over Sarah, not knowing in which category to place her, as she had in her mother's absence taken on the temporary role of housekeeper. After some thought she had had made for her a dark grey dress with a large white collar. Had she intended to subdue the girl's colouring with the shade, then her plans were thwarted, for Sarah's hair stood out like a flame above the dark material.

Isaac, as soon as he was able, took himself back to his comfortable office in Hull. Though he was still in some discomfort and walked with a limp, leaning heavily on his cane, there were times when he preferred the bustle of the busy town and the rough voices of the seamen to the constant demands of Isobel and the mindless chatter and complaints of Lucy. He thought with pleasure of the gentle care Sarah had given him before his wife and daughter had returned. She had known in some inexplicable way when the pain was unbearable and stayed by his side, soothing him with medication and soft words, and withdrawing quietly when he needed to be alone. But she'd stopped coming after his wife's return, as if sensing her displeasure, and confined herself to running the household as Mrs Masterson demanded.

'Can I talk to you, Fayther?' Deliberately Sarah had sought her father out as he walked home towards Field House after his day's work.

She had watched him as he appeared over the fields with a sack of kindling over his shoulders and a pair of rabbits tied to a stick. He walked now with a slight stoop and, although he was wearing his long, strong knee boots which Mr Masterson had made for him every year, he limped badly as if in pain. His old wound had opened up and was often raw and bloody.

'Aye, lass. What brings thee out of 'house. No work to do?'

She smiled ironically. 'There's always work to do at the Hall. Mrs Masterson never seems to be satisfied, nothing is ever quite right for her.'

'Aye, well, thy ma is about ready to go back. She seems to be 'only one who can please 'mistress. I try to keep out of her road, she's never got a civil word for me, but then she never did.'

A cold, hard look passed across his face momentarily and Sarah was surprised, for her father didn't often complain, but it was gone in seconds and his eyes, which reflected the colour of the sea, smiled down at her. 'But it doesn't matter, Sal. We are very, very lucky. Tha won't appreciate what we've got, having always had advantages. Tha's never had owt different, but had we been still in 'town, why, thy ma would have died with this fever. We might even have been in 'charity home afore now.'

'I know, Fayther.' She had heard this tale so often in one form or other, always from her father, never from her mother. It was as if he was constantly having to convince himself that he had done the right thing in bringing them here. 'That's what I want to talk to you about. About Garston Hall!'

'Aye, what about Garston Hall?'

'I – I don't think I can stay there any longer.' Her words came out in a rush. 'I don't seem to fit in any more. There isn't a place for me.'

'No place for thee? There's always a place there, for all of us, tha knows that. We have that security for ever. 'Mastersons would never turn us out, never. Look how Ma Scryven spent her last years there, even though she couldn't do much work. Nay, only if we did summat really bad – otherwise we're here for ever.'

He narrowed his eyes. 'Tha's not been upsetting Miss Lucy? Or—' A sudden possibility crossed his mind. 'Tha's not been getting into trouble in London – stepping out of turn?'

'Stepping out of turn! Would I do that, Fayther? Am I not always so careful not to offend that it's second nature to me?'

'Then what is it, lass?' It was unusual for Sarah to become so agitated.

'There isn't a place for me there any more. Miss Lucy doesn't need me. Oh, she thinks she does, when she wants someone to listen to her gossip, but she will be going away again soon and she might or might not expect me to go too. Or else I will be expected to stay here and become a housemaid under Ma.'

Will grew angry, his temper swift to rise. 'And is tha too good for that, miss? It seems to me that tha's getting ideas above thy station.'

'No, Fayther, you know that isn't true! And you were the one who said that I would be wasted just being a servant, remember?'

He did remember, and he recalled, too, how proud they had all been of her intelligence and cleverness and her ability to read and write.

'I know, lass,' he said more gently. 'But tha can go no further, at least, not unless tha leaves Monkston, and tha won't do that.'

No, she wouldn't do that. Couldn't do that. Especially not now, not whilst there was a possibility of seeing John. And that was another difficulty. When he came to visit Garston Hall they had to be so careful not to be seen alone together, but sometimes their eyes would meet and it was as if there was no-one else in the room; when she felt as if his lips were touching hers and she could hear his soft whispered words in her ears. But she knew that Lucy had eyes like a hawk and sooner or later she or Mrs Masterson would start to become suspicious.

'Sarah? Tha won't leave Monkston?' Her father repeated himself as he saw an obscure shadow flit across her face.

'What? Oh no, never. Fayther – what if I should want to get married?'

He laughed. 'Tha can't do that, lass. Tha's too good for most of 'men around here.'

'So!' She laughed back, sharing the joke with him, her lips smiling but her eyes anxious. 'I'll have to choose a gentleman then, someone rich and handsome?'

His smile died away and he shook his head. 'I'm right sorry for thee, Sarah, tha's fallen between two stools. There's no gentleman will have thee to wed, not without becoming a laughing stock.' He put both his hands around her face and lovingly stroked her cheeks, and she could smell the blood of the rabbits on his fingers. 'And don't ever think on becoming somebody's doxy – for I'd kill thee first, and him as well.'

It was a cold, bleak February before she finally made up her mind. She had spent many long, lonely hours over the last few weeks walking along the cliff top, buffeted by the strong winds which blew in vigorously from across the sea and which whipped her skirts and cloak with such ferocity it was as if they were trying to tear them from her. It was almost like a battle and she leaned into the icy gusts, forcing herself on and defying the elements to do their worst. At times she cried out aloud, 'You can't deny me, I belong here. This is mine.'

She took shelter when the weather was particularly bad in the doorway of Ma Scryven's cottage, crouched down in the corner so that the drips from the bedraggled old thatch didn't run down her neck, and it was as she was there one wild and gusty day, looking seawards at the pitching and plunging of the white seahorses on the boisterous grey water, that she remembered that she had been given the key, that the cottage now was hers, to do with as she wished.

She got up from her uncomfortable position on the doorstep and gathering her cloak around her went into the garden. It was wild and overgrown, and swathes of bramble smothered what had once been the old woman's flourishing glory of colour, scent and herbal splendour. She sadly ran her fingers through a battered lavender hedge and the perfume rose up towards her, invoking memories of her first visit here with her mother, when she'd scattered sprigs of lavender and sweet smelling rose petals and delighted in their faded and delicate colours.

'Tha must take my place,' Ma Scryven had said. 'Put aside thine own desires.' Sarah sighed deeply. She had made herbal preparations for her mother and Mr Masterson when they were ill; she had been hesitant about doing so for it had been a long time since she had made any remedies, but it had come back to her, easier than she had thought it would, as she remembered Ma Scryven's instructions from a long time ago.

'We buy it in the market.' She remembered the comment from Rose, Miss Pardoe's maid, as they'd un-packed the lavender-fragrant gowns from the travelling trunks. 'We don't have the bother of growing it.'

Well, it's no bother to me, she thought excitedly, her

heart thumping furiously as an idea grew into a positive thought. She looked more closely at the dishevelled land. Many of the shrubs had died from the harsh winters, others were straggly and neglected, but some were struggling to survive with a hardiness that came from being reared in the blustering east wind.

She'd whispered a word to John on his following visit, asking him to meet her by the old church, that she needed to talk to him, and his face had brightened at the prospect. He was there before her, a dark shadow in the church porch as she arrived breathlessly, having run all the way after being held up by some whim of Lucy's.

He didn't wait for her to speak, but gathered her up into his arms and kissed her yielding mouth and up-turned throat, and with a sigh buried his face in her soft hair, breathing in the warm fragrance of her body as she clung to him.

'Oh, Sarah, I can't go on like this. I need you so desperately. We must go away. Away from here, where no-one knows us, or cares. We'll go abroad where it won't matter who we are, and start a new life together.'

She hushed him then with a kiss and held her fingers over his lips, and he opened his mouth and gently bit them. She groaned softly as she felt the warmth of his tongue on her finger tips and the strength of his body close to hers. She pulled away. 'This is madness, John. You know that I love you and always will, there will never be another, but you know that we can't go away. You can't leave Mr Masterson, he needs you, he's old now and can't run the company alone – and the men who work for you, they need you.'

He answered her sharply. 'The men would find other work, whaling is booming, there's always a ship for a good man.' But he knew as he spoke that it would be on his conscience to leave his uncle who now relied on him totally, and who had supported him and been his guardian throughout his childhood.

'I'm sorry.' He stroked her cheek. 'We'll think of some way that we can be together. But these stolen moments are not enough for me, Sarah. I think of nothing else but being with you. You fill my mind night and day; you take over my thoughts so totally that I can't work, I can't sleep. It's as if I am not in charge of my own life any more.'

She drew back in dismay, her hand to her forehead. 'That's my fault,' she breathed. 'I've thought of you so much these last few weeks that my mind has spun out to meet yours.'

He laughed at her. 'What a darling goose you are. It's not just your mind that bothers me, it's the whole of you, the completeness of you which has captured me.'

He held her close again and kissed her tenderly, but she pushed him away. 'It wasn't meant to be funny, John, I mean it. I have tried to picture you – where you are, what you are doing, trying to make you think of me. That's why you can't think of anything else. I don't know how, but I have linked your mind to mine, tied it as securely as if it was bound by thread.'

He smiled down at her indulgently. 'You're a witch,' he whispered teasingly, 'and you have me in your power!'

'Hush, don't say that, not ever. You don't know how superstitious country folk are.' She hesitated. 'And especially not when I tell you what I am going to do.'

'Wait,' he said softly, putting his hand up in warning. 'I thought I heard something. Footsteps!'

They stood silently, holding their breath, but nothing could be heard above the sound of the wind and the waves.

'I could have sworn that I heard someone,' he breathed, 'but I must have been mistaken.'

'No-one comes here any more,' she whispered. 'Ma Scryven's funeral was the last service. They've removed the altar and the silver and taken it to Tillington.' She shivered violently and he put his arms about her, thinking that she was cold. Her voice dropped low and she spoke in hushed, ominous tones. 'The church will soon be in the sea – drowned, along with all the scattered bones of the poor dead souls in the graveyard.'

He shook her gently for he could see by the grey light filtering into the porch that she was nervous and uneasy. 'That's enough of such morbid talk. Now tell me what it is you are going to do.'

She shook her head to rid her mind of vague, melancholy thoughts and said impulsively, 'I'm going to be a herb woman, like Ma Scryven. I'm going to make potions and oils, so that the villagers can come to me when they are sick. But more than that, I'm going to sell what I grow in the markets at Hull and Beverley.'

He gazed at her in astonishment. 'What will you sell?'

'Oh, lavender and rosemary, sage and comfrey. Things that townspeople can't grow themselves.'

'But you can't, Sarah.' He was aghast. 'How can you think of it? How can you think of standing in a market selling wares? There are villains and thieves there. I know it, don't think that I don't. Men who would cut your throat for a copper. You haven't been brought up to it, you won't survive!'

She drew away from him and surveyed him coldly, then her eyes flashed. 'Don't tell me that I'm too good for that sort of life. That I have been too gently brought up!'

'That *is* what I'm saying,' he replied heatedly. 'You're not like your mother or father, or even Lizzie. They survived because that was all they knew. You have had a kinder existence!'

She gave a small sob. 'It seems then that I am just a misfit. Too good for one kind of life and not good enough for another.' She held up her head defiantly. 'But as I can't seem to please anybody, then I shall please myself. I shall live alone in Ma Scryven's cottage where I shall bother no-one, and I shall survive, you'll see. I have the strength!'

'Sarah, please, don't talk like that,' he pleaded. 'I need you, we need each other. We shall be nothing if we are apart – and I shall never have a moment's peace if I know that you are alone here with no-one to protect you.' He looked around at the ravages that the winter had wrought on the coastline, at the cracked and falling stonework of the church, at the dilapidated buildings hanging on the edge, waiting for the final crack that would precipitate them into the sea.

'My cottage won't go yet, not for some time.' She smiled as she made the decision. 'I shall be safe enough.' She stepped outside and the wind caught her cloak, billowing it out behind her like a black sail.

'You'll be lonely, there'll be no-one to talk to.' Harshly he spoke to her though he sensed that her mind was made up.

She stretched out her arms to encompass the waters lashing below. 'How can I possibly be lonely? Not here. Not when the sea is my friend, my companion.'

Will was set firmly against it. He said it was wrong that a young woman should live alone. 'If tha so much as allows a man over 'doorstep, then tha reputation is in shreds.'

'But you said that no man would marry me, Fayther, so what does it matter about my reputation?' she replied sharply.

Her mother worried about her being alone but had not decried her plan. 'There is a need, Will.' She tried to pacify him. 'Folks around here are lost without Ma Scryven. Oh, they've got their own remedies but sometimes they need something more.'

'And somebody to blame if owt goes wrong,' he grumbled.

'Make her a good stout door and shutters and she'll be all right,' Maria continued practically, ignoring his remark. 'I've some linen and fustian blankets tha can have, Sarah, and thy fayther will bring thee rabbits and game, and when Tom gets going he can supply thee with flour.' Swiftly she dispensed with minor difficulties. ' 'Only problem that I can see,' a small frown creased

414

her forehead, 'will be with 'Mastersons. They're not going to like it at all.'

Sarah gave notice to Mr Masterson first. She guessed, rightly, that he would be easier to talk to.

'We shall miss you, Sarah.' He sat hunched over the fire, a blanket around his knees. He felt the cold in his bones and had decided to stay at home until the worst of the winter was over. 'But I'm glad that you are going to do something useful, and I dare say we shall call on you when we need something.' His rheumy eyes looked at her kindly and he blew his nose on a soft white handkerchief. 'I wouldn't like to think that we were not going to see you again.'

She smiled at him and curtsied. He was a good man and she was fond of him. 'I shan't be far away, sir, and if ever you need me you only have to ask.'

'Have you any money, Sarah?'

'Just my wages, sir, when they are due. But it is enough,' she added quickly as he reached for his pocket. 'I'll grow what I need and my wants are few.'

He nodded understandingly. 'Yes? Well, you too only have to ask.'

She thanked him for his generosity. She would miss his kindness and she wished that she could kiss his tired old face.

She realized with a sudden pang that she would miss this house which had always been home, more so even than Field House, her parents' home, where she felt cramped and confined under the low smoky beams after the elegance and charm of Garston Hall. She would no longer enjoy the warmth and comfort of the huge kitchen or a walk in the rose garden, and she felt saddened at the impending loss.

Mrs Masterson and Lucy were appalled. 'How can you even think of it, Sarah?' Lucy said in a shocked tone. 'Whatever will people think? And you realize of course that I can never visit you. It wouldn't be proper.'

'I don't see why not, Miss Lucy, if you wish to. I shall

still be the same person as I am now. I'm not going to change, except that I shall be independent.'

'It will be quite unthinkable for you to call on her, Lucy,' said Mrs Masterson after Sarah had left. Her voice was cold, but her eyes glittered. At last she was rid of her, this servant girl with her gentle manner who had come to pose a threat. 'You have your future to think of. It will not do for you to mix with such a person.'

23

She couldn't do anything in the garden until the spring, when the gales would die away and the wet earth started to sprout fresh green growth, so she spent her time clearing out the cottage, sweeping out years of cobwebs and birds' nests and bringing in wood for the fire which she lit and then had to retreat, coughing and choking as the blocked chimney cast down thick black smoke.

Purposefully she kept John out of her thoughts during the day, pushing any yearning for him to the recesses of her mind, though she felt sometimes the anguish of knowing that he was thinking of her. But at night, as she lay sleepless in her bed listening to the sea, which was so much louder and more persistent in its cry below her cottage than it had been either at Field House or Garston Hall, she let her mind wander and thought only of him and imagined him in her arms, loving him, caressing him, being loved and possessed by him.

Lizzie was her first visitor. She appeared smiling on her doorstep one afternoon, her eyes bright and her manner lively.

'You look well, Lizzie, and happy. Come in and tell me all the news. Is the mill nearly ready, and how is Tom?'

Lizzie sat down and looked around the room. 'It looks grand, Sarah. I wouldn't have believed it could be made so cosy. It smells so nice.'

The cottage, once the fire had warmed it and taken away the damp musty smell, exuded the perfume of the dried flowers and oils which had been left discarded in cupboards and drawers. Sarah had scattered them on the floor with the rushes, and as she trod on them their scent rose to fill the room. To make up for the lack of furniture she had filled jars and pans with dried grasses and poppy heads and gathered the flat white heads of yarrow from the cliffs and placed them on her windowsill.

'Aye,' said Lizzie, sitting back and contemplating a sisterly chat. 'Tom's well and rarin' to start. 'Mill's almost ready, so I don't see as much of him as I'd like.'

'Once you're wed, Lizzie, and living there, you'll see as much of him as you want.' Sarah looked fondly at her. 'Then I shan't see so much of either of you.'

'I'll visit thee, Sarah, don't worry about that, me and Tom both will, when we're not too busy at 'mill.'

She frowned a little and her blue eyes looked troubled. 'I was going to ask thee – well, I'm being sick – though I feel all right in meself. I'm afeard of telling Tom, now when I'm so happy and I've got so much to look forward to – being with Tom and all that.' She blushed and looked away. 'I never thought that a man could be so kind and loving as my Tom is.'

Sarah smiled. 'I'm not ready with my herbs yet, but I have got some peppermint leaves.' She got up, reached into a cupboard and took down a box. 'Make a drink with these and you'll find it will ease the sickness.'

She laid her hand affectionately on Lizzie's shoulder. 'And I shall have a word with that brother of mine. If the mill is almost ready then I see no reason why you shouldn't be wed – and as soon as possible. I think we all deserve a celebration.'

Lizzie beamed gratefully. 'Oh, I wish you would, Sarah. He'll listen to you. It's what I want more than owt. To be married to Tom.'

A trickle of villagers called, mostly out of curiosity, to look at Miss Sarah who had lived at the big house and given up a good living to live alone in a run-down old hovel at the edge of the sea. But they knew her and guarded her privacy when pointed questions were asked by people from outside.

She told them they must come in the summer after she had gathered the flowers and fruit, but as the rains came down, making the land a morass of mud, and then the east winds blew unceasingly, battering the existing plants and drying the soil so that she couldn't put her spade into it, she wondered if anything would ever grow in time for her to harvest and gather before they were knocking on her door again.

It was a cold wet spring morning when Tom and Lizzie set off for the church in Tillington, but they didn't notice the rain as they rode hand in hand in the back of the waggon, with Will in Harris's cocked hat driving the mare, and the rest of the noisy party walking or running beside them to keep up.

Lizzie carried a sweet-smelling posy of blue forget-me-nots and shiny leaves of myrtle to signify true love, and the delicate bell-shaped lily of the valley to bring happiness. She wore a circlet of fragrant flowers in her coiled and plaited hair, and a dress which Miss Lucy had given to her. It was a pretty blue, and though Lizzie knew she would never have occasion to wear such a dress again she was grateful and delighted.

'I feel like a real lady, Maria,' she had cried as Maria helped her to dress. 'I wish, I wish that our Jimmy could have been here – and my ma.'

She'd put her head on Maria's shoulder and shed a few tears. 'It's not that I don't love thee, Maria. I do, but I sometimes wonder if ever she thinks of us.'

'I know that she'll think of thee often, Lizzie, if she's still on God's good earth.' Maria had a lump in her throat as she thought of her old friend. 'And if she isn't then she'll be watching over thee.'

'Here's our Alice, Ma. Come specially from Scarbro'.' Tom with a big grin on his face had opened the door wide to bring in Alice escorted by a husband and an infant in her arms.

'Why didn't tha tell me, lass?' Maria gathered them all up in an embrace.

'We can hardly ever afford 'fare, Ma, and I can't come

on my own now that I'm carrying again. Sam won't hear of it, wilt tha, love?'

Sam, a thick-set, red-faced fisherman of few words, had shaken his head and then nodded, 'Aye, that's right, I won't.'

Sarah walked at the side of Joe Reedbarrow, for they were both to be witnesses. He kept glancing her way as if he wanted to speak, but each time she tried to make conversation he blushed or had a fit of coughing so that he could hardly answer her, so she gave up trying and huddled further into her cloak to escape the driving rain.

Mr Masterson had supplied them with a barrel of ale, and Maria, Janey and Lizzie had been preparing a feast for weeks, baking pies and cakes, potting hare and braising well hung game. Everything had been transported to the low, red brick loading shed at the side of the new mill, which was almost complete, save for the millstones and sails, and after the ceremony they gathered together, family and friends, to toast the young couple's health and future prosperity.

A trestle table had been laid with a starched white cloth and decorated with a garland of ivy. Roast goose took place of honour, its cavities stuffed with tender knobs of pork, dried mushrooms and bittersweet juniper berries. Golden ham, its crisp, shiny surface patterned with cloves, lay waiting for destruction in the company of sweet parsnips and tender green sorrel. Trembling jellies, their vibrant colours quivering as spoons were dipped into their dimpled surfaces, vied for sweetness with honeyed mulled pears coated with cream.

They called for a speech from the groom, but Tom was already feeling the effects of the ale and elderberry wine and the events of the day, and was unable to string a dozen words together. He sat down to loud cheers, an amiable smile on his handsome face, and planted a kiss on Lizzie's cheek, put his head down on the table and promptly fell asleep.

* * *

'I'll walk thee home, Miss Sarah.' Joe fell into step with her as the wedding guests straggled their way home, shouting their goodbyes and words of encouragement to the newly-weds. 'It's dark down by 'cliffs, we don't want thee tummelling ower.'

'It's all right, Joe. There's no need to trouble yourself. I know my way well enough.'

'Tha doesn't have to worry, Miss Sarah, it's no trouble to me, none at all.'

'Joe, you don't have to keep calling me Miss Sarah,' she said a trifle sharply. 'My name is Sarah and that's quite good enough.'

'Oh, aye, but tha's not quite 'same as rest of us, is tha? But I'll try to remember. I thank thee.'

She could have cried with vexation at his humility and submissiveness, which were at odds with his tallness, his wide shoulders and massive hands.

'It was a good wedding, Miss Sarah – Sarah.' He slowed his long strides to match hers. 'They made a grand couple, they'll do well together will Tom and Lizzie.'

'Yes,' she agreed. 'They will.' She didn't want to rebuff him, for he was a mild, artless man, but she wanted him to leave her so that she could continue the walk home alone and analyse her feelings. She hadn't realized that the effect of hearing the simple vows which Tom and Lizzie had made, or seeing Alice, complacent with her docile husband and child, would cause a hopelessness to wash over her, knowing that she would spend the rest of her days alone without the love of the companion she would have chosen.

'I can manage from here, Joe. Thank you very much.' They were at the end of the lane, in sight of the cottage.

'If tha's sure then.' He nodded his big head and touched his cap. 'Good night, Miss Sarah. Be sure to lock up.' He turned away and walked back a few yards, then standing in the shadows he waited patiently until she reached her gate safely.

'Sarah!'

She jumped back as a figure came out from beside her door. 'I'm sorry, I didn't mean to startle you.' John spoke softly.

'You shouldn't be here,' she whispered back and fumbled in the darkness to put the iron key in the lock.

'May I come in for a moment? I'm cold and wet through, I've been waiting for hours.'

'Well, all right, but not for long.' She didn't trust herself to let him stay for more than a few minutes for she felt a rush of happiness mingled with despair as she saw him again.

She lit the lamp and he gently kissed her wet cheek and untangled a damp tendril of hair. 'I've missed you, Sarah. More than I can say.'

She returned his kiss and they clung together in silence. Presently she turned away. 'I can't see you any more, John. I just can't endure this situation any longer. We must part. It's the only way. We shall never have any peace of mind otherwise.'

He gazed at her unbelievingly. 'How can you possibly say that, I thought you loved me?'

'It's because I love you that I'm saying it. You must get on with your life and I with mine. We can't be together, we both know that.' She took hold of his hand with both of hers. 'I will make a vow that I shan't ever stop loving you, you will be in my thoughts until the day I die.'

He shook her away. 'All words. You don't mean what you say.' His voice was bitter with helpless frustration. 'You'll be off with some brawny farmhand as soon as my back is turned.'

She caught her breath and flushed with pain.

'I'm sorry, I'm sorry. I didn't mean it!' he said resentfully. 'It's just that I saw you with that hulking young fellow back there in the lane, and I was so envious that he could be seen with you, and I can't.'

She smiled wistfully. 'Strange that you who have so much should be envious of someone who has so little. Please go now, John. We have nothing more to say to each other.' She walked to the door and opened it, and the draught caused the yellow lamplight to flicker and almost die, then kindle again. She reached up to him and he caught her face between his hands and briefly brushed her lips with his, before departing into the night without even a backward glance.

She bolted the door and lay down on her bed consumed with despair. What a fool she was. Why hadn't she made him stay, just this once, to show how she loved him? She stared wide-eyed at the ceiling.

She sat up suddenly as she heard a sound outside the door and watched as she saw the sneck handle being tried. She jumped off the bed. He had come back! She wrenched at the iron bolt and in her hurry tore a small piece of skin from her finger. She opened the door and her welcoming smile died as she saw the lopsided grin on Paul Reedbarrow's face as he stood in front of her.

'I see'd thee. Aha, I see'd thee! With our Joe and t'other fine fellow. I see'd thee all right. See'd thee afore, up at 'old church.' He laughed, his tongue curling against his wet lips. 'Didn't see me though!'

She slammed the door shut in his leering face and with trembling fingers pushed the bolt home and threw the wooden bar across. She leant against it feeling sick and distressed. So he was still spying on her, just as he used to years ago down on the sands. He wouldn't tell what he had seen, he would be too afraid of his father's or Joe's anger, but in spite of that he would whisper veiled insinuations, and though the villagers perhaps would laugh at him, they might also listen and wonder.

She closed the shutters tightly across the window and sat huddled on her bed until her agitated breathing eased and her trembling stopped, but she kept the lamp burning all through the long night, until with tired eyes she saw the pale dawn searching its way through the cracks in the shutters, reminding her that another day was about to begin.

*   *   *

She became thinner as summer wore on, losing the round plumpness of girlhood and becoming slender and brown and lithe as she worked all hours in her garden, digging and planting, taking comfort in the feel of the earth beneath her spade and the tender plants and seeds in her hands. And when the day's work was over she took long, lonely walks along the sands, letting the wind tangle her loosened hair and the waves wash over her sandy feet.

Her mother became concerned and said she wasn't eating enough, and plied her with pies and puddings, but contrarily she wouldn't eat those which came from the Garston Hall kitchen, valuing her independence, and gave them away to the poor in the village.

She made up simple potions and medicines, but was careful at first that she gave nothing which would cause discomfort. This was because at the insistence of old Mrs Alsop, who was her first customer and had a persistent cough, she infused a herbal tea which the old woman drank down there and then, only to find after she had left that she had mistakenly given her a purgative. In trepidation Sarah waited for wrath to descend on her, but Mrs Alsop appeared the next day, a look of satisfaction on her aged face, to say she hadn't felt so good in years and demanding more of the same.

On her first visit to market she rose at dawn and packed her basket with bunches of marjoram, rosemary, mint and sage. She also put in small jars of apple jelly and rose hip syrup and a soothing cough mixture. She gathered her long thick hair into a plait and covered it with a white kerchief, wrapped her woollen shawl around her, for the morning was not yet warm, and set off to walk into Aldbrough to catch the carrier's early morning cart.

There were other country women waiting also for the ride into Hull and they looked at her curiously as she approached and nudged one another as they recognized her. She felt some antagonism towards her, but taking courage in both hands she smiled shyly and spoke to them.

'Good morning to thee. I've not been to market before, could any of thee advise me on the best place to stand?'

They stared at her for a moment then one of the women said, 'Try to get a place in 'middle of 'market, that's where 'crowds go.'

Another butted in. 'Aye, but tha has to be careful there or tha'll lose all tha stuff just as soon as tha back is turned.'

Within a few minutes there was an earnest discussion and not a few dissensions on the desirability of certain areas where she should or should not go.

'Stay by us, honey,' said a large florid woman. 'We'll watch that nobody filches from thee. It's not easy when tha's not used to it, but tha'll be all right with us.' She peered into Sarah's basket and, satisfied that there would be no competition with the contents of her own, she smiled encouragingly.

At the end of the day Sarah had an empty basket and a purse full of coins. She had sewn a hidden pocket beneath her skirt and she shook it just for the satisfaction of hearing the clinking sound. As she walked towards the Blue Bell inn to catch the cart home she stopped to look in Miss Ellie's window. At this rate, she would be able to buy herself a new bonnet. Then she dismissed the fleeting thought as she remembered that she would no longer have any occasion to wear one.

On impulse she opened the door and the bell jingled. Miss Ellie appeared immediately, a frilled handkerchief in her hand. Her fixed smile faded as she saw the market girl standing there.

'Good afternoon, Miss Ellie. You may not remember me, Sarah Foster?'

Miss Ellie wrinkled her brow. The well modulated voice was not in keeping with the plain dress and apron the girl wore. Then recognition came. 'Of course, Mrs Masterson's – er, companion, was it?'

'Not any more. I work for myself now. I grow and sell flowers and herbs and make up potions for the sick.'

425

'A herb woman? Indeed, and what can I do for you?'
Her voice was curious but mildly mocking.

'Do you remember that the last time I came here, you
gave me a silk rose? Well, I wondered if you would be
willing to buy some real flowers? Not to decorate your
hats but to display here in your salon, and perhaps some
dried flowers which keep their perfume, and which
would mask that awful smell outside.'

Miss Ellie opened her mouth in surprise and then
laughed out loud. 'You must be a mind reader, my dear!'
She put her hanky to her nose. 'I have been nearly sick
today with the smell of that boiling blubber. Wouldn't
you think that having been born and bred in this town,
I'd be used to it by now? There's no wonder that every
one who can is moving out. Sit down, my dear, and tell
me what you have to sell.'

Sarah was pleased with her day as she waved goodbye
to her fellow travellers at the top of Aldbrough hill and
set off down the road to Monkston. Her feet were aching
after standing all the day but she felt a great sense of
achievement. Miss Ellie had promised to buy a quantity
of flowers once a week and also said she would take half
a dozen posies of dried flowers to sell for her, on
condition that if no-one bought them Sarah would take
them back.

She had walked about a mile when she heard the
sound of hooves and the rattle of a carriage coming up
fast behind her. She moved to the side of the narrow
road and looked back. It was the Mastersons' carriage,
bearing down fast towards her.

Harris lifted his whip in greeting as he approached
and slightly tightened the reins as he anticipated the
signal from inside to slow down and stop, but none
came. Mrs Masterson and Lucy were either asleep or
didn't see Sarah close by the hedge, and as he looked
back over his shoulder he saw her walking briskly, her
head tossed back and her chin defiant.

*　　*　　*

John saw her quite by chance one morning as he cut through the Market Place towards the High Street. His attention was caught by a group of soldiers who were gathered around a stall, and as he saw them move laughingly away he saw that the object of their attention was Sarah. He stood for a moment watching her, absorbing every detail of her face as if he must etch it into his mind for ever. Her small chin and straight nose, the rounded curve of her cheek, the wispy spirals of red hair which had escaped from her plait.

Suddenly as if she had received a signal she looked up and saw him. She didn't smile but her mouth worked for a moment as if she was about to say something and he thought he saw a sad appeal in her brown eyes.

He walked across to her and gave her a small formal bow. 'Sarah.'

She inclined her head. 'Good day, Mr John. Are you well?'

'Quite well, thank you. And you? You look very well.' He noted her slimness and thought that though it might be considered unfashionable in some quarters, it gave Sarah an elegance which was apparent in spite of her plain gown and apron. Her skin had a soft golden glow though there were dark shadows beneath her eyes, and he saw that the soft downy hair on her brown arms had been bleached white by the sun.

'You're beautiful, Sarah.' He uttered the words softly. 'How am I going to exist without you?'

She turned her head away and looked down. 'Please. Don't make it even more difficult for me.'

'Difficult for you?' He raised his voice. 'What about me? Don't you ever think about how I feel?'

'Yes,' she replied softly. 'I think of nothing else.'

He walked swiftly away. It was an intolerable situation. How could he possibly concentrate on business when she was sitting virtually yards away from him? And what were those soldiers doing, gathering there? Supposing they came back and made a nuisance of themselves? How would she deal with that? It was impossible.

As he walked into the yard a young boy of about eight or nine years old got up from where he was sitting in a corner and taking off his cap came over to him. 'Spare me a copper, mister.'

John impatiently shooed him away.

'Got any work, then, sir?'

John put his hand to his head in frustration. He could do without begging children as well as everything else. Then his better nature came to the fore and he put his hand in his pocket.

'Wait a moment,' he said. 'You can earn this, young fellow.' He tossed a coin in the air and the boy caught it eagerly. 'If you do what I ask, then there are another two like this one at the end of the day.'

The boy couldn't believe his luck. All he had to do was sit in the Market Place and watch a young woman, a pretty one at that, and let the gentleman know if anyone bothered her. He sat in the corner of a shop doorway eating a pie which he had bought with the first coin and felt the sun on his face. He saw the young woman looking across at him and he raised his hand cheerily and waved.

November came and she made her last visit to the market. Over the past few weeks she had sometimes sold nothing at all, going home with an empty money bag. The townspeople were buying only the bare essentials as they prepared for the coming winter when work would be scarce and food costly for their meagre earnings. They had bought her cough syrup and honey as winter colds and fevers began, but her flowers and herbs they discarded. However, she was satisfied with her profits and she had a small hoard of money which would last until next spring.

As she repacked her basket she saw the young boy who had spent so much time watching her from across the street, and she beckoned him to come over. He did so reluctantly, hanging back halfheartedly amongst the carts and stalls as if he thought he was going to be reprimanded for loitering, but instead of chastising him she handed him a jar of blackberry jam.

'Here, take this to your ma. I shan't be coming again until next year.'

He thanked her, his eyes wide with gratitude, though he felt it was a pity she was going for he would now be out of work again. As he walked away carefully holding the jar she called to him, 'Be sure to give Mr Rayner my kind thanks.'

She had a sad, lovely smile, he thought, but on reflection he decided shrewdly that perhaps he would forget to give the message. Mr Rayner hadn't indicated that his presence was to be a secret from the pretty young woman, but on the other hand he hadn't said that it wasn't. After all, he had to think of next year.

He watched her as she climbed into a farm waggon and drove off, a big hulking fellow at her side. He had just decided that perhaps he wouldn't mention that either, when he saw it was too late, for as he turned he almost ran into Mr Rayner who was also watching. 'That's it for this year, sir. I don't think she'll be back until next summer.'

'No,' said John, gazing after them. 'I think you're probably right.' He gave a deep sigh, then looked down at the boy. 'Come on then, lad. Let's see if we can find you something else to do.'

'I just came to see if tha's all right, Miss Sarah. There's a right old gale blowing out there.' Joe's bulk filled her narrow doorway.

'You'd better come inside.' She admitted him reluctantly, for she had made it a policy not to allow men inside the house but to keep them on the doorstep. Joe, however, had been kind and willing, bringing her logs for the fire and making himself available for any heavy work, or collecting her from the market whenever he could.

There had been a few visits from village men who ostensibly had come on messages from their wives or mothers, but who would ask her if she had something she could recommend for their aches and pains. 'Such a pain in my back, Miss Sarah, if you would just take a look.' Or, 'If I could just come inside and show you my sore leg, arm, neck or wherever.' She had firmly kept them outside the door and charged them double for a preparation, reckoning that it would be more sensible to discourage them by hurting their pocket rather than their pride.

For the genuinely sick she made no charge, but asked them to give what they could afford, and those who could afford nothing would give her their grateful thanks, or leave a bag of kindling on her doorstep.

'Tha shouldn't be here alone.' Joe's gloom was discouraging. ' 'Cliff isn't safe. Great chunks have fallen off near our barn. We'll have to move animals' bedding out.'

'I'm sorry, Joe. What a worry for you.'

'Aye, well, at least 'house is still safe. But this cottage is a lot nearer to 'sea than I'd be happy about. Tha should move.'

She had been a little uneasy herself of late, but she didn't want to admit it. She thought that the sea sounded louder than when she first came, but it wasn't the pounding of the waves below the cliffs that disturbed her, that sound she had always found soothing and comforting, it was the slight imperceptible movement that she thought she could feel as she lay in her bed. She had told herself that it was just her imagination, that she couldn't possibly feel the shifting of the sand and clay beneath her, but her old recurring dream of falling, and the sound of rushing water filling her ears, would waken her during the night, and she would get out of bed, put on her shawl, walk to the cliff edge and look over to see if there had been another fall, trying to convince herself that the lapping water was no nearer than before.

'Where should I move to, Joe? I can't go to Field House, nor would I want to.' She couldn't possibly do that. Her parents' home was on Garston land and she was sure that Mrs Masterson wouldn't approve of villagers coming and going there, while they too would be reluctant to visit her.

Joe looked down and intently examined his carefully scraped boots, then cleared his throat nervously. 'Hast tha ever thought of getting wed?'

She watched a slow flush rise, colouring his neck and face, and he pressed his lips firmly together as if to close in any further communication.

'I did think of it once,' she answered slowly, 'only I decided against it.'

He looked at her, his gentle eyes wistful and appealing. 'Well, if tha should ever think on it again, Miss Sarah.'

'Sarah,' she gently reminded him.

He nodded and looked down at his boots again. 'It's just – well, I know tha's had a better education than me, and I'm just a rough clodhopper, but I work hard and I'd provide for thee.' He looked up again and this time she saw the eagerness in his eyes. 'I'd work all 'hours God sends if tha'd have me, Sarah. Tha'd want for nowt.'

'But I don't love thee, Joe.' Softly she slipped back into the language she knew would make him comfortable.

'But I love thee. I always have, since 'first time I saw thee. So it wouldn't matter. And in time tha maybe would come to like me.'

She smiled and touched his arm. 'But I do like thee, Joe. Tha's a dear, sweet man and I'm very fond of thee. But not enough to wed thee.'

'Aye, I understand.' He put his hand on the door and paused before he went out. 'If I ask thee again, tha won't be offended?'

She shook her head, tears rising to her eyes. 'No,' she said huskily. 'I won't be offended at all.'

He asked her again two weeks later, and laughingly she refused, and again two weeks after that and she shook her head solemnly. And right through to the beginning of the next year until finally she invited him in to sit down and talk.

'Tha'd get on well with my sister Nellie,' he said eagerly. 'She'd be glad of female company after looking after us lads and me da all her life, and tha'd share 'work so it wouldn't be too hard.'

'You mean we would live there with your father and brothers?' she said hesitantly. 'Paul as well?'

He gripped his big hands together, his knuckles showing white. 'Tha needn't worry about him, Sarah. He'll not be stopping. He's got a lass in trouble over at Tillington, and her fayther says if he doesn't marry or support her he'll come after him with his dogs.' He gazed at her with his grey, honest eyes. 'He'll not bother thee any more, I'll see to that.'

'You know then that he comes here?' She had heard often the soft footsteps at her locked door and seen the lifting of the sneck. She would shout at him to go away and he did, laughing softly to himself.

He nodded and looked away. 'I said I'd slug him if he didn't leave thee alone. He's nowt but a troublemaker.'

There was something else, for his manner was restless. 'What else, Joe? What else about Paul?'

He got up and stood over her. 'He told me about Mr Rayner, about tha meeting him at 'old church, and him being here.'

In consternation she started to explain, but he raised his hand to hush her as he continued, 'But there was no need for him to tell me. I already knew. I saw him that night after thy Tom's wedding, I watched him come in and waited till he came out.'

He put his hand on her head and gently stroked her hair. 'He'll not marry thee, Sarah, love. That sort stick to their own. Just 'same as we do!'

She turned away. How wrong Joe was. John would have taken a chance, she was the one who wouldn't. A great lassitude came over her. She was so weary of struggling with her emotions, of trying to keep them in check. Perhaps if she were married to someone else she would forget him. No – never, never. But maybe John would let her go, cut the bond which held them and set her free.

She raised her head. Dear Joe, he was willing to take her though he knew she loved someone else. She badly needed comfort, someone to take away this ache inside. She put out her hand and he grasped it tightly.

'All right Joe, I'll marry thee.'

He shook his head in amazement. After all his hopes he could hardly believe it. 'Tha means it, Sarah? Promise?' He could barely speak.

'Yes, Joe. I mean it. I promise.' Her eyes were bright and moist, but she gave him a trembling smile. It was something after all to give happiness to someone else, even though you were dying inside.

'And you'll not see him again?' His voice was anxious but she detected a command in his plea.

She felt she was bleeding as the wound cut deeper. 'Just once, Joe, to tell him. I owe him that at least.'

'Aye, that's right. Tha'll need to tell him. Then it's finished with.'

Sarah waved to Harris to stop as he was driving out of the iron gates of Garston Hall. 'Will you give this message to Mr Rayner, please. Be sure to give it to him yourself and not hand it to anyone else.'

She was sure that Harris would be discreet, but she had penned the letter to John in terms that would not give rise to suspicion if anyone else should read it.

' 'Be glad to, Miss Sarah, I'll be seeing him this morning.' He started to move off and then turned round to call to her. 'I heard thy ma say she was going to come over to see thee, she's on her way now.'

She smiled her thanks and set off down the path which wound round to the rear of the house to meet her. Maria waved to her from the kitchen door.

'Tha's saved me a journey, Sarah. I was just coming to see thee. Mr Masterson is asking after thee.'

'Oh, but—?'

'It's all right, 'mistress and Miss Lucy are away. They've gone gadding off to London again, and poor maister is in such pain with his leg.'

She pushed back a stray lock of hair beneath her linen cap and Sarah noticed the predominant silver strands, and the fine lines etched on her mother's forehead. Maria had aged since the fever and had taken a long time to recover, but the arrival of Lizzie's and Tom's bawling lusty son on Christmas Day had given her a renewed lease of energy, and while she and Lizzie and Sarah had gazed fondly at the newest Foster, Tom and Will, with the assistance of Joe and Martin Reedbarrow, had got roaring drunk as they'd wetted the baby's head.

Sarah ran her fingers along the bannister rail as she slowly climbed the wide staircase up to Mr Masterson's room. She thought of John: he'd said that he'd slid down here on the day she was born. She remembered looking down at him as he had stood in the hall on the day he told her about it, and she remembered too the strange nervous exhilaration she had felt as she listened and watched him, searching his face to know if he felt it too.

The house was quiet and restful. It smelt of beeswax and flowers, and she was saddened that she could only come here when Mrs Masterson and Lucy were away. Although she was happy in her cottage it was here at Garston in the spacious, handsome rooms that she felt as if she was at home; and soon, when she married Joe, she wouldn't be allowed to come at all.

'Sarah. How pleased I am to see you!' Isaac sat propped up with cushions and his legs stretched out on a stool. 'I can't tell you how much pain I'm in with this dratted gout. Can you bathe my legs like you did last time?'

She did what she could for him, bathing his swollen toes and swathing his legs with comfrey leaves.

'No, don't go, please stay a little longer,' he said as she prepared to leave. 'I get so little company when Mrs Masterson and Lucy are away. Tell me all that you have been doing since last I saw you.'

She sat on a low stool beside him and talked of her garden and her visits to the market, and of Tom and the mill, of the difficulties of keeping down the price of flour and of the antipathy towards millers by the general public. He discussed with her the new Humber Dock which was being dug and which he hoped to buy shares in, and the continuing hazards of the whaling industry.

He patted her hand. 'I have enjoyed our talk. Come again if you can. I wish—' He stopped and scratched his sparse grey beard as he meditated, then shook his head ruefully. 'Ah, well.'

'Yes, sir?' She waited, her brown eyes smiling fondly.

'Nothing, Sarah. It doesn't matter. It was just a fancy.'

She curtsied and left him. She hadn't mentioned that she was going to be married. She wanted John to be the first to know, although she suspected that Joe had already told his father, who in turn had told Will, for her father had put his arm around her shoulder the last time she had seen him and had spoken of his friendship with Martin Reedbarrow and what a good solid Holderness family they were.

'Just as we will be, Sarah, given time. Starting with our Tom and his son. 'First Foster to be born here.'

'No, Fayther. I was the first, don't forget!' she had objected vehemently, and her eyes flashed. Her father looked at her in surprise.

'Aye, well, I meant on 'male side. Women change their names when they wed, and if tha should decide—' He trailed off indecisively.

She had put her chin in the air and said defiantly, 'I would still be a Foster, Fayther, nothing can change that, ever.'

Gratified, he laughed. 'That's 'spirit, Sarah. Tha's a Foster all right. Tha's got red hair and temper to prove it.'

She waited by the old church each evening as dusk was falling, when the treetops stood out in shadowy silhouette against the darkening sky and the horizon was lost in a roke of grey.

On the fourth evening, as the dusk was turning to darkness and she was about to return home, she saw him walking below her on the sands. He raised his hand and smiled and she knew with sinking despair how her news would wipe away the smile from his face and bring him only misery.

She scrambled down the cliffs before he could attempt to come up to her and as she came to the bottom of the incline he reached up to help her, lifting her into his arms and holding her there. He kissed her tenderly, her face, her lips, then with a groan he drew her to him, bending her willing body to his.

'I've missed you so much, Sarah. I want you so much that it hurts.'

Unable to resist she arched her neck towards him and he kissed the long line of her throat, running his hands over her, feeling the shape of her body beneath her gown.

'I love you, love you, love you,' she whispered as her body melted against his. The words echoed in his ears with the pounding of the waves.

'Don't ever leave me again, Sarah. I am nothing without you,' he implored softly. 'My life, my being, it is nothing if you are not there to share it with me.'

Safe in his arms, she dreamily watched as a bright, white moon appeared in the night sky, highlighting a drift of clouds, touching their downy edges with silver. But as the sands turned white by its light, she felt their sharpness beneath her, and reality reasserted itself as if the moon had illuminated her mind, reminding her that her path led elsewhere and that she was promised to someone else.

She whispered her news haltingly to him and he stared, disbelieving.

'I will always love you, John,' she cried, clutching his hand. 'Even though I can't be with you. Even though we must live our lives apart, we'll be together. Nothing can separate us. We belong to one another – in spirit and mind, if not in body.'

Angrily he pushed her away. 'How can you say that? How can you join your life to someone else without thinking of me?' He seized her shoulders violently. 'I can't wait until the great hereafter and live in Hell now. I need you, Sarah.'

She wept, sobs shaking her body. 'How I wish this was another time; another place, when perhaps it wouldn't matter who we were. When we might not have to bow down to convention or society's rules, when we could please ourselves only and not think of others!'

'You're fooling yourself, Sarah, there will never be such a time. There will always be prejudice and narrow-mindedness, but it has to be faced, to be met head on, otherwise we're lost.' He pleaded with her. 'We can face it together, you and I.'

She shook her head. 'I was too afraid, and now it's too late. I've made a promise that I must keep.'

She reached out to him, imploring him to understand, but he stormed away from her and stood at the water's edge watching the waves as they broke softly on the sand.

'And what about me?' He spoke quietly as if all the fight had gone out of him.

She put her fingers over her lips and breathed softly, 'Marry Miss Pardoe, John. She'll be a fine wife for you.' Tears ran down her cheeks.

'What? What did you say?' By chance his fingers had closed on the letter that was in his pocket.

'Marry Miss Pardoe. She'll be good for you, she's kind and beautiful and she cares about you.'

He strode back to face her and pulled her up from where she crouched on the sand. 'I'll make my own decisions, and I'm making one now. I'm going away, I was coming to tell you when I received your message. I'm sailing to the Arctic. I shall be too busy trying to stay alive to even think about you.'

He took her head in his hands, kissed her fiercely and then held her at arms' length. 'We shan't meet again, don't you or your intended bridegroom worry about that, but I'll tell you this, Sarah. You'll see me in your sleep and in every waking moment. When you are lying in his arms you'll feel me there between you. You will never be rid of me, not if you live to be a hundred. You will never have any peace, not in this world or the next, I promise you.'

She stood watching as he walked swiftly away, his long strides making deep footprints in the damp sand. She watched until a prominence of broken clay ridges hid him from view, and then she slowly turned to make her solitary ascent back up the moonlit cliff.

John let the heavy door close with a bang, bringing Janey hurrying out of the kitchen.

'Oh, Mr John.' She took his cape from him. 'We've kept supper hot for you. Master's gone to bed but he asked would you go up as soon as you've eaten?'

'Bring a couple of bottles of wine and some cheese to Mr Masterson's room, nothing more.' His voice was brusque, and she dipped her knee and gazed at him anxiously. 'I shan't require anything else, thank you. Don't wait up.'

He climbed the stairs two at a time. He intended to get drunk, so drunk that he wouldn't remember anything of this evening. Not the sweetness of her lips and the drowning depths of her eyes. Not the consuming jealousy he felt that she was to marry that hulking farmhand. He couldn't bear the thought of him laying his great body next to hers, crushing her fragile form beneath his.

He might take her body but he'll never possess her mind, her thoughts, he told himself wretchedly, but he knew that it wasn't enough; he couldn't comprehend that he would never see her again, that she was gone from him for ever.

He staggered into his uncle's room, already half drunk with emotion, and Isaac looked up irritably from his bed where he lay snug beneath a fur rug, his nightcap pulled about his ears. 'What the devil are you up to? Where have you been? Janey said that you had arrived and then gone straight out again, and now you come crashing in, waking all the household!'

It didn't matter that the household consisted only of himself and the servants. Isaac did not like his tranquillity disturbed in such a manner. 'Are you drunk?'

'Not yet, sir, but I intend to be, that is if you will allow me the facilities of your cellar. I've taken the liberty of sending down for some wine.'

'Hmph. Most of it's yours anyway. I'm not allowed to drink the stuff with this dratted gout.' Isaac adjusted his cap and pulled his rug around him. 'You'd better tell me what's going on.'

John paused as Janey came in with the cheese and wine and some bread which she had brought as an afterthought. It was not like Mr John to refuse his supper.

'I don't know that I want to discuss it, Uncle,' he muttered after she had gone. 'Sufficient to say that I have had a great disappointment and that I am feeling as low as it is possible for a man to be.'

He poured a glass of wine and drank it quickly. The sooner he was drunk the better. 'I came to tell you that I am going to London for a few days, but that I shall be back in time for the *Northern Star*'s sailing.'

'Why you should want to go away on this trip anyway, I can't fathom,' Isaac said grumpily. 'You know I can't get to the office just now.'

'Another two weeks and you'll feel better, the doctor told you that, and anyway the staff are perfectly capable of running the company for a few weeks.' He poured another glass of wine and Isaac watched him curiously.

'I need to get away and I'm curious about this trip. The captain reckons on pushing further north to follow the whales, and I'd like to be there if he's going into uncharted territory. We have to think of the men's safety as well as the profits.'

'If you're going to London you might look in on Isobel and Lucy. Find out when they are coming back.'

John hesitated, he'd forgotten that his relatives were in London. 'Are they staying with the Pardoes again?'

'They've rented a house so as not to be an inconvenience to Miss Pardoe!' Sulkily he watched as John drank his wine. 'Isobel even wants me to buy a property down there so that they can go down every season, so that Lucy can meet the right company.'

He looked longingly at the wine bottle. 'Pour me just one glass, there's a good fellow. Just one can't hurt.'

He sipped the red wine appreciatively. 'I think I deserve some comfort if my wife and daughter have deserted me.'

'That's the trouble with our ladies.' John slurred over his words and poured more wine, slopping it on to the carpet. 'They always desert us when we need them most. That's my trouble, Uncle, I'll confide in you. I've been deserted.'

Isaac drummed silently on the counterpane with his gnarled fingertips and waited with narrowed eyes for the outburst. When it came it was with a rush, a torrent of words, of broken sentences and verbal confusion.

'And you say she won't have you, this woman?' asked Isaac. 'Is this the same woman you had in mind once before? The one without a dowry?'

John nodded. He was spent, drained of all feeling.

'And she's a married woman, is she?' Isaac hadn't quite got the drift of his ramblings.

'Not yet, but she soon will be. She's promised.' He put his head in his hands. 'Oh God! Sarah, how am I to live without you?'

'Sarah? She's called Sarah, is she?' The old man sighed deeply. 'It's a good name for a woman.'

Something in John's eyes as he looked up alerted him and Isaac frowned, biting his lips apprehensively. 'You don't mean it's *our* Sarah – not Sarah Foster?'

'The same, Uncle. There is only one as far as I am concerned.'

440

John sat back in his chair and closed his eyes. The oblivion he had hoped for in drunkenness had not come, he was as sober as a judge now, and more despondent than ever. When he opened his eyes to look at his uncle tears were streaming down the old man's face, running down his wrinkled cheeks and wetting his beard.

'Uncle?' He knelt beside him. 'What is it, sir? Are you ill? I'm sorry if I've upset you.'

'You're a fool, John! Why did you not say that it was Sarah you loved? Sarah, who we both love.' The old man put his head in his hands and wept. 'You know that one day all of this will be yours, if you want it. Isobel won't stay here once I'm gone. And Sarah, she would have been happy here. Sarah, who would have cared for me now that I'm old and ill – cared as no-one else would. And now she's gone, lost to us – both of us.'

He woke at the first pencil glow of daybreak, dressed and left the house as the servants were stirring, surprising them as, sleepy-eyed, they unlocked the door and let him out. He rode away from Monkston towards town, his back turned to the brushstrokes of colour which appeared in the eastern sky, as darkness fled and the virgin day stretched out its bright rays.

He packed his valise quickly at his High Street home, and changed horses, leaving his mare and taking a strong stallion, for he intended to ride fast for the two hundred miles to London.

He stopped over in Lincoln and Sleaford, paying well for the hire of other mounts at inns there, and arrived at the Pardoes' door dirty, aching and weary, having punished himself and his sweating horses by his hard riding. He had barely given thought to the question of why Matilda Pardoe should have written asking him to call on her, except to reflect curiously that it was strange that she should wish to see him now at a time when Sarah told him that he ought to marry her.

He washed, changed his clothes and went downstairs. One of the footmen greeted him and showed him through to the withdrawing room where Miss Pardoe would join him.

'Is Mr Stephen Pardoe at home?'

'No, sir. Mr Stephen is out of town at present, as is Mr Pardoe.'

He waited seated for a few moments, and then got up restlessly and examined the paintings on the wall. It was odd, he thought, that Miss Pardoe had invited him to stay when there didn't appear to be any other guests and when her father and brother were absent.

He bowed as she came into the room. She was poised and smiling as she greeted him with thanks for coming so swiftly after receiving her letter.

'It was not a question of life or death, Mr Rayner, but a matter that I would like settled fairly soon. Please, take a seat. You look very tired, I fear that the journey has overtaxed you?'

'Not at all, Miss Pardoe. I came immediately, as I am to sail to the Arctic very shortly, and it may be many months before I return.'

He watched her as she seated herself across from him. Sarah was right, she would make someone a good wife. She was handsome and charming, and he felt sure that she would take an intelligent interest in her husband's affairs. And yet there was something missing, some spark or warmth, perhaps waiting to be kindled.

'My aunt will be joining us for supper,' she said, as if reassuring him that they would not be dining alone, 'but I wished to speak with you privately, which is why I asked you to come whilst my father and brother are away.'

She took a deep breath and looked away. John detected a small movement in her throat as if she was nervously swallowing.

'I have decided to marry,' she said firmly and John's eyebrows rose in surprise. He had not heard a whisper of the news.

'My father is anxious for grandchildren to continue our family line, and as my brother does not appear to be in any hurry to be married and produce a family, I have decided to take matters into my own hands.'

Her cheeks flushed slightly and John realized that for some reason this was not an easy subject for her. He therefore kept his eyes averted, gazing at the paintings and the windows, and just occasionally glancing in her direction.

'You may have heard, as I well know how this type of gossip travels, that I have refused several offers of marriage. My reasons for this are personal, but I can tell you that I have not previously met anyone with whom I wish to share the rest of my days.'

She got up from the chair and walked across to the window, gazing out of the gauze curtains into the street below.

John too stood up and waited hesitatingly for her to continue.

'This is quite difficult for me, Mr Rayner, so you must excuse me if I do not phrase my words well.'

She turned to face him and although the cold white light was behind her, throwing her face into shadow, he could see the flush on her cheeks. 'The fact is, I have a proposition to offer you. If you do not think it presumptuous of me and if you have not already any commitments in this direction, I would ask if you would give serious consideration to taking me as your wife?'

He drew in his breath. What it must have cost her to ask such a question he couldn't begin to consider. After a moment he took her hand and led her to a chair, thinking that perhaps she might be feeling the strain of embarrassment, but once seated she sat upright, her hands folded calmly across her lap.

'You see, Mr Rayner, of all the gentlemen I have met, you are the only one that I would consider as a suitable companion, and if you will excuse my plainness of speech, as a prospective father of my children.'

John was lost for words, he wasn't sure whether he should be flattered, for she was an extremely eligible heiress, or, and this he felt more likely, simply to regard himself as a participant in a joint transaction. That this was the way things were often regarded he was quite well aware, but surely not in such a calculated or direct manner?

'I don't of course expect you to make a decision now, but if you should decide that it would be possible, then I would ask you to approach my father in the usual way.' She smiled then and her face looked softer, gentler. 'He would be horrified to think that his daughter had approached a gentleman with such an offer, so I must ask you to be completely discreet, but I must also explain that I do not intend to let anyone else make decisions which affect my life. I never have and I never will.'

He took her hand and kissed it gently. 'I think that you are very brave, Miss Pardoe, and I admire your spirit. I am honoured to have your regard.'

She interrupted him before he could say more. 'Matilda, please. As I say, I do not expect you to decide now, in fact I would prefer it if you would give it careful thought, perhaps during your voyage. It is a once in a lifetime decision, after all, not to be taken lightly.' She hesitated slightly. 'I cannot speak of love as I have not experienced it, but I have to say that I would expect and give complete fidelity. I would not tolerate any other liaison after marriage, as some I know do.'

It was during supper, during a momentary break in the garrulous chatter of her aunt, that John realized the degree of astuteness in Matilda Pardoe. She enquired if he would be visiting his aunt and cousin whilst in London, and on hearing that he would not as he wished to return north immediately the next morning, she asked quite casually the whereabouts of Sarah.

'I understand that she is no longer in your cousin's employ?'

He thought it strange that she should even enquire, but answered lightly that she was not. 'She wished to be independent. She has become a herb woman,' he said dismissively.

'I'm glad to hear it,' Matilda answered. 'She was wasted as a servant.' She glanced at him from beneath her dark lashes. 'She has not married some rich farmer?'

'No.' John's tone was curt. 'But I understand that she is to marry a poor one.'

'Such a pity.' Matilda's eyes were wide and appraising, with a dark, perceptive gleam. 'Such beauty and intelligence. She must be marrying for love?'

John stood with his arms folded, silently watching the crew as they came aboard. Some came quietly and soberly, glancing over their shoulders to wave and give a sombre smile to those waiting on the quayside, mothers, wives and children, who had braved the cold, dim morning to see their men depart.

Others of the crew came staggering on to the deck, given a helping hand by those only slightly less inebriated than themselves, as they disgorged from the warmth of the taverns where they had spent the last of their money and time on shore before leaving for less hospitable territory.

He greeted Rob Hardwick and his son as they came on board. He noticed that the older man was very stooped and his legs were bent. He couldn't surely expect to do many more trips. He was a good, reliable seaman, but this wasn't an old man's occupation. Strength and swiftness were needed as well as experience, and John sighed regretfully. He didn't like to do it, but he would have to tell him at the end of the voyage that this would be his last sailing.

He nodded, too, to Jimmy Swinburn, now out of his apprenticeship and an experienced linesman as his father had been, but he received only a grunt as the sullen young seaman averted his eyes to look down at the dockside where a pair of slatternly drabs were calling to him and blowing kisses.

No-one to wave a last goodbye to me, John brooded. No-one to wish God speed and a safe return. He dismissed the melancholy thought. There was only

445

one person he would have wished to see waving her handkerchief as they passed out of the harbour mouth into the muddy waters of the Humber, and she was miles away, no doubt just rising from her bed, for it was barely five o'clock. He imagined her stretching her brown arms above her head, her skin still warm from sleep and her hair tousled about her face and shoulders.

One day, Sarah, he meditated some hours later, as they drew away from the pilot boat and rounded the sandbanks of Spurn Head into the wide reaches of the German Ocean, one day you'll be mine. Though you may be promised to someone else in this life, I'll return for you one day, and you won't refuse me then. He saw her face before him, smiling sadly, and thought he felt a slight, soft touch on his cheek, like a loving, goodbye kiss.

Sarah rose in darkness and with the aid of a dim lantern manoeuvred the horse between the shafts of the small cart. She had persuaded Tom to loan her the mare with the promise that she would return her by midday and did nothing to correct his mistaken impression that she wanted to leave on an early excursion into Hull.

She walked at the mare's head until she was clear of the village, murmuring softly to her in the darkness, and then turned back to take the narrow road leading down the coast. The mare was as surefooted as she was and there was light enough reflected from the sea to travel by. Although Sarah hadn't before journeyed the total length of road which ended at the narrow spit of Spurn, she knew by word of mouth which areas had eroded, and which parts of the road had disintegrated under the constant battering of the sea, and how to avoid them.

Dawn was breaking as she travelled through the still sleeping village of Waxholme and skirted the deserted cottages of Owthorne which trembled on the cliff edge, and headed on towards the high cliffs of Dimlington

Heights where she would have a long view of the coastline and the sails of the ships as they sailed out of the estuary and into the German Ocean on their route to the Shetlands and the Arctic.

It had been her mother who had mentioned that Mr John was sailing on the *Northern Star* and that her father's old seamate Rob Hardwick would also be on board.

'When does she sail, Ma?' Sarah had casually asked.

'I know for a fact that it's 'day after tomorrow,' Maria had replied. 'Mr Masterson said it particularly. Said he wished he could have been there to see her go. He said it would be a hard voyage as they're pushing further north than they've ever done before, and I said I was glad that Will wasn't going, and he said particularly that it would be a day to remember.'

Sarah was determined to be there. She couldn't go to the dockside as there might be someone who would recognize her as Will Foster's daughter and wonder why she was there, and most certainly there would be people who knew John, and she didn't want to embarrass him; yet no-one would think it odd if a lone woman on a cliff top stood gazing at a ship as it ploughed its way across the sea.

She stood by the beacon at Dimlington Heights and stared across the water, but apart from the vessels returning to harbour and a few scattered fishing boats and cobbles, there were no ships sailing out from the home shores. I'm too early, she thought, there hasn't been time to clear the Humber. She looked up at the sun breaking through the clouds and decided to drive on down to Spurn where she would see the ships as they rounded the point.

She cracked the whip and urged on the mare, making good progress where the road was sound and getting down to lead her when it drew near the cliff edge. Several times she looked down and saw at the foot of the cliffs ridges and mounds of red and grey clay from previous falls, with here and there timber and thatch and old chairs sitting incongruously abandoned amongst the abundant grass and vegetation which was flourishing there.

As she drove up the hill towards the high cliffs above the village of Kilnsea, she took a long look as she passed at the spired church standing only yards from the sea shore. This was a big village, bigger than Monkston, maybe thirty or so houses and farms, but the road ran perilously close to the edge and the cliffs were cracked and fissured.

She stopped to water the mare from a fast-running stream and bent to cup her hands and take a drink herself The morning was running on fast and she worried that she might not get back in time to deliver the horse and cart to Tom as she'd promised. She rinsed her face with the clear water and looked south again down towards the headland, narrowing her eyes as she saw rounding the narrow strip of land a fleet of whaling ships, their sails spread wide.

She left the horse to graze and stood silently watching, her hand shielding her eyes against the brightness of the morning sky. There were five ships, two of which she knew belonged to the Masterson fleet, but from this distance she could not make out their names and had no means of knowing which they were.

She stood locked in calm meditation until her eyes fixed on the leading vessel, a swift, three-masted barque. She concentrated fully on this ship, clearing her mind of all thoughts and sounds as she searched, and knew for sure that this was the ship which held John.

'I know I said I wouldn't do this any more,' she whispered. 'I said I would not link my mind to yours, that I would give you some peace. But I can't help myself. I'm bound to you as if we were one flesh and blood, and if I'm not to see you again, never again to feel your arms about me, the warmth of your lips on mine, then I must say goodbye.'

She touched her fingers to her lips and spread her arms wide towards the ocean. The wind buffeted and caught her, blowing her skirts and hair wildly, gathering up the dust and sand from beneath her feet and tossing it seawards. Her thoughts were carried too, blown towards the ship as it moved gracefully out of her sight towards the horizon. She felt a sudden warmth envelop her as love reached out, and she smiled sadly and touched her lips again. 'Goodbye,' she breathed. 'God speed.'

She turned away to gather in the horse, which had wandered off in search of more succulent grass, and as she climbed back into the cart and headed for home she looked once more to the horizon. The fleet could barely be seen, had become merely smudges of white on the blue sea. As she stared, in her mind the white became bigger and colder, white sheets of ice which stretched for ever beneath an alien sky. She shivered as the coldness touched her spine, tingling her fingertips and toes, and she hugged her arms around herself to bring back some comfort from the cold, sharp, icy fear which clutched her and held her fast.

24

'We'll wed as soon as 'spring sowing is finished, Sarah.'
Joe lowered his big frame into a chair by Sarah's fireside.

'But—but that will be soon, Masterson's have nearly
finished,' she stammered. 'I shan't – I shan't be ready.'

'Aye, well, they've got plenty of help. We shall be a
week or two yet, even if 'weather holds. That'll give thee
enough time to do whatever it is tha has to do.'

He smiled at her indulgently and pulled her down
towards him to sit on his knee. He nuzzled his beard
into her neck and she grimaced as the rough bristles
rubbed her skin.

' 'Course, we don't have to wait for ceremony, Sarah,'
he said softly. 'Tha only has to say 'word and I'll stay.
I want to, tha knows that, I've telled thee plenty of
times.'

'I know, Joe,' she said awkwardly, sliding off his knee
on the pretext of putting a pan on the fire. 'But I'd rather
wait.'

He nodded glumly. That she was reluctant he could
understand, she wasn't like other women, who were
happy to tumble with their men once the banns were
read. Being brought up to act and think like a lady had
spoilt her, he decided, but she would have to change her
ways if she was to be a farmer's wife. He would expect
his marital rights, and often, for he was a normal healthy
young fellow, but he wouldn't want to compel or force
her. There would be no happiness in that for either of
them.

He sighed, it wasn't going to be easy. His sister, he
knew, would not stand for any nonsense, and if they were
all to live together Nellie would still expect to be mistress
of the house. Not that Sarah didn't work hard, he had

seen last year how she did. Never expecting any help, she'd worked her garden and collected the produce alone. He'd seen the dirt beneath her fingernails, though her hands hadn't become rough and horny like his sister's, but were still soft and smooth. Nevertheless, she had also become independent, and he could see that sparks might fly as female temperaments clashed.

When spring sowing was finished she put him off again, making the excuse that she was busy in her garden and she wanted this to be a good year so that she might have some money to bring him. He couldn't argue with this as money was short. They had lost another piece of crop-growing land to the sea and two of their pigs had died of disease.

'If this keeps on we shall have to think about renting a piece of land ower at Tillington and leaving this lot for 'sea to do what it wants wi' it.' He hunched his hands into his pocket. 'Thy Tom did well to get that land. Folks'll always need millers. He'll be getting his own hoss and carriage afore long.'

Sarah touched his arm. 'He works hard, does Tom. Day and night sometimes. Don't begrudge him, Joe.'

'I don't begrudge him,' he answered feelingly. 'Though there's some as do. It's just I feel that bitter when I see all that me da and grandfayther have worked for tummel ower cliff edge, and there's nowt I can do about it.'

Summer came, and she said she was too busy with her trips to market to think about a wedding. Miss Ellie was taking a regular supply of roses, and she was selling bottles of last year's fruit and jams and jellies in the market as well as her herbs and potions. She became known, and customers would come looking for her to buy her produce.

She noticed the small boy who had watched her last year. He was sitting in the same spot, idly whittling a piece of wood and occasionally glancing in her direction.

451

Sarah waved to him one morning and beckoned him over. 'What are you doing?' she asked.

'I'm just carving this wood, miss.' He opened his hand to show her.

'No, I meant what were you doing here, why are you still watching me?' She spoke gently, a smile in her voice. 'Don't you know that Mr Rayner is away at sea?'

'Oh, I know that, miss,' he said airily. 'But I have me orders.' He stuck his chin up in the air and his eyes gleamed proudly. 'I'm on Mastersons' payroll, same as me da and grandfayther.' He leaned towards her confidentially. 'Three generations now, that's what me grandfayther said.' He cocked his head towards the river. 'They've sailed in 'same ship as 'gaffer – Mr Rayner, I mean, miss. But Mr Rayner said as 'ow I was to still keep an eye on thee while he's away and make sure that nobody bothers thee.'

She had trouble speaking, so choked was she with emotion. 'And will you be a whaling man? I don't know your name, what is it?'

'Bob, miss, Bob Hardwick, named after me grandfayther. He knows thy da, or so he says.' He fingered the wood delicately. 'But as for 'other question, miss, about being a whaling man, Mr Rayner says he'll apprentice me to a carpenter, that's what I really want to do. He says whaling is no life for a young lad. Too cold and too bloody.'

The boy laughed. 'But I might still go as a ship's carpenter. 'Sea's in me blood, tha knows; three generations, like me grandfayther says.'

As summer wore on, Joe was too busy to take time off for a wedding; the weather was hot and dry and the harvest had to be brought home, but he was becoming increasingly irritable and deep frowns lined his normally placid face.

'As soon as harvest is ower, Sarah. I'll not wait much longer. I shall start to think tha doesn't want to be wed.'

She couldn't bring herself to tell him that she didn't. She couldn't bear to inflict sorrow on this gentle giant of a man, couldn't watch the misery that it would bring if she told him that she had changed her mind and wouldn't marry him. How would he face his friends that he had known all of his life, if she should turn him down now?

He put his arms around her. 'Sometimes I think tha still thinks on yon fine fellow.' He could never bring himself to mention John Rayner by name.

She put her head on his chest and felt the roughness of his jacket against her cheek. 'I think of a lot of things, Joe, but I said I would marry you, and I will, but please, don't rush me, give me time.'

She needed time to rid herself of the ache which she felt each time she thought of John, the persistent torment which never went away, but was with her day and night, haunting her dreams and every waking moment. She tossed restlessly in her bed each night or walked the damp sands until morning came, leaving her wide-eyed and weary yet unable to rid herself of his image.

As summer drew to a close and the smells of autumn filled the air, she became more and more uneasy. The fleet should have been straggling home by the end of September or before if they had had a successful voyage, but none of the ships had yet been sighted. All had headed further north in their attempt to catch more whales and she had heard rumblings in the Market Place that bad weather had been expected. Once John is safely home, then I'll marry Joe, she promised herself, but wondered how long she could keep delaying him, what further excuses she could make.

Christmas came and went and still no news, and the townspeople of Hull went into mourning. Three overdue ships had arrived, one of them from the Masterson fleet, but they had no further news of the *Northern Star* or the *Stellar* which had followed it up the Lancaster Sound. Isaac Masterson spent more time in Hull at his office, using John's rooms for eating and sleeping, not wanting to tear himself away from the river, and to be on hand if any news came through from other returning ships.

The local newspaper published a gloomy account of the possible hazards that they might have encountered and gave a list of names of the men and apprentices who were on board.

Will brought the newspaper home and asked Sarah to read the report to him. She did so with growing despair, and a chill filled her heart as something within her died. Her parents looked at her as she covered her face with her hands.

'Sarah? What is it, love?' Her mother's anxious voice roused her and she blew her nose and tried to stem her tears.

'I keep thinking of those poor men,' she choked, her face white. 'And their wives. That young boy; his father and grandfather, you know them, Fayther, were both on the ship, and Mr John – the Mastersons will never get over their grief.'

'Aye, that's true, it's hit us all hard. Such a fine, handsome man, a real gentleman was Mr John, there'll never be another like him.' Maria wiped away a tear and patted her daughter on the shoulder as she sat, her head bowed.

'I haven't given up hope yet,' said Will. 'Ships have taken as long as this afore and still turned up, though it's odd that nobody has seen them.' He sat silently meditating, then shook his head, a small smile on his lips. 'I used to think, when he was just a lad, that he was like a cat with nine lives!'

'Whatever does tha mean, Will? Who does tha mean?'

'Young John. Well, like 'time when he fell into 'water, when I had my accident. Tha can freeze to death in minutes in those waters, but he just came up smiling.'

Sarah raised her head, she had never heard her father speak of it, it was her mother who had told her what had happened in the year she was born.

'And then another time he almost got into a scrape because of me.' Will recalled silently the escapade near Beverley and John's verbal sparring with the soldiers. 'But, by, he was right sharp.' His expression suddenly closed up as he realized he had an interested audience in his wife and daughter.

'So he really was a friend, Fayther?'

'Aye, or he could have been if he hadn't been who he was, or if I hadn't been who I was.'

'Did it matter so much?' Sarah asked, her voice catching. 'Did it really matter?'

'Aye, lass, it did at 'time. Still does, tha can't alter how folks feel.' He looked at her keenly. 'Don't ever forget thy background. No need to be ashamed of it, tha's from good stock, but we're different from 'gentry, better in some ways than they are, but they'll always be masters and we'll always be peazuns.'

Sarah rose to leave, to go back to her own cottage and face another sleepless night. Her father was wrong. She realized that, now that it was too late, but there was no sense in saying so, nothing she said would make him alter his opinion.

'Tha looks pale, Sarah. Is tha poorly?' Maria watched her sharply.

'No, I'm all right, Ma. I'm not sleeping well, that's all. I can hear the sea battering against the cliffs, it seems to be worse at night.' She hesitated. 'Fayther. Do whales scream?'

Will looked shocked. 'What a question, Sal! Why does tha want to know?'

'Do they, Fayther? Please answer me.' She had to ask. She needed to know whether the cries which penetrated her dreams and woke her, cold and sweating, came from human or beast.

He took a deep breath. He hadn't thought about it for a long time. 'Aye, they do,' he said slowly. He looked into the depths of the fire and remembered the cold. He shivered. 'They do. When the iron hits, they moan. It's like no other sound in God's world.'

He ran his hand across the stump of his knee. 'There's some as will say that they make no sound, none that humans can hear, anyroad, but I'll tell thee, and other seamen will vouch for it, that they do, we've heard 'em.'

His eyes glazed and he was absent from the room with its smoky, flickering firelight, gone from them to a distant land. 'When we get to the ice, and whales are about, even though we're a long way off, it's as if they can hear us, even though we try to keep quiet. Then they start to sing, as if they're calling to us! I tell thee, I've never heard music like it. It's eerie and mournful and beautiful, as if it's from some other world. It carries across water and ice and seems to echo from all sides. Tha can feel it pounding through 'ship and through thy body. Men get scared and can't wait to kill 'monsters, just to get it over with.'

'Poor things,' said Sarah softly.

'Poor things?' Her father looked up from his reverie. 'What would we do without them? We'd have no lighting, no oil, no brushes or soap. No oil for manufacturing. Hull would be a dead town without 'whaling, I'll tell thee, so don't go soft in thy head and think on 'poor whales. They have to suffer or we all die.'

The banns were read in Tillington church at the end of a cold bleak February. Joe insisted that they should not wait any longer and Sarah could no longer think of a reason to say no.

'Our Sarah's sickening for summat, I'm sure.' Maria bounced her grandson on her knee and confided in Lizzie. 'Tha would never think she was about to be wed.'

'Maybe she's having a babby,' said Lizzie, looking shyly at Maria, wondering whether to tell of her own impending second pregnancy.

Maria smiled at her daughter-in-law. Motherhood suited her, she was round and plump and contented, unlike Sarah who was pale and thin. 'No, I'm sure it's not that. I would know. There's summat else bothering her.'

She knew from Joe's tense and worried frown that things were not right between him and Sarah, but Sarah would not discuss it and withdrew further into herself.

'Don't marry him, Sarah if tha's not happy about it,'

she implored her as the day drew near. 'There's nowt wrong with being an old maid. Better that than spending a lifetime regretting.'

Sarah just nodded and said nothing, feeling only ice in her veins where warm blood should be.

She had seen the Mastersons' carriage the day before as she returned from a visit to a sick child in the village, and as usual she stepped to one side and averted her eyes, but as it drew past her, Walters pulled up the team and Miss Lucy put her head out. She was alone in the carriage and she beckoned for Sarah to come over.

'How are you, Sarah?'

Sarah curtsied. 'I'm quite well, thank you, Miss Lucy. And you?'

'I'm very well indeed.' Her blue eyes shone and she laughed happily. 'Oh, Sarah, I wish things hadn't changed. I do miss you, what fun we used to have.'

'Yes, we did, Miss Lucy. When we were small and didn't understand how things had to be.' Sarah smiled back at her former friend. Lucy hadn't really changed, she was just obeying the rules.

'Do I look different, Sarah?' Lucy lifted her face for Sarah to see. She was warmly wrapped against the cold, her hands inside a fur muff and her cheeks glowing under her fur-trimmed bonnet.

'No, I don't think so, or maybe a little brighter, the wind has brought colour to your cheeks.'

'No, it's not that. Sarah. What do you think?' She smiled a brilliant smile which lit up her face. 'I'm to be married. To the most wonderful man in the world. As soon as we have news of Papa's ship we shall make the announcement.' Her smile faded slightly. 'But we will wait a suitable time, you know, because of poor dear John.'

Sarah turned her head so that Lucy wouldn't see her trembling lips or her tear-filled eyes. How strange to think that life would go on, that people went about their business, got married, had babies; whilst inside herself there was a great desolation.

'Would you come with me, Sarah?'

'Come with you? Where?' she asked blankly.

'When I'm married. I can make my own decisions then. Mama won't make them for me. We shall be living in Bath, a most beautiful town.'

Sarah had refused of course, but had been pleased to have been asked, and had told Lucy that she too was to be married, the following week.

Sarah roused to a fleeting state of melancholy. An undefined sense of loss greeted her most mornings when she woke restless from her dreams, but today her waking thoughts were disturbed by unanswered questions. Something was happening today. But what? She threw off the blanket from her bed and sat still, gathering her thoughts together.

It was her wedding day. The day when she would join her life to Joe's. She drew in a deep trembling breath. Was she being fair to him, giving him but a fragment of her being, when her spirit was lost, gone for ever? If only I knew for certain if John was alive or dead, she thought, then perhaps I would have peace. Her inner perception had deserted her these past few weeks, her mind an empty, cold void.

She unbolted the door and opened it wide. A blast of wind rushed in, bringing with it twigs and dead leaves that had gathered in the doorway overnight and deposited them about her feet. The sea was wild, lashing with angry ferocity against the cliffs below her garden. She stood for a moment defying the squall as it tried to tear the door from her grasp, and looked out at the ocean. Somewhere out there his ship was being tossed, heaving on mountainous waves or plummeting to unknown depths, or worse, frozen in, unable to move, the ribs of the whaler squeezed and crushed by the pressure of relentless, heaving ice.

Twelve months had passed since John had sailed from Hull and Sarah knew she must say her final goodbye. 'Today I start a new life,' she whispered, 'and to do justice to that life I must reach out just once more to find you.'

She unhooked her cloak from behind the door and threw it around her shoulders. Her mind was becoming calm and detached and she was oblivious of her surroundings. 'I must go now,' she murmured. A compelling urgency pulled her out of the house towards the cliff path and the old deserted church. The sea was calling her, challenging her to come and face its power or forever be defeated.

She paced the cliff top, backwards and forwards, to and fro, constantly watching the swell of the waves out at sea and the battle of angry swirling foam as it battered against the weakened structure of the cliffs. The wind tore at her hair and whipped her skirts about her, but she felt nothing, not the sharp sand as it was flung into her face nor the pain as she stubbed her bare feet on the boulders and pebbles which lay in her path.

Finally she climbed the mound where the ruined church stood alone, its graveyard sliding over the edge, and stood with her back against the decaying stonework. She closed her eyes, her ears, her mind to the sights and sounds around her, she shut out the shriek of the wind and the pounding of the waves below her feet and sent out signals, soaring, flying, across this sea to the icy waters of the Polar regions, to the strange blue light which hovered above the icecaps, past the icebergs which towered mountainlike from the clear blue water, and on to the ice field which stretched beyond.

In this other world she searched, calling plaintively, a sound which was echoed by the frantic call of sea birds as they rose in their hundreds, disturbed by her presence. She sped across the ice, her feet barely touching its frozen surface, as she saw a ship marooned fast in the ice, a hundred miles away, but as she came nearer, hope giving wings to her heels, it disappeared, a mere blue haze in the distance.

She gave a deep shuddering sigh and felt the ice

respond. It trembled and shook and cracked beneath her feet; it heaved and broke, throwing up great white mountains before her. She shielded her eyes from the brightness; flashes of blue and yellow invaded her sight as the sun appeared behind the mountains, though there was no warmth from it and she felt the marrow of her bones freeze.

Suddenly there came a haunting cry. A creature was in pain. She could see blood on the ice, pools of red which froze as it fell, making maps and patterns on the ice floe. She had to help it but she couldn't see it, couldn't find it, no matter where she looked. Frantically she ran, hither and thither, searching, calling, but all she could hear was a plaintive sound like music, and she felt the cold wind chill her blood.

She slid down on to the ice. Here she would stay, she would become one with the elements, frozen into the ice until the great thaw began, and then be washed away with the melting floes, to join the other waterbound creatures and to sing with them their sorrowful song.

'Sarah!' Joe shouted above the wind. 'Sarah! Come down from there.' He'd searched an hour for her after finding her cottage empty, the door swinging on its hinges. The wind had drawn the fire, burning it away, and the deserted room was cold and full of twigs and leaves.

He found her crouched near the old church staring out to sea, but he couldn't make her hear. She seemed to be deaf or in a trance and he was alarmed for her safety. The cliff had crumbled overnight, six yards had gone over, and part of Sarah's garden too. Maybe that was why she was here. She must be upset. Not that it mattered, for today they were to be wed and she would be coming to live with him.

'Sarah!' He called again and she turned and looked at him, though he knew she did not see him. It was as if she were frozen to the spot and couldn't move. That was it. She couldn't move. Fear had made her immobile. She was sitting with her feet over the edge of the cliff and he dared not go too near in case he startled her. The piece of cliff that she was sitting on had a deep crack running through it, creeping insidiously towards the ruined church.

'Sarah?' He lowered his voice as if speaking to a child. 'Just sit very still and I'll go and get some help. I'll bring a rope for thee to hold on to. Don't be afeard, I'll not be long. I'll soon have thee back safely.' He sought to give her comforting words. 'Then we'll be off to church. Hast tha forgotten we're to be wed today?'

He moved slowly away and then turned to run, knowing in his heart that she hadn't heard him, that she was lost elsewhere.

'Will! For God's sake help me!' He burst into the kitchen at Garston Hall where Maria was putting the finishing touches to the baking for the party after the ceremony.

'He's out in 'foldyard, Joe. Whatever's 'matter?'

He didn't reply but raced out again slamming the door behind him. She wiped her hands on her apron and watched out of the window as he ran in search of Will.

He stammered out his request, his face flushed with alarm. Will stared at him uncomprehendingly, then, galvanized into furious action as he realized what Joe was saying, shouted at him, 'Don't just stand there, man, fetch a rope for her to catch hold of. What's she doing up there on a day like this?'

Joe shook his head and shouted against the wind as they ran. 'I don't know, Will, she's been acting that strange lately. I can't make her out. She's been odd for months now.' He stopped so that Will could catch his breath. 'I came for thee. I thought tha could talk to her, would know what to say.'

'What to say? What does tha mean? We've got to get her down before we can talk to her. I'm afeard of 'cliff breaking away, there's a strong tide running and 'water's deep!'

'Aye, but there's summat strange. It's as if she didn't see me. As if she were somewhere else.' He choked back

461

a sob. 'It's no good, Will. She doesn't want me. She still loves other yon chap. I'll not keep her to 'bargain. I can't do that to her.'

Will stopped. He could see Sarah sitting motionless on the cliff, her red hair tangled and disarrayed, staring out to sea.

'Yon chap? Which chap does tha mean?' A pain struck his chest and he drew in his breath sharply. He was getting too old for running across cliff tops, and his leg hurt. The new boots were tight and rubbed the sore, he could feel it throbbing.

'Yon Mr Rayner. She's never stopped wanting him, I know it, though she never said. I'm not a fool.'

'But he's—' Will put his hand to his head.

'Aye, dead most like, but it won't stop her feelings for him, will it?' Joe's eyes were wet. 'Feelings don't stop hurting just because somebody's gone away,' he said softly. 'I know all about that.'

'What a fool I've been! My own daughter, and I didn't know, didn't know that she was hurting inside.' Will stumbled forward. 'Sarah!' he shouted. 'Sarah! It's all right, I'm coming, I'm coming. My poor bairn, I'm coming.'

Startled, she turned to face them, then as she saw her father she smiled and put out her hands in a childlike gesture, as she used to when she was small and wanted him to carry her.

Joe was the first to reach the ruins of the church, his heavy strides vibrating on the soft wet clay. He stretched out his hand to throw the rope towards Sarah and felt the ground tremble beneath him. The stonework behind him shuddered and rumbled. A wide crack appeared in the wall and he turned and watched, unable to move in a brief unconscious moment in time, as it slithered and fell towards him, striking him and pushing him into Sarah so that together they fell over the cliff to the sea below.

'No!' Will screamed, and a gull overhead caught his cry and wheeled in alarm, flying swiftly away from the heaving waters to the sanctuary of the fields and gardens surrounding Garston Hall.

'No. No. Sarah!'

He scrambled up the mound, tripping painfully over the broken stone of the church and clawing his way over the deep fissures in the ground. He gazed helplessly over the edge at the wash of foaming brown water. Then the ground cracked below him and gave way, plummeting him down with the mass of clay and boulder stone, falling, falling into a bottomless void.

He felt the sea close over him and drag him down, but his instinct for survival was strong and he held his breath and pushed up through the water, though his boots were heavy and pulling at him.

His hands came into contact with something firm and he grabbed it. He felt folds of cloth wrapping around him and seaweed in his face. Then he realized that it wasn't seaweed but Sarah's hair. He took hold of her and pushed against her, holding her body above his, forcing her up by the strength of his arms and shoulders. He felt her slip away from him, and reached out to bring her back, felt the tightness in his chest as his lungs filled with water.

He saw through the mist of pain some faces that he knew, and they signalled to him to come. Young Richard Bewley, what was he doing here? And Jimmy – thy Lizzie's been right bothered about thee, Jim. And there's a devil's grinning face I never wished to see again, but there, he's gone; and here's my lovely Maria. He felt a vague sense of loss as she beckoned to him. She looks so sad, don't cry, my lovely lass, for I'm with good friends. Here's Rob Hardwick and his lad. I'm glad to see thee, Rob, me old mate, I was afeard tha'd gone down on 'ship. Why's tha smiling like that? Tell us 'joke, there's a good fellow.

They started to move away from him and he called to them. Hey, wait on, wait for me. I'm coming. He heard a familiar comforting sound, a plaintive vibrant echo, like music, calling him. He felt the soothing rhythmic rocking of the waters carry him onwards. By, lads, it's grand to be at sea again. This is where we belong.

It was Martin Reedbarrow who found Sarah, alerted by Paul who'd gone wandering along the cliffs, thrown out of the house by his shrill, nagging wife, and come back to Monkston to see what was doing.

Paul was so frightened that he was incomprehensible, and Martin hadn't at first understood his breathless gabbling. When at last what he said made sense, Martin shouted at him to fetch help from the village, then ran towards the sea as fast as his heavy frame would allow him, for he had become fat and short-winded as he'd grown older.

Paul had told his father that Joe and Sarah had gone over together, he had seen her red hair streaming behind her. He had been watching from behind an old gravestone as she sat on the cliff top, staring out to sea. He'd seen Joe come and go, and then come back again with Will, and his muddled mind couldn't decide whether Joe had pushed her or whether he was trying to catch her.

The cliffs were high by the old church and the water was raging, dashing great plumes of white foam against the cliff face, but Martin placed his large feet surely and carefully as he scrambled down the broken surface, and reached the fresh fall of clay, which lay in peaks and ridges, breaking the full force of the sea's raw energy which gathered momentum and flung Sarah's light form towards him.

Waist-deep in water he reached out towards her. Her cloak and gown were heavy with water and the waves sucked at her, trying to tear her from his grasp, to gather her back. Desperately he held on, feeling the sand moving beneath his feet, dragging him down, and just as he felt that he too would succumb to the power of the sea, and his arms burnt as if on fire, he heard the sound of other voices and men from the village took her from him and pulled him back.

He carried her himself, back to her mother, cradling

her like the daughter she now would never be. They had heard her moan, and turning her over pumped the sea water out of her until she retched and cried and they knew they had saved her.

Some of the men wanted to take a boat out and look for Joe, but Martin shook his head. It was useless, no sense in risking more lives. He knew his son wouldn't stand a chance. His big landsman's body would be dragged down. Joe hated the water, he always had. He was a countryman and had had no affinity with the sea despite living within sight of it all of his life.

Maria cried as they laid Sarah on a blanket on the floor in the warm kitchen at Garston Hall, and after hurrying to get brandy and hot water rocked her in her arms.

'But where's her da? Where's Will? He was with Joe. They went running off together. Dear God. Don't say he's gone too.'

They found Paul and he nodded nervously. Aye, he did see Will go over, he fell with the cliff. He hadn't stopped to look but had run to fetch his father.

A search party set out, but they found nothing, not that day or the next, but on the third day a message came from down the coast for them to come. It was Joe, an enormous blow on the back of his head and mud from the land still caked on the soles of the heavy boots which had dragged him down. The sea had returned him and deposited him gently back on the shore.

'They'll not find my Will.' Maria's eyes had dark shadows beneath them and her hair was more white than black. She smiled wistfully. ' 'Sea will keep him. I always knew it would. He'll sleep soundly beneath those 'waters. I have no fear of that.'

She sighed. 'I always thought that one day I would leave this place. I always meant to ask Will to take me back to Hull, to see that old brown river, and to wave to King Billy on his golden hoss, and finally to lie with my own folk. I realize now that it wasn't meant to be. Here I'll stay with my bairns and wait. 'Sea doesn't frighten me any more, not now, in fact it's quite a comfort – knowing that Will is out there.'

She put her sorrow to one side to care for her daughter, who lay wan and lifeless, not eating, not sleeping, and locked in silent distress.

Isaac Masterson had insisted that Sarah should stay at Garston Hall, that they make up a bed for her and give her everything she needed. He was beside himself with grief. So much sorrow, so much waste of life – John, Foster, Reedbarrow's son, and Sarah so sick that they feared for her mind. He ordered the doctor to come and attend her, and he stood at her bedside and shook his head.

'We could try bleeding her, get rid of the poisons which are obviously affecting her mind.'

But Maria wouldn't let him near with his jar of leeches, and he didn't come again.

Lucy came to see her and gently stroked her cheek and held her hand. 'Please get better, Sarah. I can't bear to see you like this.'

Sarah gave a small sad smile of recognition and then turned away.

'You're making so much of the girl, Isaac. I don't understand you.' Isobel was sharp and irritable at Isaac's distress. 'I'm sad too, for goodness sake, over poor John. And it isn't as if Sarah was one of the household any more. She cut herself off from us, we didn't make he go.'

'Sarah might well have been one of us,' he replied wearily. He was too old to deal with such troubles, and told her all he knew. 'John loved her and she him, this is why she is so sick, she thinks there is nothing left to live for.'

She stared at him, angry and confused, her pride battling with her fondness for John.

'Then it's a pity we didn't know sooner,' she said bitterly. 'If he had married her, at least he would still be here with us, and not gone to his death on some foolhardy voyage.'

25

Sarah opened her eyes reluctantly. The sun was shining through the curtains and falling on to the mirror on the chest across the room, sending bright reflections flitting across her face. The brightness reminded her of something, some white, bright light that she had seen she knew not where. But that had been a cold, hard light, without colour or warmth, unlike this pale gold glow which bathed the room.

Maria came in and sat by the bed. She stroked Sarah's forehead and smoothed the hair away from her face.

'Ma. Where is this room?'

Maria was startled for a moment, then a sudden joy returned to her, for this was the first response they had had from Sarah since she had been brought here so many weeks ago. She smiled delightedly. 'Why, Sarah, tha's been in here many times, surely? Tha's at Garston Hall. Doesn't tha know this place better than thine own?'

'Yes, Ma. But this room, how else do I know it?' she whispered. There was a pounding in her weakened body, an awareness coming fast and strong that she was alive after all, and not trapped, cold and alone, beneath the icy waters.

She had known without them telling her that her father was gone. She had felt his body beneath hers as they struggled deep in the watery blackness, felt him pushing her with all the strength of his muscular arms, forcing her up against the savage waves, and just as she was about to learn the truth and solve the wondrous secrets of the universe, he had heaved her out of the water to face life and its pain.

There was some other person also, someone kind and loving who in his eagerness to save her from herself had gone too, and she felt the guilt weigh heavily upon her. Someone who had gathered her into his arms to cushion her body as they plunged down the cliff and sank beneath the waves. She hadn't remembered who he was until she saw the tear-stained, saddened face of Janey, who spoke in whispers of her lost brother.

'Ma?'

She saw her mother wipe away a tear, but she turned a smiling face towards her. 'I'll tell thee a secret then, Sarah. This is 'same room as tha was born in. Only Mastersons never knew. We never told them that tha was born here.'

Maria saw the question on Sarah's face. 'Tha was in such a hurry to come into this world, that there wasn't time to get me home to Field House. Mr John had been using this room, for he'd come unexpected and we weren't ready for him. It didn't have a fine bed like this, though, just a truckle bed and a chest, but he brought me in here, and here tha was born.'

She looked down at her daughter and patted her hand. 'I'm going to fetch thee some soup. Tha looks so much better, perhaps tha might eat?'

Sarah lay back on the pillow. There had to be a reason why she at last felt comforted, why she now felt warmth flowing through her bones where before there had been only a lifeless chill.

John had been here. Here he had slept, walked the floor and sat in the chair, touched the door knob and left part of himself indelibly stamped in the fabric of the walls and the air that she breathed.

She pushed the sheets and hangings to one side and cautiously rose from the bed. Her legs were weak and she clung to the chair and windowsill as she looked out of the window. Spring was almost there, tender green growth was pushing its way out of the frosty earth, the first signs of an abundant vitality fighting for existence. She could see the sea. Where the cliff had fallen away there was a wide band of silver and grey glistening in the morning sun. She heard the soft breathing of the surf, and it no longer menaced her as it had when they brought her here and she had hidden, cold and lost, cowering beneath the sheets.

She could go on now, she wanted to live. She sensed John near, felt his presence, and knew now that he would always be with her, would never leave her, that through endless time they were united.

It was Harris who heard the clatter of hooves in the stable yard and the crunch of gravel as the messenger dismounted, and looked down from his narrow window above the stables into the darkness of the yard below.

He listened intently to what the man had to say and bade him wait whilst he went to the house. Not wanting to wake the whole household, he threw gravel up at Janey's window, hoping that he wouldn't break the glass. He saw her face appear behind it, and beckoned her to come, his finger on his lips.

She came, a guttering candle in her hand, prepared to scold at being woken at such an hour, but wrapped her shawl tightly over her nightshift and went to waken the master as she was requested. She made Mr Masterson a warm drink and wrapped a hot brick in a piece of old blanket, whilst he hurriedly dressed and Harris harnessed the horses to the carriage. She nodded obediently when her master told her not to discuss with anyone why he had departed so rapidly in the middle of the night.

No-one else heard them go. Not Maria, dreaming of Will as she slept in Mrs Scryven's old room, unable to face going back alone to Field House. Not the other servants, who would sleep soundly for the next few hours until dawn. Not Isobel Masterson, who slept high on her pillow to save disturbing her hair, and not Lucy, who smiled as she turned beneath her soft sheets. And not Sarah, who slept peacefully for the first time in weeks.

I'm too old for this, thought Isaac, and tried to ease his burning joints as the carriage rattled through still, sleeping villages, too old to deal with difficulties such as this. He shivered in spite of his warm greatcoat and warmed his bony hands on the hot brick, pulling the rug which Janey had given him around his narrow shoulders. *Dare I hope for good news? No, I dare not, in case I am disappointed.*

There was news of a ship, but not his: the *Stellar* which had been lost with the *Northern Star*. *If I hear that all is lost, then I shall sell my ships and my company and retire to oblivion in Monkston and wait for death,* he told himself. He trembled as he climbed down from the carriage and leant heavily on Harris's supporting arm.

There was only a handful of men waiting in the yard, and the watchman told him that the *Stellar* had been sighted late last evening just off the Humber, and that even now she had dropped sail and was being escorted by the pilot boat through the mud and sand flats round the stump of Spurn towards the mouth of the River Hull and the harbour entrance.

'I would like to be there,' said Isaac, 'as she comes in,' and a sedan chair was sent for to carry him there.

A small group of women was already waiting as the ship drifted in on the tide, pulled by a small cobble. They waited silently and patiently, with a glimmer of hope where previously all hope had been abandoned. As dawn broke and the eastern sky lightened, showing streaks of rosy gold and the promise of a fine day, the *Stellar* moved slowly towards the dock, cleaving her way through the muddy water, passing through the huddle of boats which filled the narrow waterway and sweeping up the mist which drifted there, sending it floating high over the rooftops of the riverside warehouses into the dense mass of buildings in the town.

Isaac was bent low over his stick as the crew came ashore, narrowing his eyes in a vain effort to recognize any of the faces. The only men he would likely know were those who had served on his vessels since boyhood, men like Hardwick who had been with the company all of his working life. Isaac had little to do with the crews these days, he had left so much to John.

Beside the gangboard he saw Carstairs, the owner of the whaler, greeting the crew as they appeared. Isaac slowly walked towards him to ask if he had news of the *Northern Star*.

Carstairs shook his hand, holding it with both of his in sympathy. 'I haven't heard all the details, but I understand she is lost, my friend, broken up off Lancaster Sound. It's only by the grace of God that the *Stellar* has returned.'

As shock and despair showed on Isaac's grey face Carstairs added quietly, 'But I understand that some of the men were saved, the *Stellar* took them on board. They have had a dreadful time, but they have opened up new territories if we wish to pursue them – if it is worth the risk.'

'My nephew was on board.' Isaac spoke in barely a whisper. 'Have you news of him?'

'I know little more than you.' Carstairs shook his head. 'We must wait and watch.'

There were tears of happiness as the men tumbled ashore to be greeted by their families, and also tears of sorrow as they gave news of those who wouldn't be returning. Twenty lives had been lost from the *Northern Star* and eight from the *Stellar*.

Isaac had almost given up hope as the last straggle of men came down the gangboard and he carefully scrutinized each face as they passed him. 'Your pardon.' He raised his hand towards a tall thin man with a thick beard who walked slowly towards him and gazed at him with tired, haunted eyes. 'I know you are anxious to be with your family, but do you have any news of John Rayner who sailed with the *Northern Star*?'

The man smiled and for a moment there was a bright flash of humour about his lips. 'Have I changed so much, sir, that my own kith and kin cannot recognize me?'

'Can it be you?' Isaac peered into the thin face.

'Indeed it is, Uncle,' said John, putting down his box and enveloping the old man in his arms.

* * *

'We must go home now.' Isaac had waited whilst John took his papers into the office and was greeted warmly by his staff who had feared him dead, forgetting their places sufficiently to crowd round him and shake him vigorously by the hand. 'You must rest and get your strength back. Isobel and Lucy will be so thankful to see you. They know nothing of your return, I crept from the house before dawn.'

He was bursting with delight at seeing his nephew safe and well and had to keep reminding himself that there were many others whose lot would be sorrow and grief. In a day or two he would visit the relatives of the lost seamen himself, to give them his support and what comfort he could.

They had spoken only briefly of the ill-fated voyage. The details would emerge piece by piece as John relaxed, but now, Isaac surmised, he was exhausted, and his words came out haltingly.

The ship had sailed up the Davis Strait where there was good open water, and, as the weather seemed to be holding, they continued on further north than they had been before, into Lancaster Sound.

'We were then hit by the most awful weather I have known,' said John. 'Thick fog made navigation difficult and the ice started to close in. We were lifted above it, high and dry, unable to move until the thaw set in. There was no other ship within sight, but we had food and water in plenty at that time, enough to last several months, so we were not unduly worried. We set about our usual tasks and prepared to wait.'

He gave a shiver. 'Then the ice started to break up in front of us but it still lay thick behind, so the captain decided to move forward. We found whales in plenty, they surrounded the ship, almost as if they were looking for us, and we captured four on the first day of fishing. We were by now in waters unknown to us. We found dozens of small islands, without name or number, but again we were beset by bad weather, and for days and sometimes weeks we were unable to make any progress.

The men went on to the ice to shoot duck, for by now we were running short of food and had even resorted to eating whale meat.'

'You don't have to say more, John.' Isaac watched anxiously as John wearily rubbed his eyes. 'It will keep.'

'No. It's better that I tell you,' he replied. 'I may want to forget it otherwise, erase it from my memory. If I don't, I may never sail again.'

He leaned back against the soft leather of the upholstery and shut his eyes as the motion of the carriage rocked him gently.

'When the ice floes started to break again we had the choice, either to continue forward and round Baffin Island bearing south, or to turn and retrace our direction back through the Sound towards Baffin Bay. We decided on the second choice, mainly because by then the men were weak and unable to stand a voyage of indeterminate length. These were strange waters, and besides, the ship had taken a terrible battering from the pressure of the ice, and we feared what might be in front of us.'

'Quite right,' said Isaac, his mind going back to his own whaling days. 'Quite right.'

'So we turned about, but once more we were beset by ice and had to wait, and now the men were becoming ill. There was scurvy on board, and men with severe frostbite, and one morning a party of six went out hunting and never returned, so as you can imagine we were in desperate spirits. Then just as we thought that we would never see home again, the ice field started to break and we were able to move forward once more, and it was then that we saw the *Stellar*. She was a long way off but she saw us and waited, three, maybe four days. We discovered later that she too had been beset by ice and had considered herself lost.'

He laughed softly. 'We thought then that our troubles were over, but in fact they were only just beginning. We were within a day of reaching the *Stellar* when the ice began to close in again. We could see that she was already in trouble, but what we didn't see was the iceberg floating towards us and by the time we did see it it was too late. It hit us with such force that within minutes we were sinking. Some of the men were thrown overboard and died of the cold or drowning. We had no time for saving anything but ourselves, and we watched from the ice as she went down.'

Isaac looked out at the fields with their covering of new green shoots where the corn and barley were pushing up through the brown earth; and also saw the frozen ice field as he remembered it. 'And so you walked across the ice to reach the *Stellar*?' he murmured. 'And were taken on board.'

John nodded. 'If she hadn't been there, we would have been finished. There was nothing else. Not another ship, not another living thing to be seen.'

He heaved a deep sigh. 'That's about the sum of it, sir, the rest you know. We waited again for the thaw, we shared what little food they had left, we shared their bunks and their clothing, for we had only what we were wearing, and each of us hoped and prayed that we would have the strength to hold on.'

He too looked out of the carriage window. It seemed an unreal world, of warm sun and green fields, but he was not heartened by it. What was he coming back to? He was bereft with hopelessness, lonely and stricken with despair. There had been times out there, in that other crystal world, when he had forgotten that Sarah was no longer his, when she had been near to him, giving him strength by her loving, but he knew now that it had been only an illusion.

He put his hand in his pocket and felt the cold smoothness of ivory; the whale tooth had been the only reminder he had. No lacy handkerchief or pretty ribbon, but something ageless and indestructible, and he carried it always.

'Well, we have had our ups and downs,' said Isaac. 'We too have had our share of tragedy.'

John looked at him with dull eyes.

474

'And I must tell you! What about this? Little Lucy is to be married!'

'That's a tragedy?' John raised his eyebrows.

'No, no. You misunderstand. We are very pleased about it. A fine gentleman from Bath. She was introduced, I gather, at the Pardoes' home, so he comes highly recommended.'

The Pardoes' home. What a lifetime ago it was when he was last there. John recalled that a decision had to be made, but not yet. Matilda would have to wait a little longer, if indeed she hadn't given up hope already and married someone else.

'We had a letter from Miss Pardoe some months ago, asking if we had heard news of you. She appeared most anxious for your safety.'

Isaac looked at John from the corner of his eyes. 'Some other news also. As I said, we too have had our tragedies out at Monkston. If you are up to it, I will tell you about them.'

Sarah stood inside the cottage door. Her mother had said not to come, that she would be upset by the desolation.

The room was as she had left it all those weeks ago, before the tragedy. The blanket was still crumpled on the bed, the grey ash in the hearth. No-one had had the heart to come, so it had been left, the door locked on its memories.

Her mother had been right, she could no longer live here. The earth around was cracked and broken, and the shallow foundations of the walls undermined by the power of the sea. But apart from that, as she looked around, there were so many memories there to torment her; she could see vestiges of her father, the shelves he had made, the stout bar for the door; and the small chair where Joe had sat, his large body straining the frame.

Poor, loving Joe, he had died trying to save her; her father, who could have saved himself, saving her life when she didn't really care about living. And John. She

475

remembered how he had waited here in the rain on the night of Tom's wedding. They had held each other, and then she had sent him away. Three men who had loved her, three men lost because of her.

She folded up the blanket and opened the cupboard doors, taking down the boxes and jars of herbs and oils and stacking them neatly on the table. She opened the door wide and let in the sunshine and then took a broom and swept out the crisp dead leaves that littered the floor. 'I'm glad Ma Scryven isn't here to see it,' she murmured to herself. 'How saddened she would be.' She still thought of it as the old woman's cottage, feeling herself just the keeper until the day she had to give it back.

One day the sea will claim it, she thought sadly. It will carry it off to the bottom of the cliffs and out on the waves. The memories and lives of those who lived here will be carried out to sea and no-one will remember them. All will be forgotten. She started to hum an old song that her father used to sing, but she only remembered the tune and none of the words.

She went outside, feeling the sun warm on her face, and looked at the remains of the garden. Part of the land had slithered over the edge and deep fissures broke the ground, deep enough to fall into and break a foot or ankle. She bent down to inspect the cracks and saw inside the layers of brown mud and yellow sand the roots of shrubs, lavender and elder, and bulbs of wild daffodils stretching down their tensile roots and pushing tender shoots upwards through the clay.

She picked up a spade that was leaning against the wall and with her foot firm on the iron blade dug out clumps of snowdrops and primroses with a large clod of earth round each to cushion them. She eased from the ground violet roots, the plant of everlasting love, broke off twigs of hawthorn bursting with new growth, and carefully gathered heads from last year's poppies and put them in her pocket. Then, when she was finished, she brought out the old chair from inside the house and placed it facing the sea and sat there gently rocking, the sun glinting on her hair.

I've been guilty of too much self-importance, she thought. I've thought only of myself. I've not been humble enough or considerate of other people's feelings. But I'll change. I'll take my pride in my hands and ask the Mastersons if I can have Field House to live in and make my living. They have been very kind to me whilst I have been ill, and I feel sure they will grant me this one request. My mother won't want it now, she'll stay at Garston Hall, or perhaps live with Lizzie and Tom. I know they have asked her.

She sat rocking gently, the sun moving around her, warming her head and shoulders. She watched through half-closed eyes as the waves washed gently up the sands, softly caressing, softly shushing, the creamy white flecks curling and falling rhythmically.

'I thought you were my friend,' she said softly. 'I knew your every mood, your every whim. Why, then? Why did you have to be so cruel, so vicious, taking away those I love, when you can be so loving, so playful, as you are today?'

The waves, as if amused, rose and fell, tossing capriciously on to the sand then running playfully back.

'We'll not give in, you know. You shan't beat us.'

A large ripple rose and threw itself defiantly against the shore, crashing against the broken mounds of clay at the bottom of the cliff.

'We won't go away. We shall keep on moving back, but you won't get rid of us. We belong here. We're part of this landscape just as much as you are.'

She smiled as a shadow fell across her, and she raised her hand without turning, thinking that it was Tom or her mother come to fetch her. 'I'm just explaining a few things,' she said. 'Reasons for being here.' She gave a deep sigh. 'There has to be a reason, hasn't there?'

Turning, she shielded her eyes from the sun which threw into shadow the face of the man who stood there.

John smiled, the smile lighting up his face, easing away

the pain and crinkling the corners of his eyes. He saw the band of sun-kissed freckles sliding across her nose and the look of hope slowly dawning in her dark eyes.

He took her eager outstretched hands as she rose from the chair and drew her towards him, and this time she knew that he was real, warm and living, not insubstantial and shadowy as he had been in her dreams. His image blurred through her tears. She blinked, the tears fell away and he was still there.

'There is always a reason, Sarah, that must be what brought me back.' He put his arms round her and kissed the top of her head, and held her close, breathing in the scent of the coming summer and the salt of the sea. 'Come. It's time we went home.'

Their heads were close as they walked up the cliff path, their backs to the sea. The cottage door, caught by the breeze, creaked on its hinges. Twigs and leaves blew inside followed by a swirl of golden sand which settled in a fine layer on the floor, and the sea, turning on the ebb tide, drew away from the shore breathing softly like a sigh.

THE END

ANNIE
by Valerie Wood

Annie Swinburn had killed a man – the killing was timely and well-deserved, for Francis Morton had been evil in every possible way. But Annie knew that however justified her crime, only the rope and the gibbet awaited her if she remained in the slums of Hull. And so she ran – up river, along the wild and secretive paths of the great Humber – a new and unfamiliar territory which was to lead her into a new and unfamiliar life.

Her first refuge was with Toby Linton, well-born, estranged from his father, and – with his brother Matt – earning a dangerous living as a smuggler. Annie led a double life, as smuggler, and as a pedlar roaming the remote countryside of the Wolds. It was this new existence which led her, once more, into allowing herself to love, in spite of all the things that had gone before.

By the bestselling author of *The Doorstop Girls*, *Far from Home* and *The Hungry Tide*, winner of the Catherine Cookson Prize for Fiction.

0 552 14263 8

A SELECTED LIST OF FINE NOVELS AVAILABLE FROM CORGI BOOKS

THE PRICES SHOWN BELOW WERE CORRECT AT THE TIME OF GOING TO PRESS. HOWEVER TRANSWORLD PUBLISHERS RESERVE THE RIGHT TO SHOW NEW RETAIL PRICES ON COVERS WHICH MAY DIFFER FROM THOSE PREVIOUSLY ADVERTISED IN THE TEXT OR ELSEWHERE.

☐	14058 9	**MIST OVER THE MERSEY**	*Lyn Andrews*	£6.99
☐	14974 8	**COOKLEY GREEN**	*Margaret Chappell*	£6.99
☐	14712 5	**ROSIE OF THE RIVER**	*Catherine Cookson*	£5.99
☐	14452 5	**PARADISE PARK**	*Iris Gower*	£5.99
☐	15066 5	**TROUBLE IN PARADISE**	*Pip Granger*	£5.99
☐	14538 6	**A TIME TO DANCE**	*Kathryn Haig*	£5.99
☐	14906 3	**MATTHEW & SON**	*Ruth Hamilton*	£5.99
☐	14566 1	**THE DREAM SELLERS**	*Ruth Hamilton*	£5.99
☐	14686 2	**CITY OF GEMS**	*Caroline Harvey*	£5.99
☐	14535 1	**THE HELMINGHAM ROSE**	*Joan Hessayon*	£5.99
☐	14603 X	**THE SHADOW CHILD**	*Judith Lennox*	£5.99
☐	13910 6	**BLUEBIRDS**	*Margaret Mayhew*	£6.99
☐	14872 5	**THE SHADOW CATCHER**	*Michelle Paver*	£5.99
☐	14752 4	**WITHOUT CHARITY**	*Michelle Paver*	£5.99
☐	12607 1	**DOCTOR ROSE**	*Elvi Rhodes*	£5.99
☐	15051 7	**A BLESSING IN DISGUISE**	*Elvi Rhodes*	£5.99
☐	14903 9	**TIME OF ARRIVAL**	*Susan Sallis*	£5.99
☐	15050 9	**FIVE FARTHINGS**	*Susan Sallis*	£6.99
☐	15052 5	**SPREADING WINGS**	*Mary Jane Staples*	£5.99
☐	15138 6	**FAMILY FORTUNES**	*Mary Jane Staples*	£5.99
☐	14990 X	**DATING GAME**	*Danielle Steel*	£6.99
☐	14506 8	**JOURNEY**	*Danielle Steel*	£6.99
☐	14263 8	**ANNIE**	*Valerie Wood*	£5.99
☐	14476 2	**CHILDREN OF THE TIDE**	*Valerie Wood*	£5.99
☐	14640 4	**THE ROMANY GIRL**	*Valerie Wood*	£5.99
☐	14740 0	**EMILY**	*Valerie Wood*	£5.99
☐	14845 8	**GOING HOME**	*Valerie Wood*	£5.99
☐	14846 6	**ROSA'S ISLAND**	*Valerie Wood*	£5.99
☐	15031 2	**THE DOORSTEP GIRLS**	*Valerie Wood*	£5.99
☐	15032 0	**FAR FROM HOME**	*Valerie Wood*	£5.99

All Transworld titles are available by post from:

Bookpost, P.O. Box 29, Douglas, Isle of Man IM99 1BQ

Credit cards accepted. Please telephone +44(0)1624 836000, fax +44(0)1624 837033, Internet http://www.bookpost.co.uk or e-mail: bookshop@enterprise.net for details.

Free postage and packing in the UK.
Overseas customers allow £2 per book (paperbacks) and £3 per book (hardbacks).